BEAU SABREUR

by the same author

FOREIGN LEGION STORIES

Beau Geste
Beau Ideal
The Wages of Virtue
Uniform of Glory

OMNIBUS VOLUMES

Stories of the Foreign Legion
Dead Men's Boots

OTHER NOVELS

Soldiers of Misfortune
The Man of a Ghost
Spanish Maine
Fort in the Jungle

P. C. WREN

Beau Sabreur

"A man may escape from his
enemies or even from his
friends, but how shall a man
escape from his own nature?"

John Murray
FIFTY ALBEMARLE STREET
LONDON

First published 1926
Nineteenth impression 1957
This edition 1961

Printed in Great Britain by
Cox & Wyman, Ltd., London, Fakenham and Reading
and published by John Murray (Publishers) Ltd.

To
"NOBBY"
True Comrade,
To Whom This Book Owes Much

NOTE

THE Author would like to anticipate certain of the objections which may be raised by some of the kindly critics and reviewers who gave so friendly and encouraging a chorus of praise to *Beau Geste*, *The Wages of Virtue*, and *The Stepsons of France*.

Certain of the events chronicled in these books were objected to, as being impossible.

They were impossible.

The only defence that the Author can offer is that, although perfectly impossible, they actually happened.

In reviewing *The Wages of Virtue*, for example, a very distinguished literary critic remarked that the incident of a girl being found in the French Foreign Legion was absurd, and merely added an impossibility to a number of improbabilities.

The Author admitted the justice of the criticism, and then, as now, put forth the same feeble defence that, although perfectly impossible, it was the simple truth. He further offered to accompany the critic (at the latter's expense) to the merry town of Figuig in Northern Africa, and there to show him the tombstone (with its official epitaph) of a girl who served for many years, *in the Spahis, as a cavalry trooper*, rose to the rank of Sergeant, and remained, until her death in battle, quite unsuspected of being what she was—a European woman.

And in this book, nothing is set forth as having happened which has not happened—including the adoption of two ex-Legionaries by an Arab tribe, and their rising to Sheikhdom and to such power that they were signatories to a treaty with the Republic.

One of them, indeed, was conducted over a French troopship, and his simple wonder at the marvels of the *Roumi* was rather touching, and of pleasing interest to all who witnessed it. . . .

The reader may rest assured that the deeds narrated, and the scenes and personalities pictured, in this book, are not the vain outpourings of a film-fed imagination, but the rearrangement of actual happenings and the assembling of real people who have actually lived, loved, fought and suffered—and some of whom, indeed, live, love, fight and suffer to this day.

Truth *is* stranger than fiction.

CONTENTS

PART ONE

Failure

THE MAKING OF A BEAU SABREUR

PART TWO

Success

THE MAKING OF A MONARCH

PART ONE

Failure

THE MAKING OF A BEAU SABREUR

Out of the unfinished *Memoirs* of
MAJOR HENRI DE BEAUJOLAIS
of the *Spahis* and the French Secret Service

" *To set the cause above renown,*
To love the game beyond the prize,
To honour, while you strike him down.
The foe that comes with fearless eyes;
To count the life of battle good,
And clear the land that gave you birth,
Bring nearer yet the brotherhood
That binds the brave of all the earth. . . ."

SIR HENRY NEWBOLT

CHAPTER I

"OUT OF THE DEPTHS I RISE"

I WILL start at the very nadir of my fortunes, at the very lowest depths, and you shall see them rise to their zenith, that highest point where they are crowned by Failure.

Behold me, then, clad in a dirty canvas stable-suit and wooden clogs, stretched upon a broad sloping shelf; my head, near the wall, resting on a wooden ledge, a foot wide and two inches thick, meant for a pillow; and my feet near the ledge that terminates this beautiful bed, which is some thirty feet long and seven feet wide. It is as long as the room, in fact, and about two feet from the filthy brick floor.

Between my pampered person and the wooden bed, polished by the rubbing of many vile bodies, is nothing. Covering me is a canvas "bread-bag", four feet long and two wide, a sack used for the carrying of army loaves. As a substitute for sheets, blankets and eider-down quilt, it is inadequate.

The night is bitterly cold, and, beneath my canvas stable-suit, I am wearing my entire wardrobe of under-clothes, in spite of which my teeth are chattering and I shiver from head to foot as though stricken with ague.

I am not allowed to wear my warm regimentals and cloak or overcoat, for, alas! I am in prison.

There is nothing else in the prison but myself and a noisy, *nouveau riche*, assertive kind of odour.

I am wrong—and I wish to be strictly accurate and per-fectly truthful—there are hungry and insidious insects, number unknown, industrious, ambitious, and successful.

Some of my fellow troopers pride themselves on being men of intelligence and reason, and therefore believe only in what they can see. I cannot see the insects, but I, in-telligent or not, believe in them firmly.

Hullo! there is something else. . . . A rat has run across

my face. . . . I am glad so rude a beast is in prison. Serve him right. . . . On the whole, though, I wish he were not in prison, for he is nibbling at my ambrosial locks. . . . If I smite at him wildly I shall administer a severe blow to the brick wall, with my knuckles. . . .

The door, of six-inch oak, is flung open, and by the light of the lantern in the hands of the Sergeant of the Guard, I see a man and a brother flung into my retreat. He falls heavily and lies where he falls, in peaceful slumber. He has been worshipping at the shrine of Bacchus, a false god. The door clangs shut and leaves the world to darkness and to me, and the drunken trooper, and the rat, and the insects.

I shiver and wriggle and scratch and wonder whether the assertive odour will conquer, or my proud stomach rise victorious over . . . Yes, it is rising . . . Victorious? . . . No. . . .

Again the door opens and a trooper enters, thanking the Sergeant of the Guard, in the politest terms, for all his care and kindness. The Sergeant of the Guard, in the impolitest terms, bids the trooper remove his canvas trousers.

He does so, and confirms what the Sergeant had feared—that he is wearing his uniform trousers beneath them. The Sergeant of the Guard confiscates the nethermost garments, consigns the prisoner to the nethermost regions, gives him two extra days in this particular region, and goes out.

As the door clangs, the new-comer strikes a match, produces half a candle, lights it, and politely greets me and the happy sleeper on the floor.

"Let us put this one to bed," he suggests, sticking his candle on the pillow-shelf; and I arise, and we lift the bibulous one from the hard floor to the harder, but less damp and filthy, "bed."

Evidently a humane and kindly soul this. I stand rebuked for my callousness in leaving the drunkard on the ground.

But he does not carry these virtues to excess, for, observing that the Bacchanal has been cast into prison in his walking-out uniform (in which he was evidently brought helpless into barracks), he removes the man's tunic, and puts it on over his own canvas stable-jacket.

"The drunk feel nothing," he observes sententiously. "Why should the sober feel cold?"

4

I no longer stand rebuked.

By the light of his candle, I study the pleasing black hole in which we lie, its walls decorated by drawings, poems, aphorisms, and *obiter dicta* which do not repay study.

It is a reeking, damp and verminous cellar, some thirty feet square, ventilated only by a single grated aperture, high up in one of the walls, and is an unfit habitation for a horse or dog.

In fact, Colonel du Plessis, our Commanding Officer, would not have one of the horses here for an hour. But I am here for fifteen days (save when doing punishment-drill) and serve me jolly well right.

For I have *tirée une bordée*—absented myself, without leave, for five days—the longest period that one can be absent without becoming a deserter and getting three years' hard labour as such.

Mind, I am not complaining in the very least. I knew the penalty and accepted it. But there was a lady in the case, the very one who had amused us with her remark to de Lannec, anent a stingy Jew politician of her acquaintance—"When a man with a Future visits a lady with a Past, he should be thoughtful of the Present, that it be acceptable—and expensive." She had written to me, beseeching me in the name of old kindnesses, to come quickly to Paris, and saying that she knew nothing but Death would keep me from helping her in her terrible need. . . .

And Death stayed his hand until I had justified this brave and witty little lady's faith; and now, after the event, sends his fleas, and odours, and hideous cold too late. . . . Dear little Véronique Vaux! . . .

There is a great commotion without, and the candle is instantly extinguished by its owner, who pinches the wick.

Evidently one foolishly and futilely rebels against Fate, and more foolishly and futilely resist the Guard.

The door opens and the victim is flung into the cell with a tremendous crash. The Sergeant of the Guard makes promises. The prisoner makes sounds and the sounds drown the promises. He must be raging mad, fighting-drunk, and full of vile cheap canteen-brandy.

The humane man re-lights his candle, and we see a huge and powerful trooper gibbering in the corner.

What *he* sees is, apparently, a gathering of his deadliest

5

foes, for he draws a long and of nasty knife from the back his trouser-belt, and, with a wild yell, makes a rush for us.

The humane man promptly knocks the candle flying, and leaps off the bed. I spring like a—well, *flea* is the most appropriate simile, just here and now—in the opposite direction, and take up an attitude of offensive defence, and to anybody who steps in my direction I will give of my best —where I think it will do most good. . . .

Apparently the furious one has missed the humane one and the Bacchanalian one, and has struck with such terrific force as to drive his knife so deeply into the wood that he cannot get it out again.

I am glad that my proud stomach, annoyed as I am with it, was not between the knife and the bed. . . .

And I had always supposed that life in prison was so dull and full of *ennui*. . . .

The violent one now weeps, the humane one snores, the Bacchanalian one grunts chokingly, and I lie down again, this time without my bread-bag.

Soon the cruel cold, the clammy damp, the wicked flea, the furtive rat, the noisy odour, and the proud stomach combine with the hard bench and aching bones to make me wish that I were not a sick and dirty man starving in prison.

And a few months ago I was at Eton! . . . It is all very amusing. . . .

CHAPTER II

UNCLE

DOUBTLESS you wonder how a man may be an Etonian one year and a trooper in a French Hussar Regiment the next.

I am a Frenchman, I am proud to say; but my dear mother, God rest her soul, was an Englishwoman; and my father, like myself, was a great admirer of England and of English institutions. Hence my being sent to school at Eton.

On my father's death, soon after I had left school, my uncle sent for me.

He was even then a General, the youngest in the French Army, and his wife is the sister of an extremely prominent and powerful politician, at that time—and again since—Minister of State for War.

My uncle is fantastically patriotic, and *La France* is his goddess. For her he would love to die, and for her he would see everybody else die—even so agreeable a person as myself. When his last moments come, he will be frightfully sick if circumstances are not appropriate for him to say, "*I die—that France may live*"—a difficult statement to make convincingly, if you are sitting in a Bath chair at ninety, and at Vichy or Aix.

He is also a really great soldier and a man of vision. He has a mind that plans broadly, grasps tenaciously, sees clearly.

Well, he sent for me, and, leaving my mother in Devonshire, I hurried to Paris and, without even stopping for *déjeuner*, to his room at the War Office.

Although I had spent all my holidays in France, I had never seen him before, as he had been on foreign service, and I found him to be my *beau idéal* of a French General—tall, spare, hawk-like, a fierce dynamic person.

He eyed me keenly, greeted me coldly, and observed—"Since your father is spilt milk, as the English say, it is useless to cry over him."

"Now," continued he, after this brief exordium, "you are a Frenchman, the son of a Frenchman. Are you going to renounce your glorious birthright and live in England, or are you going to be worthy of your honoured name?"

I replied that I was born a Frenchman, and that I should live and die a Frenchman.

"Good," said my uncle. "In that case you will have to do your military service. . . . Do it at once, and do it as I shall direct. . . .

"Some day I am going to be the master-builder in consolidating an African Empire for France, and I shall need

7

tools *that will not turn in my hand*. . . . Tools on which I can rely *absolutely*. . . . If you have ambition, if you are a *man*, obey me and follow me. Help me, and I will make you. . . . Fail me, and I will break you. . . ."

I stared and gaped like the imbecile that I sometimes choose to appear.

My uncle rose from his desk and paced the room. Soon I was forgotten, I think, as he gazed upon his splendid Vision of the future, rather than on his splendid Nephew of the present.

"France . . . France . . ." he murmured. "A mighty Empire . . . Triumphant over her jealous greedy foes. . . .

"England dominates all the east of Africa, but what of the rest—from Egypt to the Atlantic, from Tangier to the Gulf? . . . Morocco, the Sahara, the Soudan, all the vast teeming West. . .

"Algeria we have, Tunisia, and corners here and there. . . . It is not enough. . . . It is nothing. . . ."

I coughed and looked more imbecile.

"Menaced France," he continued, "with declining birthrate and failing manpower . . . Germany only awaiting *The Day*. . . . Africa, an inexhaustible reservoir of the finest fighting material in the world. The Sahara—with irrigation, an inexhaustible reservoir of food. . . ."

It was lunch-time, and I realized that I, too, needed irrigation and would like to approach an inexhaustible reservoir of food. If he were going to send me to the Sahara, I would go at once. I looked intelligent, and murmured:

"Oh, *rather*, Uncle!"

"France must expand or die," he continued. And I felt that I was just like France in that respect.

"The Soudan," he went on, "could be made a very Argentine of corn and cattle, a very Egypt of cotton—and ah! those Soudanes! What soldiers for France! . . .

"The Bedouin must be tamed, the Touareg broken, the Senussi won over. . . . *There* is where we want trained emissaries—France's secret ambassadors at work among the tribes . . .

"Shall the West come beneath the Tri-colour of France, or the Green Banner of Pan-Islamism? . . ."

At the moment I did not greatly care. The schemes of irrigation and food-supply interested me more. Corn and

8

cattle . . . suitably prepared, and perhaps a little soup, fish and chicken too. . . .

"We must have safe Trans-Saharan Routes; and then Engineering and Agricultural Science shall turn the desert to a garden—France's great kitchen-garden. France's orchard and cornfield. And the sun's very rays shall be harnessed that their heat may provide France with the greatest power-station in the world. . . ."

"Oh, yes, Uncle," I said. Certainly France should have the sun's rays if I might have lunch.

"But conquest first! Conquest by diplomacy. . . . Divide and rule—that Earth's poorest and emptiest place may become its richest and fullest—and that France may triumph. . . ."

Selfishly I thought that if my poorest and emptiest place could soon become the richest and fullest, *I* should triumph. . . .

"Now, Boy," concluded my uncle, ceasing his swift pacing, and impaling me with a penetrating stare, "I will try you, and I will give you such a chance to become a Marshal of France as falls to few. . . . Listen. Go to the Headquarters of the military division of the *arrondissement* in which you were born, show your papers, and enlist as a *Volontaire*. You will then have to serve for only one year instead of the three compulsory for the ordinary conscript—because you are the son of a widow, have voluntarily enlisted before your time, and can pay the *Volontaire's* fee of 1,500 francs. . . . I will see that you are posted to the Blue Hussars, and you will do a year in the ranks. You will never mention my name to a soul, and you will be treated precisely as any other private soldier. . . .

"If you pass out with high marks at the end of the period, come to me, and I will see that you go to Africa with a commission in the Spahis, and your foot will be on the ladder. . . . There, learn Arabic until you know it better than your mother-tongue; and learn to know the Arab better than you know yourself. . . . *Then* I can use you!"

"Oh, *yes*, Uncle," I dutifully responded, as he paused.

"And some day—some day—I swear it—you will be one of France's most valuable and valued servants, leading a life of the deepest interest, highest usefulness and greatest danger. . . . You will be tried as a cavalryman, tried as a

9

Spahi officer, tried as my aide-de-camp, tried as an emissary, a negotiator, a Secret-Service officer, and will get such a training as shall fit you to succeed me—and I shall be a Marshal of France—and Commander-in-Chief and Governor-General of the great African Empire of France. . . .

"But—fail in any way, at any one step or stage of your career, and I have done with you. . . . Be worthy of my trust, and I will make you one of France's greatest servants. . . . And, mind, Boy—you will have to *ride alone*, on the road that I shall open to you. . . ." He fell silent.

His fierce and fanatical face relaxed, a sweet smile changed it wholly, and he held out his hand.

"Would you care to lunch with me, my boy?" he said kindly.

"Er—*lunch*, Uncle?" I replied. "Thank you—yes, I think I could manage a little lunch perhaps. . . ."

CHAPTER III

THE BLUE HUSSAR

EXCELLENT! I would be worthy of this uncle of mine, and I would devote my life to my country. (Incidentally I had no objection to being made a Marshal of France, in due course.)

I regarded myself as a most fortunate young man, for all I had to do was my best. And I *was* lucky, beyond belief—not only in having such an uncle behind me, but in having an English education and an English training in sports and games. I had won the Public Schools Championship for boxing (Middle-weight) and for fencing as well. I was a fine gymnast, I had ridden from childhood, and I possessed perfect health and strength.

Being blessed with a cavalry figure, excellent spirits, a perfect digestion, a love of adventure, and an intense zest for Life, I felt that all was for the best in the best of all possible worlds. As for "riding alone"—excellent . . . *I* was not going to be the sort of man that allows his career to be hampered by a woman!

§ 2

A few weeks after applying at the proper military headquarters, I received orders to appear before the *Conseil de Revision* with my papers, at the Town Hall of my native district; and, with a hundred or so other young men of every social class and kind, was duly examined, physically and mentally.

Soon after this, I received a notice directing me to present myself at the cavalry barracks, to be examined in equitation. If I failed in the test, I could not enter a cavalry regiment as a one-year *Volontaire*.

I passed all right, of course, and, a little later, received my *feuille de route* and notification that I was posted to the Blue Hussars and was to proceed forthwith to their barracks at St. Denis, and report myself.

I had spent the interval, partly with my mother and her people, the Carys; and partly in Paris with a Lieutenant de Lannec, appointed my guide, philosopher and friend by my uncle, under whom de Lannec was then working at the War Office. To this gentleman I was indebted for much good advice and innumerable hints and tips that proved invaluable. Also for the friendship of the dear clever little Véronique Vaux, and, most of all, for that of Raoul d'Auray de Redon, at a later date.

To de Lannec I owed it that if in my raw-recruit days I was a fool, I was not a sanguinary fool; and that I escaped most of the pitfalls digged for the feet of the unwary by those who had themselves only become wary by painful experience therein.

Thanks to him, I also knew enough to engage permanently a private room for myself at a hotel in St. Denis, where I could have meals and a bath; to have my cavalry boots and uniform privately made for me; and to equip myself with a spare complete outfit of all those articles of clothing and of use, the loss or lack of which brings the private soldier to so much trouble and punishment.

§ 3

And one fine morning I presented myself at the great gates of the barracks of the famous Blue Hussars, trying to look happier than I felt.

I beheld an enormous parade ground, about a quarter of a mile square, with the Riding School in the middle of it, and beyond it a huge barracks for men and horses. The horses occupied the ground-floor and the men the floors above—not a nice arrangement I thought. (I continued to think it, when I lived just above the horses, in a room that held a hundred and twenty unwashed men, a hundred and twenty pairs of stable-boots, a hundred and twenty pairs of never-cleaned blankets—and windows that had been kept shut for a hundred and twenty years, to exclude the exhalations from the stable (because more than enough came up through the floor).

I passed through the gates, and Sergeant came out from the Guard-Room, which was just beside them.

"Hi, there! Where d'ye think you're going?" he shouted.

"I have come to report myself, Sergeant," I replied meekly, and produced my *feuille de route*.

He looked at it.

"One of those anointed *Volontaires*, are you?" he growled. "Well, my fine gentleman, I don't like them, d'you understand? . . . And I don't like you. . . . I don't like your face, nor your voice, nor your clothes, nor anything about you. D'you see? . . ."

Mindful of de Lannec's advice, I held my tongue. It is the one thing of his own that the soldier may hold. But a good Sergeant is not to be defeated.

"Don't you dare to stand there and sulk, you dumb image of a dead fish," he shouted.

"No, Sergeant," I replied.

"And don't you back-answer me either, you chattering baboon," he roared.

"You have made a bad beginning," he went on menacingly, before I could be either silent or responsive, "and I'll see you make a bad end too, you pimply *pékin*! . . . Get out of this—go on—before I . . . ?"

12

"But, Sergeant," I murmured, "I have come to join . . ."

"You *will* interrupt me, will you?" he yelled. "That's settled it! Wait till you're in uniform—and I'll show you the inside of a little stone box I know of. That'll teach you to contradict Sergeants. . . . Get out of this, you insubordinate rascal—and take your *feuille de route* to the Paymaster's Office in the *Rue des Enfants Abandonnés*. . . . I'll deal with you when you come back. Name of an Anointed Poodle, I will! . . ."

In silence I turned about and went in search of the *Rue des Enfants Abandonnés*, and the Paymaster's Office, feeling that I was indeed going to begin at the bottom of a fairly steep ladder, and to receive some valuable discipline and training in self-control.

I believe that, for the fraction of a second, I was tempted to seek the train for Calais and England, instead of the Street of the Abandoned Children and the Office of the Paymaster. (Were they Children of Abandoned Character, or Children who had Been Abandoned by Others? Alas, I knew not; but feeling something of a poor Abandoned Child myself, I decided that it was the latter.)

Expecting otherwise, I had found the non-commissioned officer who was the Paymaster's Clerk, a courteous person. He asked me which Squadron I would like to join, and I replied that I should like to join any Squadron to which the present Sergeant of the Guard did not belong.

"Who's he?" asked the clerk.

I described the Sergeant as a ruffianly brute with a bristly moustache, bristly eyebrows, bristly hair, and bristly manners. A bullying blackguard in fact.

"Any private to any Sergeant," smiled the clerk; "but it sounds like Blüm. Did he swear by the name of an Anointed Poodle, by any chance?"

"That's the man," said I.

"Third Squadron. I'll put you down for the Second. . . . Take this paper and ask for the Sergeant-Major of the Second Squadron. And don't forget that if you can stand well with the S.S.M. and the *Adjudant* of your Squadron, you'll be all right. . . ."

On my return to the Barracks, I again encountered the engaging Sergeant Blüm at the Guard-Room by the gates.

"To what Squadron are you drafted?" he asked.

"To the Second, Sergeant," I replied innocently.

"And that's the worst news I have heard this year," was the reply. "I hoped you would be in the Third. I'd have had you put in my own *peloton*. I have a way with aristocrats and *Volontaires*, and *maquereaux*. . . ."

"I did my best, Sergeant," I replied truthfully.

"*Tais donc ta sale gueule*," he roared, and turning into the Guard-Room, bade a trooper do some scavenging work by removing me and taking me to the Office of the Sergeant-Major of the Second Squadron.

I followed the trooper, a tall fair Norman, across the great parade ground, now alive with men in stable-kit, carrying brooms or buckets, wheeling barrows, leading horses, pumping water into great drinking-troughs, and generally fulfilling the law of their being, as cavalry-men.

"Come along, you gaping pig," said my guide, as I gazed around the pleasing purlieus of my new home.

I came along.

"Hurry yourself, or I'll chuck you into the manure-heap, after the S.S.M. has seen you," added my conducting Virgil.

"Friend and brother-in-arms," said I, "let us go to the manure-heap at once, and we'll see who goes on it. . . . I don't know why you ever left it. . . ."

"Oh—you're one of those beastly *bullies*, are you?" replied the trooper, and knocked at the door of a small bare room which contained four beds, some military accoutrements, a table, a chair, and the Squadron Sergeant-Major, a small grey-haired man with an ascetic lean face, and moustache of grey wire, neatly clipped.

This was a person of a type different altogether from Sergeant Blüm's. A dog that never barked, but bit hard, Sergeant-Major Martin was a cold man, forceful and fierce, but in manner quiet, distant, and almost polite.

"A *Volontaire*!" he said. "A pity. One does not like them, but such things must be. . . ."

He took my papers, asked me questions, and recorded the answers in the *livret* or regimental-book, which every French soldier must cherish. He then bade the trooper conduct me to Sergeant de Poncey with the bad news that I was to be in his *peloton*.

"Follow me, bully," said the trooper after he had saluted the Sergeant-Major and wheeled from the room. . . .

Sergeant de Poncey was discovered in the exercise of his duty, giving painful sword-drill to a punishment-squad, outside the Riding School. He was a handsome man who looked as though life held nothing for him but pain. His voice was that of an educated man.

The troopers, clad in canvas uniform and clogs, looked desperately miserable.

They had cause, since they had spent the night in prison, had had no breakfast, and were undergoing a kind of torture. The Sergeant would give an order, the squad would obey it, and there the matter would rest—until some poor devil, sick and half-starved, would be unable to keep his arm, and heavy sword, extended any longer. At the first quiver and sinking down of the blade, the monotonous voice would announce:

"Trooper Ponthieu, two more days *salle de police*, for not keeping still," and a new order would be given for a fresh form of grief, and another punishment to the weakest.

Well—they were there for punishment, and they were certainly getting it.

When the squad had been marched back to prison, Sergeant de Poncey attended to me. He looked me over from head to foot.

"A gentleman," said he. "Good! I was one myself, once. Come with me," and he led the way to the *quartiers* of the Second Squadron, and the part of the room in which his *peloton* slept.

Two partitions, some eight feet in height, divided the room into three, and along partitions and walls were rows of beds. Each bed was so narrow that there was no discomfort in eating one's meals as one sat astride the bed, as though seated on a horse, with a basin of *soupe* before one.

It was thus that, for a year, I took all meals that I did not have at my hotel.

At the head of each bed hung a cavalry-sword and bag of stable-brushes and cleaning-kit; while above each were a couple of shelves bearing folded uniforms covered with a canvas bag on which was painted their owner's *matricule* number. Crowning each edifice was a *shako* and two pairs of boots. Cavalry carbines stood in racks in the corners of the room. . . . As I stared round, the Sergeant put his hand on my arm.

"You'll have a rough time here," he said. "Your only chance will be to be rougher than the time."

"I am going to be a real rough, Sergeant," I smiled. I liked this Sergeant de Poncey from the first.

"The worst of it is that it *stays*, my son," replied Sergeant de Poncey. "Habit becomes second nature—and then first nature. As I told you, I was a gentleman once; and now I am going to ask you to lend me twenty francs, for I am in serious trouble. . . . Will you?"

"No, Sergeant," I said, and his unhappy face darkened with pain and annoyance. "I am going to give you a hundred, if I may. . . . Will you?"

"You'll have a friend in me," was the reply, and the poor fellow positively flushed—I supposed with mingled emotions of gratitude, relief and discomfort.

And a good friend Sergeant de Poncey proved, and particularly valuable after he became Sergeant-Major; for though a Sergeant-Major may not have power to permit certain doings, he has complete power to prevent Higher Authority from knowing that they have been done. . . .

A Corporal entering the room at that minute, Sergeant de Poncey called him and handed me over to him with the words:

"A recruit for your *escoude*, Lepage. A *Volontaire*—but a good fellow. Old friend of mine. . . . See?"

The Corporal saw. He had good eyesight; for the moment Sergeant de Poncey was out of earshot, he added:

"Come and be an 'old friend' of mine too," and led the way out of the *quartiers*, across the great barrack-square, to the canteen.

Cheaply and greasily handsome, the swarthy Corporal Lepage was a very wicked little man indeed, but likeable, by reason of an unfailing sense of humour and a paradoxical trustworthiness. He had every vice and would do any evil thing—except betray a trust or fail a friend. Half educated, he was a clerk by profession, and an ornament of the city of Paris. Small, dissipated and drunken, he yet had remarkable strength and agility, and was never ill.

In the canteen he drank neat cognac at my expense, and frankly said that his goodwill and kind offices could be purchased for ten francs. I purchased them, and, having pouched the gold piece and swallowed his seventh cognac, the worthy man inquired whether I intended to jabber there the *entire* day, or to go to the medical inspection to which he was endeavouring to conduct me.

"This is the first I have heard of it, Corporal," I protested.

"Well, it won't be the last, Mr. Snipe, unless you obey my orders and cease this taverning, chambering and wantonness," replied the good Lepage. "Hurry, you idle apprentice and worthless *Volontaire*."

I hurried.

Pulling himself together, Corporal Lepage marched me from the canteen to the dispensary near by.

The place was empty save for an Orderly.

"Surgeon-Major not come yet, Corporal," said the man Lepage turned upon me.

"Perhaps you'll let me finish my coffee in peace another time," he said, in apparent wrath, and displaying sharp little teeth beneath his waxed moustache. "Come back and do your duty."

And promising the Orderly that *I* would give him a cognac if he came and called the Corporal from the canteen as soon as the Surgeon-Major returned, he led the way back.

In the end, I left Corporal Lepage drunk in the canteen, passed the medical examination, and made myself a friend for life by returning and getting the uplifted warrior safely back to the barrack-room and bed.

An amusing morning.

§ 5

I shall never forget being tailored by the *Sergent-Fourrier* that afternoon. His store was a kind of mighty shop in which the Regimental Sergeant-Tailor, Sergeant-Boot-maker Sergeant-Saddler and Sergeant-Storekeeper were his shop assistants.

Here I was given a pair of red trousers to try on—"for size." They were as stiff, as heavy, and nearly as big, as a diver's suit and clogs, and from the knees downward were of solid leather.

They were not riding-breeches, but huge trousers, the legs being each as round as my waist. As in the case of an axiom of Euclid, no demonstration was needed, but since the Sergeant-Tailor bade me get into them—I got.

When the heavy leather ends of them rested on the ground, the top cut me under the arm-pits. The top of that inch-thick, red felt garment, hard and stiff as a board, literally cut me.

I looked over the edge and smiled at the Sergeant-Tailor.

"Yes," he agreed, "*excellent*," and handed me a blue tunic to try on, "for size." The only faults in this case were that my hands were invisible within the sleeves, and that I could put my chin inside the collar after it had been hooked. I flapped my wings at the Sergeant-Tailor.

"Yes, you go into that nicely, too," he said, and he was quite right. That there was room for him, as well, did not seem to be of importance.

The difficulty now was to move, as the trousers seemed to be like jointless armour, but I struggled across the store to where sat the Sergeant-Bootmaker, with an entire range of boots of all sizes awaiting me. The "entire range" consisted of four pairs, and of these the smallest was two inches long, but would not permit the passage of my instep.

They were curious leather buildings, these alleged boots. They were as wide as they were long, were perfectly square at both ends, had a leg a foot high, heels two and a half inches thick, and great rusty spurs nailed on to them.

The idea was to put them on under the trousers.

"You've got deformed feet, oh, *espèce d'imbécile*," said the Sergeant-Bootmaker, when his complete range of four sizes had produced nothing suitable. "You ought not to be in the army. The likes of you are a curse and an undeserved punishment to good Sergeants, you orphaned Misfortune of God. . . . . Put on on the biggest pair. . . ."

18

"But, Sergeant," I protested, "they are exactly five inches longer than my feet!"

"And is straw so dear in a cavalry regiment that you cannot stuff the toes with it, Most Complete Idiot?" inquired the man of ideas.

"But they'd simply fall off my feet if I tried to walk in them," I pointed out.

"And will not the straps of your trousers, that go underneath the boots, keep the boots on your feet, Most Polished and Perfected Idiot?" replied this prince of bootmakers. "And the trousers will hide the fact that the boots are a little large."

As all I had to do was to get from the barracks to my hotel, where I had everything awaiting me, it did not so much matter. But what of the poor devil who had to accept such things without alternative?

When I was standing precariously balanced inside these boots and garments, the *Sergent-Fourrier* gave me a Hussar shako which my ears insecurely supported; wound a blue scarf round my neck, inside the collar of the tunic, and bade me go and show myself to the Captain of the Week—who was incidentally *Capitaine en Second* of my Squadron.

Dressed as I was, I would not willingly have shown myself to a mule, lest the poor animal laugh itself into a state of dangerous hysteria.

Walking as a diver walks along the deck of a ship, I plunged heavily forward, lifting and dropping a huge boot, that hung at the end of a huge trouser-leg, at each step.

It was more like the progression of a hobbled clown-elephant over the tan of a circus, than the marching of a smart Hussar. I felt very foolish, humiliated and angry.

Guided by a storeroom Orderly, I eventually reached the door of the Captain's office, and burst upon his sight.

I do not know what I expected him to do. He did not faint, nor call upon Heaven for strength.

He eyed me as one does a horse offered for sale. He was of the younger school—smart, cool and efficient; a handsome spare man, pink and white above a shaven blueness. In manner he was of a suavely sinister politeness that thinly covered real cruelty.

"Take off that tunic," he said.

I obeyed with alacrity.

"Yes, the trousers are too short," he observed, and added: "Are you a natural fool, that you come before me with trousers that are too short?"

"*Oui, mon Capitaine*," I replied. I felt I *was* a natural fool, to be there in those, or in any other, trousers.

"And look at your boots. Each is big enough to contain both your feet. Are you an *un*natural fool to come before me in such boots?"

"*Oui, mon Capitaine*," I replied. I felt I *was* an unnatural fool, to be there in those, or in any other, boots.

"I will make a note of it, recruit," said the officer, and I felt he had said more than any roaring Sergeant, shouting definite promises of definite punishments.

"Have the goodness to go," he continued in his silky-steely voice, "and return in trousers twice as large and boots half as big. You may tell the *Sergent-Fourrier* that he will shortly hear something to his disadvantage. . . . It will interest him in you. . . ."

It did. It interested all the denizens of that horrible store-room, that stank of stale leather, stale fustian, stale brass, and stale people.

("I would get them into trouble, would I? . . . I would bring reprimands and punishments upon senior Sergeants, would I? . . . Oh, Ho! and Ah, Ha! Let me but wait until I was in their hands! . . . ")

A little later, I was sent back to the Captain's room, in the identical clothes that I had worn on the first visit. My trousers were braced to my chin, the leather ends of the legs were pulled farther forward over the boots, a piece of cloth was folded and pushed up the back of my tunic, my sleeves were pulled back, and a fold or tuck of the cloth was made inside each elbow. A crushed-up ball of brown paper relieved my ears of some of the weight of my shako.

"You come back here again, unpassed by the Captain, and I swear I'll have you in prison within the week," promised the *Sergent-Fourrier*.

I thanked him and shuffled back.

My Captain eyed me blandly across the table, as I saluted.

"Trousers are now too big," he observed, "and the tunic too small. Are you *really* determined to annoy me, recruit?" he added. "If so, I must take steps to protect myself. . . . Kindly return and inform the *Sergent-Fourrier* that I will interview him later. . . ."

Pending that time, the *Sergent-Fourrier* and his myrmidons interviewed *me*. They also sent me back in precisely the same garments; this time with trousers braced only to my breast and with the sleeves of my tunic as they had been at first.

My Captain was not in his room, and I promptly returned and told the truth—that he had found no fault in me this time. . . .

Eventually I dragged my leaden-footed, swaddled, creaking carcase from the store, burdened with an extra tunic, an extra pair of incredible trousers, an extra pair of impossible boots, a drill-jacket, a *képi*, two canvas stable-suits, an overcoat, a huge cape, two pairs of thick white leather gauntlets big enough for Goliath of Gath, two terrible shirts, two pairs of pants, a huge pair of clogs, and no socks at all.

Much of this impedimenta was stuffed into a big canvas bag.

With this on my back, and looking like Bunyan's *Christian* and feeling like no kind of Christian, I staggered to my room.

Here, Corporal Lepage, in a discourse punctuated with brandified hiccups, informed me that I must mark each article with my *matricule* number, using for that purpose stencils supplied by the *Sergent-Fourrier*.

Feeling that more than stencils would be supplied by that choleric and unsocial person, if I again encountered him ere the sun had gone down upon his wrath, I bethought me of certain advice given me in Paris by my friend de Lannec—and cast about for one in search of lucrative employment.

Seated on the next bed to mine, and polishing his sword, was a likely-looking lad. He had a strong and pleasing face, calm and thoughtful in expression, and with a nice fresh air of countrified health.

"Here, comrade," said I, "do you want a job and a franc or two?"

"Yes, sir," he replied, "or two jobs and a franc or three . . . I am badly broke, and I am also in peculiar and particular need to square Corporal Lepage."

I found that his name was Dufour, that he was the son of a horse-dealer, and had had to do with both horses and gentlemen to a considerable extent.

From that hour he became my friend and servant, to the day when he gave his life for France and for me, nearly twenty years later. He was very clever, honest and extremely brave; a faithful, loyal, noble soul.

I engaged him then and there; and his first job in my service was to get my kit stencilled, cleaned and arranged *en paquetage* on the shelves.

He then helped me to make myself as presentable as was possible in the appalling uniform that had been issued to me, for I had to pass the Guard (and in full dress, as it was now noon) in order to get out to my hotel where my other uniforms, well cut by my own tailor, were awaiting me, together with boots of regulation pattern, made for me in Paris.

To this day I do not know how I managed to waddle past the Sergeant of the Guard, my sword held in a gloved hand that felt as though cased in cast iron, my big shako wobbling on my head, and the clumsy spurs of my vast and uncontrollable boots catching in the leather ends of my vaster trousers.

I did it however, with Dufour's help; and, a few minutes later, was in my own private room and tearing the vile things from my outraged person.

As I sat over my coffee, at a quarter to nine that evening, after a tolerable dinner and a bottle of *Mouton Rothschild*, dreaming great dreams, I was brought back to hard facts by the sudden sound of the trumpeters of the Blue Hussars playing the *retraite* in the *Place*.

That meant that, within a quarter of an hour, they would march thence back to Barracks, blowing their instant summons to all soldiers who had not a late pass—and that I must hurry.

My return journey was a very different one from my last, for my uniform, boots, and shako fitted me perfectly; my gauntlets enabled me to carry my sword easily ("*in left hand; hilt turned downwards and six inches behind hip; tip of scabbard in front of left foot,*" etc.), and feeling that I could salute any officer or non-commissioned officer otherwise than by flapping a half-empty sleeve at him.

Once more I felt like a man and almost like a soldier. My spirits rose nearly to the old Eton level.

They sank to the new Barrack level, however, when I entered the room in which I was to live for a year, and its terrific and terrible stench took me by the throat. As I stood at the foot of my bed, as everybody else did, awaiting the evening roll-call, I began to think I should be violently unwell; and by the time the Sergeant of the Week had made his round and received the Corporal's report as to absentees (stables, guard, leave, etc.) I was feeling certain that I must publicly disgrace myself.

However, I am a good sailor, and when the roll-call (which has no "calling" whatever) was finished, and all were free to do as they liked until ten o'clock, when the "*Lights out*" trumpet would be blown, I fled to the outer air, and saved my honour and my dinner.

I had to return, of course, but not to stand to attention like a statue while my head swam; and I soon found that I could support life with the help of a handkerchief which I had had the forethought to perfume.

While I was sitting on my bed (which consisted of two trestles supporting two narrow planks, and a sausage-like roll of straw-mattress and blankets, the whole being only two feet six inches wide), gazing blankly around upon the specimen of my fellow-man in bulk, and wondering if and when and where he washed, I was aware of a party approaching me, headed by the fair trooper who had been my guide to the office of the Squadron Sergeant-Major that morning.

"That is it," said their leader, pointing to me. "It is a *Volontaire*. It is dangerous too. A dreadfully bully. Tried to throw me into the muck-heap when I wasn't looking . . ."

"Behold it," said a short, square, swarthy man, who looked, in spite of much fat, very powerful. "Regard it. It uses a scented handkerchief so as not to smell us."

"Well, we are not roses. Why *should* he smell us?" put in a little rat-like villain, edging forward.

He and the fat man were pushed aside by a typical hard-case fighting-man, such as one sees in boxing-booths, fencing-schools and gymnasia.

"See, *Volontaire*," he said, "you have insulted the Blue Hussars in the person of Trooper Mornec and by using a handkerchief in our presence. I am the champion swordsman of the Regiment, and I say that such insults can only be washed out in . . ."

"Blood," said I, reaching for my sword.

"No—*wine*," roared the gang as one man, and, rising, I put one arm through that of the champion swordsman and the other through that of Trooper Mornec, and we three headed a joyous procession to the canteen, where we solemnly danced the *can-can* with spirit and abandon.

I should think that the whole of my *peloton* (three *escouades* of ten men each) was present by the time we reached the bar, and it was there quickly enriched by the presence of the rest of the Squadron.

However, brandy was only a shilling a quart, and red wine fourpence, so it was no very serious matter to entertain these good fellows, nor was there any fear that their capacity to pour in would exceed mine to pay out.

But, upon my word, I think the combined smells of the canteen—rank tobacco-smoke, garlic, spirits, cooking, frying onions, wine, burning fat and packed humanity—were worse than those of the barrack-room; and it was borne in upon me that not only must the soldier's heart be in the right place, but his stomach also. . . .

The "*Lights out*" trumpet saved me from death in the canteen, and I returned to die in the barrack-room, if I must.

Apparently I returned a highly popular person, for none of the usual tricks was played upon me, such as the jerking away (by means of a rope) of one of the trestles supporting the bed, as soon as the recruit has forgotten his sorrows in sleep.

De Lannec had told me what to expect, and I had decided to submit to most of the inflictions with a good grace and cheerful spirit, while certain possible indignities I was determined to resist to the point of serious bloodshed.

With Dufour's help, I inserted my person into the sausage precariously balanced on the planks, and fell asleep in spite of sharp-pointed straws, the impossibility of turning in my cocoon, the noisy illness of several gentlemen who had spent the evening unwisely, the stamping and chain-rattling of horses, the cavalry-trumpet snoring of a hundred cavalry noses, and the firm belief that I should in the morning be found dead from poisoning and asphyxiation.

All very amusing. . . .

CHAPTER IV

A PERFECT DAY

I FOUND myself quite alive, however, at five o'clock the next morning, when the Corporal of the Week passed through the room bawling, "Anyone sick here?"

I was about to reply that although I was not being sick at the moment, I feared I shortly should be, when I realized that the Corporal was collecting names for the Sergeant-Major's morning report, and not making polite inquiries as to how we were feeling after a night spent in the most mephitic atmosphere that human beings could possibly breathe, and live.

There is no morning roll-call in the Cavalry, but the Sergeant-Major gets the names of those who apply for medical attention, and removes them from the duty-list of each *peloton*.

For half an hour I lay awake wondering what would happen if I sprang from my bed and opened a window— or broke a window if they were not made for opening. I was on the point of making this interesting discovery when the *réveille* trumpets rang out, in the square below, and I was free to leave my bed—at five-thirty of a bitter cold morning.

Corporal Lepage came to me as I repressed my first yawn (fearing to inhale the poison-gas unnecessarily) and bade me endue my form with canvas and clogs, and hie me to the stables.

Hastily I put on the garb of a gutter-scavenger and, guided by Dufour, hurried through the rain to my pleasing task.

In the stable was a different smell, but it was homogeneous and, on the whole, I preferred the smell of the horses to that of their riders. (You see, we clean the horses thoroughly, daily. In the Regulations it is so ordered. But as to the horse*men*, it says, "*A Corporal must sleep in the same room with the troopers of his escouade and must see that his troopers wash their heads, faces, hands and feet.*" This much would be something, at any rate, if only he carried out the Regulations.)

At the stables I received my first military order.

"Clean the straw under those four horses," said the Sergeant on stable-duty.

An unpleasing but necessary work.

Someone had to do it, and why not I? Doubtless the study of the art of separation of filthy straw from filthier straw, and the removal of manure, is part of a sound military training.

I looked round for implements. I believed that a pitchfork and shovel were the appropriate and provided tools for the craftsman in this line of business.

"What the hell are you gaping at? You . . ." inquired the Sergeant, with more liberty of speech than fraternity or equality.

"What shall I do it with, Sergeant?" I inquired.

"Heaven help me from killing it!" he moaned, and then roared: "Have you no *hands*, Village Idiot? D'you suppose you do it with your toe-nails, or the back of your neck?"

And it was so. With my lily-white hands I laboured well and truly, and loaded barrows until they were piled high. I took an artistic interest in my work, patting a shapely pyramid upon the barrow, until:

"Dufour," I said, "I am going to be so *very* sick. What's the punishment? . . ."

The good Dufour glanced hastily around.

"Run to the canteen," he whispered. "I can do the eight stalls easy. Have a hot coffee and cognac."

I picked up a bucket and rushed forth across the barrack-square, trying to look like one fulfilling a high and honourable function. If anybody stopped me, I would say I was going to get the Colonel a bucket of champagne for his bath. . . .

At the canteen I found a man following a new profession. He called himself a Saviour-from-Selfish-Sin, and explained to me that the basest thing a soldier could do was to *faire Suisse*, to drink alone.

No one need drink alone when *he* was there, he said, and he gave up his valuable time and energy to frequenting the canteen at such hours as it might be empty, and a man might come and fall into sin.

I drank my coffee and cognac and then went outside,

inhaled deeply for some minutes and soon felt better. Catching up my bucket, I returned to the stables, trying to look like one who has, by prompt and determined effort, saved the Republic.

Dufour finished our work and told me we must now return to the barrack-room in time to get our bags of grooming-implements before the trumpets sounded "*Stables*" at six o'clock.

"You begin on the horse that's given you, sir," said Dufour, "and as soon as the Sergeant's back is turned, clear out again, and I'll finish for you."

"Not a bit of it," I replied. "I shall be able to groom a horse all right. It was loading those barrows with my bare hands that made me feel so sea-sick."

"You'll get used to it," Dufour assured me.

But I doubted it. "Use is second nature," as de Poncey said, but I did not think it would become my second nature to scavenge with my bare hands. . . . Nor my third. . . .

At six o'clock we returned to the stables, and the Lieutenant of the Week allotted me my horse and ordered me to set about grooming him.

Now I have the horse-gift. I love and understand horses, and horses love and understand me. I was not, therefore, depressed when the horse laid his ears back, showed me a white eye, and lashed out viciously as I approached the stall. It merely meant that the poor brute had been mishandled by a bigger brute, and that fear, instead of love, had been the motive appealed to.

However, I had got to make friends with him before he could be friendly, and the first step was to enter his stall—a thing he seemed determined to prevent. I accordingly slipped into the next one, climbed over, and dropped down beside him. In a minute I was grooming him, talking to him, handling him, making much of him, and winning his confidence.

I swore to myself I would never touch him with whip nor spur: for whip and spur had been his trouble. He was a well-bred beast, and I felt certain from his colour, socks, head, eye and general "feel" that he was not really vicious. I don't know how I know what a horse thinks and feels and *is*, but I do know it.

I groomed him thoroughly for nearly an hour, and then

fondled him and got him used to my voice, hands and smell. I rather expected trouble when I took him to water, as Dufour had put his head round the partition and warned me that *Le Boucher* was a dangerous brute who had sent more than one man on a stretcher to hospital.

At seven o'clock the order was given for the horses to be taken to the water-troughs, and I led *Le Boucher* out of his stall. Seizing a lock of his mane, I vaulted on to his bare back and prepared for trouble.

He reared until I thought he would fall; he put down his head and threw up his heels until I thought that *I* should; and then he bucked and bounded in a way that enabled me to give an exhibition of riding.

But it was all half-hearted. I felt that he was going through the performance mechanically, and, at worst, finding out what sort of rider I was.

After this brief period of protest he trotted off to the watering-tank, and I never again had the slightest trouble with *Le Boucher*. I soon changed the stupid name of "The Butcher", to "Angelique", partly in tribute to one of the nicest of girls, and partly in recognition of the horse's real temper and disposition. . . .

After "Stables", I was sent to get the rest of my kit, and was endowed with carbine, saddle, sword-belt cartridge-box and all sorts of straps and trappings. I found my saddle to be of English make and with a high straight back, behind which was strapped the cylindrical blue portmanteau, with the regimental crest at each end.

I also found that the bridle was of the English model, not the "9th Lancer" pattern, but with bit and snaffle so made that the head-stall remained on the horse when the bit-straps were taken off.

It was ten o'clock by the time that I had received the whole of the kit for myself and horse, and that is the hour of breakfast. Our trumpets sang "*Soupe*" and the bucket was lowered from the hand of the soldier who crossed the wide plain—of the barrack-square.

Everybody rushed to put away whatever he held in his hand, and to join the throng that poured into the Regimental kitchen and out by another door, each man bearing a *gamelle* (or saucepan-shaped tin pot), of *soupe* and a loaf of

28

bread. Having washed my hands, without soap, at the horse-trough, I followed.

Holding my own, I proceeded to my room, placed it on my bed, sat astride the bed with the *gamelle* before me, and fell to.

It wasn't at all bad, and I was very hungry in spite of my previous nausea.

The meal finished, the Orderly of the *Caporal d'Ordin-aire* collected the pots and took them back to the kitchen.

My immediate desire now was a hot-and-cold-water lavatory and a good barber. It was the first day of my life that had found me, at eleven o'clock, unwashen and un-combed, to say nothing of unbathed. At the moment I wanted a shave more ardently than I wanted eternal salva-tion.

"And now, where is the lavatory, Dufour?" I asked, as that youth stowed away his spare bread behind his *paquet-age*.

"Beside the forage-store, sir," he replied, "and it is a grain-store itself. There is an old Sergeant-pensioner at the hospital, who remembers the day, before the Franco–Prussian War, when it was used as a lavatory, but no one else had ever seen anything in it but sacks of corn."

"Isn't washing compulsory, then?" I asked.

"Yes. In the summer, all have to go, once a fortnight, to the swimming-baths," was the interesting reply.

"Do people ever wash voluntarily?" I asked.

"Oh, yes," said Dufour. "Men going on guard, or on parade, often wash their faces, and there are many who wash their hands and necks as well, on Sundays, or when they go out with their girls. . . . You must not think we are dirty people. . . ."

"No," said I. "And where can this be done?"

"Oh, under the pump, whenever you like," was the reply, and I found that it was the unsullied truth.

No one was hindered from washing under the pump, if he he wished to do such a thing. . . .

At twelve o'clock, Corporal Lepage sent me to join the Medical-Inspection Squad, as I must be vaccinated.

After that operation, dubiously beneficial by reason of the probability of one's contracting tetanus or other sor-rows as well as immunity from smallpox, I returned to my bright home to deal with the chaos of kit that adorned my bedside; and with Dufour's help had it reduced to order and cleanliness by three in the afternoon, when "*Stables*" was again the pursuit in being.

After "Stables" we stood in solemn circles around our respective *Caporaux-fourriers* to hear the Regimental Orders of the Day read out, while Squadron Sergeant-Majors eyed everybody with profound suspicion and sure conviction of their state of sin.

So far as I could make out, the Regimental Orders of that particular day consisted of a list of punishments inflicted upon all and sundry (for every conceivable, and many of inconceivable, military offence), including the officers themselves—which surprised me.

So far as I remember, the sort of thing was:

"*Chef d'Escadron* de Montreson, fifteen days' *arrêts de rigueur* for being drunk and disorderly in the town last night.

"*Capitaine Instructeur* Robert, eight days' *arrêts simples* for overstaying leave and returning with uniform in untidy condition.

"*Adjudant* Petit, four days' confinement to room for allowing that room to be untidy.

"*Trooper* Leduc, eight days' *salle de police* for looking resentful when given four days' *salle de police*.

"*Trooper* Blanc, eight days' *salle de police* for possessing and reading a newspaper in *quartiers*.

'*Trooper* Delamer, thirty days' extra *salle de police* from the Colonel for having received sixteen days' extra *salle de police* from his Captain because he had received four days' extra *salle de police* from Sergeant Blüm, who caught him sleeping in the stables when he should have been sleeping in the *salle de police*.

"*Trooper* Mangeur, eight days' confinement to Barracks for smiling when given four days' Inspection with the Guard Parade."

And so on.

When the joyous parade was finished, I was free, and having cleaned and beautified myself, I passed the Sergeant of the Guard in full-dress uniform, and sought mine inn for dinner, peace, and privacy.

But oh! how my heart ached for any poor soul who,

being gently nurtured, had to remain in that horrible place for three years, and without the privilege, even if he could afford it, of a private place to which he could retire to bathe and eat, to rest and be alone.

CHAPTER V

BECQUE—AND RAOUL D'AURAY DE REDON

I SETTLED into the routine of my new life very quickly, and it was not long before I felt it was as though I had known no other.

At times I came near to desperation, but not so near as I should have come had it not been for my private room at the hotel, the fact that I did much of my work with other *Volontaires* in a special class, and the one great certainty, in a world of uncertainty, that there are only twelve months in a year.

From 6.30 to 8 we *Volontaires* were in "school"; from 8 to 10 we drilled on foot; from 10 to 11 we breakfasted; from 11 to 12 we were at school again; from 12 to 1 we had gymnastics; from 1 to 2 *voltige* (as though we were going to be circus riders); from 2.30 to 5 "school" once more; from 5 to 6 dinner; from 6 to 8 mounted drill—and, after that, kit-cleaning!

It was some time before my days grew monotonous and shortly after they had begun to do so, I contrived to brighten the tedium of life by pretending to kill a man, deliberately, in cold blood, and with cold steel. I fear I give the impression of being a bloodthirsty and murderous youth, and I contend that at the time I had good reason.

It happened like this.

Dufour came to me one night as I was undressing for bed, and asked me whether I would care to spend an interesting evening on the morrow.

Upon inquiry it turned out that he had been approached by a certain Trooper Becque, a few days earlier, and invited to spend a jolly evening with him and some other good fellows.

Having accepted the invitation, Dufour found that Becque and the good fellows were a kind of club or society that met in a room above a little wine shop in the Rue de Salm.

Becque seemed to have plenty of money and plenty of ideas—of an interesting and curious kind. Gradually it dawned upon the intrigued Dufour that Becque was an "agent," a Man with a Message, a propagandist, and an agitator.

Apparently his object was to "agitate" the Regiment, and his Message was that Law and Order were invented by knaves for the enslavement of fools.

Dufour, I gathered, had played the country bumpkin that he looked; had gathered all the wisdom and wine that he could get; and had replied to Becque's eloquence with no more than profound looks, profounder nods, and profoundest hiccups as the evening progressed; tongues were loosened, and, through a roseate, vinous glow, the good Becque was seen for the noble friend of poor troopers that he professed to be.

Guided by a proper love of sound political philosophy and sound free wine, Dufour had attended the next meeting of this brave brotherhood, and had so far fallen beneath the spell of Becque's eloquence as to cheer it to the echo, to embrace him warmly and then to collapse, very drunk, upon a bench; and to listen with both his ears.

After his third or fourth visit, he had asked the good Becque if he might formally join his society, and bring a friend for whom he could vouch as one who would listen to Becque's sentiments with the deepest interest. . . . Would I come?

I would—though I feared that if Becque knew I was a *Volontaire*, it would be difficult to persuade him that I was promising anarchistic material. However, I could but try, and if I failed on my own account, I could still take what action I thought fit, on the word of Dufour.

On the following evening, having arrayed myself in the uniform that had been issued to me by the *Sergent-Fourrier* when I joined, I accompanied Dufour to the rendezvous. Becque I did not know, nor he me, and I received a hearty welcome. Watching the man, I decided that he was a half-educated "intelligent". He had an evil, fanatical face and a most powerful muscular frame.

I played the gullible brainless trooper and took stock of Becque and his gang. The latter consisted of three classes, I decided: First, the malcontent dregs of the Regiment—men with grievances, real or imaginary, of the kind known as "hard cases" and "King's hard bargains" in England; secondly, men who in private life were violent and dangerous "politicians"; and thirdly, men who would go anywhere, agree with anything, and applaud anybody—for a bottle of wine.

Becque's talk interested me.

He was clearly a monomaniac whose whole mental content was *hate*—hate of France; hate of all who had what he had not; hate of control, discipline and government; hate of whatsoever and whomsoever did not meet with his approval. I put him down as one of those sane lunatics, afflicted with a destruction-complex; a diseased egoist, and a treacherous, dangerous mad dog. Also a very clever man indeed, an eloquent and forceful personality. . . . The perfect *agent-provocateur*, in fact.

After a certain amount of noisy good fellowship in the bar of this low wine shop, part of the company adjourned to the room above, the door was locked, and the business of the evening began.

It appeared that Dufour had not taken the Oath of Initiation, and it was forthwith administered to him and to me. We were given the choice of immediate departure or swearing upon the Bible, with terrific oaths and solemnities, that we would never divulge the secret of the Society nor give any account whatsoever of its proceedings.

The penalty for the infringement of this oath was certain death.

We took the oath, and settled ourselves to endure an address from Becque on the subject of The Rights of Man—always meaning unwashen, uneducated, unpatriotic and wholly worthless Man, *bien entendu*.

Coming from the general to the particular, Becque inveighed eloquently against all forms and manifestations of Militarism, and our folly in aiding and abetting it by conducting ourselves as disciplined soldiers. What we ought to do was to "demonstrate", to be insubordinate, to be lazy, dirty, inefficient, and, for a start, to be passively mutinous. By the time we had spread his views throughout the Regiment and each man in the Regiment had written unsigned letters to a man in another Regiment, with a request that these might again be forwarded to other Regiments, the day would be in sight when passive mutiny could become active.

Who were a handful of miserable officers, and more miserable N.C.O.'s, to oppose the will of eight hundred united and determined men? . . .

After the address, as proper to an ignorant but inquiring disciple, I humbly propounded the question:

"And what happens to France when her army has disbanded itself? What about Germany?"

The reply was enlightening as to the man's honesty, and his opinion of our intelligence.

"The German Army will do the same, my young friend," answered Becque. "Our German brothers will join hands with us. So will our Italian and Austrian and Russian brothers, and we will form a Great Republic of the Free Proletariat of Europe. All shall own all, and none shall oppress any. There shall be no rich, no police, no prisons, no law, no poor. . . ."

"And no *Work*," hiccupped a drunken man, torn from the arms of Morpheus by these stirring promises.

As the meeting broke up, I buttonholed the good Becque, and, in manner mysterious, earnestly besought him to meet me *alone* outside the Hotel Coq d'Or tomorrow evening at eight-fifteen. I assured him that great things would result from this meeting, and he promised to come. Whereupon, taking my sword, I dragged my mighty boots and creaking uniform from his foul presence, lest I be tempted to take him by the throat and kill him.

§ 2

At eight-fifteen the next evening I was awaiting Becque outside my hotel, and when he arrived I led him, to his great mystification, to my private room.

"So you are a *Volontaire*, are you?" he began. "Are you a spy—or——"

"Or what?" I asked.

He made what I took to be a secret sign.

With my left hand I patted my right elbow, each knee, the top of my head, the back of my neck and the tip of my nose.

Becque glared at me angrily.

I raised my eyebrows inquiringly, and with my right hand twice patted my left shin, my heart, my stomach, and the seat of my trousers. . . . I also could make "secret signs"! I then rang for a bottle of wine wherewith I might return his hospitality of the previous night—before I dealt with him.

When the waiter retired I became serious, and got down to business promptly.

"Are you a Frenchman?" I asked.

"I am, I suppose," replied Becque. "My mother was of Alsace, my father a Parisian—God curse him! . . . Yes . . . I am a Frenchman. . . ."

"Good," said I. "Have you ever been wrongfully imprisoned, or in any way injured or punished by the State?"

"*Me?* . . . *Prison?* . . . *No!* What d'you mean? . . . Except that we're *all* injured by the State, aren't we? There didn't ought to be any State."

"And you hold your tenets of revolution, anarchy, murder, mutiny, and the overthrow and destruction of France and the Republic, firmly, and with all your heart and soul, do you?" I asked.

"With all my heart and soul," replied Becque, and added. "What's the game? Are you fooling—or are you from the Third Central? Or—or——"

"Never mind," I replied. "Are you prepared to die for your faith? That's what I want to know."

"I am," answered Becque.

"*You shall*," said I, and arose to signify that the conversation was ended.

Opening the door, I motioned to the creature to remove itself.

§ 3

At that time, you must know, duelling was not merely permitted but, under certain conditions, was compulsory, in the French Army, for officers and troopers alike.

It was considered, rightly or wrongly, that the knowledge that a challenge to a duel would follow insulting conduct, must tend to prevent such conduct, and to ensure propriety of behaviour among people of the same rank.

(Unfortunately, no one was allowed to fight a duel with any person of a rank superior to his own. There would otherwise have been a heavy mortality among Sergeants, for example!)

I do not know whether it may be the result or the cause of this duelling system, but the use of fists is regarded, in the French cavalry, as vulgar, ruffianly and low. Under no circumstances would two soldiers "come down and settle it behind the Riding School", in the good old Anglo-Saxon way. If they fought at all, they would fight with swords, under supervision, with seconds and surgeons present, and "by order".

A little careful management, and I should have friend Becque where I wanted him, give him the fright of his life, and perhaps put him out of the "agitating" business for a time.

I told Dufour exactly what I had in mind, and, on the following evening, instead of dining at my hotel, I went in search of the scoundrel.

He was no good to me in the canteen, on the parade ground, nor in the street. I needed him where the eye of authority would be quickly turned upon any unseemly *fracas*.

Dufour discovered him doing a scavenging *corvée* in the Riding School, under the eye of Sergeant Blüm. This would do excellently. . . .

As the fatigue-party was dismissed by the Sergeant, Dufour and I strolled by, passing one on either side of Becque, who carried a broom. Lurching slightly, Dufour pushed Becque against me, and I gave him a shove that sent him sprawling.

Springing up, he rushed at me, using the filthy broom as though it had been a bayonet. This I seized with one hand, and, with the other, smacked the face of friend Becque right heartily. Like any other member of the snake tribe, Becque spat, and then, being annoyed, I really hit him.

As he went head-over-heels, Sergeant Blüm rushed forth from the Riding School, attracted by the scuffling and the shouts of the fatigue-party and of Dufour, who had certainly made noise enough for six.

"What's this?" he roared. "Are you street curs, snapping and snarling and scrapping in the gutter, or soldiers of France? . . . Take eight days' *salle de police* both of you. . . . Who began it, and what happened?"

The excellent Dufour gabbled a most untruthful version of the affair, and Sergeant Blüm took notes. Trooper Becque had publicly spat upon *Volontaire* de Beaujolais, who had then knocked him down. . . .

The next evening's orders, read out to the troopers by the *Caporaux-Fourriers*, contained the paragraph, by order of the Colonel:

"The Troopers Becque and de Beaujolais will fight a duel on Monday morning at ten o'clock, with cavalry-swords, in the Riding School, in the presence of the Major of the Week, the Captain of the Week, and of the Second Captains of their respective Squadrons, of Surgeon-Major Philippe and Surgeon-Major Patti-Reville, and of the Fencing-Master, in accordance with Army Regulation 869: *If a soldier has been gravely insulted by one of his comrades, and the insult has taken place in public, he must not hesitate to claim reparation for it by a duel. He should address his demand to his Captain Commanding, who should transmit it to the Colonel. But it must not be forgotten that a good soldier ought to avoid quarrels.* . . .

"The successful combatant in this duel will receive fifteen days' imprisonment, and the loser will receive thirty days'."

On hearing the order, I was of opinion that the loser would disappear from human ken for more than thirty days.

§ 4

On entering the Riding School with Dufour on the Monday morning, I was delighted to see Sergeant Blüm in the place of the Fencing-Master, who was ill in hospital.

This was doubly excellent, as my task was rendered easier and Sergeant Blüm was placed in an unpleasant and risky situation. For it was the Fencing-Master's job, while acting as Master of Ceremonies and referee, to stand close by, with

37

a steel scabbard in his hand, and prevent either of the combatants from killing, or even dangerously wounding the other!

Severe punishment would follow his failing to do his duty in this respect—and the noisy, swaggering Blüm was no *maître d'armes*.

As instructed, we were "in stable-kit, with any footwear preferred," so I had tucked my canvas trousers into socks, and put on a pair of gymnasium shoes.

Scrutinizing Becque carefully, I came to the conclusion that he would show the fierce and desperate courage of a cornered rat, and that if he had paid as much attention to fencing as to physical culture and anarchistic sedition, he would put up a pretty useful fight. I wondered what sort of a swordsman he was, and whether he was in the habit, like myself and a good many troopers, of voluntarily supplementing the compulsory attendance at fencing-school for instruction in "foils and sabres".

When all the officers and official spectators were present we were ordered to strip to the waist, were given heavy cavalry-swords, and put face to face, by Sergeant Blüm who vehemently impressed upon us the imperative duty of instantly stopping when he cried "*Halt!*"

Blüm then gave the order "*On guard*", and stood with his steel scabbard beneath our crossed swords. Throughout the fight he held this ready to parry any head-cuts, or to strike down a dangerous thrust. (And they called this a *duel!*)

My great fear was, that with the clumsy lout sticking his scabbard into the fight and deflecting cuts and thrusts, I should scratch Becque or Becque would scratch me. This would end the preposterous fight at once, as these glorious affairs were "first-blood" duels—and my object was to incapacitate Becque, and both frighten and punish a viperous and treacherous enemy of my beloved country.

I stared hard into Becque's shifty eyes. Blüm gave the word—"*Go!*" and Becque rushed at me, making a hurricane attack and showing himself to be a very good and determined fighter.

I parried for dear life, and allowed him to tire his arm and exhaust his lungs. Blüm worried me nearly as much as Becque, for he leapt around yelling to us to be "careful", and swiping at both our swords. He made me laugh, and that made me angry (and him furious), for it was no laughing matter.

"*Halt!*" he cried, and I sprang back, Becque aiming another cut at my head, after the order had been given.

"You, Becque," he shouted, "be more careful, will you? D'you think you are beating carpets, or fighting a duel, you . . ."

Becque was pale and puffing like a porpoise. He had not attempted a single thrust or feint, but had merely slashed with tremendous speed, force and orthodoxy. He was a strong, plain swordsman, but not a really good and pretty fencer.

Provided neither of us scratched the other's arm, nor drew blood prematurely, I could put Becque where I wanted him—unless the fool Blüm foiled me. It was like fighting two men at once. . . .

"*On guard!*" cried Blüm. "*Go!*" . . .

Becque instantly cut, with a *coup de flanc*, and, as I parried, struck at my head. He was fighting even more quickly than in the first round, but with less violence and ferocity. He was tiring, and my chance was coming. . . . I could have touched him a dozen times, but that was not my object. . . . I was sorely tempted, a moment later, when he missed my head, and the heavy sword was carried out of guard, but the wretched Blüm's scabbard was between us in a second. . . .

Becque was breathing heavily, and it was my turn to attack. . . . *Now!* . . . Suddenly Becque sprang backward and thrust the point of his sword into the ground. Quite unnecessarily, Blüm struck my sword down, and stepped between us.

"What's the matter, you?" snapped Major de Montreson.

"I am satisfied," panted Becque. This was a trick to get a much-needed breathing-space.

"Well, I'm not," replied the Major sourly. "Are you?" he asked, pointing to me.

"It is a duel *au premier sang*, Monsieur le Majeur," I replied, "and there is no blood yet."

"Quite so," agreed the Major. "The duel will continue at once. And if you, Becque, retreat again like that, you shall fight with your back to a corner. . . ."

"*On guard!*" cried Sergeant Blüm, and we crossed swords again. "*Go!*" . . . Becque made another most violent assault. I parried until I judged that his arm was again tired, and then feinted at his head. Up went his sword and Blum's scabbard, and my feint became a thrust—beneath the pair of them, and through Becque's right breast. . . .

France, my beautiful France, my second Mother, had one active enemy the less for quite a good while.

"I'll do that for you again, when you come out of hospital, friend Becque," said I, as he staggered back.

§ 5

There was a most tremendous row, ending in a *Conseil de discipline*, with myself in the dock, Becque being in the Infirmary. As all was in order, however, and nothing had been irregular (except that the duellists had really fought), I was not sent, as my comrades had cheerfully prophesied, to three years' hard labour in the *Compagnies de discipline* in Algeria. I was merely given fifteen days' prison, to teach me not to fight when duelling another time; and, joy of joys, Sergeant Blüm was given *retrogradation*—reduction in rank.

I walked most warily in the presence of Corporal Blüm, until, as the result of my being second in the April examination (in Riding, Drill and Command, Topography, *Voltige*, Hippology and Gymnastics) for *Volontaires*, I became a Corporal myself.

Life, after that promotion, became a little less complex, and improved still further when I headed the list of *Volontaires* at the October examination, and became a Sergeant.

§ 6

After hanging between life and death for several weeks, Becque began to mend, and Surgeon-Major Patti-Reville pronounced him to be out of danger.

That same day I received an order through Sergeant de Poncey to visit the junior officer of our squadron, *Sous-*

Lieutenant Raoul d'Auray de Redon, in his quarters, after stables.

"And what the devil does that mean, Sergeant?" I asked.

"I know no more than you," was the reply, "but I do know that Sub-Lieutenant d'Auray de Redon is one of the very finest gentlemen God ever made. . . . He has often saved me from suicide—simply by a kind word and his splendid smile. . . . If only our officers were all like him!"

I, too, had noticed the young gentleman, and had been struck by his beauty. I do not mean prettiness nor handsomeness, but *beauty*. It shone from within him, and illuminated a perfectly formed face. A light of truth, strength, courage and gentleness burned like a flame within the glorious lamp of his body. He radiated friendliness, kindness, helpfulness, and was yet the best disciplinarian in the Regiment—because he had no need to "keep" discipline. It kept itself, where he was concerned. And with all his gentle goodness of heart he was a strong man. Nay, he was a lion of strength and courage. He had the noble *élan* of the French and the cool forceful determination and bull-dog tenacity of the Anglo-Saxon.

After a wash and some valeting by Dufour, I made my way to Sub-Lieutenant d'Auray de Redon's quarters. . . .

He was seated at a table, and looked up with a long appraising stare, as I saluted and stood at attention.

"You sent for me, *mon Lieutenant*," I murmured.

"I did," replied de Redon, and the brilliant brown eyes smiled, although the strong handsome face did not.

"Why did you want to fight this Becque?" he suddenly shot at me.

I was somewhat taken aback.

"Er—he—ah—he has dirty finger-nails, *mon Lieutenant*," I replied.

"Quite probably," observed de Redon. "Quite. . . . And are you going to start a Clean Finger-nail Crusade in the Blue Hussars, and fight all those who do not join it and live up to its excellent tenets?"

"No, *mon Lieutenant*," I admitted.

"Then why Becque in particular, out of a few hundreds?" continued de Redon.

41

"Oh!—he eats garlic—and sometimes has a cast in his eye—and he jerks at his horse's mouth—and had a German mother—and wipes his nose with the back of his hand—and grins sideways exposing a long yellow dog-tooth, *mon Lieutenant*," I replied.

"Ah—you supply one with interesting information," observed my officer dryly. "Now I will supply you with some, though it won't be so interesting—because you already know it. . . . In addition to his garlic, cast, jerks, German mother, nose-wiping and dog-tooth, he is a seditious scoundrel and a hireling spy and agitator, and is trying to seduce and corrupt foolish troopers. . . . You have attended his meetings, taken the oath of secrecy and fidelity to his Society, and you have been closeted with him in private at your hotel."

I stared at de Redon in astonishment, and said what is frequently an excellent thing to say—nothing.

"Now," continued my interlocutor, "perhaps you will answer my questions a little more fully. . . . Why did you challenge Becque, after you had joined his little Society for engineering a mutiny in the Regiment, for achieving the destruction of the State, and for encompassing the ruin of France?"

"Because of the things I have already mentioned, *mon officier* and because I thought he would be the better for a rest," I replied. "I considered it a good way to end his little activities. My idea was to threaten him with a duel for every meeting that he held. . . ."

"Ah—you did, eh?" smiled de Redon. "And now I want you to tell me just what happened at these meetings, just what was said, and the names of the troopers who were present."

"I cannot do that, sir," I replied. . . . "As you seem to be aware, I took a solemn oath to reveal nothing whatsoever."

Sub-Lieutenant Raoul d'Auray de Redon rose from his chair, and came round to where I was standing. Was he—a gentleman—going to demand with threats and menaces that I break my word—even to such a rat as Becque?

"Stand at ease, Trooper Henri de Beaujolais," he said, "and shake hands with a brother of the Service! . . . Oh,

yes, I know all about you, old chap. . . . From de Lannec
—though I don't know whether your uncle is aware of the
fact. . . ."

I took the proffered hand and stammered my thanks at
this honour from my superior officer.

"Oh, nonsense, my dear boy. You'll be *my* 'superior
officer' some day, I have no doubt. . . . I must say I admire your pluck in coming to *Us* by way of the ranks. . . .
How soon will you come to Africa? . . . I am off next
month . . . Spahis . . . until I am perfect in language
and disguises. . . . Isn't it a glorious honour to be one of
your uncle's picked men? . . . And now about this Becque.
You needn't pursue him any more. I have been giving myself a little Secret Service practice and experiment. Much
easier here in France than it will be in Africa, by Jove! . . .
Well, we know all about Becque, and when he leaves hospital he will go where there will be nothing to distract his
great mind from his great thoughts for two or three years. . . .
He may be a mad dog, as you say, but I fancy that the mad
dog has some pretty sane owners and employers."

"Someone has denounced him, then?" I said.

"No, my dear de Beaujolais, not yet. But someone is
going to do so. Someone who attended his last meeting—
and who was too drunk to take any oaths. . . . So drunk
that he could only giggle helplessly when invited to swear!"

"*You?*" I asked.

"Me," replied Sub-Lieutenant d'Auray de Redon.
"'And no *Work*'! You may remember my valuable con-
tribution to the great ideas of the evening. . . ."

Such was my first encounter with this brilliant and
splendid man, whom I came to love as a brother is rarely
loved. I will tell you in due course of my last encounter with
him.

§ 7

A letter from de Lannec apprised me of the fact that my
uncle had heard of the duel, and seemed amused and far
from displeased with me. . . .

Poor old de Lannec! He wrote that his very soul was dead
within him, and his life "but dust and ashes, a vale of woe

and mourning, a desert of grief and despair in which was no oasis of joy or hope. . . ."

For he had lost his adored Véronique Vaux. . . . She had transferred her affections to a colonel of Chasseurs d'Afrique and departed with him to Fez . . . !

CHAPTER VI

AFRICA

At the end of the year, my uncle was pleased grimly to express himself as satisfied, and to send me forthwith to the Military School of Saumur, where selected Cavalry-Sergeants of good family and superior education are made into officers.

Here nothing amusing occurred, and I was glad when, once more, wires were pulled and I was instructed to betake myself and my new commission to Algeria and present myself at the *Quartier des Spahis* at Sidi-bel-Abbès.

I shall never forget my first glimpse of my new home. It is indelibly etched upon the tablets of my memory.

I stood at the great gates in the lane that separates the Spahis' barracks from those of the Foreign Legion, and thought of the day—so recently passed—when I had stood, a wretched civilian, at those of the Blue Hussars in St. Denis. . . .

Outside the red-white-and-blue-striped sentry-box stood a bearded dusky giant, a huge red turban crowning the snowy linen *kafiya* that framed his face; a scarlet be-medalled Zouave jacket covering a gaudy waistcoat and tremendous red sash; and the most voluminous skirt-like white baggy trousers almost concealing his great spurred cavalry-boots. A huge curved cavalry-sabre hung at his left side, and in his right hand he bore a carbine.

"And so this is the type of warrior I am to lead in cavalry-charges!" thought I, and wondered if there were any to equal it in the world.

He saluted me with faultless smartness and precision, and little guessed how I was thrilled to the marrow of my bones as I returned the first salute I had received from a man of my own Regiment.

Standing at the big open window of the *Salle de Rapport* in the regimental offices near the gate, was a strikingly smart and masculine figure—that of an officer in a gold-frogged white tunic (that must surely have covered a pair of corsets), which fitted his wide shoulders and narrow waist as paper fits the walls of a room.

Beneath a high red *tarbush* smiled one of the handsomest faces I have ever seen. So charming was the smile, so really beautiful the whole man, that it could be none other than Raoul d'Auray de Redon, here a couple of years before me.

I know now that one man *can* really love another with the love that is described as existing between David and Jonathan. . . . I do not believe in love "at first sight", but tremendous attraction, and the strongest liking at first sight, soon came, in this case, to be a case of love at second sight. . . . To this day I can never look upon the portrait of Raoul d'Auray de Redon, of whom more anon, without a pang of bitter-sweet pain and a half-conscious prayer. . . .

By the Guard-Room stood a group that I can see now—a statuesque *sous-officier* in spotless white drill tunic and trousers, white shoes and a *tarbush* (miscalled a fez cap)—*l'Adjudant* Lescault; an elderly French Sergeant-Major in scarlet patrol-jacket, white riding-breeches with a double black stripe down the sides, and a red *képi* with a gold band; an Arab Sergeant, dressed like the sentry, save for his chevrons; and the Guard, who seemed to me to be a mixture of Arabs and Frenchmen—for some of them were as fair in complexion as myself.

Beyond this group stood a Lieutenant, examining a horse held by an Arab groom, and I was constrained to stare at this gentleman, for beneath a red tunic he wore a pair of the colossal Spahi white skirt-trousers, and these were gathered in at the ankle to reveal a pair of tiny pointed-toed patent shoes. His other extremity was adorned by a rakish peaked *képi* in scarlet and gold.

My future brothers-in-arms these. . . .

I glanced beyond them to the Oriental garden, tree-embowered, which lay between the gates and the distant low-colonnaded stables that housed the magnificent grey Arab horses of the Regiment; and feeling that I could embrace all men, I stepped forward and entered upon my heritage. . . .

§ 2

Neverthless, it was not very long before life at the depot in Sidi-bel-Abbès grew very boring indeed. One quickly grew tired of the mild dissipations of our club, the *Cercle Militaire*, and of the more sordid ones of the alleged haunts of pleasure boasted by that dull provincial garrison-town.

Work saved me from weariness, however, for I worked like a blinded well-camel—at Arabic—in addition to the ordinary duties of a cavalry-officer.

To the Spahis came Dufour, sent by my uncle at my request, and together we pursued our studies in the language and in disguises. Nor was I sorry when, at the earliest possible moment, my uncle again pulled wires, and I was ordered to Morocco.

In that fascinating country I was extremely lucky—lucky enough, after weary garrison-duty at Casa Blanca, or rather Ain Bourdja, outside its walls, Rabat, Mequinez, Fez, Dar-Debibagh and elsewhere—to be at the gory fight of R'fakha and to charge at the head of a squadron; and to play my little part in the Chaiova campaigns at Settat, M'koun, Sidi el Mekhi, and the M'karto.

After the heavy fighting round, and in, Fez, I was a Captain, and had two pretty little pieces of metal and ribbon to hang on my tunic; and in the nasty little business with the Zarhoun tribe (who took it upon them to close the roads between Fez and Tangier and between Meknes and Rabat) I was given command of the squadron that formed part of the composite battalion entrusted with the job. . . .

With this squadron was my good Dufour, of course, a non-commissioned officer already wearing the *médaille militaire* for valour. Of its winning I must briefly tell the tale, because the memory of it was so cruelly and poignantly before my mind in the awful hour when I had to leave him

46

to his death, instead of dying with him as I longed to do. . . .

On that black day I saw again, in clear and glowing colours, this picture:

I am charging a great *harka* of very brave and fanatical Moors, at the head of my squadron. . . . We do not charge in line as the English do, but every man for himself, hell-for-leather, at the most tremendous pace to which he can spur his horse. . . . Being the best mounted, I am naturally well ahead. . . . The earth seems to tremble beneath the thundering onrush of the finest squadron in the world. . . . I am wildly happy. . . . I wave my sabre and shout for joy. . . . As we are about to close with the enemy, I lower my point and straighten my arm. (Always use the point until you are brought to a standstill, and then use the edge with the speed and force of lightning.) The Moors are as cunning as they are brave. Hundreds of infantry drop behind rocks and big stones and into nullahs, level their long guns and European rifles, and blaze into the brown of us. Hundreds of cavalry swerve off to right and left, to take us in flank and surrounded us, when the shock of our impact upon the main body has broken our charge and brought us to a halt. They do not know that we shall go through them like a knife through cheese, re-form and charge back again—and even if we do not scatter them like chaff, will effectually prevent their charging and capturing our silent and almost defenceless little mountain-guns. . . .

We thunder on, an irresistible avalanche of men and horses, and, like a swimmer diving from a cliff into the sea— I am into them with a mighty crash. . . . A big Moor and his Barbary stallion go head-over-heels, as my good horse and I strike them amidships, like a single projectile; and, but for the sword-knot whose cord is round my wrist, I should have lost my sabre, pulled from my hand as I withdrew it from beneath the Moor's right arm. . . .

I spur my horse; he bounds over the prostrate horse and man; I give another big Moslem my point—right in the middle of his long black beard as I charge past him—and then run full tilt into a solid mass of men and horses. I cut and parry; slash, parry and cut; thrust and strike, and rise in my stirrups and hack and hew—until I am through and spurring again to a gallop. . . . And then I know that my horse is hit and going down, and I am

47

flying over his head and that the earth rises up and smashes my face, and strikes my chest so cruel a blow that the breath is driven from my body, and I am a living pain. . . .

Oh! the agony of that struggle for breath, after the smashing crash that has broken half my ribs, my right arm and my jaw-bone. . . . And, oh! the torture of my dead horse's weight on my broken leg and ankle. . . .

And why was my throat not being cut? Why no spears being driven through my back? Why was my skull not being battered in? . . .

I got my dripping face from out of the dust, wiped it with my left sleeve, and got on to my left elbow. . . .

I was the centre of a terrific "dog-fight", and, standing across me, leaping over me, whirling round and round, jumping from side to side like a fiend and a madman, a grand athlete and a great hero—was Dufour. . . . Sick and shattered as I was, I could still admire his wonderful swordsmanship, and marvel at his extraordinary agility, strength, and skill. . . . Soon I realized that I could do more than admire him. I could help, although pinned to the ground by my horse and feeling sick, shattered, and smashed. . . . With infinite pain I dragged my revolver from its holster, and rejoiced that I had made myself as good a shot with my left hand as with my right.

Then, lying on my right side, and sighting as well and quickly as I could in so awkward a position, I fired at a man whose spear was driving at Dufour's back; at another whose great sword was swung up to cleave him; at a third, whose long gun was presented at him; and then, after a wave of death-like faintness had passed, into the very face of one who had sprung past him and was in the act of driving his big curved dagger into my breast. . . .

As I aimed my last shot—at the man whose sword was clashing on Dufour's sabre—the squadron came thundering back, headed by Lieutenant d'Auray de Redon, and never was I more glad to see the face of my beloved Raoul. . . .

He and several of the Spahis drew rein, scattered our assailants and pursued them, while Dufour caught a rider-less troop-horse and—I am told—lifted me across the saddle, jumped on its back, behind the saddle, and galloped back to our position.

It seems that he had been behind me when my horse came down, had deliberately reined up, dismounted, and run to rescue me—when he was attacked. Nor had he striven to cut his way out from among the few who were surrounding him, but had stood his ground, defending me until he was the centre of the mob of wild fanatics from which Raoul's charge saved us in the nick of time. He was bleeding from half a dozen sword-cuts by the time he got me away, though not one of them was severe. . . .

Yes—this was the picture that burned before my eyes on the dreadful day of which I shall tell you.

Duty is a stern and jealous God. . . .

§ 3

I made a quick recovery, and thanked Heaven and our splendid surgeons when I found that I was not, as I had feared, to be lame for life.

I got back to work, and when my uncle, punctual to his life's programme, came out to Africa, I was able to join his Staff as an officer who knew more than a little about the country and its fascinating towns and people; an officer who could speak Arabic and its Moorish variant like a native; and who could wander through *sūq* and street and bazaar as a beggar; a pedlar; a swaggering Riffian *askri* of the *bled*; a nervous, cringing Jew of the *mellah*; a fanatic of Mulai Idris; a camel-man, or donkey-driver—without the least fear of discovery.

And I believe I could tell him things that no other officer in all Morocco could tell him of subterranean tribal politics; gutter intrigues of the fanatical mobs of towns that mattered (such as Meknes, for example, where I relieved my friend Captain de Lannec and where I was soon playing the Jew pedlar, and sending out messengers up to the day of its rising and the great massacre); and the respective attitudes, at different times, of various parts of the country and various classes of the people towards the Sultan Abd-el-Aziz; the would-be Sultan, Mulai Hafid; the Pretender Mulai Zine, his brother; or the great powerful *marabout* Ibn Nualla.

My uncle was pleased with the tool of his fashioning—

the tool that would *never* "turn in his hand", and my name was writ large in the books of the *Bureau des Affaires Indigènes* at Rabat. . . .

Nor do I think that there was any jealousy or grumbling when I became the youngest Major in the French Army, and disappeared from human ken to watch affairs in Zaguig and in the disguise of a native of that mean city. . . .

I entered it on foot, in the guise of a hill-man from the north, and as I passed through the tunnel of the great gate in the mighty ramparts, a camel-driver rose from where he squatted beside his beast and accosted me.

We gave what I think was an unexceptionable rendering of the meeting of two Arab friends who had not seen each other for a long time.

"Let me be the proud means of giving your honoured legs a rest, my brother," said the man loudly, as he again embraced me and patted my back with both hands. "Let my camel bear you to the lodging you honour with your shining presence. . . . God make you strong. . . . God give you many sons. . . . God send rain upon your barley crops. . . ." And he led me to where his kneeling camel snarled.

And may I be believed when I say that it was not until he had patted my back (three right hand, two left, one right, one left) that I knew that this dirty, bearded, shaggy camel-man was Raoul d'Auray de Redon, whom I was to relieve here! I was to do this that he might make a long, long journey with a caravan of a certain Sidi Ibrahim Maghruf, a Europeanized Arab merchant whom our Secret Service trusted—to a certain extent.

Raoul it was, however, and, at Sidi Ibrahim Maghruf's house, he told me all he could of local politics, intrigues, under-currents and native affairs in general.

"It's high time we made a plain gesture and took a firm forward step," he concluded. "It is known, of course, that we are coming and that the Military Mission will be a strong one—and it is anticipated that it will be followed by a column that will eventually remark *J'y suis—J'y reste*. . . . Well, the brutes have asked for it, and they'll get it—but I think it is a case of the sooner the quicker. . . .

"I'll tell you a curious thing, my friend. I have been attending some very interesting gatherings, and at one or two of them was a heavily-bearded fanatic who harangued the audience volubly and eloquently—but methought his Arabic had an accent. . . . I got Sidi Ibrahim Maghruf to let me take his trusted old factotum, Ali Mansur, with me to a little fruit-party which the eloquent one was giving.

"When old Ali Mansur had gobbled all the fruit he could hold and we sat replete, listening to our host's harangue upon the greatness of Islam and the littleness (and nastiness) of Unbelievers—especially the *Franzawi* Unbelievers who have conquered Algeria and penetrated Tunisia and Morocco and intended to come to Zaguig—I asked old Ali if he thought the man spoke curious Arabic and was a foreigner himself.

"'He is an Egyptian or a Moor or a Turk or something else, doubtless,' grunted Ali. 'But he is a true son of Islam and a father of the poor and the oppressed. *Wallahi*, but those melons and figs and dates were good—Allah reward him.'

"So I decided that I was right and that this fellow's Arabic *was* a little queer. . . . Well, I followed him about, and, one evening, saw him meet another man, evidently by appointment, in the Zaouia Gardens. . . . And the other man made a much quicker job of tucking his legs up under him on the stone seat, and squatting cross-legged like a true native, than my suspect did. He was a little slow and clumsy about it, and I fancied that he would have sat on the seat in *European* fashion, if he had been alone and unobserved. . . . Whereupon I became a wicked cut-purse robber of a mountaineer, crept up behind those two, in barefooted silence, and suddenly fetched our eloquent friend a very sharp crack on the head with my heavy *matrack* stick. . . . He let out one word and sprang to his feet. The hood of my dirty *burnous* was well over my ingenuous countenance and the evening was growing dark, but I got a clear glimpse of his face, and then fled for my life. . . . I am a good runner, as you know, and I had learned what I wanted—or most of it."

I waited, deeply interested, while Raoul paused and smiled at me.

"When a man has an exclamation fairly *knocked* out of him, so to speak, that exclamation will be in his mother-tongue," continued Raoul. "And if a man has, at times, a very slight cast in his eye, that cast is much enhanced and emphasized in a moment of sudden shock, fright, anger or other violent emotion."

"True," I agreed.

"My friend," said Raoul, "that man's exclamation, when I hit him, was '*Himmel!*' and, as he turned round, there was a most pronounced cast in his left eye. He almost squinted, in fact. . . ."

"The former point is highly interesting," I observed. "What of the other?"

"Henri," replied Raoul. "Do you remember a man who—let me see—had dirty finger-nails, ate garlic, jerked his horse's mouth, had a German mother, wiped his nose with the back of his hand, revealed a long dog-tooth when he grinned sideways, and had a cast in his eye . . .? A man in the Blue Hussars, a dozen years and more ago . . .? Eh, *do* you?"

"*Becque!*" I exclaimed.

"Becque, I verily believe," said Raoul.

"But wouldn't he exclaim in French, under such sudden and violent shock?" I demurred.

"Not if he had been bred and born speaking the German of his German mother in Alsace," replied my friend. "German would be literally his mother-tongue. He would learn from his French father to speak perfect French, and we know that his parents were of the two nationalities."

"It *may* be Becque, of course," I said doubtfully.

"I believe it is he," replied Raoul, "and I also believe you're the man to make certain. . . . What about continuing that little duel—with no Sergeant Blüm to interrupt, eh?"

"If it is he, and I can manage it, the duel will be taken up at the point where it was stopped owing to circumstances beyond Monsieur Becque's control," I remarked.

"Yes. I think *ce bon* Becque ought to die," smiled Raoul, "as a traitor, a renegade and a spy. . . . For those things he is—as the French-born son of a Frenchman, and as a soldier who has worn the uniform of France and taken the oath of true and faithful service to the Republic."

"Where was he born?" I asked.

"Paris," replied Raoul. "Bred and born in Paris.

He was known to the police as a criminal and an anarchist from his youth, and it appears that he got into the Blue Hussars by means of stolen or forged papers in this name of Becque. . . . They lost sight of him after he had served his sentence for incitement to mutiny in the Blue Hussars. . . ."

And we talked on far into the night in Sidi Ibrahim Maghruf's great moonlit garden.

Next day, Raoul departed on his journey of terrible hardships—a camel-man in the employ of Sidi Ibrahim Maghruf, to Lake Tchad and Timbuktu, with his life in his hands and all his notes and observations to be kept in his head.

§ 4

Of the man who might or might not be Becque, I saw nothing whatever in Zaguig. He may have taken fright at Raoul's sudden and inexplicable assault upon him, and thought that his secret was discovered, or he may have departed by reason of the approach of the French forces. On the other hand he may merely have gone away to report upon the situation in Zaguig, or again, he may have been in the place the whole time.

Anyhow, I got no news nor trace of him, and soon dismissed him from my mind. In due course I was relieved in turn by Captain de Lannec and returned to Morocco, and was sent thence into the far south, ostensibly to organize Mounted Infantry companies out of mules and the Foreign Legion, but really to do a little finding-out and a little intelligence-organizing in the direction of the territories of our various southern neighbours, and to travel from Sengal to Wadai, with peeps into Nigeria and the Cameroons. I was in the Soudan a long while.

Here I had some very instructive experiences, and a very weird one at a place called Zinderneuf, whence I went on leave *via* Nigeria, actually travelling home with a most excellent Briton named George Lawrence, who had been my very senior and revered fag-master at Eton!

It is a queer little world, and very amusing.

.   .   .   .   .

53

And everywhere I went, the good Dufour, brave, staunch and an extraordinarily clever mimic of any kind of native, went also, "seconded for special service in the Intelligence Department"—and invaluable service it was. At disguise and dialect he was as good as, if not better than, myself; and it delighted me to get him still further decorated and promoted as he deserved.

And so Fate, my uncle, and my own hard, dangerous and exciting work, brought me to the great adventure of my life, and to the supreme failure that rewarded my labours at the crisis of my career.

Little did I dream what awaited me when I got the laconic message from my uncle (now Commander-in-Chief and Governor-General):

"*Return forthwith to Zaguig and wait instructions.*"

Zaguig, as I knew to my sorrow, was a "holy" city, and like most holy cities, was tenanted by some of the un-holiest scum of mankind that pollute the earth.

Does not the Arab proverb itself say, "*The holier the city, the wickeder its citizens*"?

CHAPTER VII

ZAGUIG

AFTER the cities of Morocco, the Enchantress, I hated going back to Zaguig, the last-won and least-subdued of our Saharan outposts of civilization; and after the bold Moor I hated the secretive, furtive, evil Zaguigans, who reminded me of the fat, fair and false Fezai.

Not that Zaguig could compare with Fez or Marrakesh, of course, that bright jewel sunk in its green ocean of palms, with its wonderful gardens, Moorish architecture, cool marble, bright tiles, fountains and charming hidden *patios*.

This Zaguig (now occupied by French troops) was an ash-heap populated with vermin, and very dangerous vermin, too.

I did not like the position of affairs at all. I did not like the careless over-confident attitude of Colonel Levasseur; I did not like the extremely scattered disposition of the small garrison, a mere advance-guard; and I did not like the fact that Miss Mary Hankinson Vanbrugh was, with her brother, the guest of the said Colonel Levasseur.

You see, I *knew* what was going on beneath the surface, and what I did not know from personal observation, Dufour could tell me.

(When I was not Major de Beaujolais, I was a water-carrier, and when Dufour was not Adjudant Dufour of the Spahis, he was a seller of dates and melons in the *sūq*. When I was here before, I had been a blind leper—when not a coolie in the garden of Sidi Ibrahim Maghruf, the friend of France.)

Nor could I do more than lay my information before Colonel Levasseur. He was Commanding Officer of the troops and Governor of the town, and I was merely a detached officer of the Intelligence Department, sent to Zaguig to make arrangements for pushing off "into the blue" (on *very* Secret Service) as soon as word came that the moment was ripe. . . .

Extracts from a letter, written by my uncle at Algiers, and which I found awaiting me at Zaguig, will tell you nearly as much as I knew myself.

". . . . *and so, my dear Henri, comes your chance—the work for which the tool has been fashioned. . . . Succeed and you will have struck a mighty blow for France (and you will not find France ungrateful). But mind—you will have to be as swift and as silent as you will have to be clever, and you must stand or fall absolutely alone. If they fillet you and boil you in oil—you will have to boil unavenged. A desert column operating in that direction would rouse such a howl in the German Press (and in one or two others) as would do infinite harm at home, and would hamper and hinder my work out here for years. The Government is none too firmly seated, and has powerful enemies, and you must not provide the stick wherewith to beat the dog.*

"*On the other hand, I am expecting, and only waiting for, the dispatch which will sanction a subsidy of a million francs, so long as this Federation remains in alliance with France and rejects*

*all overtures to Pan-Islamism. That is the fear and the danger, the
one great menace to our young and growing African Empire.*

"*God grant that you are successful and that you are before
Bartels, Wassmuss or any Senussi emissaries.*

"*What makes me anxious, is the possibility of this new and remarkable Emir el Hamel el Kebir announcing himself to be that
very* Mahdi *whom the Bedouin tribes of that part are always expecting—a sort of Messiah.*

"*As you know, the Senussi Sidi el Mahdi, the holiest prophet
since Mahommet, is supposed to be still alive. He disappeared at
Garu on the way to Wadai, and an empty coffin was buried with
tremendous pomp and religious fervour at holy Kufara. He reap-
pears from time to time, in the desert, and makes oracular pro-
nouncements—and then there is a sort of 'revival' hysteria where he
is supposed to have manifested himself.*

"*If this Emir el Hamel el Kebir takes it into his head to announce
that he is the* Mahdi, *we shall get precisely what the British got
from their* Mahdi *at Khartoum—(and that son of a Dongola
carpenter conquered 2,000,000 square miles in two years)—for he
has got the strongest tribal confederation yet known. . . .*

"*Well—I hope you won't be a Gordon, nor I a Wolseley-
Kitchener, for it's peace we want now, peace—that we may con-
solidate our Empire and then start making the desert to bloom like
the rose. . . .*

"*You get a treaty made with this Emir—whereby he guarantees
the trade routes, and guarantees the friendship of his tributary
tribes to us, and a 'hostile* neutrality' *towards the Senussi and any
European power in Africa, and you will have created a buffer-state,
just where France needs it most.*

"*Incidentally you will have earned my undying gratitude and
approbation—and what you like to ask by way of recognition of such
invaluable work. . . . We* must *have peace in the East in view of the
fact that the Riffs will* always *give trouble in the West. . . .*

"*. . . Sanction for the subsidy may come any day, but you will
have plenty of time for your preparations. (When you get word,* be
gone in the same hour, *and let* nothing *whatsoever delay you
for a minute.) . . . d'Auray de Redon came through from Kufara
with one of Ibrahim Maghruf's caravans and saw this* Mahdi *or
Prophet himself. . . . He also takes a very serious view, and thinks it
means a jehad sooner or later. . . . And, mind you, he may be
Abd el Kadir (grandson of the Great Abd el Kadir, himself),
though I believe that devil is still in Syria.*

"*The fellow is already a very noted miracle-monger and has a tremendous reputation as a warrior. He is to the Emir Mohammed Bishri bin Mustapha Korayim abd Rabu what the eagle is to the hawk—a dead hawk too, according to an Arab who fell in with Ibrahim Maghruf's caravan, when fleeing from a great slaughter at the Pass of Bab-el-Haggar, where this new 'Prophet' obliterated the Emir Mohammed Bishari. . . . The said Arab was so bitter about the 'Prophet', and had such a personal grudge, that d'Auray de Redon cultivated him with talk of revenge and gold, and we may be able to make great use of him. . . . I shall send him to you at Zaguig with d'Auray de Redon who will bring you word to start, and any orders that I do not care to write. . . .*

"*In conclusion—regard this as* THE *most important thing in the world—to yourself, to me, and to France. . . .*"

Attached to this letter was a sheet of notepaper on which was written that which, later, gave me furiously to think, and at the time, saddened and depressed me. I wondered if it were intended as a warning and "*pour encourager les autres*," for it was not like my uncle to write me mere Service news.

"*By the way, I have broken Captain de Lannec, as I promised him (and you too) that I would do to anyone who, in any way, failed me. . . . A woman, of course. . . . He had my most strict and stringent orders to go absolutely straight and instantly to Mulai Idris, the Holy City, and establish himself there, relieving Captain St. André, with whom it was vitally important that I should have a personal interview within the month.*

"*Passing through the Zarhoun, de Lannec got word from one of our friendlies that a missing Frenchwoman was in a village among the mountains. She was the* amie *of a French officer, and had been carried off during the last massacre, and was in the* hareem *of the big man of the place. . . . It seems de Lannec had known her in Paris. . . . One Véronique Vaux. . . . Loved her, perhaps. . . . He turned aside from his duty; he wasted a week in getting the woman; another in placing her in safety; and then was so good as to attend to the affairs of his General, his Service and his Country . . .!*

"*Exit de Lannec. . . .*"

Serve him right, of course . . . Yes—of course. . . . A little hard? . . . Very, very sad—for he was a most promising officer, a tiger in battle, and a fox on Secret Service; no braver, cleverer, finer fellow in the French Army. . . . But yes, it served him right, certainly. . . . He had acted very wrongly—putting personal feelings and the fate of *a woman* before the welfare of France, before the orders of his Commander, before the selfless, self-effacing tradition of the Service. . . . Before his *God*—Duty, in short.

He deserved his punishment. . . . Yes. . . . He had actually put a mere woman before *Duty*. . . . "*Exit de Lannec.*" . . . Serve him right, poor devil. . . .

And then the Imp that dwells at the Back of my Mind said to the Angel that dwells at the Front of my Mind:

"*Suppose the captured woman, dwelling in that unthinkable slavery of pollution and torture, had been that beautiful, queenly and adored lady, the noble wife of the stern General Bertrand de Beaujolais himself?*"

Silence, vile Imp! *No one* comes before Duty.

Duty is a Jealous God. . . .

I was to think more about de Lannec ere long.

§ 2

I confess to beginning with a distinct dislike for the extremely beautiful Miss Vanbrugh, when I met her at dinner, at Colonel Levasseur's, with her brother. Her brother, by the way, was an honorary ornament of the American Embassy at Paris, and was spending his leave with his adventurous sister and her maid-companion in "doing" Algeria, and seeing something of the desert. The Colonel had rather foolishly consented to their coming to Zaguig "to see something of the *real* desert and of Empire in the making", as Otis Hankinson Vanbrugh had written to him.

I rather fancy that the *beaux yeux* of Miss Mary, whom Colonel Levasseur had met in Paris and at Mustapha Supérieur, had more to do with it than a desire to return the Paris hospitality of her brother.

Anyhow, a young girl had no business to be there at that time. . . .

Probably my initial lack of liking for Mary Vanbrugh was prompted by her curious attitude towards myself, and my utter inability to fathom and understand her. The said attitude was one of faintly mocking mild amusement, and I have not been accustomed to regarding myself as an unintentionally amusing person. In fact, I have generally found people rather chary of laughing at me.

But not so Mary Vanbrugh. And for some obscure reason she affected to suppose that my name was "*Ivan*". Even at dinner that first evening, when she sat on Levasur's right and my left, she addressed me as "*Major Ivan*".

To my stiff query, "Why *Ivan*, Miss Vanbrugh?" her half-suppressed provoking smile would dimple her very beautiful cheeks as she replied:

"But surely? . . . You *are* really *Ivan What's-his-name* in disguise, aren't you? . . . Colonel Levasseur told me you are a most distinguished Intelligence Officer on Secret Service, and I think that must be one of the Secrets. . . ."

I was puzzled and piqued. Certainly I have played many parts in the course of an adventurous career, but my duties have never brought me in contact with Russians, nor have I ever adopted a Russian disguise and name. Who was this "*Ivan What's-his-name*"? However, if the joke amused her . . . and I shrugged my shoulders.

"Oh, *do* do that again, Major Ivan," she said. "It *was* so delightfully French and expressive. You dear people can talk with your shoulders and eyebrows as eloquently as we barbarous Americans can with our tongues."

"Yes—we are amusing little funny foreigners, Mademoiselle," I observed. "And if, as Ivan What's-his-name, I have made you smile, I have not lived wholly in vain. . . ."

"No. You have not, Major Ivan," she agreed. A cooler, calmer creature I have never encountered. . . . A man might murder her, but he would never fluster nor discompose her serenity while she lived.

Level-eyed, slow-spoken, unhurried, she was something new and strange to me, and she intrigued me in spite of myself.

Before that evening finished and I had to leave that wide moonlit verandah, her low rich voice, extreme self-possession, poise, grace, and perfection almost conquered my dislike of her, in spite of her annoying air of ironic mockery, her mildly contemptuous amusement at me, my sayings and my doings.

As I made my way back to my quarters by the Bab-el-Souq, I found myself saying, "Who the devil *is* this *Ivan What's-his-name?*" and trying to recapture an air that she had hummed once or twice as I sat coldly silent after some piece of slightly mocking irony. How did it go?

Yes, that was it.

§ 3

Miss Vanbrugh's curiosity and interest in native life were insatiable. She was a living interrogation-mark, and to me she turned, on the advice of the over-worked Levasseur, for information—as it was supposed that what I did not know about the Arab, in all his moods and tenses, was not worth knowing.

I was able to bring that sparkling dancing flash of pleasure to her eyes, that seemed literally to light them up, although already as bright as stars, by promising to take her to dinner with my old friend Sidi Ibrahim Maghruf.

At his house she would have a real Arab dinner in real Arab fashion, be able to see exactly how a wealthy native lived, and to penetrate into the innermost arcana of a real *hareem*.

I had absolute faith in old Ibrahim Maghruf, and I had known him for many years and in many places.

Not only was he patently and provenly honest and reliable in himself—but his son and heir was in France, and much of his money in French banks and companies. He was a most lovable old chap, and most interesting too —but still he was a *native*, when all is said, and his heart was Arab.

It was difficult to realize, seeing him seated cross-legged upon his cushions and rugs in the marble-tiled French-Oriental reception-room of his luxurious villa, that he was a self-made man who had led his caravans from Siwa to Timbuctu, from Wadai to Algiers, and had fought in a hundred fights for his property and life against the Tebu, Zouaia, Chambaa, Bedouin, and Touareg robbers of the desert. He had indeed fulfilled the Arab saying, *"A man should not sleep on silk until he has walked on sand."*

Now he exported dates to France, imported cotton goods from Manchester, and was a merchant-prince in Islam. And I had the pleasant feeling that old Ibrahim Maghrui loved me for myself, without *arrière pensée*, and apart from the value of my reports to Government on the subject of his services, his loyalty, and his influence.

In his house I was safe, and in his hands my secret (that I was a French Intelligence Officer) was safe; so if in the maximum of gossip, inquiry and research, I told him the minimum of truth, I told him no untruth whatsoever. He, I believe, responded with the maximum of truth and the minimum of untruth, as between a good Mussulman and a polite, friendly, and useful Hell-doomed Infidel.

Anyhow, my disguise, my *hejin* camels—of the finest breed, brindled, grey-and-white, bluish-eyed, lean, slender greyhounds of the desert, good for a steady ten kilometres an hour—and my carefully selected outfit of necessities, watched night and day by my Soudanese orderly, Djikki, were safe in his charge.

§ 4

It was on calling at the Vanbrughs' quarters in the big house occupied by Colonel Lavasseur, to take Miss Vanbrugh to Sidi Maghruf's, that I first encountered the pretty and piquant "Maudie", an artless and refreshing soul. She met me in the verandah, showed me into the drawing-room, and said that Miss Vanbrugh would be ready in half a minute. I wondered if she were as flirtatious as she looked. . . .

. . . . .

Maudie Atkinson, I learned later, was a London girl, —a trained parlour-maid who had attracted Miss Vanbrugh's notice and liking by her great courage, coolness and resource on the occasion of a disastrous fire in the English country house at which Miss Vanbrugh was visiting. Maudie had been badly burnt in going to the rescue of a fellow-servant, and had then broken an arm in jumping out of a window.

Visiting the girl in the cottage-hospital, and finding that she would be homeless and workless when she left the hospital, Miss Vanbrugh had offered her the post of maid-companion, and in her democratic American way, treated her much more as companion than maid. . . .

When asked in Paris, by Miss Vanbrugh, if she were willing to accompany her to Africa, Maudie had replied,

"Oh, Miss! That's where *the Sheikhs* live, isn't it?" And on being assured that she need not be afraid of falling into the hands of Arabs, had replied.

"Oh, Miss! I'd give anything in the world to be carried off by a Sheikh! They *are* such lovely men. I *adores* Sheikhs!"

Further inquiry established the fact of Maudie's belief that Sheikhs were wealthy persons, clad in silken robes, exhaling an odour of attar of roses, residing on the backs of wondrous Arab steeds when not in more wondrous silken tents—slightly sunburnt Young Lochinvars in fact, and, like that gentleman, of most amazingly oncoming disposition; and, albeit deft and delightful, amorous beyond all telling.

"Oh, *Miss*," had Maudie added, "they catches you up into their saddles and gallops off with you into the sunset! No good smacking their faces neither, for they don't take 'No' for an answer, when they're looking out for a wife . . ."

"Or wives," Miss Vanbrugh had observed.

"Not if you're the first, Miss. They're true to you. . . . And they fair *burn* your lips with hot kisses, Miss."

"You can do that much for yourself, with hot tea, Maudie. . . . Where did you learn so much about Sheikhs?"

"Oh—I've got a book all about a Sheikh, Miss. By a lady . . ."

"Wonder whether the fair sob-sister ever left her native shores—or saw all her Sheikhs on the movies, Maudie?" was Miss Vanbrugh's damping reply.

And when she told me all this, I could almost have wished that Maudie's authoress could herself have been carried off by one of the dirty, smelly desert-thieves; lousy, ruffianly and vile, who are much nearer the average "Sheikh" of fact than are those of the false and vain imaginings of her fiction. . . .

Some Fiction is much stranger than Truth. . . .

The dinner was a huge success, and I am not sure which of the two, Sidi Ibrahim Maghruf or Miss Mary Vanbrugh, enjoyed the other the more.

On my translating Ibrahim's courteous and sonorous, "*Keif halak*, Sitt Miriyam! All that is in this house is yours," and she had replied,

"What a bright old gentleman! Isn't he too cute and sweet? I certainly should like to kiss him," and I had translated this as,

"The Sitt admires all that you have and prays that God may make you strong to enjoy it," we got down to it, and old Ibrahim did his best to do us to death with the noblest and hugest feast by which I was ever defeated. . . .

A gazelle stalked solemnly in from the garden and pattered over the marble floor.

"Major Ivan, it isn't gazelles that Grandpapa Maghruf should pet. It's boa-constrictors . . ." groaned Miss Vanbrugh, as the thirty-seventh high-piled dish was laid on the red cloth at our feet. . . .

The feast ended at long last and we got away, surprised at our power to carry our burden, and staggered home through the silent moonlit night, preceded by Dufour and followed by Achmet (my splendid faithful servant, loving and beloved, Allah rest his brave soul!)—and Djikki, for I was taking no chances.

For next day, at an hour before sunset, the good Colonel Levasseur, in his wisdom, had decreed a formal and full-dress parade of the entire garrison, to salute the Flag, and "to impress the populace". It seemed to me that he would certainly impress the populace with the fact of the utter inadequacy of his force, and I told him so.

He replied by officiously ordering me to be present, and "thereby render the garrison adequate to anything".

The good Levasseur did not like me and I wondered whether it was on account of Miss Vanbrugh or the fact that he was twenty years my senior and but one grade my superior in rank. . . . Nor did I myself greatly love the good Levasseur, a man very much *du peuple*, with his stubble hair, goggle-eyes, bulbous nose, purple face and enormous moustache, like the curling horns of a buffalo.

But I must be just to the brave Colonel—for he died in Zaguig with a reddened sword in one hand and an emptied revolver in the other, at the head of his splendid Zouaves; and he gave me, thanks to this officious command of his, some of the best minutes of my life. . . .

Cursing *ce bon* Levasseur, I clattered down the wooden stairs of my billet, in full fig, spurred calvalry-boots and sword and all, out into a narrow stinking lane, turned to the right—and began running as I believe I have never run before or since, not even when I won the senior quarter-mile at Eton—in somewhat more suitable running-kit.

For I had seen a sight which made the blood run cold throughout my body and yet boil in my head.

A woman in white riding-kit, on a big horse, followed by a gang of men, was galloping across an open space.

One of the men, racing level with her and apparently holding to her stirrup with one hand, drove a great knife into her horse's heart with the other, just as she smashed him across the head with her riding-crop.

As the horse lurched and fell, the woman sprang clear and dashed through the open gate of a compound.

It all happened in less time than it takes to tell, and by the time she was through the gate, followed by the Arabs, I was not twenty yards behind.

Mon Dieu! How I ran—and blessed Levasseur's officiousness as I ran—for there was only one woman in Zaguig who rode astride officer's chargers; only one who wore boots and breeches, long coat and white solar-topi.

By the mercy of God I was just in time to see the last of her pursuers vanish up a wooden outside stair that led to the flat roof of a building in this compound—a sort of firewood-and-hay store, now locked up and entirely deserted, like the streets, by reason of the Review.

When I reached the roof, with bursting lungs and dry mouth, I saw Miss Vanbrugh in a corner, her raised riding-crop reversed in her hand, as, with set mouth and protruding chin, she faced the bloodthirsty and bestial fanatics, whom, to my horror, I saw to be armed with swords as well as long knives.

In view of the stringent regulations of the Arms Act, this meant that the inevitable rising and massacre was about to begin, or had already begun.

It was no moment for kid-gloved warfare, nor for the niceties of chivalrous fighting, and I drove my sword through the back of one man who was in the very act of yelling, "Hack the . . . in pieces and throw her to the dogs," and I cut half-way through the neck of another before it was realized that the flying feet behind them had not been those of a brother.

My rush carried me through to Miss Vanbrugh, and as I wheeled about, I laid one black throat open to the bone and sent my point through another filthy and ragged *jellabia* in the region of its owner's fifth rib.

And then the rest were on me, and it was parry, and parry, and parry, for dear life, with no chance to do anything else—until suddenly a heavy crop fell crashing on an Arab wrist and I could thrust home as the stricken hand swerved.

Only two remained, and, as I took on my hilt a smashing blow aimed at my head, dropped my point into the brute's face and thrust hard—the while I expected the other man's sword in my side—I was aware, with the tail of my eye, of a pair of white-clad arms flung round a black neck from behind. As the great sword of the disconcerted Arab went wildly up, I sprang sideways, and thrust beneath his arm-pit. . . .

Then I sat me down, panting like a dog, and fought for breath—while from among seven bodies, some yet twitching in the pool of blood, a spouting Thing dragged itself by its fingers and toes towards the stairs. . . . Had I been a true Hero of Romance, I should have struck an attitude, leaning on my dripping sword, and awaited applause. In point of actual fact, I felt sick and shaky.

"The boys seem a little—er—*fresh*," complained a cool quiet voice, and I looked up from my labours of breath-getting. She was pale, but calm and collected, though splashed with blood from head to foot.

"*Some* dog-fight, Major Ivan," she said. "Are you hurt?"

"No, Miss Vanbrugh," I answered. "Scratched and chipped a bit, that's all. . . . Are you all right? . . . You are the coolest and bravest woman I have ever met. . . . You saved my life. . . ."

"Nonsense!" was the reply. 'What about mine? I certainly was in some trouble when you strolled in. . . . And I was *mad* that I couldn't explain to these beauties that this was the first time I had ever come out without my little gun! . . . I could have wept at myself. . . .

"Major, I'm going to be just a bit sick. . . . I've got to go home right now. . . . Steward! *Basin* . . ."

I wiped my sword (and almost kissed it), sheathed it, picked the girl up, and carried her like a baby, straight to my quarters. . . . That I had heard no rifle-fire nor mob-howling, showed that the revolt had not begun. . . .

Achmet was on guard at my door, but Dufour had taken his place at the Review as I had told him.

I laid her on my bed, brought congnac and water, and said, "Listen, Miss Vanbrugh. I am going to bring your maid here. Don't you dare go out of this room till I return with her—in fact Achmet won't let you. There's going to be Hell tonight—or sooner—and you'll be safer here than at the Governor's house, until I can get *burkahs* and *barracans* for you and the maid, and smuggle you down to Ibrahim Maghruf's. . . ."

"But what about all the pretty soldier-boys, won't they deal with the Arabs?" interrupted the girl.

"Yes, while they're alive to do it," I replied, and ran off. . . .

§ 6

Not a soul in the streets! A very bad sign, though fortunate for my immediate purpose of getting Maudie to my quarters unseen.

I had not far to go, and was thankful to find she was at home. Otis Vanbrugh had gone out. I noted that the maid was exhilarated and thrilled rather than frightened and anxious, when I explained that there was likely to be trouble.

"Just like Jenny What's-her-name, the Scotch girl in the Indian Mutiny. . . . You know, sir, the Siege of Lucknow and the bagpipes and all that. . . . I know a bit of po'try about it. . . . Gimme half a mo', sir, and I'll put some things together for Miss Mary. . . . *Lumme!* What a lark!" and as the droll, brave little soul bustled off, I swear she murmured "*Sheikhs!*"

Sheikh! A lark! *Une escapade!* . . . And suppose the house of Sidi Ibrahim Maghruf was the first that was looted and burnt by a victorious blood-mad mob, as being the house of a rich, renegade friend of the Hell-doomed Infidel? . . .

"Hurry, Maudie," I shouted, and out she came—her pretty face alight and alive at the anticipation of her "lark"—with a big portmanteau or suitcase. Taking this, I hurried her at top speed back to the Bab-el-Souq.

"Oh, my *Gord!* Look!" ejaculated poor Maudie as we came to where the slaughtered horse lay in its blackening pool, and a Thing still edged along with toes and fingers, leaving a trail. It must have rolled down those stairs. . . .

Some of the bloom was gone from the "lark" for the gay little Cockney, and from her bright cheeks too. . . .

For me a stiff cognac and off again, this time to the house of Sidi Ibrahim Maghruf. It was useless to go to

Colonel Levasseur yet. I had said all I could say, and he had got all his men—for the moment—precisely where they ought to be, all in one place, under one command; and if the rising came while they were there, so much the better.

I would see Sidi Ibrahim Maghruf, and then, borrowing a horse, ride to Levasseur, tell him of the attack on Miss Vanbrugh, assure him that the rising would be that night, and beg him to act accordingly.

Sidi Ibrahim Maghruf's house, as usual, appeared to be deserted, empty and dead. From behind high blind walls rose a high blind house, and from neither of the lanes that passed the place could a window be seen.

My private and particular knock with my sword-hilt— two heavy, two light, and two heavy—brought a trembling ancient to the iron-plated wicket in the tremendously heavy door. It was good old Ali Mansur.

I stepped inside and the old mummy, whose eye was still bright and wits keen, gave me a message which I doubt not was word for word as his master and owner had delivered it to him.

"Ya, Sidi, the Protection of the Prophet and the Favour of Allah upon Your Honour's head. My Master has been suddenly called away upon a journey to a far place, and this slave is alone here with Djikki, the Soudanese soldier. This slave is to render faithful account to you Excellency of his property in the camel-sacks; and Djikki, the Soudanese, is ready with the beautiful camels. The house of my Master, and all that is in it, is at the disposal of the Sidi, and these words of my Master are for the Sidi's ear. '*Jackals and hyenas enter the cave of the absent lion to steal his meat!*'". . .

Quite so. The wily Ibrahim knew more than he had said. He had cleared out in time, taking his family and money, until after the massacre of the tiny garrison and the subsequent looting was over, the town had been recaptured, a sharp lesson taught it, and an adequate garrison installed. . . . There is a time to run like the hare and a time to hunt with the hounds.

No—this would be no place to which to bring the two women.

I ordered the ancient Ali to tell Djikki to saddle me a horse quickly, and then to fetch me any women's clothing he could find—*tobhs, aabaias, foutas, guenaders, haiks, lougas, melah'af, mendilat, roba, sederiya, hezaam, barracan*—any mortal thing he could produce, of female attire.

My big Soudanese, Private Djikki, grinning all over his hideous face, brought the horse from the huge stables in the big compound, reserved for camels, asses, mules, well-bullocks, milch-cows and goats, and I once again gave him the strictest orders to have everything absolutely ready for a desert journey, at ten minutes' notice.

"It always is, Sidi," he grinned. "On my head and my life be it."

There are times when I love these huge, fierce, staunch Soudanese, childish and lazy as they are. (I had particular reason to love this one.) They are like coal-black English bull-dogs—if there are such things. . . .

I again told him where to take the camels and baggage, by way of the other gate, if the mob attacked the house.

The ancient returning with the bundle of clothing, I bade Djikki run with it to my quarters and give it to his old pal Achmet, and to come back at once.

I then mounted and rode off through the strangely silent town, to where Colonel Levasseur was holding his futile parade in the vast market-square—a poor handful consisting of his 3rd Zouaves, a company of *Tirailleurs Algériens*—possibly none too loyal when the Cry of the Faith went up and the Mulahs poured forth from the mosques to head a Holy War—and a half-squadron of *Chasseurs d'Afrique*. What were these against a hundred thousand fanatics, each anxious to attain remission of sins, and Paradise, by the slaying of an Infidel, a *giaour*, a *meleccha*, a dog whose mere existence was an affront and an offence to the One God?

There should have been a strong brigade and a battery of artillery in the place. . . .

The old story of the work of the soldier ruined by the hand of the politician—not to mention the subject of mere lives of men. . . .

.   .   .   .   .

A dense and silent throng watched the review, every house-top crowded, every balcony filled, though no women were visible, and you could have walked on the heads of the people in the Square and in every street and lane leading to the square, save four, at the ends of which Levasseur had placed pickets—for the easier scattering of his little force after the parade finished!

By one of these empty streets I rode, and, through an ocean of sullen faces, to where the Governor sat his horse, his *officier d'ordonnance* behind him, with a bugler and a four of Zouave drummers.

The band of the 3rd Zouaves was playing the *Marseillaise*, and I wondered if its wild strains bore any message to the silent thousands who watched motionless, save when their eyes turned expectantly to the minaret of the principal mosque. . . . To the minaret. . . . Expectantly? . . . Of course!

It was from there that the signal would come. On to that high-perched balcony, like a swallow's next on that lofty tower, the muezzin would step at sunset. The deep diapason of his wonderful voice would boom forth the *shehada*, the Moslem profession of faith, "*Ash hadu illa illaha ill Allah, wa ash hadu inna Mohammed an rasul Allah*"; he would recite the *mogh'reb* prayer, and *then*—then he would raise his arms to Allah and call curses on the Infidel; his voice would break into a scream of "*Kill! Kill!*" and from beneath every dirty *jellabia* would come sword and knife, from every house-top a blast of musketry. . . . I could see it all. . . .

"You are late, Major," growled the Governor, accusingly and offensively, as I rode up.

"I am, Colonel," I agreed, "but I am alive. Which none of us will be in a few hours unless you'll take my advice and expect to be attacked at odds of a hundred to one, in an hour's time." And I told him of Miss Vanbrugh's experience.

"Oh, you Intelligence people and your mares'-nests! A gang of rude little street-boys I expect!" laughed this wise man; and ten minutes later he dismissed the parade—the men marching off in five detachments, to the four chief gates of the city and to the Colonel's own headquarters respectively.

As the troops left the Square, the mob, still silent, closed in, and every eye was turned unwaveringly to the minaret of the mosque. . . .

§ 7

I rode back towards my quarters, cudgelling my brains as to the best thing to do with the two girls. The Governor's house would be in the thick of the fighting, and it was more than probable that Ibrahim Maghruf's house would be looted and burnt. . . .

Yes, they would perhaps be safest in my quarters, in Arab dress, with Achmet to defend them with tongue and weapons. . . . I had better send for Otis Vanbrugh too, and give him a chance to save himself—if he'd listen to reason—and to look after his sister. . . . But my house was known as the habitation of a *Franzawi* officer. . . .

And I myself would be in an awkward dilemma, for it was no part of my duty to get killed in the gutters of Zaguig when my uncle was relying on me to be setting off on the job of my life—that should crown the work of *his*. Nor was it any part of my inclination to sit cowering in an upper back room with two women and a civilian, while my comrades fought their last fight. . . . Hell! . . .

As I swung myself down from my horse, by the door in the lane at the back of my house, I was conscious of a very filthy and ragged Arab, squatting against the wall on a piece of foul old horse-blanket, his staff, begging-bowl, and rosary beside him. He begged and held out his hand, quavering for alms in the name of Allah, the Merciful, the Compassionate—"*Bismillah arahman arahmim!*" in Arabic—and in French, "*Start at once!*". . .

The creature's eyes were bloodshot and red-rimmed, his mangily-bearded cheeks were gaunt and hollow, his ribs showed separate and ridged through the rents in his foul *jellabia*, and a wisp of rag failed to cover his dusty shaggy hair. And at the third stare I saw that it was my friend, the beautiful and smart Captain Raoul d'Auray de Redon.

I winked at him, led my horse to the stable on the other

side of the courtyard, and ran up the wooden stair at the back of the house. . . . So it had come! I thought of my uncle's letter and the underlined words—"*begone in the same hour.*"

I tore off my uniform, pulled on my Arab kit, the dress of a good-class Bedouin, complete from *agal*-bound *kafiyeh* to red-leather *fil-fil* boots—and, as I did this and rubbed dye into my face and hands, I thought of a dozen things at once—and chiefly of the fate of the girls.

I could not leave them alone in this empty house, and it would be delivering them to death to take them back to the Governor's villa. . . .

I shouted for Achmet and learned that he had given the Arab clothing to Miss Vanbrugh.

"Run to the house of his Excellency the Governor, and tell the Roumi Americani lord, Vanbrugh, the brother of the Sitt Miriyam Vanbrugh, to come here in greatest haste. Tell him the Sitt is in danger here. Go on the horse that is below, and give it to the Americani. . . ."

This was ghastly! I should be *escaping in disguise* from Zaguig, at the very time my brothers-in-arms were fighting for their lives. . . . I should be leaving Mary Vanbrugh to death or worse than death. . . .

I ran down the stairs again and glanced round the court-yard, beckoning to Raoul who was now sitting just inside the gate. Turning back, I snatched up a cold chicken and a loaf from my larder and, followed by Raoul, hurried back to my room to make a bundle of my uniform. Wringing Raoul's hand, I told him to talk while he ate and I worked. He told me all about the Emir upstart and about the guide, as he drew a route on my map.

"The tribes are up, all round the north-west of here," he said later, "and hurrying in. It's for sunset this evening —as I suppose you have found out. . . ."

"Yes—and warned Levasseur. . . . He's besotted. . . . Says they'd never dare do anything while *he* and his Zouaves are here! And he's got them scattered in small detachments—and, Raoul, there are two *white* girls here. . . ."

"Where?" interrupted my friend.

"In the next room," I answered, and hurriedly told him about them.

"God help them," he said. "They'll be *alone* in an hour. . . ."

"What are you going to do?" I asked. "Are you to come with me?"

"No—the General doesn't want us both killed by this Emir lad, he says. And he thinks you're the man to pull it off, now that poor de Lannec's gone. . . . I confess I begged him to let me go, as it was I who brought him confirmation of the news. . . . He said it was your right to have the chance, Henri, on your seniority as well as your record, apart from the fact that you'd handle the situation better than I. . . . Said it was such almost-certain death too, that he'd prefer to send his own nephew! I nearly wept, old chap, but he was absolutely right. You *are* the man. . . ."

Noble loyal soul! Steel-true and generous—knowing not the very name of jealousy. He gave me every ounce of help, information and guidance that it lay in his power to do.

"No—I'm not even to come with you, Henri. . . . I shall join the mob here and lead them all over the shop on false scents. Confuse their councils and start rumours that there's a big French army at the gates, and so on. . . . Then I'll get back with the news of what's happened here. . . . There's one thing—it'll strengthen the General's hand and get more troops into Africa, so poor Levasseur and his men won't have . . ."

There came a bang at the door, Raoul crouched in a dark corner and Otis Vanbrugh burst in, followed by Achmet.

"Where's my sister!" he shouted, looking wildly round and seeing two Arabs, as he thought.

"I am Major de Beaujolais, Mr. Vanbrugh," said I. "Your sister and her maid are in the next room—putting on Arab dress. There will be a rising this evening and a massacre. . . . The worst place for you and your sister will be the Governor's house. Will you hide here until it's over—and try to keep alive somehow until the French troops arrive? Levasseur will start telegraphing the moment fighting begins, but it'll be a matter of days before they can get here—even if the wires aren't cut already—and you and the two girls will be the sole living white people in the

73

city. . . . If you don't starve and aren't discovered. . . .
Anyhow, your only chance is to hide here with the girls. . . ."

"Hide nothing, sir!" burst out Vanbrugh. "I shall fight
alongside my host and his men."

"And your sister?" I asked.

"She'll fight too. Good as a man, with a gun."

"And when the end comes?" I said gently.

"Isn't there a chance?" he asked.

"Not the shadow of a ghost of a chance," I said. "Five
little scattered detachments—each against ten thousand!
They'll be smothered by sheer numbers. . . . And you
haven't seen an African mob out for massacre and
loot. . . ."

"Let's talk to my sister," he answered, and dashed out
of the room.

"*Un brave*," said Raoul as we followed.

He was—and yet he was a gentle, refined and scholarly
person, an ascetic-looking bookman and ornament of
Chancelleries. I had thought of James Lane Allen and
"Kentucky Cardinals", for some reason, when I first met
him. He had the eyes and forehead of a dreaming philosopher—but he had the mouth and chin of a *man*. . . .

In the next room were two convincing Arab females
each peering at us through the muslin-covered slit in the
all-enveloping *bourkah* that covered her from head to
foot.

"Say, Otis, what d'you know about *that*," said one of the
figures, and spun round on her heel.

"Oh, *sir*," said the other, "*isn't* it a lark! Oh, *Sheikhs*!"

"Oh, Shucks! you mean," replied Vanbrugh, and hastily
laid the situation before his sister.

"And what does Major Ivan say?" inquired she. "I
think we'd better go with him. . . . Doesn't he look cunning in his Arab rags?"

I think I should have turned pale but for my Arab
dye.

"I'm leaving Zaguig at once," I said.

"Not *escaping*?" she asked.

"I am leaving Zaguig at once," I repeated.

"Major de Beaujolais has just received dispatches,"
said Raoul in English, "and has to go."

"How *very* convenient for the Major!" replied Mary

Vanbrugh. . . . "And who's *this* nobleman, anyway, might one ask?"

"Let me present Captain Raoul d'Auray de Redon," said I, indicating the filthy beggar.

"Well, don't present him too close. . . . Pleased to meet you, Captain. You *escaping* too?"

"No, Mademoiselle, I am not escaping," said Raoul, and added, "Neither is Major de Beaujolais. He is going on duty, infinitely against his will at such a time. But he's also going to dangers quite as great as those in Zaguig at this moment. . . ."

I could have embraced my friend.

Miss Vanbrugh considered this.

"Then, I think perhaps I'll go with him," she said. "Come on, Maudie. Grab the grip. . . . I suppose you'll stay and fight, Otis? Good-bye, dear old boy, take care of yourself . . ." and she threw her arms round her brother's neck.

"*Mon Dieu,* what a girl!" Raoul laughed.

"You have heard of the frying-pan and the fire, Miss Vanbrugh?" I began.

"Yes, and of pots and pans and cabbages and kings. I'm quite tired of this gay city, anyway, and I'm coming along to see this Where-is-it place. . . ."

Vanbrugh turned to me.

"For God's sake take her," he said, "and Maudie too."

"Oh, *yes*, sir," said Maudie, thinking doubtless of Sheikhs.

"Why—surely," chimed in Miss Vanbrugh. "Think of Major Ivan's good name. . . . He *must* be chaperoned."

"I'm sorry, Vanbrugh," I said. "I can't take your sister . . . I'm going on a Secret Service mission—of the greatest importance and the greatest danger. . . . My instructions are to go as nearly alone as is possible—and I'm only taking three natives and a white subordinate as guide, camel-man and cook and so forth. . . . It's *impossible* . . ."

(No *de Lannec* follies for Henri de Beaujolais!)

But he drew me aside and whispered, "Good God, man, I'm her brother! I *can't* shoot her at the last. You are a stranger. . . . There is a *chance* for her, surely, with you. . . ."

"Impossible," I replied.

Someone came up the stair and to the door. It was Dufour in Arab dress. He had hurried back and changed, in his quarters.

"We should be out of this in a few minutes, sir, I think," he said. "They are only waiting for the muezzin. Hundreds followed each detachment to the gates. . . ."

"We *shall* be out of it in a few minutes, Dufour," I answered. "Get on down to Ibrahim Maghruf's. Take Achmet. Don't forget anything—food, water, rifles, ammunition, compasses. See that Achmet takes my uniform. . . . I'll be there in ten minutes."

"Let the gentle Achmet take the grip, then," said Miss Vanbrugh, indicating her portmanteau.

Raoul touched my arm.

"Take the two girls in a *bassourab*," he whispered. "It would add to your plausibility, in a way, to have a *hareem* with you. . . . You might be able to hand them over to a north-bound caravan too, with promise of a tremendous reward if they're taken safe to a French outpost."

"Look here, couldn't Vanbrugh ride north-west with them himself?" I suggested. "He's a plucky chap and . . ."

"And can't speak a word of Arabic. Not a ghost of a chance—the country's swarming, I tell you. They wouldn't get a mile. Too late . . ."

"Wouldn't *you* . . . ?" I began.

"Stop it, Henri," he answered. "I'm not de Lannec . . . My job's here, and you know it. . . . I may be able to do a lot of good when they get going. Mobs always follow anybody who's got a definite plan and a loud voice and bloody-minded urging. . . ."

"De Beaujolais—what can I say—I *implore* you . . ." began Vanbrugh.

"Very well," I said. "On the distinct understanding that I take *no* responsibility for Miss Vanbrugh, that she realizes what she is doing, and that I shall not deviate a hairbreadth from what I consider my duty. . . . Not to save her from death or torture. . . ."

There could be no harm in my taking her out of the massacre—but neither was *I* a de Lannec!

"Oh, Major! you *are* so pressing. . . . Come on, Maudie, we're going from certain death to sure destruction, so cheer up, child, and let's get busy . . ." said the girl.

I turned away as Vanbrugh crushed his sister to his breast, and with a last look round my room, I led the way down the stairs, and out into the deserted silent street, my ears tingling for the first mob-howl, the first rifle-shot.

That poor unworthy fool, de Lannec! ...

CHAPTER VIII

FEMME SOUVENT VARIE

"Somewhere upon that trackless wide, it may be we shall meet
The Ancient Prophet's caravan, and glimpse his camel fleet."
A. FARQUHAR

WE were quite an ordinary party. Two sturdy desert Bedouins, Dufour and I, followed by two heavily shrouded females and trailed by a whining beggar—Raoul.

I had refused to let Vanbrugh come to Ibrahim Maghruf's house with us, partly because his only chance of not being torn to pieces in the streets was to get quickly back to the Governor's, where he could use a rifle with the rest; partly because I wanted him to take a last message and appeal to the Governor; and partly because I did not want a European to be seen going into Ibrahim's, should the place be watched.

I had taken farewell of him in the compound of my quarters, repeating my regrets that I could take *no* responsibility for his sister, and feeling that I was saying good-bye to a heroic man, already as good as dead.

He would not listen to a word about escaping from the town and taking his chance with my party until we were well away, and then shifting for himself.

He didn't desert friends in danger, he said; and with a silent hand-grip and nod, we parted, he to hurry to his death, and I to take his sister out into the savage desert and the power of more savage fanatics—if she were not killed or captured on the way. ...

All was ordered confusion and swift achievement at Ibrahim Maghruf's house, as the splendid riding-camels were saddled and the special trotting baggage-camels were loaded with the long-prepared necessities of the journey.

Here Raoul presented to me a big, powerful and surly Arab, apparently, named "Suleiman the Strong", who was to be my guide. He was the man who had escaped from one of this new Mahdi's slaughters, and been picked up by the caravan in which Raoul had been carrying on his work, disguised as a camel-driver. . . .

This Suleiman the Strong actually knew the Mahdi, having had the honour of being tortured by him personally; and apparently he only lived for his revenge. I thought he should be an extremely useful person, as he knew the wells and water-holes on the route, though I did not like his face and did not intend to trust him an inch farther than was necessary. Anyhow, he would lead me to the Great Oasis all right, for he had much to gain in the French Service—pay, promotion and pension—and nothing to lose.

Luckily there were spare camels, left behind by Ibrahim Maghruf, as well as my own: and Djikki and Achmet soon had a *bassourab* (a striped hooped tent—shaped something like a balloon) on to a riding-camel for the girls, and another baggage-camel loaded with extra sacks of dates, *girbas* of water, and bags of rice, tea, coffee, sugar and salt, as well as tinned provisions.

As I was helping the girls into the *bassourab*, showing them how to sit most comfortably—or least uncomfortably—and giving them strictest injunctions against parting the curtains until I gave permission, Raoul touched my arm.

"Better go, Major," he said. "*It's begun*—hark! . . ."

As he spoke, a growing murmur, of which I had been subconsciously aware for some minutes—a murmur like the sound of a distant sea breaking on a pebble beach—rose swiftly to a roar, menacing and dreadful, a roar above which individual yells leapt clear like leaping spray above the waves. Rifles banged irregularly and then came crash after crash of steady volley-firing. . . .

"*En avant—marche!*" said I; the old mummy opened

78

the compound gate; and I rode out first, on my giant camel, followed by Djikki leading the one that bore the two girls. After them rode Suleiman, in charge of the baggage-camels, behind which came Achmet. Last of all rode Dufour.

For a minute, Raoul ran along the narrow lane in front of us. As we turned into the street that led to the south-eastern gate—luckily not one of the four at which poor Levasseur had stationed detachments—a mob of country-dwelling tribesmen came running along it, waving swords, spears, long guns and good rifles above their heads, and yelling " *Kill! Kill!* "

" *Halt! Back!* " I shouted to Djikki, and brought my little caravan to a standstill at the mouth of the lane, wondering if our journey was to end here in Zaguig. I had my rifle ready, and Dufour, Djikki, Achmet and Suleiman pushed up bedside me with theirs. . . .

The mob drew level.

" *Good-bye, Henri,* " said a voice from below me, and out in front of them bounded Captain Raoul d'Auray de Redon—a filthy dancing-dervish—span round and round, and then, with his great staff raised in one hand and his rosary in the other, yelled:

" *The Faith! The Faith! The Faith! Kill! Kill!* This way, my brothers! *Quick! Quick!* I can show you where there are infidel dogs! . . . *White women!* . . . *Loot!* " and he dashed off, followed by the mob, down a turning opposite to ours, across the main street.

That was the last I ever saw of Raoul.

It was the last ever seen of him in life by any French-man, save for the glimpses that Levasseur and his comrades got, by the light of burning houses, of a wild dervish that harangued the mob just when it was about to charge—or led great sections of it off from where it could do most harm to where it could do least.

One cannot blame poor Levasseur that he supposed the man to be a blood-mad fanatical ringleader of the mob —and himself ordered and directed the volley that riddled the breast of my heroic friend and stilled for ever the noblest heart that ever beat for France.

As the mob streamed off after their self-constituted leader,
I gave the word to resume the order of march, and led
the way at a fast camel-trot towards and through the gate,
and out into the open country.

I breathed more freely outside that accursed City of the
Plain. . . . Another small mob came running along the
road, and I swerved off across some irrigated market-
gardens to make a chord across the arc of the winding
road.

A few scoundrels detached themselves from the mob
and ran towards us, headed by a big brute with a six-foot
gun in one hand and a great sword in the other. I did not
see how he could use both. He showed me.

As they drew nearer, I raised my rifle.

"Get your *own* loot," I snarled. "There's plenty more
in Zaguig. . . ." There was a laugh, and half of them
turned back.

The leader, however, stuck his sword in the ground, knelt,
and aimed his long gun at my camel. Evidently his simple
system was to shoot the beasts of mounted men and then
hack the head off the rider as he came to earth.

However, rifles are quicker than *jezails*, blunderbusses,
snap-haunces or arquebusses, and without reluctance I shot
the gentleman through the head.

My followers, who, with a disciplined restraint that delighted me, had refrained from shooting without orders,
now made up for lost time, and the remainder of the
tribesmen fled, doubtless under the impression that they
had stirred up a hornet's nest of loot-laden Toureg. . . .

I again pushed forward quickly, smiling to myself as I
remembered the small voice that had issued from the
bassourab after I had fired, remarking, "A bell-ringer for
Major Ivan!"

Evidently those *bassourab* curtains had been opened in
spite of what I had said. . . .

A red glare lit the sky. The mob-howl—that most
terrible and soul-shaking of all dreadful sounds—rose higher
and louder, and the crashing volleys of disciplined fire-

control answered the myriad bangings of the guns and rifles of the mob.

At a bend of the road, I found myself right into another hurrying crowd, and I visualized the northern roads as covered with them. There was no time to swerve, and into them we rode.

"Hurry, brothers, or you'll be too late," I shouted, and behind me my four followers yelled "*Kill! Kill!*" and we were through the lot, either before they realized that we were so few, or because they took us for what we were—a well-armed band from whom loot would only be snatched with the maximum of bloodshed.

And to these wild hill-tribesmen, the glare of the burning city was a magnet that would have drawn them almost from their graves.

On once again, and, but for a straggler here and there, we were clear of the danger-zone.

In a couple of hours we were as much in the lonely uninhabited desert as if we had been a hundred miles from the town.

I held the pace however, and as we drove on into the moonlit silence, I tried to put from me the thoughts of what was happening in Zaguig, and of the fate of my beloved friend and of my comrades whom harsh Duty had made me desert in their last agony. . . . I yearned to flee from my very self. . . . I could have wept. . . .

§ 3

It was after midnight when I drew rein and gave the word to *barrak* the camels and to camp.

Before I could interfere, Djikki had brought the girls' camel to its knees, with a gutteral "*Adar-ya-yan*", and with such suddenness that poor Maudie was shot head foremost out of the *bassourab* on to the sand, as a tired voice within said,

"What is it *now*? Earthquakes? . . ."

Maudie laughed, and Miss Vanbrugh crawled out of the *bassourab*. "Major," she observed, "I'm through with the cabin of the Ship of the Desert. . . . The deck for me. I don't ride any more in that wobbling wigwam after tonight. . . . And there isn't real *room* for two. Not to be sea-sick in solid comfort."

"You'll ride exactly where and how I direct, Miss Vanbrugh," I replied, "until I can dispose of you somehow."

"*Dear* Major Ivan," she smiled. "I *love* to hear him say his little piece," and weary as she was, she hummed a bar of that eternal irritating air.

In a surprisingly short time we had the little *tentes d'arbri*, which should have been mine and Dufour's, up and occupied by the girls; fires lighted; water on to boil for tea; a pot issuing savoury odours, as its contents of lamb, rice, butter, vegetables and spice simmered beneath the eye of Achmet, who turned a roasting chicken on a stick.

Maudie wanted to "wait" on Miss Vanbrugh and myself, but was told by her kind employer and friend to want something different. So the two girls, Dufour, and I made a *partie-carrée* at one fire, while Achmet ministered to us; and Djikki and Suleiman fed the camels, and afterwards did what Miss Vanbrugh described as their "chores" about another.

After we had eaten, I made certain things clear to Miss Vanbrugh and Maudie, including the matter of the strictest economy of water for their ablutions, when we were away from oases; and the absolute necessity of the promptest and exactest obedience to my orders.

After supper the girls retired to the stick-and-canvas camp-beds belonging to Dufour and myself; and I allotted two-hour watches to Djikki, Achmet, and Suleiman, with "rounds" for Dufour and myself at alternate hours.

Visiting the camels and stacked loads, I saw that all was well—as I expected from such experienced desertmen as my followers. . . .

None of the water-*girbas* appeared to be leaking. . . . I rolled myself in a rug and lay down to count the stars. . . .

§ 4

"Good-morning, Major Ivan," said a cool voice, at daybreak next morning, as I issued stores and water for breakfast. "Anything in the papers this morning?"

"I hope you and Maudie slept well, Miss Vanbrugh," I replied. "Have you everything you want?"

"No, Kind Sir, she said," was the reply. "I want a hot bath and some tea, and a chafing-dish—and then I'll show you some *real* cookery."

She looked as fresh as the glorious morning, and as sweet in Arab dress as in one of her own frocks.

"You may perhaps get a bath in a week or two," I replied.

"A *hot* bath?" she asked.

"Yes. In a saucepan," I promised.

"And today we're going to make a forced march," I added, "with you and Maudie safe in the *bassourab*. After that it will have to be the natural pace of the baggage-camels and we'll travel mostly by night—and you can ride as you please—until we bid you farewell."

"Why at night?" asked the girl. "Not just for my whims?"

"No. . . . Cooler travelling," I replied, "and the camels go better. They can't see to graze—and our enemies can't see *us*."

"Of course. I was afraid you were thinking of what I said about the *bassourab*, Major, and planning to save the women and children. . . ."

"How's Maudie?" I asked.

"All in, but cheerful," she replied. "She's not used to riding, and her poor back's breaking."

"And yours?" I asked.

"Oh, I grew up on a horse," she laughed, "and can grow old on a camel. . . . Let me dye my face and dress like a man, and carry a rifle, Major. Maudie could have the *bassourab* to herself then, with the curtains open."

"I'll think about it," I replied.

All that day we marched, Suleiman riding far ahead, as scout and guide. . . .

After going my rounds that night, I had a talk with this fellow, and a very interesting and illuminating talk it was.

I learned, in the first place, that the Emir el Hamel el Kebir was a desert "foundling", of whom no one knew anything whatsoever.

This looked bad, and suggested one of the "miraculous"

83

appearances of the Mahdi el Senussi or an imitation of it.

Also, from Suleiman's grudging admissions, and allowing for his obvious hatred, the Emir appeared to be a mighty worker of miracles in the sight of all men—an Invincible Commander of the Faithful in battle, and a man of great ability and power.

He was evidently adored by his own tribe—or the tribe of his adoption, to whom he had appeared in the desert—and apparently they regarded their present importance, success and wealth, as their direct reward from Allah for their hospitable acceptance of this "Prophet" when he had appeared to them.

I reflected upon my earlier studies of the British campaigns in Egypt against Osman Digna, and Mohammed Ahmed the Mahdi, and the Khalifa—and upon the fate of any Englishman who had ridden—with two white women—into the camp of any of these savage and fanatical warriors.

On my trying to get some idea of the personality and character of the Emir, Suleiman could only growl:

"He is a treacherous Son of Satan. He poisoned the old Sheikh whose salt he had eaten, and he tortured me. *Me*, who should have succeeded the good old man—to whom I was as a son. . . ."

This sounded bad, but there are two sides to every story, and I could well imagine our Suleiman handsomely earning a little torture.

"I fled from the Tribe," continued Suleiman, "and went to the Emir Mohammed Bishari bin Mustapha Korayim abd Rabu, who took me in and poured oil and wine into my wounds. . . .

"Him also this *Emir* el Hamel el Kebir slew, falling upon him treacherously in the Pass of Bab-el-Haggar, and again I had to flee for my life. A caravan found me weeks later, at the point of death in the desert, and they took me with them. . . .

"The man who brought me to you befriended me from the first, and showed me how to make a living as well as how to get my revenge on this foul pretender and usurper. This '*Emir*' el Hamel"—and the gentle Suleiman spat vigorously.

"Are you a *Franzawi*, Sidi?" he asked, after a brief silence.

"Like you, I work for them," I replied. "They pay, splendidly, those who serve them well; but their vengeance is terrible upon those who betray them—and their arm is long," I added.

"Allah smite them," he growled; and asked, "Will they send an army and wipe out this el Hamel?"

"What do I know?" I replied. "It is now for us to spy upon him and report to them, anyhow."

"Let him beware my knife," he grunted, and I bethought me that were I a Borgia, or my country another that I could mention, here would be one way of solving the problem of the new Mahdi menace.

"The *Franzawi* hire no assassins, nor allow assassination," I replied coldly. . . . "Keep good watch . . ." and left him, pondering many things in my heart. . . .

Oh for a friendly north-bound caravan to whose leader I might give these two girls, with a reasonably easy mind, and every hope that they would be safe. . . .

Poor old de Lannec. . . . None of that nonsense for *me*!

§ 5

Day followed lazy day and night followed active night, as weeks become a month and we steadily marched south-east; but no caravan gladdened my eyes, nor sight of any human being, away from the few oases, save once a lonely Targui scout, motionless on his *mehara* camel on a high sand-hill at evening.

After seeing this disturbing sight, I made a forced march all through the night and far into the next day, and hoped that we had escaped unseen and unfollowed.

I was very troubled in mind during these days.

Not only was my anxiety as to the fate of the two girls constant, but I was annoyed to find that I thought rather more about Mary Vanbrugh than about the tremendously important work that lay before me.

My mind was becoming more occupied by this slip of a girl, and less by my mission, upon which might depend the issues of Peace and War, the lives of thousands of men, the loss or gain of an Empire perhaps—certainly of milliards of francs and years of the labour of soldiers and statesmen. . . .

I could not sleep at night for thinking of this woman, and for thinking of her fate; and again for thinking of how she was disturbing my thoughts which should have been concentrated on Duty. . . .

And she was adding to my trouble by her behaviour towards me personally.

At times she appeared positively to loathe me, and again at times she was so kind that I could scarcely forbear to take her in my arms—when she called me "*Nice Major Ivan*", and showed her gratitude—though for what, God knows, for life was hard for her and for poor Maudie, the brave uncomplaining souls.

For the fact that her brother's fate must be a terrible grief to her I made allowance, and ascribed to it her changeful and capricious attitude towards me.

Never shall I forget one perfect night of full moon, by a glorious palm-shaded desert pool, one of those little oases that seem like Paradise and make the desert seem even more like Hell.

It was an evening that began badly, too.

While fires were being lighted, camels fed, and tents pitched, the two girls went to bathe.

Strolling, I met Maudie returning, and she looked so fresh and sweet, and my troubled soul was so full of admiration of her, for her courage and her cheerfulness, that, as she stopped and, with a delightful smile, said:

"Excuse me, sir, but is that Mr. Dufour a *married* man?" I laughed and, putting a brotherly arm about her, kissed her warmly.

With remarkable speed and violence she smacked my face.

"*Maudie!*" said I aghast, "you misunderstood me entirely!"

"Well, you won't misunderstand *me* again, sir, anyhow!" replied Maudie, with a toss of her pretty head, and marched off, chin in air.

As she did so, a tinkling laugh from among the palms

apprised me of the fact that Miss Vanbrugh had been an interested witness of this romantic little episode!

Nothing was said at dinner that evening, however, and after it, I sat apart with Mary Vanbrugh and had one of the delightfullest hours of my life.

She began by speaking of her brother Otis, and the possibilities of his being yet alive, and then of her parents and of her other brother and sister.

Papa was what she called "a bold bad beef-baron", and I gathered that he owned millions of acres of land and hundreds of thousands of cattle in Western America.

A widower, and, I gathered, a man the warmth of whose temper was only exceeded by the warmth of his heart. The other girl, in giving birth to whom his beloved wife had died, was, strangely enough, the very apple of his eye, and she it was who kept house for him while Mary wandered.

The older brother had apparently been too like his father to agree with him.

"Dad surely was hard on Noel," she told me, "and Noel certainly riled Dad. . . . Would he go to school or college? Not he! He rode ranch with the cowboys and was just one of them. Slept down in their bunk-house too. Ran away from school as often as he was sent—and there Dad would find him, hidden by the cowboys, when he thought the boy was 'way East.

"Dad was all for education, having had none himself. Noel was all for avoiding it, having had some himself. . . .

"One merry morn he got so fresh with Dad that when he rode off, Dad pulled himself together and lassoed him —just roped him like a steer—pulled him off his pony and laid into him with his quirt!

"Noel jumped up and pulled his gun. Then he threw it on the ground and just said, '*Good-bye, Dad. I'm through*,' and that was the last we saw of brother Noel. . . . How I did cry! I worshipped Noel, although he was so much older than I. So did Dad—although Otis never gave him a minute's trouble, and took to education like a duck. . . . He's a Harvard graduate and Noel's a 'roughneck', if he's alive. . . ."

"And you never saw Noel again?" I said. I wanted to keep her talking, to listen to that beautiful voice and watch that lovely face.

"Never. Nor heard from him. We heard *of* him though once —that after hoboing all over the States he was an enlisted man in a cavalry regiment, and then that a broncho-buster, whom our overseer knew, had seen him on a cattle-ship bound for Liverpool."

"And now you roam the wide world o'er, searching for the beloved playmate of your youth?" I remarked, perhaps fatuously.

"Rubbish!" was the reply. "I've almost forgotten what he looked like, and might not know him if I met him. . . . I'd just love to see him again though—dear old Noel. He never had an enemy but himself and never did a mean thing. . . . And now tell me all about *you*, Major Ivan, you stern, harsh, terrible man!" . . .

I talked about myself, as a man will do—to the right woman. And by-and-by I took her hand and she did not withdraw it—rather clasped it as I said:

"Do you know, the devil tried to tempt me last night to give the order to saddle up and ride north, and put you in a place of safety. . . ."

"Did you fall, Major?" she asked quietly—and yes, she did return my pressure of her strong little hand.

"I did not even listen to the tempter," I replied promptly. "But I'm feeling horribly worried and frightened and anxious about you. . . ."

"Business down yonder urgent, Major?" she asked.

"Very."

"And your chief's trusting you to put it through quick, neat and clean?"

"Yes."

"Then defy the devil and all his works, Major," she said, "and don't let my welfare interfere with yours. . . ."

"I shan't, Miss Vanbrugh," I replied. "But if we could only meet a caravan . . ."

"Nonsense! You don't play Joseph's Brethren with *me*, Major."

"How can I take you into the power of a man who, for all I know, may be a devil incarnate. . . . I should do better to shoot you myself. . . ."

"I was going to say, 'Make a camp near the oasis and ride in alone,' but I shan't let you do that, Major."

"It is what I had thought of—but a man like this Emir would know all about us and our movements, long before we were near his territory. . . . And what happens to you, if I am made a prisoner or killed? Dufour would not go without me—nor would Achmet and Djikki for that matter."

"You are going to carry on, just as if I were not here, my friend," she said, "and I'm coming right there with you —to share and share alike. I can always shoot myself when I'm bored with things. . . . So can Maudie. She's got a little gun all right . . . I wouldn't be a drag on you, Major, for anything in the world . . . Duty before pleasure —of course. . . ."

And as she said those words, and rubbed her shoulder nestlingly against mine, I took her other hand . . . I drew her towards me . . . I nearly kissed her smiling lips . . when she snatched her hand away, and, springing up, pointed in excitement towards the oasis.

"What is it?" I cried in some alarm, for my nerves were frayed with sleeplessness.

"I thought I saw a kind of winged elephant cavorting above the trees. You know—like a flying shrimp or whistling water-rat of the upper air, Major Ivan. . ."

And as I raged, she laughed and sang that cursed air again, *with* words this time—and the word were:

> "There are heroes in plenty, and well known to fame
> In the ranks that are led by the Czar;
> But among the most reckless of name or of fame
> Was *Ivan* Petruski Skivah.
> He could imitate Irving, play euchre, or pool,
> And perform on the Spanish guitar:—
> In fact, quite the cream of the Muscovite team
> Was *Ivan* Petruski Skivah."

Damn the girl, she had been laughing at me the whole time!

I gave the order to saddle up and did a double march, on towards the south of the rising sun—when it did rise—to punish her for her impertinence and to remind her that she was only with me on sufferance. . . . She should see who was the one to laugh last in *my* caravan. . . . .

And, *mon Dieu!* What a fool de Lannec was!

CHAPTER IX

THE TOUAREG—AND "DEAR IVAN"

ONE or two days later, as we jogged along in the "cool" of the evening, Dufour, the trusty rearguard of my little caravan, rode up to me.

"We're followed, sir," said he. "Touareg, I think. I have sent Djikki back to scout."

"If they're Touareg they'll surround our next camp and rush us suddenly," I said. "Our night-travelling has upset them, as there has been no chance for the surprise-at-dawn that they're so fond of."

"They'll follow us all night and attack when they think we are busy making camp tomorrow morning," said Dufour.

"We'll try to shake them off by zig-zagging and circling," I replied. "If it weren't for the women, it would be amusing to ride right round behind them and attack. . . . They may be only a small gang and not a *harka*."

Mary Vanbrugh closed up. I had been riding ahead in haughty displeasure, until Dufour came to me.

I had done with Mary Vanbrugh. "What is it, Major?" she asked.

"Nothing, Miss Vanbrugh," I replied.

"What men-folk usually wag their heads and their tongues about," she agreed.

Maudie's *bassourab*-adorned camel overtook us as we dropped into a walk and then halted.

"What is it, Mr. Dufour?" I heard her ask.

"*Sheikhs!*" replied Dufour maliciously, and I wondered if his face had also been slapped.

I looked at Maudie. Methought she beamed joyously.

Half an hour later, Djikki of the wonderful eyesight came riding up at top-speed.

"Veiled Touareg," he said. "The Forgotten of God. About five hands of fingers. Like the crescent moon," from which I knew that we were being followed by about five and twenty Touareg, and that they were riding in a curved line—the horns of which would encircle us at the right time.

There was nothing for it but to ride on. We were five rifles—six counting Mary Vanbrugh—and shooting from behind our camels we should give a good account of ourselves against mounted men advancing over open country.

Nor would so small a gang resolutely push home an attack upon so straight-shooting and determined a band as ourselves.

But what if they managed to kill our camels?

"Ride after Suleiman as fast as you can, Miss Vanbrugh, with Maudie. Achmet will ride behind you," said I. "You and I and Djikki will do rearguard, Dufour. . . ."

"Don't be alarmed if you hear firing," I added to the girls.

"Oh, Major, I shall jibber with fright, and look foolish in the face," drawled Mary Vanbrugh, and I was under the impression that Maudie's lips parted to breathe the word "Sheikhs!"

We rode in this order for an hour, and I then left D'ikki on a sand-dune, with orders to watch while the light lasted. I thought he would get our pursuers silhouetted against the sunset and see if their numbers had increased, their formation or direction changed, and judge whether their pace had quickened or slackened.

"As soon as it is dark, we'll turn sharp right, for a couple of hours, and then left again," I said to Dufour.

"Yes, sir," said he. "They won't be able to follow tracks in the dark. Not above a walking pace."

He had hardly spoken when a rifle cracked. . . . Again twice. . . . Aimed from us, by the sound. . . . . Djikki! We wheeled round together and rode back along our tracks. We passed Djikki's *barracked* camel and saw the Soudanese lying behind the crest of a sand-hill. He stood up and came down to us.

"Three," he said. "Swift scouts in advance of the rest. I hit one man and one camel. The others fled. Four hundred metres."

For a Soudanese it was very fine marksmanship.

"It'll show them we're awake, anyhow," said Dufour; and we rode off quickly, to overtake the others.

As soon as it was as dark as it ever is in the star-lit desert, I took the lead, and turned sharply from our line as we were riding over a rocky stone patch that would show no print of the soft feet of camels.

For an hour or two I followed the line, and then turned sharply to the left, parallel with our original track.

Thereafter I dropped to the rear, leaving Dufour to lead. I preferred to rely upon his acquired scientific skill rather than upon Suleiman's desert sense of direction, when I left the head of the caravan at night. Dropping back, I halted until I could only just see the outline of the last rider, Achmet, sometimes as a blur of white in the star-shine, sometimes as a silhouette against the blue-black starry sky. . . .

Vast, vast emptiness. . . . Universes beyond universes. . . . Rhythmic fall of soft feet on sand. . . . Rhythmic swaying of the great camel's warm body. . . . World swaying. . . . Stars swaying. . . .

I will not falsely accuse myself of having fallen asleep, for I do not believe I slept—though I have done such a thing on the back of a camel. But I was certainly slightly hypnotized by star-staring and the perfect rhythm of my camel's tireless changeless trot. . . . And I had been very short of sleep for weeks. . . . Perhaps I did sleep for a few seconds?

Anyhow, I came quite gradually from a general inattentiveness toward the phenomena of reality, to an interest therein, and then to an awareness that gripped my heart like the clutch of a cold hand.

First I noted dully that I had drawn level with Achmet and was some yards to his right. . . . Then that Djikki or Suleiman perhaps, was riding a few yards to my right. . . . And then that someone else was close behind me.

I must have got right into the middle of the caravan. Curious. . . . *Why, what was this . . .?* I rubbed my eyes. . . . None of *us* carried a lance or spear of any kind!

It was then that my blood ran cold, for I knew I was *riding with the Touareg*!

I pulled myself together and did some quick thinking. Did each of them take me for some other member of their band who had ridden to the front and been overtaken again? Or were they chuckling to themselves at the poor fool whom they had outwitted, and who was now in their power? . . .

Was their object to ride on with me, silently, until the Touareg band and the caravan were one body—and then each robber select his victim and slay him?

What should I do? My rifle was across my thighs. No; I could not have been asleep or I should have dropped it.

I slowly turned my head and looked behind me. I could see no others—but it was very dark and others might be near, besides the three whom I could distinguish clearly.

Achmet was not in sight. What *should* I do? . . .

Work, poor brain, work! Her life depends on it. . . .

Could I draw ahead of them sufficiently fast to overtake the caravan, give a swift order, and have my men wheeled about and ready to meet our pursuers with a sudden volley and then rapid fire?

I could try, anyhow. I raised the long camel-stick that dangled from my wrist, and my camel quickened its pace instantly. There is never any need to strike a well-trained *mehara*. . . . The ghostly riders to right and left of me kept their positions. . . . I had gained nothing. . . .

I must not appear to be trying to escape. . . . With faint pressure on the left nose-rein of my camel, I endeavoured to edge imperceptibly towards the shadow on my left. I would speak to him as though I were a brother Targui, as soon as I was close enough to shoot with certainty if he attacked me.

The result showed me that the raiders had not taken me for one of themselves—I could get no nearer to the man, nor draw farther from the rider on my right. . . .

Wits against wits—and Mary Vanbrugh's life in the balance. . . .

Gently I drew rein, and slowed down very gradually. My silent nightmare companions did the same.

This would let the caravan draw ahead of us, and give

my men more time for action, when the time for action came.

Slower and slower grew my pace, and I drooped forward nodding like a man asleep, my eyes straining beneath my *haik* to watch these devils who shepherded me along.

My camel dropped into a walk, and very gradually the two shadows converged upon me to do a silent job with sword or spear. . . .

And what of the man behind me? The muscles of my shoulder-blades writhed as I thought of the cold steel that even then might be within a yard of my back. . . .

Suddenly I pulled up, raised my rifle, and fired carefully, and with the speed that has no haste, at the rider on my right. I aimed where, if I missed his thigh, I should hit his camel, and hoped to hit both. As my rifle roared in the deep silence of the night, I swung left for the easier shot, fired again, and drove my camel bounding forward. I crouched low, as I worked the bolt of my rifle, in the hope of evading spear-thrust or sword-stroke from behind.

As I did so a rifle banged behind me, at a few yards range, and I felt as though my left arm had been struck with a red-hot axe.

With the right hand that held the rifle, I wheeled my camel round in a flash, steadied the beast and myself and, one-handed, fired from my hip at a camel that suddenly loomed up before me. Then I wheeled about again and sent my good beast forward at racing speed.

My left arm swung useless, and I could feel the blood pouring down over my hand, in a stream. . . .

This would not do. . . .

I shoved my rifle under my thigh and with my right hand raised my left and got the arm up so that I could hold it by the elbow, with the left hand beneath my chin.

I fought off the feeling of faintness caused by shock and the loss of blood—and wondered if Suleiman, Djikki, Achmet and Dufour would shoot first and challenge afterwards, as I rode into them. . . .

Evidently I had brought down the three camels at which I had aimed—not a difficult thing to do, save in darkness, and when firing from the back of a camel, whose very breathing sways one's rifle. . . .

I was getting faint again. . . . It would soon pass off. . . .

If I could only plug the holes and improvise a sling. . . .
As the numbness of the arm wore off and I worried at it,
I began to hope and believe that the bone was not broken. . .
Fancy a shattered elbow-joint, in the desert, and with the
need to ride hard and constantly. . . .

I was aware of three dark masses in line. . . .

"Major! *Shout!*" cried a voice, and with great prompt-
itude I shouted—and three rifles came down from the
firing position.

"Where is she?" I asked.

"I made her ride on with Achmet, hell-for-leather,"
replied Dufour. "I swore she'd help us more that way,
till we can see what's doing. . . . What happened, sir?"

I told him.

"They'll trail us all right," said Dufour. "Those were
scouts and there would be a line of connecting-links between
them and the main body. Shall we wait, and get them
one by one?"

"No," I replied. "They'd circle us and they'd get the
others while we waited here. It'll be daylight soon. . . ."

It was in the dim daylight of the false dawn that we
sighted the baggage-camels of the caravan.

"Those baggage-camels will have to be left," said Dufour.

"You can't ride away from Touareg," I answered.
"It's hopeless. We've got to fight, if they attack. They
may not do so, having been badly stung already. But the
Targui is a vengeful beast. It isn't as though they were
ordinary Bedouin. . . ."

The light grew stronger, and we drew near to the others.
I told Djikki to drop back and to fire directly he saw
anything of the robbers—thus warning us, and standing
them off while we made what preparations we could.

I suddenly felt extremely giddy, sick, and faint. My
white *burnous* made a ghastly show. I was wet through,
from my waist to my left foot, with blood. I must have
lost a frightful lot . . . artery. . . .

Help . . . !

The next thing that I knew was that I was lying with
my head on Maudie's lap, while Mary Vanbrugh, white of
face but deft of hand, bandaged my arm and strapped it

95

across my chest. She had evidently torn up some linen garment for this purpose. Mary's eyes were fixed on her work, and Maudie's on the horizon. The men were crouched each behind his kneeling camel.

"*Dear* Major Ivan," murmured Mary as she worked.

I shut my eyes again, quickly and without shame. It was heavenly to rest thus for a few minutes.

"Oh, is he *dead*, Miss?" quavered poor Maudie.

"We shall all be dead in a few minutes, I expect, child," replied Mary. "Have you a safety-pin? . . . Dead as cold mutton. . . . *Sheikhs*, my dear! . . . Shall I shoot you at the last, Maudie, or would you rather do it yourself?"

"Well—if you wouldn't *mind*, Miss? Thank you very much, if it's not troubling you."

Silence.

"*Dear* Major Ivan," came a sweet whisper. "Oh, I *have* been a beast to him, Maudie. . . . Yes, I'll shoot you with pleasure, child. . . . How *could* I be such a wretch as to treat him like that. . . . He is the bravest, nicest, sternest . . ."

I felt a cad, and opened my eyes—almost into those of Mary, whose lips were just . . . were they . . . *were* they? . . .

"Yes, Miss," said Maudie, her eyes and thoughts afar off. "He is a beautiful gentleman. . . ."

"Hallo! the patient has woken up!" cried Mary, drawing back quickly. "Had a nice nap, Major? How do you feel? . . . Here, have a look into the cup that cheers and inebriates"; and she lifted a mug, containing cognac and water, to my lips.

I drank the lot and felt better.

"My heart come into my mouth it did, sir, when I saw you fall head-first off that camel. You fair *splashed* blood, sir," said Maudie. "Clean into me mouth me heart come, sir."

"Hope you swallowed the little thing again, Maud. Such a sweet *garden* of romance as it is! . . . '*Come into the maud, Garden!*' for a change. . . . That's the way, Major. . . . Drinks it up like milk and looks round for more. Got a nice clean flesh wound and no bones touched, the clever man. . . ."

I sat up.

"Get those camels farther apart, Dufour," I shouted. "Absolute focal point to draw concentrated fire bunched like that . . ."

Nobody must think that I was down and out, and that the reins were slipping from a sick man's grasp.

The men were eating dates as they watched, and Mary had opened a tin of biscuits and one of sardines.

"Hark at the Major saying his piece," a voice murmured from beneath a flowing *kafiyeh* beside me. "Isn't he fierce this morning!"

I got to my feet and pulled myself together. . . . Splendid. . . . Either the brandy, or the idea of a kiss I foolishly fancied that I had nearly received, had gone to my head. I ate ravenously for the next ten minutes, and drank cold tea from a water-bottle.

"There's many a slip between the kiss and the lip," I murmured anon, in a voice to match the one that had last spoken.

I was unwise.

"Wrong again, Major Ivan Petruski Ski*vah*! I was just going to blow a smut off your grubby little nose," was the prompt reply, and I seemed to hear thereafter a crooning of:

> "*But among the most reckless of name and of fame*
> *Was Ivan Petruski Skivah*
>
> . . . .
>
> *. . . and perform on the Spanish guitar*
> *In fact, quite the cream of 'Intelligence' team*
> *Was Ivan Petruski Skivah . . .*"

as Miss Vanbrugh cleaned her hands with sand and then re-packed iodine and boric lint in the little medicine-chest.

I managed to get on to my camel, and soon began to feel a great deal better, perhaps helped by my ferocious anger at myself for collapsing. Still, blood is blood, and one misses it when too much is gone.

"Ride on with Achmet again," I called to Miss Vanbrugh, and bade the rest mount. "We'll keep on now, just as long as we can," I said to Dufour, and ordered Djikki to hang as far behind us as was safe. In a matter of that sort, Djikki's judgement was as good as anybody's. . . .

Dufour then told me a piece of news.

A few miles to the south-east of us was, according to Suleiman, a *shott*, a salt-lake or marsh that extended to the base of a chain of mountains. The strip of country between the two was very narrow.

We could camp there.

If the Touareg attacked us, they could only do so on a narrow front, and could not possibly surround us. To go north round the lake, or south round the mountains, would be several days' journey.

"That will be the place for us, sir," concluded Dufour.

"Yes," I agreed, "if the Touareg are not there before us."

CHAPTER X

MY ABANDONED CHILDREN

THAT would have been one of the worst days of my life, and that is saying a good deal, had it not been for a certain exaltation and joy that bubbled up in my heart as I thought of the look in Miss Vanbrugh's eyes when I had opened mine. . . .

What made it so terrible was not merely the maddening ache in my arm that seemed to throb in unison with the movement of my camel, but the thought of what I must do if this pass was what I pictured it to be, and if the Touareg attacked us in strength.

It would be a very miserable and heart-breaking duty— to ride on and leave my men to hold that pass—that I might escape and fulfil my mission. How could I leave Dufour to die that I might live? How could I desert Achmet and Djikki, my servants and my friends? . . .

However—it is useless to attempt to serve one's country in the Secret Service, if one's private feelings, desires, loves, sorrows, likes and dislikes are to be allowed to come between one and one's country's good. . . . Poor de Lannec! How weak and unworthy he had been. . . .

There was one grain of comfort—nothing would be gained by my staying and dying with my followers. . . . It would profit them nothing at all. . . . They would die just the same. . . .

If the Touareg could, by dint of numbers, overcome four, they could overcome five. I could not save them by staying with them. . . .

But oh, the misery, the agony, of ordering them to hold that pass while I rode to safety!

How could I give the order: "Die, but do not retire—until *I* have had time to get well away"?

And the girls? Would they be a hindrance to me on two of the fleetest camels. . . . And perhaps any of my little band who did not understand my desertion of them would think they were fighting to save the women, whom I was taking to safety—*if I decided to take them.*

But it would be ten times worse than leaving my comrades in Zaguig. . . .

How could I leave *Mary Vanbrugh*—perhaps to fall, living, into the hands of those bestial devils?

The place proved an ideal spot for a rearguard action, and the Touareg were not before us.

Lofty and forbidding rocks rose high, sheer from the edge of a malodorous swamp, from whose salt-caked edge grew dry bents that rattled in the wind.

Between the swamp and the stone cliffs was a tract of boulder-strewn sand, averaging a hundred yards in width.

Here we camped, lit fires, and prepared to have a long and thorough rest—unless the Touareg attacked—until night.

Achmet quickly pitched the little *tentes d'abri,* fixed the camp-beds for the girls, and unrolled the "flea-bags" and thin mattresses, while his kettle boiled. It was a strangely peaceful and domestic scene—in view of the fact that sudden death—or slow torture—loomed so large and near.

Dufour himself ungirthed and fed the camels while Suleiman stood upon a rock and stared out into the desert. He could probably see twice as far as Dufour or I. . . .

"*Into* that tent, Major," said the cool sweet voice that I was begining to like again. "I have made the bed as comfy as I can. Have Achmet pull your boots off. I'll come in ten minutes or so, and dress your arm again."

"And what about *you*?" I replied. "I'm not going to take your tent. I am quite all right now, thanks."

"Maudie and I are going to take turns on the other bed," she replied. "And you *are* going to take 'my' tent, and lie down too. What's going to happen to the show if you get ill? Suppose you get fever? Suppose your arms mortifies and falls into the soup? . . . Let's get the wound fixed again, before those low-brow Touareg shoot us up again. . . . You'll find a cold-water compress very soothing. . . . Go along, Major. . . ."

I thought of something more soothing than that—the touch of cool deft fingers.

"I'd be shot daily if you were there to bind me up, Miss Vanbrugh," I said as I gave in to her urgency, and went to the tent.

"Well—perhaps they'll oblige after breakfast, Major, and plug your other arm," observed this most unsentimental young woman.

"But, my dear!" I expostulated. "If I had no arms at all, how could I? . . . "

"Just what *I* was thinking, Major," was the reply, as, to hide a smile, she stooped over the big suit case and extracted the medicine chest. . . .

As we hastily swallowed our meal of dates, rice, biscuits and tinned milk, I gave my last orders to Dufour. . . .

"You'll hold this pass while there is a man of you alive," I said.

"*Oui, mon Commandant*," replied the brave man, with the same quiet nonchalance that would have marked his acknowledgement of an order to have the camels saddled.

"Should the Touareg abandon the attempt (which they will not do), any survivor is to ride due south-east until he reaches the Great Oasis."

"*Oui, mon Commandant*."

"Even if Suleiman is killed, there will be no difficulty in finding the place, but we'll hear what he has to say about wells and water-holes—while he is still hale and hearty."

"*Oui, mon Commandant*."

"But I fear there won't be any survivors—four against

a *harka*—say, a hundred to one. . . . But you must hold them up until I am well away. . . . They won't charge while your shooting is quick and accurate. . . . When they do, they'll get you, of course. . . . Don't ride for it at the last moment. . . . See it through here, to give the impression that you are the whole party. I must not be pursued. . . . Die here. . . ."

"*Oui, mon Commandant.*"

"Excuse me, Major de Beaujolais," cut in the voice of Miss Vanbrugh, icily cold and most incisive, "is it possible that you are talking about *deserting your men* . . .? Leaving them to die here while you escape . . .? *Ordering* them to remain here to increase your own chance of safety, in fact. . . ."

"I was giving instructions to my subordinate, who will remain here with the others, Miss Vanbrugh," I replied coldly. "Would you be good enough to refrain from interrupting. . . ."

My uncle's words burned before my eyes—"*A woman, of course! . . . He turned aside from his duty. . . . Exit de Lannec. . . .*"

Miss Vanbrugh put her hand on Dufour's arm.

"If you'll be so kind as to enrol me, Mr. Dufour—I am a very good rifle shot," she said. "I shall dislike perishing with you intensely, but I should dislike deserting you infinitely more," and she smiled very sweetly on my brave Dufour.

He kissed her hand respectfully and looked inquiringly at me.

"And Maudie?" I asked Miss Vanbrugh. "Is she to be a romantic heroine, too? I hope she can throw stones better than most girls, for I understand she has never fired a rifle or pistol in her life. . . ."

"I think you really are the most insufferable and detestable creature I have *ever* met," replied Miss Vanbrugh.

"Interesting, but hardly germane to the discussion," I replied.

"Listen, Miss Vanbrugh," I continued. "If the Touareg are upon us, as I have no doubt they are, I am going to ride straight for the Great Oasis. Dufour, Achmet, Djikki and Suleiman will stand the Touareg off as long as possible. Eventually my men will be rushed and slaughtered. If sufficiently alive, when overcome and seized, they will be tortured unbelievably. The Touareg may or may not then follow me, but they will have no chance of overtaking me as I shall have a long start. I shall have the best of the riding camels, and I shall make forced marches. . . . Now—I see no reason why you and Maudie should not accompany me *for just as long as you can stand the pace.* . . ."

"Oh, Major—we might conceivably hinder you and so imperil your most precious life, endanger your safety—so essential to France and the world in general. . . ."

"I'll take good care you don't do that, Miss Vanbrugh," I replied. "But, as I say, there is no reason why you and your maid should not ride off with me—though, I give you fair warning, I shall probably ride for twenty-four hours without stopping—and you will be most welcome. In fact, I pray you to do so. . . . Trust me to see to it that you are no hindrance nor source of danger to the success of my mission. . . ."

"Oh—I fully trust you for *that*, Major de Beaujolais," she replied bitterly.

"Then be ready to start as soon as we get word from Djikki that they are coming," I said. "Once again, there is no reason why you should not come with me. . . ."

"Thank you—but there is a very strong reason. I would sooner die twice over. . . . I remain here," was the girl's reply. "I can think of only one thing worse than falling alive into the hands of these beasts—and that is deserting my *friends*, Mr. Dufour, Achmet and Djikki. . . . Why, I wouldn't desert even that evil-looking Suleiman after he had served me faithfully. . . . I wouldn't desert a dog. . . ."

"And Maudie?" I asked.

"She shall do exactly as she pleases," answered the girl.

Turning to Maudie, who was listening open-mouthed, she said:

"Will you ride off with Major de Beaujolais, my child, or will you stay with me? You may get to safety with this gallant gentleman—if you can keep him in sight. . . . It is death to stay here, apparently, but I will take care that it *is* death and not torture for you, my dear."

"Wouldn't the Sheikhs treat us well, Miss?" asked Maudie.

"Oh, *Sheikhs*!" snapped Miss Vanbrugh. "These are two-legged *beasts*, my good idiot. They are human wolves, torturing *devils*, merciless *brutes*. . . . What is the worst thing you've got in your country?"

"Burglars, Miss," replied Maudie promptly.

"Well, the ugliest cut-throat burglar that ever hid under your bed or came in at your window in the middle of the night, is just a dear little woolly lambkin, compared with the best of these murderous savages. . . ."

Maudie's face fell.

"I thought perhaps these was Sheikhs, Miss. . . . Like in the book. . . . But, anyhow, I was going to do what you do, Miss, and go where you go—of course, please, Miss."

"I am afraid you are another of those ordinary queer creatures that think faithfulness to friends and loyalty to comrades come first, dear," said Miss Vanbrugh, and gave Maudie's hand a squeeze. "But you'll do what I tell you, Maudie, won't you?"

"That's what I'm here for, please, Miss, thank you," replied the girl.

"Well, you're going with Major de Beaujolais," said Miss Vanbrugh. "I hate sending you off with a gentleman of his advanced views and superior standards—but I should hate shooting you, even more."

"Yes, Miss, thank you," answered Maudie, and I rose and strolled to my tent.

Ours is not an easy service. Duty is a *very* jealous God. . . .

Miss Vanbrugh came and dressed my arm, and we spoke no word to each other during the process. How I *hated* her! . . . The unfair, illogical little vixen! . . . The *woman*! . . .

A few minutes later Suleiman uttered a shout. He could see a rider on the horizon. I hurried towards him.

"It is Djikki, the black slave," he said.

"Djikki, the French Soudanese soldier, you dog," I growled at him, and at any other time would have fittingly rewarded the ugly scowl with which he regarded me.

"They are coming," shouted Djikki as his swift camel

drew near; and we all rushed to work like fiends at packing-up and making preparations, for flight and fight respectively.

"They are more than ten hands of five fingers now," said Djikki, as he dismounted. . . . "More than a battalion of soldiers in numbers. . . . They are riding along our track. . . . Here in an hour."

"Miss Vanbrugh," said I, "I have got to go. If you stay here I shall go on and do my work. When that is successfully completed, I shall come back to this spot and shoot myself. . . . Think of Maudie, too—if you won't think of yourself or me. Do you want the girl to meet some of her 'Desert Sheikhs' at last?"

"*Can* you leave Dufour and the Brown Brothers, Major de Beaujolais? . . . I love that little Djikki-bird. . . ."

"I can, Miss Vanbrugh, because I *must*. And if I, a soldier, can do such a thing, a girl can. What could you do by stopping to die here?"

"Shoot," she replied, "as fast and as straight as any of them."

"My dear lady," I said, "if four rifles won't keep off a hundred, five won't. If five can, four can. . . . And I must slink off. . . ."

I could have wept. We stood silent, staring at each other.

"Your say goes, Major. I suppose you are right," answered the girl, and my heart leapt up again. "But I *hate* myself—and I *loathe* you. . . ."

All worked like slaves to get the four swiftest camels saddled and loaded with light and indispensable things. The fourth one, although a *mehara*, had to carry one *tente d'abri* and bed, water, and food.

I could hardly trust myself to speak as I wrung Dufour's hand, nor when I patted the shoulder of my splendid Achmet. Djikki put my hand to his forehead and his heart, and then knelt to kiss my feet.

The drop of comfort in the bitter suffering of that moment was my knowledge that these splendid colleagues of mine—white man, brown man, and black—knew that what I was doing was my Duty and that what they were about to do was theirs. . . .

I bade Suleiman fight for his life; he was too new a

recruit to the Service to be expected to fight for an ideal. . . .

Miss Vanbrugh and Maudie mounted their *mehari*—Maudie still as cheerful and plucky as ever, and, I am certain, thrilled, and still hopeful of tender adventure.

I should be surprised if her novelette-turned brain and rubbish-fed imagination did not even yet picture the villainous desert wolves, who were so close on our trail, as the brave band of a "lovely" Desert Sheikh in hot pursuit of one Maudie Atkinson, of whose beauty and desirability he had somehow heard. . . .

There was a shout from Suleiman again. Something moving on the horizon.

I gave the word to start, and took a last look round.

My men's camels were *barraked* out of danger. Each man had a hundred rounds of ammunition, a *girba* of water, a little heap of dates, and an impregnable position behind a convenient rock. . . .

Four against scores—perhaps hundreds. . . . But in a narrow pass. . . . If only the Touareg would content themselves with shooting, and lack the courage to charge.

"Say, Major," called Mary, "let those desert dead-beats hear six rifles for a bit! They may remember an urgent date back in their home-town, to see a man about a dog or something. . . . Think we're a regular sheriff's posse of *vigilantes* or a big, bold band of Bad Men. . . ."

Dare I? It would take a tiny trifle of the load of misery from my shoulders. . . .

I would!

We brought our camels to their knees again, and rejoined the garrison of the pass, the men of this little African Thermopylae. . . .

Miss Vanbrugh chose her rock, rested her rifle on it, sighted, raised the slide of her back-sight a little—all in a most business-like manner.

Maudie crouched at my feet, behind my rock, and I showed her how to work the bolt of my rifle, after each shot. I was one-handed, and Maudie had, of course, never handled a rifle in her life.

I waited until we could distinguish human and animal forms in the approaching cloud of dust, and then gave the range at 2,000 metres. *"Fixe!"* I cried coolly there-after, for the benefit of my native soldiers. *"Feux de salve. . . . En Joue! . . . Feu!"*

It was an admirable volley, even Suleiman firing exactly on my word, *"Feu,"* although he knew no word of French.

Three times I repeated the volley, and then gave the order for a rapid *feu de joie* as it were, at 1,500 metres, so that the advancing Touareg should hear at least six rifles, and suppose that there were probably many more.

I then ordered my men, in succession, to fire two shots as quickly as possible, each firing as soon as the man on his left had got his two shots off. This should create doubt and anxiety as to our numbers.

I then ordered rapid independent fire.

The Touareg had deployed wildly, dismounted, and opened fire. This rejoiced me, for I had conceived the quite unlikely possibility of their charging in one headlong overwhelming wave. . . .

It was time to go.

"Run to your camel, Maudie. Come on, Miss Van-brugh," I shouted; and called to Dufour, "God watch over you, my dear friend."

I had to go to the American girl and drag her from the rock behind which she stood, firing steadily and methodically, changing her sights occasionally, a handful of empty cartridge-cases on the ground to her right, a handful of cartridges ready to her hand on the rock. . . .

I shall never forget that picture of Mary Vanbrugh —dressed as an Arab girl and fighting like a trained soldier. . . .

"I'm not coming!" she cried.

I shook her as hard as I could and then literally dragged her to her camel.

"Good-bye, my children," I cried as I abandoned them.

§ 2

We rode for the rest of that day, and I thanked God when I could no longer hear the sounds of rifle-fire, glad though I was that they had only died away as distance weakened them, and not with the suddenness that would have meant a charge, massacre and pursuit.

I was a bitter, miserable and savage man when at last I was compelled to draw rein, and Miss Vanbrugh bore my evil temper with a gentle womanly sweetness of which I had not thought her capable.

She dressed my arm again (and I almost hoped that it might never heal while she was near) and absolutely insisted that she and Maudie should share watches with me. When I refused this, she said:

"Very well, Major, then instead of one watching while two sleep, we'll both watch, and Maudie shall chaperon us—and that's the sort of thing Euclid calls *reductio ad absurdum*, or plumb-silly." And nothing would shake her, although I could have done so willingly.

What with the wound in my arm and the wound in my soul, I was near the end of my tether. . . .

We took a two-hour watch in turn, poor Maudie nursing a rifle of which she was mortally afraid.

CHAPTER XI

THE CROSS OF DUTY

WE rode hard all the next day, and the two girls, thanks the the hard training of the previous weeks, stood the strain well.

It was for the sake of the camels and not for that of the two brave women that I at length drew rein and halted for a four-hour rest at a water-hole

As I strode up and down, in misery and grief at the thoughts that filled my mind—thoughts of those splendid men whom I had left to die, Mary Vanbrugh came from the little *tente d'abri* which I had insisted that she and Maudie should use.

"Go and lie down," she said. "You'll get fever and make that arm worse. . . . You must rest *sometimes*, if you are to carry on at all."

"I can't," I said. "They were like brothers to me and I *loved* each one of them."

"Talk then, if you can't rest," replied the wise woman. "Tell me about them. . . ."

"Go and lie down yourself," I said.

"It's Maudie's turn for the bed," she answered. "Tell me about them. . . . Sit down here. . . ."

I told her about Dufour and his faithful service of nearly twenty years; of how he had offered his life for mine, and had saved it, more than once.

"And Djikki?" she asked.

"He, too," I replied. "He is a Senegalese soldier, and I took him for my orderly because of his great strength and endurance, his courage, fidelity and patience. . . . He was with me when I was doing some risky work down Dahomey way. . . . There was a certain king who was giving trouble and threatening worse trouble—and it was believed that he was actually getting Krupp guns from a German trading-post on the coast. . . .

"We were ambushed in that unspeakable jungle, and only Djikki and I survived the fight. . . . We were driven along for days, thrashed with sticks, prodded with spears, tied to trees at night, and bound so tightly that our limbs swelled and turned blue.

"We were given entrails to eat and carefully defiled water to drink. . . . And one morning, as they untied us, that we might stagger on—towards the king's capital—Djikki snatched a *machete*, a kind of heavy hiltless sword, from a man's hand, and put up such a noble fight as has rarely been fought by one man against a crowd. In spite of what we had been through he fought like a fiend incarnate. . . . It was Homeric. . . . It was like a gorilla fighting baboons, a tiger fighting dogs.

"That heavy razor-edged blade rose and fell like lightning, and every time it descended, a head or an arm was almost severed from a body—and he whirled and sprang and slashed and struck until the whole gang of them gave ground, and as he bellowed and charged and then smote their leader's head clean from his shoulders, they broke and ran. . . . And Djikki—dripping blood, a mass of gashes and gaping wounds—ran too. . . . With me in his arms. . . .

"And when he could run no longer, he laid me down and cut the hide thongs that bound my wrists and elbows behind me, and those that cut into the flesh of my knees and ankles. Then he fainted from loss of blood. . . .

"I collapsed next day with fever, dysentery, and blood-poisoning, and Djikki—that black ex-cannibal—carried me in his arms, like a mother her baby, day after day, for five weeks, and got food for the two of us as well. . . .

"During that time I tasted the warm blood of monkeys and the cold flesh of lizards. . . . And when, at last, we were found, by pure good luck, near a French post on the Great River, he had not, as I discovered later, eaten for three days (although I had) and he had not slept for four nights. . . . But he had not left me and saved himself, as he could so easily have done. . . .

"Instead of doing thirty miles a day and eating all he got, he did ten miles a day with me in his arms, and gave me the food—pretending he had eaten. . . . The doctor at the Fort said he had never seen anyone so starved and emaciated, and yet able to keep his feet. . . . No, he never left me. . . ."

"And *you* have left *him*," said Miss Vanbrugh.

"I have left him," I replied. . . .

"And Achmet?" she asked.

"The most faithful servant a man ever had," I said. "He has nursed me through fever, dysentery, blindness, wounds, and all sorts of illnesses, as gently and tirelessly as any woman could have done.

"He is a Spahi and a brave soldier. . . . Once I was getting my squadron across a deep crocodile-infested river, swollen and swift, very difficult and dangerous work if you have not had plenty of practice in handling a swimming horse. . . . I crossed first and then returned. Finally, I came over last, and a huge crocodile took my horse—the noise and splashing of the crossing squadron having subsided—and I went down with the pair of them, heavily weighted too. . . . It was my Achmet who spurred his horse back into the water, swam to the spot and dived for me, regardless of crocodiles and the swift current. . . . We were both pretty well dead by the time he managed to grab an overhanging branch, and they dragged us out. . . ."

A silence fell between us. . . .

"Another time, too," I went on, "Achmet and Dufour undoubtedly saved my life—and not only at the risk of their own, but at the cost of horrible suffering.

"We were besieged in a tiny entrenched bivouac, starving and nearly dead with thirst. All that came into that little hell was a hail of tribesmen's bullets by day and a gentle rain of snipers' bullets by night. . . .

"Had we been of the kind that surrenders—which we were not—we should only have exchanged the tortures of thirst for the almost unimaginable tortures of the knives and red-hot irons of the tribesmen and their women. . . . Day by day our sufferings increased and our numbers diminished, as men died of starvation, thirst, dysentry, fever heat-stroke, wounds—or the merciful bullet. . . .

"The day temperature was rarely much above 120° and never below it, and from the sun we had no shelter. Generally a sirocco was blowing at fifty miles an hour, as hot as the blast from the open door of a furnace, and the sun was hidden in the black clouds of its dust. . . . Often it was as though night fell ere noon; and men, whose ration of water was a teacupful a day, had to breathe this dust. Our mouths, nostrils, eyes, ears were filled with it. . . . And, on dark nights, those devils would place fat *girbas* of water where, at dawn, they would be in full view of men dying of thirst . . . in the hope of luring them from the shelter of rocks and sand-trenches to certain death . . . and in the certainty of adding to their tortures. . . . But my men were Spahis, and not one of them complained, or grumbled, or cast off discipline to make a dash for a *girba* and death. . . .

"Dufour asked to be allowed to crawl out at night and try to get one of those skins—in which there might still remain a few drops of water—or possibly catch one of the fiends placing a *girba*—and I would not allow it. . . . I would not weigh Dufour's life against the ghost of a chance of getting a little water—and that poisoned, perhaps. . . . Nor did I feel that I had any right to go myself, nor to send any of my few remaining men. . . .

"Then Achmet volunteered to try. . . .

"But I am wandering . . . what I started to say was this . . . Three days before we were relieved I was shot in the head, and for those three days Dufour not only maintained the defence of that post, garrisoned by dying men, but *devoted half his own tiny ration of water to me and my wound*. . . . Achmet threatened to knife him when Dufour tried to prevent him from contributing *the whole* of his! . . .

"And when the relief-column arrived there was not a man on his feet, except Dufour, though there were several lying, still alive, gripping their rifles and facing their foes. . . .

"Dufour could give no information to the Colonel commanding the relief-column, because he could not speak, and when he sat down to write an answer to a question, he collapsed, and the surgeons took him over. . . ."

"You *accepted* half Dufour's and the whole of Achmet's water-ration?" asked Mis Vanbrugh.

"I was unconscious from the time I was hit until the day after the relief," I replied. "I should never have recovered consciousness at all had not the excellent Surgeon-Major arrived—nor should I have lived until he did arrive, but for Achmet's bathing my head and keeping it clean and 'cool'—in a temperature of 120° and a howling dust-storm. . . . I learnt all about it afterwards from a Spahi Sergeant who was one of the survivors. . . . Achmet did not sleep during those three days. . . . Nor did he taste water. . . .

"And I have left *him* too," I added.

Mary Vanbrugh was silent for a while.

"Major de Beaujolais," she said at length, "suppose there had been only one camel, when you—er—departed from the pass. Suppose the Touareg had contrived to shoot the rest. . . . Would you have taken that camel and gone off alone?"

"Yes," I replied.

"Leaving Maudie—and me?"

"Unhesitatingly," I replied.

She regarded me long and thoughtfully, and then, without speaking, returned to the tent where Maudie slept, dreaming, doubtless, of Sheikhs.

Of course I would have left them. Was I to be another de Lannec and turn aside from the service of my country, imperil the interests and welfare of my Motherland, be false to the traditions of my great and noble Service, stultify the arduous and painful training of a lifetime,

fail the trust reposed in me, and betray my General—
for a woman?

But, oh, the thought of that woman struggling and
shrieking in the vile hands of those inhuman lustful
devils!

And, oh, my splendid, brave Dufour; simple, unswerv-
ing, inflexible devotee of Duty—who loved me. . . . Oh,
my great-hearted faithful Djikki, who had done for me
what few white men could or would have done; Djikki,
who loved me. . . .

Oh, my beloved Achmet, strong, gentle soul, soldier,
nurse, servant and friend . . . who loved me. . . .

Yes—*of course* I would have taken the last camel, and
with only one rider, too, to give it every chance of reaching
the Great Oasis by forced marches.

And, *of course*, I would leave those three to die alone,
tomorrow, if they survived today. . . .

Hard? . . .

Indeed, and indeed, ours is a hard service, a Service for
hard men, but a noble Service. And—Duty is indeed a
jealous God.

§ 2

And, one weary day, as we topped a long hill, we saw a
sight that made me rub my eyes and say, "This is fever
and madness!"

For, a few hundred yards from us, rode a Camel Corps—
a drilled and disciplined unit that, even as we crossed their
skyline, deployed from column to line, at a signal from their
leader, as though they had been Spahis, *barraked* their
camels, in perfect line and with perfect intervals, and sank
from sight behind them, with levelled rifles.

Surely none but European officers or drill-sergeants had
wrought that wonder?

I raised my hands above my head and rode towards their
leader, as it was equally absurd to think of flight or of
fight. . . .

Caught! . . . Trapped! . . .

The commander was a misshapen dwarf with huge
hunched shoulders and big head.

"*Aselamu, Aleikum,*" I called pleasantly and coolly. "Greeting to you."

"*Salaam aleikum wa Rahmat Allah,*" growled the Bedouin gutterally, and staring fiercely from me to the *bourkah*-covered women. "Greeting to you, and the peace of Allah."

"*Keif halak?*" I went on. "How do you do?" and wondered if this were the end. . . . Would Mary shoot herself in time . . .? Did my mission end here . . .?

No—discipline like this did not go hand-in-hand with foul savagery. There was a hope. . . .

"*Taiyib,*" replied the dwarf. "Well"—and proceeded to ask if we were alone.

"Quite," I assured him, swiftly rejecting the idea of saying there was an army of my friends close behind, and asked in turn, with flowery compliments upon the drill and discipline of his squadron, who he was.

"Commander of a hundred in the army of my Lord *the Emir el Hamel el Kebir*, Leader of the Faithful, and Shadow of the Prophet of God," was the sonorous reply; and with a falsely cheerful ejaculation of surprise and joy, I announced that I was the emissary of a Great Power to the Court of the Emir. . . .

We rode on, prisoner-guests of this fierce, rough, but fairly courteous Arab, in a hollow-square of riflemen whose equipment, bearing and discipline I could not but admire. . . .

And what if this Emir had an army of such—and chose to preach a *jehad,* a Holy War for the establishment of a Pan-Islamic Empire and the overthrow of the power of the Infidel in Africa?

CHAPTER XII

THE EMIR AND THE VIZIER

"And all around, God's mantle of illimitable space . . ."
A. FARQUHAR

IN a few hours we reached the Great Oasis, an astounding forest of palm-trees, roughly square in shape, with a ten-mile side.

My first glimpse of the Bedouin inhabitants of this area showed me that here was a people as different in spirit from those of Zaguig as it was possible to be.

There was nothing here of the furtively evil, lowering suspicious fanaticism that makes "holy" places so utterly damnable.

Practically no notice was taken of our passage through the tent-villages and the more permanent little *qsars* of sand-brick and baked mud. The clean orderliness, prevalent everywhere, made me rub my eyes and stare again.

At the "capital" we were, after a long and anxious waiting, handed over to a person of some importance, a *hadji* by his green turban, and, after a brief explanation of us by our captor—addressed as Marbruk ben Hassan by the *hadji*—we were conducted to the Guest-tents.

To my enormous relief, the girls were to be beneath the same roof as myself, and to occupy the *anderun* or *hareem* part of a great tent, which was divided from the rest by a heavy partition of felt. Presumably it was supposed that they were my wives.

This Guest-tent stood apart from the big village and near to a group of the largest and finest tents I ever saw in use by Arabs. They were not of the low black Bedouin type, spreading and squat, but rather of the pavilion type, such as the great Kaids of Morocco, or the Sultan himself, uses.

Not very far away was a neat row of the usual kind of low goatskin tent, which was evidently the "lines" of the soldiers of the bodyguard.

Flags, flying from spears stuck in the ground, showed

that the pavilions were those of the Emir—and a Soudanese soldier who came on sentry-go near the Guest-tent, that we were his prisoners.

The *hadji* (a man whom I was to know later as the Hadji Abdul Salam, a *marabout* or *mullah* and a *hakim* or doctor), returned from announcing our arrival to the Emir.

"Our Lord the Emir el Hamel el Kebir offers you the three days' hospitality, due by Koranic Law—and by the generosity of his heart—to all travellers. He will see you when you have rested. All that he has is yours," said he.

"Including the edge of his sword," I said to myself.

But this was really excellent. I thought of poor Rohlfs and contrasted my reception at the Great Oasis with his at Kufara, near where he was foully betrayed and evilly treated.

Not long afterwards, two black slave-women bore pots of steaming water to the *anderun*, and a boy brought me my share, less picturesquely, in kerosene-oil tins.

"Can I come in, Major?" called Miss Vanbrugh. "I've knocked at the felt door. . . . More felt than heard. . . . I want to dress your arm."

I told her that I was feeling happier about her than I had done since we started, for I was beginning to hope and to believe that we were in the hands of an enlightened and merciful despot, instead of those of the truculent and destructive savage I had expected to find.

"How do you like this hotel?" I inquired as she pinned the bandage.

"Nothing like it in N'York," she replied. "Maudie's sitting on cushions and feeling she's half a Sheikhess already. . . ."

"I'm going to put on my uniform," I announced. "Will you and she help a one-armed cripple?"

They did. And when the Hadji Abdul Salam, and a dear old gentleman named Dawad Fetata, came with one or two more *ekhwan* to conduct me to the presence of the Emir, I was a French Field-Officer again, bathed, shaven, and not looking wholly unworthy of the part I had to play.

Seated on dyed camel-hair rugs piled on a carpet, were the Emir el Hamel el Kebir and his Vizier, the Sheikh el Habibka, stately men in fine raiment.

I saw at a glance that the Emir, whatever he might claim to be, was no member of the family of Es Sayed Yussuf Haroun es Sayed es Mahdi es Senussi, and that if he pretended to be the expected "Messiah", Sidi Sayed el Mahdi el Senussi, he was an imposter.

For he was most unmistakably of Touareg stock, and from nowhere else could he have got the grey eyes of Vandal origin, which are fairly common among the Touareg, many of whom are blue-eyed and ruddy-haired.

I liked his face immediately. This black-bearded, black-browed, hawk-faced Arab was a man of character, force and power. But I wished I could see the mouth hidden beneath the mass of moustache and beard. Dignified, calm, courteous, strong, this was no ruffianly and swash-buckling fanatic.

My hopes rose high.

The Vizier, whose favour might be most important, I took to be of Touareg or Berber-Bedouin stock, he too being somewhat fair for a desert Arab. He was obviously a distaff blood-relation of the Emir.

These two men removed the mouthpieces of their long-stemmed *narghilehs* from their lips and stared *and* stared *and* stared at me, in petrified astonishment—to which they were too stoical or too well-bred to give other expression.

I suppose the last person they expected to see was a French officer in uniform, and they sat in stupefied silence.

Had not the idea been too absurd, I could almost have thought that I saw a look of fear in their eyes. Perhaps they thought for a moment that I was the herald of a French army that was even then getting into position round the oasis!

Fear is the father of cruelty, so I hoped that my fleeting impression was false one. I would have disabused their minds by plunging straight *in medias res*, and announcing my business forthwith, but that this is not the way to handle Arabs.

Only by devious paths can the goal be reached, and much meaningless *faddhling* (gossip) must precede the real matter on which the mind is fixed.

I greeted the Emir with the correct honorifics and in the Arabic of the educated.

He replied in an accent with which I was not familiar, that of the classical Arabic of the *Hejaz*, I supposed, called "the Tongue of the Angels" by the Arabs.

Having exchanged compliments and inquired after each other's health, with repeated "*Keif halaks?*" and "*Taiyibs*", I told the Emir of the attack upon us by the Touareg at the Salt Lake, and of my fears as to the fate of my followers.

"The Sons of Shaitan and the Forgotten of God! May they burn in Eblis eternally! Do they dare come within seven days of *me*!" growled the Emir, and clapped his hands.

A black youth came running.

"Send me Marbruk ben Hassan, the Commander of a Hundred," said the Emir, and when the deformed but powerful cripple came, and humbly saluted his Lord, the latter gave a prompt order.

"A hundred men. Ten days' rations. Ride to the Pass of the Salt Lake. A band of the Forgotten of God were there three days ago. Start within the hour . . ." He then whispered with him apart for a moment, and the man was gone.

The Vizier had not ceased to stare unwaveringly at me, but he uttered no word.

The Emir and I maintained a desultory and pointless conversation which concluded with an invitation to feast with him that night.

"I hear that you are accompanied by two Nazrani ladies. I am informed that wives of *Roumis* eat with their Lords and in the presence of other men. I shall be honoured if the Sitts—your wives doubtless?—will grace my poor tent. . . ."

One thing I liked about the Emir was the gentlemanly way in which he had forborne to question me on the subject of the astounding presence of two white women. I accordingly told him the plain truth at once, thinking it wisest and safest.

"You will receive no such treatment here as they of Zaguig meted unto you," said the Emir, when I had finished my story. "They who come in peace may remain in peace. They who come in war remain in peace also —the peace of Death." His voice was steely if not menacing. "Do you come in peace or in war, *Roumi*?" he then asked, and as I replied,

"On my head and my life, I come in peace, bearing a great and peaceful message," I fancied that both he and the Vizier looked relieved—and I again wondered if they imagined the presence or approach of a French army.

§ 3

Whatever I may forget, I shall remember that night's *diffa* of *cous-cous*; a lamb stuffed with almonds and raisins, and roasted whole; *bamia*, a favourite vegetable of the Arabs; stewed chicken; a *pillau* of rice, nuts, raisins and chopped meat; *kaibabs* of kid; camel-milk curds; a paste-like macaroni cooked in butter, and heavy shortbread fried in oil and eaten with sugar. Between the courses, we drank bowls of lemon-juice to aid our appetites, and they needed aid as the hours wore on.

When we were full to bursting, distended, comatose, came the ceremonial drinking of mint tea. After that, coffee. Finally we were offered very large cakes of very hard plain sugar.

Only five were present, the Emir, the Vizier, Mary, Maudie, and myself. We sat cross-legged on a carpet round a red cotton cloth upon which was a vast brass tray, laden with blue bowls filled to overflowing, and we ate with our fingers.

As I entered with Miss Vanbrugh and Maudie, and they dropped their *barracans*, thus exposing the two Paris frocks which the latter had put in the portmanteau at Zaguig, the effect upon the two Arabs was electrical. They were as men dreaming dreams and seeing visions.

I thought the Emir was going to collapse as he looked at Mary; and I watched the Vizier devouring her with hungry eyes. I grew a little nervous.

"The Lady Sitt Miryam Hankinson el Vanbrugh,"

said I, to make an imposing and sonorous mouthful of title, "and the Sitt Moad el Atkinson."

I suppose they were the first white women the Arabs had seen, and they were struck dumb and senseless by their beauty.

Nor was the effect of their hosts much less upon the girls. Miss Vanbrugh stared, fascinated, at the gorgeous figure of the Emir, while poor Maudie did not know whether she was on her head or her heels.

"*Sheikhs!*" she murmured. "*Real* Sheikhs! Oh, sir, *isn't* the big one a lovely man! . . ." The Emir, dragging his eyes from Mary, smiled graciously at the other fair woman, and murmured:

"*Bismillah! Sitt Moad. Oua Aleikoume Esselema, 'lham-doula!*" and to me in his classic Arabic, "sweet as the dates of Buseima is her presence," which I duly translated.

And then Mary found her voice.

"Well! Well! Major," she observed. "Aren't they sure-enough genuine Parlour Sheikhs of song and story!" and before I could stop her, she offered her hand to the Emir, her eyes dancing with delight.

Probably neither the Emir nor the Vizier had ever "shaken hands" before, but Mary's smile, gesture and "*Very* pleased to meet you, Sheikh," were self-explanatory, and both the Arabs made a good showing at this new ceremonial of the strange *Roumis* and their somewhat brazen, unveiled females.

Indeed the Vizier seemed to know more about holding Mary's hand than releasing it, and again I grew nervous.

When the Emir said to me, "Let the other Lady, the Sitt Moadi, lay her hand upon my hands also," and I translated, I thought Maudie would have swooned with pleasure and confusion. Not only did the Emir "shake hands"—he stroked hands, and I grew less and less happy.

An amorous Arab is something very amorous indeed. With these desert despots, to desire is to take, and if I were an obstacle it would be very easy to remove me. And what of the girls *then*? . . . As the meal progressed and the sense of strangeness and shyness wore off, I was glad that the Sheikh and his Vizier could not possibly know a word of English, for Miss Vanbrugh's criticisms were pungent and Maudie's admiration fulsome.

E   119

I was kept busy translating the Emir's remarks to the girls, and mistranslating the girls' remarks concerning the appearance, manner, and probable customs of their hosts.

At times I was in a cold perspiration of fear, as I thought of how utterly these two women were in the power of these men, and again at times, watching their faces, I saw no evil in them. Hard they were, perhaps relentless and ruthless, but not cruel, sensual nor debauched.

"Major," Miss Vanbrugh remarked, "d'you think these Parlour Sheikhs would like to hear a little song? . . . Tell them it's grace after meat," and before I could offer my views on the propriety of thus entertaining our hosts, or translating her remark, I once more heard the familiar air, but this time to the words:

> " *The Sons of the Prophet are hardy and bold,*
> *And quite unaccustomed to fear ;*
> *But of all—the most reckless of life and of limb,*
> *Was Abdul the Bul-bul Emir . . .!*
> *When they wanted a man to encourage the van,*
> *Or to shout* '*Attaboy!*' *in the rear,*
> *Or to storm a redoubt,*
> *They always sent out*
> *For Abdul the Bul-bul Emir!*

The Arabs stared, almost open-mouthed, and I explained that after-dinner singing was a custom with the *Roumis* and that the song, out of compliment to our hosts, described the greatness, wisdom, virtue, and courage of another famous Emir.

When we were at last permitted to cease from eating, and white-clad servants removed the remains of the *diffa*, the Emir bade me request Mary Vanbrugh to talk of her country and her home, that I might translate her words to him.

He then asked many questions through me.

Thereafter he directed that Maudie should talk.

But having almost realized the ambition of her life, Maudie was shy and could only stammer incoherently while gazing bright-eyed, flushed, with parted lips and quickened breathing, at the huge, handsome, and gorgeously arrayed Emir.

The Vizier, the Sheikh el Habibka, scarcely uttered a word the whole evening, but he hardly took his eyes from Miss Vanbrugh's face.

In the bad moments to which I have alluded, I felt that if the worst came to the worst, Maudie would be imprisoned in the Emir's *hareem*, and Mary in that of this Sheikh el Habibka—unless the Emir took them both. . . .

The sooner I could dangle before their eyes the million francs and the enormous advantages of an *entente* and an alliance with France, the better it would be; and the less they saw of the girls the better it would be also. . . .

"Well, Major, it's time you went to bed," said Mary. "Remember you're a sick man!"

"We can't move till the Emir gives the hint," I replied.

"Well, I wish he'd do it, the great old coot. Tell him what I'm saying, Major—that he fancies he's some punkins, but he's not the perfect little gentleman he thinks he is, or he'd see I'm tired to death," and she yawned heavily. . . .

Luckily the Emir shortly afterwards suggested that we might be weary, and though I told him that no one could be weary in his presence, he hinted that *he* was so in mine.

The leave-taking made it clear that Maudie's hand delighted the Emir, while that of Mary was precious in the sight of the Sheikh el Habibka. There was a look of determination in that man's eye. . . .

As we entered the Guest-tent I said to Miss Vanbrugh, "Scream if there's any trouble in the night."

"Scream? I shall *shoot*. Let the 'trouble' do the screaming. Good night, Major," was this independent and courageous young lady's reply.

§ 4

The next day I had an interview with the Emir, in the presence, as always, of the Vizier, and, after infinite meanderings around all subjects but the real one, we came to it at last.

I made it clear that what I offered him was the friendship of a most powerful protector, great wealth, and all the advantages that would ensue if a caravan-road were made and guarded from the Great Oasis to Zaguig, and trade-relations opened up between his people and the North.

I glanced at the possibility of our supplying him with arms, including machine-guns and, possibly, light artillery —later on.

I grew eloquent in showing him how the friendship of France could raise him to a safe independence, and how, in the role of protégé of France, he could benefit his people and give them the blessings of civilization.

The Emir repeated my phrase, but with a peculiar intonation.

"The blessings of civilization!" he mused. "Drink. . . . Disease. . . . Unrest. . . . Machine-guns. . . . Has the civilization of the *Roumis* always proved such a blessing to the darker races who have come in contact with it?"

The two stroked their beards, and eyed me long and thoughtfully. I assured the Emir that it would be in his power to pick and choose. Isolated as his people were, there need be no "contact". All France wanted was his friendship.

Provided he were loyal and kept the terms of the treaty exactly, he could use the subsidy as he pleased, and could discriminate between the curses and the real blessings of western civilization.

Surely he could see to it that only good ensued? Nothing was further from the thoughts of the French Government than interference—much less conquest, or even "peaceful penetration". All we asked was that the Confederation which he ruled should be a source of strength and not of weakness to us—that the Great Oasis should be an outpost of France in the hands of the Emir el Hamel el Kebir. . . . And I hinted at his own danger from others who would not come to him thus, with offers of gold and protection, but with armies. . . .

"We will talk of these matters again," said the Emir at length. "*Khallas!* It is finished. . . ."

That evening, a riding-party was arranged, and, mounted on beautiful horses, the Sheikh el Habibka and Miss Vanbrugh rode together; the Emir, on a white camel, rode with Maudie—who, very wisely, would not get on a horse; and I rode with a party of fine courteous

Arabs who were minor sheikhs, officers of the soldiery, councillors, friends and hangers-on of the Emir and the Vizier.

We rode through the oasis out into the desert.

I did not enjoy my ride, for before very long, I lost sight of the two girls, and could only hope for the best while fearing the worst. . . . Women are so attracted by externals and so easily deceived by a courteous and gallant manner.

One comfort was that neither girl could speak a word of Arabic, so there was nothing to fear from plausible tongues.

Any love-making would have to be done in dumb-show and I was beginning to feel that there was no likelihood of *force majeure*—both men giving me the impression of innate gentlemanliness and decency.

Still—Arabs are Arabs and this was the Sahara—and, as I noted that the Emir returned with Miss Vanbrugh and the Vizier with Maud, I wanted nothing so much as to get safely away with my women-folk and a signed treaty of alliance.

But this was just what I could not do.

Time after time, I sought audience with the Emir, only to find that he was engaged or sleeping or busy or absent from the Oasis.

Time after time, when his guest at meat, riding, or *faddhling* with him on the rug-strewn carpet before the pavilions, I tried to get him to discuss the object of my visit—but in vain.

Always it was, "We will talk of it tomorrow, *Inshallah*."

His eternal "*Bokra! Bokra!*" was as bad as the *mañana* of the Spaniards. And "tomorrow" never came. . . .

The return of Marbruk ben Hassen and his camel-squadron brought me news that depressed me to the depths and darkened my life for days. I was given understanding of the expression "a broken heart".

Evidently my heroes had fought to their last cartridge and had then been overwhelmed. Beneath a great cairn of stones, Marbruk and his men had buried the tortured, defiled, mangled remains of Dufour, Achmet and Djikki.

It was plain to me that Suleiman had deserted, for the parts of only three corpses were found, and the track of a single camel fleeing south-eastward from the spot.

That he had not fought to the last, and then escaped or been captured alive by the Touareg, was shown by the fact that, where he had lain, there were but few empty cartridge-cases, compared with the number lying where my men had died; and by the fact of the track of the fleeing camel.

I retired to my tent, saying I wished to see no one for a day, and that I wanted no food.

It was a black and dreadful day for me, the man for whom those humble heroes had fought and died; and, for hours, I was hard put to it to contain myself.

I did see someone however—for Miss Vanbrugh entered silently, dressed my rapidly healing wound, and then stroked my hair and brow and cheek so kindly, so gently, and with such deep understanding sympathy that I broke down.

I could almost have taken her in my arms, but that I would not trade on my misery and her sympathy—and without a word spoken between us she went back to the *anderun* . . . the blessed, beautiful, glorious woman.

Did she understand at last . . .? Duty. . . . My duty to my General, my Service, and my Country.

That evening she was visited by the future Sheikh of the tribe that had first accepted the Emir, a charming and delightful little boy, dressed exactly like a grown man.

With him came his sister, a most lovely girl, the Sitt Leila Nakhla.

Her, the two girls found haughty, distant, disapproving. and I gathered that the visit was not a success—apart from the question of the language difficulty.

Bedouin women do not go veiled in their own villages and camps, and I saw this Arab "princess" at a feast given by her guardian, the white-bearded, delightful old gentleman, Sidi Dawad Fetata.

It was soon very clear to me that the Sitt Leila Nakhla worshipped the Emir; that the grandson of old Sidi

Dawad Fetata worshipped the Sitt Leila Nakhla; and that the latter detested our Maudie, from whose face the Emir's eye roved but seldom.

The little London sparrow was the hated rival of a princess, for the hand of a powerful ruler! Oh, Songs of Araby and Tales of fair Kashmir! What a world it is!

But what troubled me more than hate was love—the love that I could see dawning in the eyes of the Sheikh el Habibka as he sat beside Miss Vanbrugh and plied her with tit-bits from the bowls.

I watched him like a lynx, and he me. How he *hated* me . . . !

Time after time I saw him open his lips to speak, sigh heavily, and say nothing. But if he said nothing he did a good deal—including frequent repetitions of the *Roumi* "shake-hands" custom, which he misinterpreted as a hold-hands habit.

He had learnt the words, and would say, "*Shakhand, Mees*," from time to time, in what he thought was English.

And Mary? She was infinitely amused. Amused beyond all cause that I could see; and I was really angry when she glanced from me to the Sheikh el Habibka—he holding her hand warmly clasped in both of his—and quietly hummed, in a conversational sort of voice:

> "*Said the Bul-bul, 'Young man, is your life then so dull*
> *That you're anxious to end your career?*
> *For Infidel, know—that you've trod on the toe*
> *Of Abdul, the Bul-bul Emir!'*
> *The Bul-bul then drew out his trusty chibouque,*
> *And shouting out 'Allah Akbar!'*
> *Being also intent on slaughter he went*
> *For Ivan Petruski Skivah!*" . . .

This interested the Sitt Leila Nakhla not at all. She watched Maudie, while young Yussuf Latif Fetata watched Leila. To me this girl was most charming, but became a little troublesome in her demands that I should translate every remark that Maudie made. I believe the Sitt's position in the Tribe was unique, owing to her relationship to the future Sheikh, and the kind indulgence of the Emir, who treated her as a child.

The chief result of this feast was to increase my anxiety and to add to my determination to bring my business to an issue and depart.

CHAPTER XIII

"CHOOSE"

BUT now, alas! the attitude of the Emir, and of his all-important and powerful Vizier towards me began to change. They grew less friendly and my position less that of guest than prisoner-guest, if not prisoner.

The most foolish proverb of the most foolish nation in the world is, "When you get near women you get near trouble," but in this instance it seemed to apply.

Mary and Maudie were the trouble; for the Emir was undoubtedly falling in love with Maudie, and the Vizier with Mary.

I wondered what would have happened if they had both fallen in love with the same girl. I suppose one of them would have died suddenly, in spite of the fact that they appeared to be more like brothers than master and servant.

And there was no hope in me for Maudie. Maudie blossomed and Maudie bloomed. If ever I saw a wildly-quietly, composedly-distractedly, madly-sanely happy woman, it was our Maudie.

She grew almost lovely. How many of us have an incredibly impossible beautiful dream—and find it come impossibly true? Maudie had dreamed of attar-scented, silk-clad, compelling but courtly Sheikhs, ever since she had read some idiotic trash; and now an attar-scented, silk-clad, compelling but courtly Sheikh *was* (in Maudie's words) "after" Maudie!

And Miss Vanbrugh? She, too, seemed happy as the day was long, albeit capricious; and though she did not apparently encourage the Sheikh el Habibka, nor "flirt" exactly, she undoubtedly enjoyed his society, as well as that of the Emir, and rode alone with either of them, without fear. They must have been silent rides—with a strange dumb alphabet! Nor would she listen to my words of warning.

"Don't you worry, Major de Beaujolais," she would say, "I tell you they are *all right*. Yes, *both* of them. I am just as safe with them as I am with you. . . . And I'm *awfully* safe with you, Major, am I not?"

Women always know better than men—until they find they know nothing about the matter at all.

The next thing that I did not like, was the giving of feasts to which the girls alone were invited; and then feasts at which Mary alone, or Maudie alone, was the guest.

However, such invitations were commands, of course; the feasts were held in the Emir's pavilion, which was but a few yards from our tent; I took care that the girls had their pistols, and I always sat ready for instant action if I should hear a scream when either of them was there alone.

Nor was there any great privacy observed, for servants were in and out with dishes, and unless there was a strong *gibli* blowing, the pavilion entrance was open.

But more and more I became a prisoner, and now when I took my daily ride it was with Marbruk ben Hassan and an escort—for my "protection".

One night, as I lay awake, the horrible thought occurred to me of using Miss Vanbrugh and Maudie to further my ends—and I was almost sick at the bare idea. Whence come these devilish thoughts into clean minds?

No. At that I drew the line. My life for France, but not a girl's honour. . . . I thrust the vile thought from me.

Soon afterwards I fell asleep and had a curious dream. . . .

I was in a vast hall, greater than any built by mortal hands. At the end to which I faced were vast black velvet curtains. As I stood gazing at these, expectant, they parted and rolled away, revealing a huge pair of golden scales, in each great cup of which was seated a most beautiful woman.

One, a noble and commanding figure, wore the Cap of Liberty and I knew her to be the Genius and Goddess and Embodiment of France. . . . The other, a beautiful and beseeching figure, I saw to be Mary Vanbrugh.

Each of these lovely creatures gave me a smile of ineffable sweetness and extended a welcoming hand. . . . A great voice cried "*Choose*", and, as I strode forward, the great curtains fell—and the dream became a nightmare in which a colossal brazen god stretched a vast hand from a brazen sky to destroy me where I stood in the midst of an illimitable arid desert. . . .

§ 2

Then to me, one night, came the Emir and the Vizier, clearly on business bent. There was no *faddhling*. As soon as I had offered them seats upon the rugs and produced my last Turkish cigarettes, the Emir got to business.

"Touching the treaty with your Excellency's great country," he began, and my heart leapt with hope. "I will sign it—on terms. . . . On terms further than those named hitherto."

He stopped and appeared to be enjoying the Turkish cigarette intensely.

"And they are, Commander of the Faithful and Shadow of the Prophet?" I inquired.

"That you take the treaty, signed and sealed by me, and witnessed by my Vizier and twelve ekhwan—*and leave the two Sitts whom you brought here.*"

So it had come! I was faced with the decision of a lifetime!

"*That is impossible*, Emir el Hamel el Kebir," I seemed to hear myself reply, after a minute of acute agony, which bathed me in perspiration from head to foot.

The Emir raised his big black eyebrows and gave me a supercilious, penetrating hawk-stare of surprise and anger.

"And why?" he inquired quietly.

"Because they put themselves under my protection," I replied, "and I have put myself and them under yours. . . ."

"And I am merely suggesting that they remain there," interrupted the Emir.

"For how long?" I sneered.

"That is for *them* to say," was the reply.

"Then let them say it," I answered. "Emir, I have treated you as a Bedouin Chief, a true Arab of the Desert, a man of chivalry, honour, hospitality, and greatness. Would you, in return, speak to me of trafficking in women . . ."?

To Hell with their treaty and their tribes—and then the face of my uncle, the words of his letters, and memories of my life-work rose before my eyes. . . . Neither of these girls was a Frenchwoman. . . . I had not asked them to come here. . . . I had warned them *against* coming. . . . I had told them plainly that I was going on a mission of national importance. . . . And de Lannec. . . . "*Exit de Lannec*"! . . .

I strode up and down the tent, the two Arabs, calm, imperturbable, stroking their beards and watching me. . . . I reasoned with myself, as a Frenchman should, *logically*.

Glorious logic—the foe of sloppiness, emotionalism, sentimentality.

I can but hope, looking back upon this crucial moment of my life, that such matters as my utter ruin and disgrace; my loss of all that made life good; my fall from a place of honour, dignity, and opportunity, to the very gutters of life; my renunciation of ambition, reward and success—weighed with me not at all, and were but as dust in the balance. . . .

I can but hope that, coolly and without bias, I answered the question as to whether the interests of France, the lives of thousands of men, the loss of incalculable treasure should, or should not, out-weigh the interests of two foreign women.

Should thousands of French soldiers suffer wounds and death—or should these two girls enter the *hareems* of Arab Sheikhs . . .?

Should I fulfil the trust reposed in me or betray it?

"*I want tools that will not turn in my hand. . . . Tools on which I can absolutely rely*," my uncle—my General, the representative of my Country—had said to me; and I had willingly offered myself as a tool that would *not* turn in his hand . . . that would *not* fail him. . . .

And if "it is expedient that one man shall die for the people," was it not expedient that two foreign women should be sacrificed to prevent a war, to save an Empire?

Two lives instead of two thousand, twenty thousand, two hundred thousand. . . .

If, as my uncle said, there would always be danger in Morocco to the French African Empire, and if, whenever that danger arose, this great Tribal Confederation became a source of even greater danger? . . .

"And for what was I *here*? For what had I been fashioned and made, taught and trained, hammered on the hard anvil of experience? . . . Why was I *in* my Service —*but to do the very thing that it now lay to my hand to do?*"

As an honest and honourable man, I must put the orders of my General, the honour and tradition of my Service, and, above all, the welfare of my Country, before everything—and *everybody*.

Logic showed me the truth—and, suddenly, I stopped in my stride, turned and shook my fist in the Emir's very face and shouted: "*Damn your black face and blacker soul, you filthy hound! Get out of my tent before I throw you out, you bestial swine! . . .* WHITE WOMEN! *You black dogs and sons of dogs! . . .*" and, shaking with rage, I pointed to the doorway of my tent.

They rose and went—and, with them, went all my hopes of success. What had I done? What *had* I done? . . . But Mary—sweet, lovely, brave, fascinating Mary . . . *and that black-bearded dog!*

Let France sink beneath the sea first. . . .

But what *had* I done? . . . What had I *done?* . . . What is "Right" and what is "Wrong"? What voice had I obeyed?

Anyhow, I was unfit, utterly unfit, for my great Service —and I would break my sword and burn my uniform, go back to my uncle, confess what I had done and enlist in the Foreign Legion. . . .

Oh, *splendid de Lannec! . . . He was right, of course. . . .*

But this was ruin and the end of Henri de Beaujolais.

Then a voice through the felt wall that cut off my part of the tent from the *anderun* said,

"Your language certainly sounded bad, Major! I am glad I don't understand Arabic!"

I was not very sure that *I* was glad she did not.

And as little as she understood Arabic did I understand whether I had done right or wrong.

But one thing I understood. I was a Failure. . . . I had failed my General, my Service, and my Country—but yet I somehow felt had not failed my higher Self. . . .

§ 3

It was the next morning that Miss Vanbrugh greeted me with the words:

"Major, you haven't congratulated me yet. I had an honest-to-God offer of marriage from a leading citizen of this burg yesterday. . . . I'm blushing still. . . . Inwardly. . . ."

I was horrified. . . . What next?

"From whom?" I asked.

"The Sheikh el Habibka el Wazir."

"Good God!" I groaned. "Miss Vanbrugh, we shall have to walk very very delicately. . . ."

"So'll the Sheikh-lad," observed Mary grimly.

"But how did he make the proposal?" I inquired, knowing that no one in the place could translate and interpret except myself.

"By signs and wonders," answered the girl. "*Some* wonders! He certainly made himself clear! . . ."

"Was he? . . . Did he? . . ." I stammered, hardly knowing how to ask if the ruffian had seized her in his hot, amorous embrace and made fierce love to her. . . . My blood boiled, though my heart sank, and I knew that depth of trembling apprehension that is the true Fear—the fear for another whom we—whom we—esteem.

"Now don't you go prying heavy-hoofed into a young thing's first love affair, Major—because I shan't stand for it," replied Miss Vanbrugh.

"Had you your pistol with you?" I asked.

"I had, Major," was the reply. "I don't get caught that way twice."

And I reflected that if the Sheikh el Rabibka el Wazir was still alive, he had not been violent.

That day I was not allowed to ride out for exercise, and a big Soudanese sentry was posted closer to my tent door.

Hitherto I had felt myself under strict surveillance; now I was under actual arrest.

The girls were invited, or ordered, to go riding as usual, and my frame of mind can be imagined.

Nothing could save them. . . . Nothing could now bring about the success of my mission—unless it were the fierce greed of these Arabs for gold. . . . I was a wretchedly impotent puppet in their hands. . . .

Now that I had mortally insulted and antagonized these fierce despots, what could I do to protect the woman . . . the women . . . whom I had brought here, and whose sole hope and trust was in me . . . ?

I realized that a mighty change had been slowly taking place in my mind, and that it had been completed in the moment that the Emir had offered to sell me the treaty for the bodies of these girls. . . . I knew now that—instead of the fate of Mary Vanbrugh being an extra anxiety at the back of a mind filled with care concerning the treaty—the fate of the treaty was an extra anxiety at the back of a mind filled with care concerning the fate of Mary Vanbrugh!

Why should this be?

I had begun by disliking her. . . . At times I had hated her . . . and certainly there were times she appeared to loathe me utterly. . . . Why should life, success, duty, France herself, all weigh as nothing in the balance against her safety? . . .

De Lannec? Fool, trifler, infirm of purpose, devoid of sense of proportion, broken reed and betrayer of his Service and his Motherland—*or unselfish hero and gallant gentleman*?

And what mattered the answer to that question, if I was an impotent, prisoner absolutely helpless in the power of this outraged Emir—and she was riding with him, alone. . . .

CHAPTER XIV

A SECOND STRING

THAT night I was honoured by a visit from the Hadji Abdul Salam, the chief *marabout* and *hakim* of this particular tribe, and a man whose immense influence and power seemed disproportionate to his virtues and merits. (One of the things the Occidental mind can never grasp, is the way in which the Oriental mind can divorce Faith from Works, the office from its holder, and yield unstinted veneration to the holy *priest*, knowing him to be, at the same time, a worthless and scoundrelly *man*.)

The good Hadji crept silently into my tent, in the dead of night, and very nearly got a bullet through his scheming brain.

Seeing that he was alone and apparently unarmed, I put my pistol under my pillow again, and asked him what he wanted.

The Reverend Father-in-Islam wanted to talk—in whispers—if I would take a most solemn oath to reveal nothing that he said. I was more than ready, and we talked of Cabbages and Kings, and also of Sealing-Wax and Whether Pigs have Wings. . . . And, after a while, we talked of Murder—or rather the Holy One did so. . . . He either trusted my keeping faith with him or knew he could repudiate anything I might say against him later.

I had a touch of fever again, and I was still in the state of mental turmoil natural to one who has just seen the edifice of a life's labour go crashing to the earth, and yet sits rejoicing among the ruins—thanking God for failure; his mind moaning a funeral dirge over the grave of all his hopes and strivings—his heart chanting a paean of praise and thanksgiving over the saving of his Self. . . .

> "*Come, let us sit upon the ground*
> *And tell sad stories of the death of Kings,*
> *How some have been deposed, some sleeping killed,*"

I quoted, from Etonian memories of Shakespeare's *Richard the Second*.

The Reverend Father looked surprised, and said he had a proposal to make.

This was that he should contrive to effect my escape, and that I should return with an army, defeat the Emir, and make the Hadji Abdul Salam ruler in his place.

An alternative idea was suggested by the probable assassination of the Emir by one Suleiman the Strong, "of whom I knew," and who was even now somewhere in the Great Oasis, *and had visited the tents of the Holy Hadji!*

Would I, on the death of the Emir, help the Hadji to seize the Seat of Power? He could easily poison Suleiman the Strong when he had fulfilled his vengeance—and his usefulness—or denounce him to the Tribe as the murderer of the Emir, and have him impaled alive. . . .

The pious man swore he would be a true and faithful friend to France.

"As you are to your master, the Emir?" I asked.

The Hadji replied that the Emir was a usurper, and that no one owed fealty to a usurper.

Moreover this was positively my only chance, as I was to be put to death shortly. . . . The Emir might then send a deputation to the Governor-General of French Africa, offering to make an alliance on receipt of a subsidy of a million francs and other advantages, and swearing that no emissary of the Governor-General's had ever reached him.

Or he might just let the matter rest—merely keeping the women, killing me, and washing his hands of French affairs, or, rather, declining to dirty his hands with them. . . . Or, of course, Suleiman might get him—and then the Wazir could be eliminated, and the good Hadji, with French support, could become the Emir and the Friend of France. . . .

"Supposing you could enable me to escape," I said when the good Hadji had finished. "I should not do so without the women. Could you effect their escape with me?"

He could not and would not. Here the Holy One spat and quoted the unkind words of the great Arab poet, Imr el Kais:

> "One said to me, '*Marry!*'
> I replied, 'I am *happy*—
> Why take to my breast
> A sackful of serpents?
> May Allah curse all woman-kind!'"

Two faithful slave-women always slept across the entrance to the *anderun*, where the girls were. Even if the slaves could be killed silently, it would be impossible to get so big a party away from the place—many camels, much food, *girbas* of water. . . . No, he could only manage it for me alone.

He could visit me at night and I could leave the tent in his *burnous* and green turban. . . . He could easily bribe or terrify a certain Arab soldier, now on sentry-go outside, and who was bound to be on duty at my tent again sooner or later. I could simply ride for dear life, with two good camels, and take my chance.

But the women—*no*. Besides, if it ever came out that he had helped *me* to escape, it would not be so bad. . . . But as for getting the women away, he simply would not consider it. . . .

No—if I were so extremely anxious about the fate of my two women ("and, Merciful Allah! what are women, that serious men should bother about them?"), the best thing I could do was to consider his firm and generous offer —the heads of the Emir and his Vizier on a charger, and the faithful friendship to France of their successor in power, the Hadji Abdul Salam. . . . The Emir had announced his intention of making the boy-Sheikh not only Sheikh of his Tribe, but eventually Emir of the Confederation also. The Hadji would be the young prince's Spiritual Guide, Tutor, Guardian and Regent—until the time came to cut the lad's throat. . . .

"So Suleiman the Strong is here—and is going to assassinate the Emir, is he?" I said, after we had sat eyeing each other, warily and in silence, for some minutes.

(*I must warn the Emir as soon as possible.*)

"Yes," replied the Hadji. "And where will you be *then*, if I am your enemy?"

"Where I am now, I expect," I replied, yawning with a nonchalance wholly affected.

"*And* your women?" asked the good man.

I ground my teeth, and my fingers itched to seize this scoundrel's throat.

"Take my advice and *go*," he continued. "Go in the certainty that you will have done what you came for—made an indissoluble and everlasting treaty of alliance between the *Franzawi* and the Great Confederation, through their real ruler, the Hadji Abdul Salam, Regent for the young Emir after the assassination of the Emir el Hamel el Kebir, imposter and usurper. . . . And if he is not assassinated, no matter—come with an army—and a million francs, of course—kill him, and make the boy nominal Emir. . . . I swear by the Sacred names of God that France shall be as my father and my mother, and I will be France's most obedient child. . . . *Go*, Sidi, while you can. . . ."

"Get two facts clearly and firmly into your noble mind, Holy One," I replied. "The first is that I do not leave this place without the lady Sitts; and the second is that France has no dealings whatsoever in assassination —nor with assassins!"

Then the reverend gentleman played his trump card.

"You are in even greater danger than you think, Sidi," he murmured, smiling wryly with his mouth and scowling fiercely with his eyes. "And our honourable, gracious and fair-dealing Lord, the Emir el Hamil el Kebir, is but playing with you as the cat with the mouse. . . . *For you are not only the mouse in his trap*—oh, no! Not by any means. . . . What are *Roumi* brains against those of the Arabs, the most wise, learned, subtle and ancient of all the races on the earth? . . . Why, you poor fool, *there are other messengers from another Power, here, in the Great Oasis*—and our fair-spoken Lord gives them audience daily in their camp. . . ."

I sprang to my feet. . . . Could this scoundrel be speaking the truth. . . . A cold fear settled on my heart. . . . What likelihood was there of my leaving this place alive, if this were true and my own folly and madness had driven the Emir into the arms of these agents of some other Power?

My life was nothing—but what of the fate of Mary Vanbrugh, when my throat was cut? . . . I broke out into a cold perspiration, and the fever left me. . . . My brain grew clearer and began to act more quickly. I smiled derisively and shook an incredulous head.

"And supposing I showed you their camp, Sidi?" sneered the Hadji. "Suppose I gave you the opportunity to *see* a disguised *Roumi* and *to speak to him*?"

"Why—then I should be convinced," I replied, and added—"And that would certainly change my—er—attitude towards you and your proposal. . . . When I have seen these men, and spoken with them—you may visit me again, with advantage to your purse. . . ." I must play this foul-feeding fish on a long line, and match his tricks with tricks of my own. If it was to be *Roumi* brains against Arab brains here also—well, we would see what we should see. . . .

"What manner of man is the leader of these emissaries of another Power?" I asked. "How many of them are there . . .? What is the Emir's attitude . . .? Tell me all you can. . . . I can buy true information at a high price. . . ."

"So can these others," grinned the pious Hadji. "The leader has already shaken a bag of good fat Turkish *medjidies* before my eyes, and promised it in return for my help."

"I could shake a bag of something better than that dirty depreciated Turkish rubbish before your eyes, Hadji," I replied, "and pour it into your lap too. . . . Fine new coins of pure gold! French twenty-franc pieces! Beautiful for women's chains and bangles, and even more beautiful to spend on fine raiment, tents, camels, weapons, food, servants, rugs, horses . . ."

The rascal's eyes glittered.

"How many, Sidi?" he asked.

"As many as you earn. . . . As many as your help is worth. . . . Now talk. . . ."

"It is a small caravan, Sidi," began this saintly *marabout*, "but very well equipped. There is plenty of money behind it. . . . I never saw better camels nor weapons, and their hired camel-men are well-paid and content. . . . I do not know from whom they really come, but they have the blessing of the Father of the Faithful, God's Vicar upon Earth, who rules at Stamboul, and of the Great

Sheikh of the Senussi. They say this openly in *mejliss*—and prove it with documents, passes, *firmans* and letters—but they talk privately, at night, with the Emir and the Wazir. . . ."

"What do they offer, openly?" I asked.

"The friendship and protection of the King of Kings, the Sultan of the Ottoman Empire, Father of the Faithful, who dwells at Stamboul; and the friendship and alliance of the powerful Sheikh el Senussi. . . . A great Pan-Islamic Alliance is being formed, in readiness for a certain Day of *Jehad*. . . ."

"And in private?" I asked.

"That I do not know," was the reply. "Only that dog of a Wazir—may swine defile the graves of his ancestors —knoweth the mind of the Emir; and he alone accompanies him to the tents of the *Roumi*."

"But this I *do* know," he continued, "*they will give me wealth untold if I poison you and the two Sitts*, whom they declare to be female spies of the French—sent to debauch and beguile the Emir with their charms. . . ."

"How do they know of our presence here?" I asked quietly, though my blood boiled.

"Oh, I visit them! . . . I visit them! . . . And we talk. . . . We talk. . . ." replied this treacherous reptile. "They say I might, if I preferred, kill you and seize the Sitts for my *hareem* for a while, before I either slay them or cut out their tongues. . . . Dumb women are the only discreet ones . . ." and the Hadji laughed merrily.

I managed to smile coldly, while I burned hotly with fierce rage, and changed the subject.

"Are they Great Men, Lords, Sidis, Nobles, Officers, Born Leaders, these emissaries?" I asked.

"No," replied the Hadji. "They are low men on high horses. They do not walk, speak, look, give, ride, eat nor act as men of noble birth. . . ."

Through a narrow aperture at the entrance to my tent I could see that the stars were paling.

"You shall take me to their camp—now—Hadji," I said, and pulled on *burnous*, *haik*, *kafiyeh*, and *fil-fil* boots.

The Hadji seemed a little startled.

"It would not look well for me to be seen visiting their camp now," he said. "It will soon be light. . . ."

"You need not visit their camp," I replied. "Take me to where I can see it, and then disappear."

The good man sat a while in thought.

"How much, Sidi?" he asked.

"I am not like those others," I replied. "I do not shake bags of money in the faces of pious and honest men, nor haggle and bargain. I richly reward those who serve me well—very richly—when their service is completed. . . . Now do as I say, or go away, and let me sleep in peace, for this chatter wearies me . . ." and I yawned.

The Hadji went to the doorway and collogued with the soldier without.

Returning, he said that he had dispatched my sentry to inform the guard at the camp of the emissaries that a man would shortly visit the latter, and must not be challenged, as he came from the Emir on secret business. The countersign was "Stamboul".

"This fellow, one Gharibeel Zarrug, is entirely faithful to me, Sidi," he added. "You can always send me messages by his mouth. I can arrange that he is very frequently on guard over your tent."

We sat in silence for a few minutes, a silence broken by the Hadji's request for a taste of the *sharab* of the Infidels. I gave the good man a nip of cognac and I believe this bound him to my interests (until they clashed with his) more strongly than gold would have done. He had all the stigmata of the secret drunkard, and his tongue continually flickered at his lips like that of a snake.

The soldier returned and whispered.

"Come, Sidi," said the Hadji, "I will take you as far as is safe."

"Safe for me or for you?" I asked.

"Nowhere is safe for *you*, Sidi," was the reply. "Take my advice and flee for your life—to return with an army, and a treaty which I will sign as Regent. . . ."

I did my best by careful noting of direction, the stars, clumps of trees, tents, water-runnels and stones, to ensure my being able to make the return journey. . . .

After we had walked for about a mile, the Hadji stopped in the black shadow of some palms and pointed to an orderly cluster of tents, just visible from where we stood.

"That is their camp, Sidi," said the Hadji, "and beyond

those palms are their camel-lines and servants' quarters and the bivouac of a Camel Corps section—provided for the—ah—protection of the party . . ." and without another word the Reverend Father vanished.

§ 2

I walked boldly across to the principal tent, ignored the distant sentry, and entered.

Two men slept on rugs, one an obvious Oriental, the other slightly fairer of complexion and with heavy moustache and huge beard.

I studied his face by the light of the lantern that hung from the tent-pole, and learned nothing from it—but I suspected a disguised European. The man's hands were larger than those of an Arab and there was more colour, in what I could see of his cheeks, than I should expect in those of a native.

Turning to the lamp, I unhooked it and held it to his face, so that the light fell upon it while mine was in the shadow thrown by the back of the lamp—a common bazaar affair of European make, such as hangs on the walls of the cheap hotels of Algeria and Tunis. I then drew a bow at a venture.

I struck the sleeper heavily on the chest, and, as he opened his eyes and sat up, said coolly:

"*Bon jour, mon cher Monsieur Becque!*"

My shaft winged true.

"*Himmel!*" he exclaimed, half awake and startled into unguarded speech. And then, collecting his scattered wits, said in French—"*What is it? Who are you?*" and his hand went under his pillow.

"Keep still!" I said sternly, and my revolver came from under my *burnous*, and he looked into the muzzle of it.

And, as he looked, the cast in his left eye was obvious.

' Who *are* you?" he said again in French.

And then a third voice added, in the same tongue, "Whoever you are, drop that pistol. *Quick*—I have you covered."

Like a fool, I had absolutely forgotten the second man

in my excitement at discovering that it was indeed *Becque*, the man whom Raoul d'Auray de Redon had seen in Zaguig before its occupation by the French. . . . My old friend, *Becque!* . . .

An awkward dilemma! . . . If I dropped my revolver I should be at their mercy, and if I did not I should probably be shot in the back and buried in the sand beneath their tent—for even if they did not know who I was, they knew (thanks to the triple traitor, Abdul Salam) that I was a rival and an enemy. . . . Who else would speak French in that place?

How neatly should I be removed from their path!

None but the rogue Abdul Salam knew that I was aware of their existence—much less that I had actually entered their tent. . . . The sentry, of course, did not know me, in my disguise, and the sound of the pistol-shot could easily be explained, if it were heard and inquiries were made. . . . An accident. . . . A shot at a prowling pariah cur or jackal that had entered the tent and alarmed one of them, suddenly awakened. . . .

I should simply *disappear*, and my disappearance would be a soon-forgotten mystery, and probably ascribed to sudden flight prompted by fear—for had I not abused the Emir with unforgettable and unforgivable insults? . . . And then what of Mary Vanbrugh and Maudie—the French female spies sent to beguile and debauch the Emir and win his consent to the treaty? . . . *Mary Vanbrugh would think I had fled, deserting her—in the name of Duty!*

All this flashed through my mind like lightning. What should I do? . . . What about a shot into Becque's vile heart and a swift wheel about and a shot at the Arab?

No—he would fire in the same second that I shot Becque, and he could not miss me at a range of six feet. . . . Nor could I, even in such a situation, shoot a defenceless man in his bed. . . .

Perhaps I could have done so in the days before Mary Vanbrugh had made me see Life and Honour and true Duty in so different a light. . . .

Then I should have said, "What would France have me do?" Now I said, "What would Mary Vanbrugh have me do?"

And I somehow felt that Mary would say: "Live if

you can, and die if you must—but not with this defenceless man's blood on your hands, his murder on your conscience . . ." even if she knew what he had plotted and proposed concerning her and her maid.

Perhaps a couple of seconds had passed—and then the voice behind me spoke again with sharp menace.

"*Quick*—I am going to shoot! . . ."

"*So am I*," said yet a fourth voice coolly, in Arabic, and even, in that moment, I marvelled that the Arab speaker should so aptly have gathered the import of the French words—though actions, of course, speak louder than words.

I recognized the voice of the Emir.

"Everybody shooting everybody this morning," added the Vizier—inevitable shadow of his master.

Keeping Becque covered I turned my head. Two excellent European revolvers threatened the fellow who, green with fright, put his automatic on the ground.

I put my own back into the holster beneath my *burnous*. Evidently the Emir was making one of his unobtrusive visits to the excellent Becque—and he had come in the nick of time. Or was he so well served that he had known of my visit here, and come to catch me and Becque together?

"*Keif halak*, Emir el Hamel el Kebir," I said coolly. "The sound of thy voice is sweet in my ears and the sight of thy face as the first gleam of the rising sun."

"In the circumstances, I do not doubt it, *Roumi*," was the reply, "for you stood at the Gates of Death. . . . What do you here?"

"I am visiting an old friend, Sidi Emir," I replied, "and my purpose is to resume a discussion, interrupted, owing to circumstances beyond his control, many years ago."

The Emir and the Vizier, their inscrutable, penetrating eyes fixed on mine, stared in thoughtful silence.

"Explain," said the Emir at length.

"Lord Emir of Many Tents and Ruler of many Tribes, Leader of the Faithful and Shadow of the Prophet," I said, "you are a person of honour, a warrior, a man of your hands as well as a man of your word. . . . Like me, you are a soldier. . . . Now, I once honoured this dog—for an excellent reason—by crossing swords with him. For an even better and greater reason I would cross swords with him again—and finish, utterly and completely, the duel begun so long ago. . . . I tell you, a lover of your People, that this cur would betray his people. I tell you, a respecter of women, that his white reptile is trying to achieve the dishonour and death of two white women. . . . You may think I wish merely to kill one who is a rival for your favour and alliance. Were that all he is, I would not try to defeat him thus. I would meet a fair adversary with fair attempts to out-bid and out-manœuvre him. . . . But as he has secretly plotted most foully against my country (and his own), against the lives and honour of the lady Sitts, and against my life—I ask you to let me meet him face to face and foot to foot and sword to sword—that I may punish him and rid my country of a matricidal renegade. . . ."

The two Sheikhs stared in silence, stroking their beards, their hard unreadable eyes, enigmatic, faintly mocking, watching my face unwaveringly.

"Swords are sharp and final arguments—and some quarrels can only be settled with them," mused the Emir. "What says our other honoured guest . . .?"

"Oh, I'll fight him!" spoke up Becque. "It will give me real pleasure to kill this chatter-box. . . ."

He turned to me with a smile that lifted one corner of his mouth and showed a gleaming dog-tooth.

"And so you are the bright *de Beaujolais*, are you?" he marvelled. "Well, well, well! Think of that now! . . . De Beaujolais—the Beau Sabreur of the Blue Hussars! . . . De Beaujolais, the Beau Sabreur of the Spahis and the Secret Service! . . . De Beaujolais, the Hero of Zinderneuf! . . . Well, my friend, I'll make you de Beaujolais of a little hole in the sand, shortly, and see you where the birds won't trouble you—and you won't trouble *me*! . . . The great and clever de Beaujolais! . . . Ha! Ha! Ha!" And the brave, brazen rogue roared with laughter.

(But how in the name of his father, the Devil, did he know anything of the affair at Zinderneuf?)

"You shall fight as soon as the light is good," said the Emir. "And you shall fight with Arab swords—a strange weapon to each of you, and therefore fair for both"; and, calling to Yussuf Fetata, he bade him send for two swords of equal length and weight and of exactly similar shape.

CHAPTER XV

"MEN HAVE THEIR EXITS . . ."

HALF an hour later, Becque and I stood face to face in the shadow, cast by the rising sun, of a great clump of palms.

We were stripped to the waist, and wore only baggy Arab trousers and soft boots.

Each held a noble two-edged sword, pliant as cane, sharp as a razor, exact model of those brought to the country by Louis the Good and his Crusaders. I verily believe they *were* Crusaders' swords, for there are many such in that dry desert where nothing rusts and a good sword is more prized, cared for, and treasured, than a good woman.

I looked for a knightly crest on the blade of mine. Had there been one, and had it been the very crest of the de Beaujolais family (for I have ancestors who went on Crusade)—what an omen! What a glorious and wonderful coincidence! What a tale to tell!

But I will be truthful and admit that there was no private mark whatever. Such things do not happen in real life—though it is stark fact that a venerable friend of mine killed a Dahomeyan warrior in Dodd's advance on Dahomey, and took from him the *very Gras rifle that he himself had carried as a private in 1870*! (He knew it both by its number and by a bullet-hole in the butt. It had evidently been sold to these people by some dealer in condemned army stores.)

The only fault I had to find with my beautiful Crusader-sword was that it had no hand-guard, nothing between handle and blade but a thin straight cross-piece. However, the same applied to Becque's weapon.

I looked at Becque. He "peeled well" as English boxers say, was finely muscled, and in splendid condition. Whether the strangeness of our weapons would be in his favour as a stronger if less finished swordsman, or in mine, remained to be seen.

He spat upon his right hand—coarse and vulgar as ever—and swung his sword mightily, trying its weight and balance.

In a little group under the trees stood the Emir, the Vizier; young Yussuf Fetata (to whose family the swords belonged); the powerful dwarf who had first captured me, Marbruk ben Hassan; the Emir's body-servant, El R'Orab the Crow; the Egyptian-Arab colleague of Becque, and a few soldiers.

"Hear my words," said the Emir, and his hawk-like stare was turned to Becque, "for the least attempt at foul play, I will shoot you dead. . . . When I say *'Begin'*—do so. When I say *'Stop'* do so instantly. . . . I shall not say *'Stop'* while both of you are on your feet, unless one of you does anything unbecoming a chivalrous warrior. . . ."

I bowed and gave the Emir the sword-salute. . . .

"*Begin!*" he said a moment later, and Becque repeated the very tactics of our previous duel.

He rushed at me like a tiger, his sword moving like forked lightning, and I gave my whole mind and body to parry and defence. I was not in the best of health and strength, thanks to my wound, my sleepless nights of anxiety, and my confinement to the tent—and if Becque chose to force the pace and tire himself, I was content.

All critics of my "form" have praised my foot-work, and I used my feet and brain to save my arm, for the swords were heavy.

At the end of his first wild whirling attack, when his sword ceased for a moment to rise and fall like a flail in the hands of a madman, I feinted for his head, and, as his sword went up, I lunged as though I held a sabre. He sprang back like a cat, and then made a Maltese-cross pattern with his sword—as though he were a Highlander wielding a light claymore—when I pursued.

Nothing could pass that guard—but it was expensive work, costly in strength and breath, and he was very welcome to make that impressive display—and I kept him at it by light and rapid feints. . . .

Suddenly his sword went up and back, as to smite straight down upon my skull, and, judging that I had time for the manœuvre, I did not parry—but sprang to my left and slashed in a smart *coup de flanc* that took him across the ribs beneath the raised right arm. A little higher and he would never have lifted his arm again; but, as it was, I gave him a gash that would mean a nice little blood-letting. In the same second, his sword fell perpendicularly on my right thigh, merely slicing off an inconsiderable—shall I say "rasher"—and touching no artery nor vein of importance.

I had drawn first blood—first by a fraction of a second—and I had inflicted a wound and received a graze.

"*Mary Vanbrugh*," I whispered.

I saw momentary fear in Becque's eyes, but knew it was only fear that I had wounded him too severely for him to continue the fight.

He began to retreat; he retreated quickly; he almost ran backward for a few paces—and, as I swiftly followed, he ducked, most cleverly and swiftly, below my sword—as it cut sideways at his neck—and lunged splendidly at my breast. A side step only just saved me, for his point and edge ploughed along the flesh of my left side and the other edge cut my upper arm as it rested for the moment against my body. . . . But the quick *riposte* has always been my strong point, and before his sword returned on guard, I cut him heavily across the head.

Unfortunately it was only a back-handed blow delivered as my sword returned to guard, and it was almost the hilt that struck him. Had it been the middle of the edge—even at such close quarters and back-handed—the cut would have been more worthy of the occasion. As it was, it did friend Becque no good at all.

"*Mary Vanbrugh*," I whispered, a second time.

And then my opponent changed his tactics and used his sword two-handed.

One successful stroke delivered thus would lop off a limb or sever a head from a body—but though the force of every blow is doubled in value, the quickness of every parry is halved, and, since my opponent chose to turn his weapon into a mace, I turned mine into a foil, instead of obediently following his tactics.

It was rhinoceros against leopard now, strong dog against quick cat—possibly Goliath against David. . . .

Hitherto we had crossed swords point downward, as in "sabres", now I held mine point upward as in "foils," and dodged and danced on my toes, feinting for a thrust.

Cut or thrust? . . .

A cut from Becque would be death for de Beaujolais—and I was very sure a thrust from de Beaujolais would be death for Becque. . . .

My foe forced the pace again. . . . He rushed like a bull, and I dodged like a matador. A hundred times his sword swept past my head like a mighty scythe, and so swift was he that never had I a chance for the matador's stroke—the *coup de grâce*. We were both panting, our breath whistling through parched throats and mouths, our bare chests heaving like bellows. . . . We were streaming with sweat and blood—and, with glaring glassy eye, Becque was fiercely scowling, and he was hoarsely croaking:

"*Curse you!* you damned dancing-master! *God smite you!* . . . *Blast you,* you jumping monkey!" with each terrific stroke; and de Beaujolais was smiling and whispering "*Mary Vanbrugh . . . Mary . . . Mary . . .*" but, believe me, de Beaujolais was weakening, for he had lost a lot of blood, his left arm was a useless weight of lead, he was growing giddy and sick and faint—and suddenly Becque, with a look a devilish hate and rage upon his contorted face, swept his sword once more above his head, and this time swept it up too far!

It was well above his head—and pointing downward behind him—for a stroke that should cleave me to the chin, when I dropped my point and lunged with all my strength and speed. . . . "*Mary Vanbrugh! . . .*"

I had won. My sword stood out a foot behind him. . . .

He tottered and fell. . . . My knees turned to water and I collapsed across his body.

"*Exit Becque!*" thought I, as I went down—"and perhaps de Beaujolais too! . . .*"

I recovered in a few minutes, to find that the Emir himself was holding my head and pouring glorious cold water on my face, chest and hands. . . . The Vizier was washing my cuts. . . .

Becque was not dead—but, far from surgeons and

hospitals, no man could long survive the driving of that huge sword through his body. . . .

Poor devil!—but he *was* a devil!

"The Sitt has bandages and cordials," I said to the Emir, as I rose to my feet, and he at once despatched R'Orab the Crow to bid the slave-girls of the *anderun* to ask the lady Sitt to send what was needed for a wounded man.

I did what I could for the unconscious Becque and then I resumed my *jelabia*, *haik*, *kafiyah* and *burnous*, after drinking deeply of the cool water, and dabbing my bleeding wounds.

The congratulatory Arabs crowded round me, filled with admiration of the victor. Would they have done the same with Becque, if he had won . . .? Nothing succeeds like success. . . . To him that hath shall be given. . . . *Væ victis*. . . . Thumbs down for the loser. . . .

"Do you send for medicaments for yourself or for your enemy, Sidi?" asked the Emir.

"For my enemy, Emir," I replied. "It is the Christian custom."

"But he *is* your enemy," said the Emir.

"Anyone can help an injured *friend*," I replied. "If that is held to be a virtue, how much more is it a virtue to help a fallen foe?"

Sententious—but suitable to the company and the occasion.

The Emir smiled and shook my hand in European fashion, and the Vizier followed his example.

I was in high favour and regard—for the moment—as the winner of a good stout fight. . . . *For the moment!* . . . What of the morrow, when their chivalrous fighting blood had cooled—and my foul insults and abuse were remembered? . . .

§ 2

And then appeared Mary Vanbrugh, following El R'-Orab, who carried the medicine chest and a bottle and some white stuff—lint or cotton-wool and bandages.

I might have known that she would not merely send

the necessary things, when she heard of wounds and injuries.

She glanced at the semi-conscious Becque, a hideous gory spectacle, and then at me. I suppose I looked haggard and dishevelled and there was a little blood on my clothes—also I held the good sword, that had perhaps saved her life and honour, in my hand.

"*Your* work?" she said in a voice of ice and steel.

I did not deny it.

"More *Duty*?" she asked most bitterly, and her voice was scathing. "Oh, you *Killer*, you professional paid hireling *Slayer*. . . . Oh, you *Murderer* in the sacred name of your noble *Duty*! . . . Tell these men to bring me a lot more water—and to make a stretcher with spears or tent-poles and some rugs . . ." and she got to work like a trained nurse.

"Tear up a clean *burnous*, or something, in long strips," she said as I knelt to help her, "and then get out of my sight—you *sicken* me. . . ."

"Are you hurt, too?" she asked a moment later, as more blood oozed through from my thigh, ribs and arm.

"A little," I replied.

"I am glad you *are*," said Miss Vanbrugh; "it serves you right,"—and then . . . "Suppose it had been *you* lying here dying . . .?"

I supposed it, and thanked the good God that it was not—for her sake.

When she had cleaned, sterilized and bandaged Becque's ghastly wound, she bade me tell the Arabs to have him carried to the Guest-tents and laid on my bed, that she might nurse him! Her orders were obeyed, and, under her superintendence, the wounded man was carried away with all possible care.

I noticed that the Emir bade Yussuf Fetata conduct the Egyptian-Arab back to his tent, and see that he did not leave it.

When everything possible had been done for Becque, and he lay on my bed motionless and only imperceptibly breathing, Mary Vanbrugh turned to me.

"I'll attend to *you* now, Killer," said she.

"Thank you, Miss Vanbrugh," I replied, "I can attend to what scratches I have quite well."

She looked at me, as in doubt. Her instinctive love of mothering and succouring the injured seemed to be at war with her instinctive hatred of those who cause the injury.

"Let me see the wound in your side," she said. "If you can look after your leg yourself, you cannot dress and bandage a wound in the ribs properly."

"I wouldn't trouble you for worlds, Miss Vanbrugh," I replied. "Doubtless the noted Doctor Hadji Abdul Salam will treat me. . . . These Arab specialists have some quite remarkable methods, such as making one swallow an appropriate quotation from the *Q'ran*, written on paper or rag, correctly blessed and suitably sanctified. . . . Do me a lot of good, I should think. . . . And possibly Maudie would lend a hand if the Doctor thinks a bandage . . ." And then loss of blood, following a terrific fight (on an empty stomach) had its humiliating effect on my already enfeebled body, and down I went in a heap. . . .

When I recovered consciousness, Mary Vanbrugh and a very white-faced Maudie were in the tent, and I was lying, bandaged, on some rugs.

Dear Becque and I—side by side!

"Brandy," said Mary Vanbrugh to Maudie, as I opened my eyes. Maudie poured some out, and gave it to me. I drank the cognac, and was very soon my own man again. How often was this drama to be repeated? . . . First the Touareg bullet; now Becque's sword. What would the third be?

I was soon to know.

I sat up, got to my feet, stiff, sore, bruised, and giddy, but by no means a "cot-case".

"Lie down again at once, Killer," said Mary Vanbrugh sharply.

"Thank you, Miss Vanbrugh," I replied. "I am all right again now, and very greatly regret the trouble I have given you. I am most grateful. . . ."

"I do not desire your gratitude, Killer," interrupted the pale, competent, angry girl.

". . . To Becque—I was going to say—for being so tender with me," I continued. And then I said a thing that I have regretted ever since—and when I think of it,

I have to find some peace in the excuse that I was a little off my balance.

"It is not so long since you were fairly glad of the killing-powers of a Killer, Miss Vanbrugh," I went on, and felt myself a cad as I said it. . . . "On a certain roof in Zaguig, the Killer against eight, and your life in the balance. . . . I apologize for reminding you. . . . I am ashamed . . ."

"*I* am ashamed . . . *I* apologize—humbly, Major de Beaujolais," she replied, and her eyes were slightly suffused as I took her hand and pressed it to my lips. . . . "But oh! why *do* you . . . why *must* you . . . all these fine men . . . that Mr. Dufour, Achmet, Djikki, and now this poor mangled, butchered creature. . . . Can you find *no* Duty that is help and kindness and love, instead of this Duty of killing, maiming, hurting? . . ."

Yes—I was beginning to think that I could find a Duty that was Love. . . .

§ 3

Becque rallied that night, incredibly. His strong spirit flickered, flared up, and then burnt clearly.

I was getting myself a drink, being consumed with thirst, when he spoke:

"So you win, de Beaujolais," he said quietly.

"I win, Becque," I replied.

I would not rejoice over a fallen foe, and I would not express regret to a villainous renegade and a treacherous cur—who, moreover, had plotted the death, mutilation and dishonour of two white girls (and one of them *Mary Vanbrugh*).

"It's a queer world," he mused. "You all but shot me that day, and I all but got you hanged. . . . The merest chance saved me, and luck saved you. . . ."

I supposed this to be the semi-delirious wanderings of a fevered mind. . . . But the brave evil Becque did not look, nor sound, delirious.

"What do you mean?" I said, more for the sake of saying something than seriously to ask a question.

"Ah—the brilliant de Beaujolais—Beau Sabreur of the Blue Hussars and the Spahis! . . . Bright particular star of the *Bureau Arabe*, the Secret Service, the Intelligence Department of the French Army in Africa! . . . You think you know a lot, don't you, and you're very pleased with your beautiful self—but you don't know who it was that turned your own men from down-trodden slaves into bloodthirsty mutineers, do you? . . . And you were never nearer death in all your days. . . . Do you know, my clever friend, that if those cursed Arabs had not attacked at that moment, nothing could have saved you—thanks to *me*? . . . Do you know that your own men were going to hang you to the flag-staff and then burn the place and march off? . . . '*Another mutiny in the discontented and rotten French Army . . .*!' Headlines in the foreign Press! . . . Encouragement to the enemies of France! . . . That would have been splendid, eh?"

I thought hard, and cast back in my memory. . . .

Most certainly I had never attempted to shoot Becque, and still more certainly I had never been in danger of hanging, at the hands of the gentleman.

In spite of his apparent command of his faculties, he must be wandering in his mind—indeed, a place of devious and tortuous paths in which to wander.

Silence fell, disturbed only by the droning of the flies which I whisked from his face.

A few minutes later the closed eyes opened and glared at me like those of a serpent.

"Beautiful, brainy de Beaujolais," the hateful voice began again. "How nearly I got you that day and how I have cursed those Arabs ever since—those black devils from Hell that saved you. . . ."

Delirium, undoubtedly. . . . I brushed the flies again from the sticky lips and moistened them with a corner of a handkerchief dipped in lemon-juice.

"And when and where was that, Becque?" I asked conversationally.

"I suppose the mighty warrior, the Beau Sabreur, the brain of the French Army, has forgotten the little episode of Zinderneuf ?. . ."

Zinderneuf! . . .

What *could* this Becque know of Zinderneuf? . . .

Was yet another mystery to be added to those that clustered round the name of that ill-omened shambles?[1]

Zinderneuf! ... *Mutiny* ...

What was it Dufour had said to me when I ordered the parade before entering that silent fort, garrisoned by the Dead, every man on his feet and at his post. . . . ("The Dead forbidden to die. The Fallen who were not allowed to fall?") He had said "*There is going to be trouble. . . . . They are rotten with* cafard *and over-fatigue. . . . They will shoot you and desert* en masse! . . ."

Could this Becque have been there? . . . Utterly impossible. . . .

Again I thought hard, cast back in my memory, and concentrated my whole mind upon the events of that terrible day. . . .

Dufour was there, of course. . . .

Yes, and that excellent Sergeant Lebaudy, I remembered, the man who was said to have the biggest voice in the French Army. . . .

And that punishing Corporal Brille whom I once threatened with a taste of the *crapaudine*, when I found him administering it unlawfully. . . . I could see their faces. . . . Yes. . . . And that trumpeter who volunteered to enter that House of the Dead. . . . Of course . . . he was one of the three Gestes, as I learned when I went to Brandin Abbas in England to be best man at George Lawrence's wedding. . . . Lady Brandon was their aunt. . . .

Yes, and I remembered two fine American soldiers with whom I spoke in English—men whom I had, alas, sent to their deaths by thirst or Arabs, in an attempt to warn St. André and his Senegalese, that awful night.

I could recall no one else. . . . No one at all. . . .

"And what do *you* know about Zinderneuf, Becque?" I asked.

His bitter sneering laugh was unpleasant to hear.

"Oh, you poor fool," he replied. "I know this much about Zinderneuf—that you nearly stepped into your grave there. . . . Into the grave that *I* dug for you there. . . . However, this place will do equally well."

With my mind back in Zinderneuf, I absently replied:

[1] *Vide "Beau Geste"* (John Murray).

"You think I shall find my grave *here*, do you, Becque?"

"I most earnestly hope so," replied Becque. "I truly hope, and firmly believe, this Emir will do to you and your women what I have urged him—and tried to bribe him—to do."

I kept silent, for the man was dying.

"You are not out of the wood yet, Beautiful de Beaujolais, Beau Sabreur," the cruel, bitter voice went on. . . . "My colleague has a brain—if he hasn't much guts—and he has money too. And the power to put down franc for franc against you or anybody else, and then double it. . . . Oh, we shall win. . . . And I'd give my soul to survive to see the hour of success—and you impaled living on a sharpened palm-trunk and *your Secret Service women given to the Soudanese soldiers*. . . ."

I bit my lips and kept silence, for the man was surely dying.

§ 4

In spite of the considered opinion of which Miss Vanbrugh had delivered herself, I am a humane man, and if I fight my foe as a soldier should fight him, I try to be *sans rancune* when the fight is over.

While Becque was awake and conscious, I would sit with him, bear with his vileness, and do what I could to assuage the sufferings of his last hours. . . . Sometimes men change and relent and repent on their death-beds. . . . I am not a religious man, but I hold tenaciously to what is good and right, and if approaching death brought a better frame of mind to Becque, I would do everything in my power to encourage and develop it. . . . I would meet him more than half-way, and if his change of heart were real, I would readily forgive him, in the name of France and of Mary Vanbrugh. . . .

"Well, Becque," I said, "I shall do my best against your colleague—and *I* would give a great deal to survive to see the hour of success, and you, not impaled living, but speeded on your way, with a safe conduct, back to whence you came."

"You mealy-mouthed liar," replied my gentleman. "You have killed me, and there you sit and *gloat*. . . ."

154

"Nonsense, Becque," I replied. "I am glad I won the fight—but I'd do anything I could to help or ease or comfort you, poor chap. . . ."

"Another lie, you canting hypocrite and swine," Becque answered me.

"No," I said. "The simple truth."

"Prove it, then," was the quick answer.

"Well?" I asked, and rose to get him anything he wanted or to do anything that he might desire.

"Look you, de Beaujolais," he said, "you are a soldier. So am I. . . . We have both lived hard—and my time has come. . . . Nothing can possibly save me— here in the desert without surgeons, anaesthetics, oxygen, antiseptics—and I may linger for days—wounded as I am. . . . I *know* that nothing on God's earth can save me—so do you. . . . Then let me die now and like a soldier. . . . Not like a sick cow in the straw. . . . Shoot me, de Beaujolais. . . ."

"I can't," I replied.

"No—as I said—you are a mealy-mouthed liar, and a canting hypocrite, full of words and words . . ." answered Becque; and then in bitter mockery he mimicked my "*I'd do anything I could for you, poor chap! . . .*"

"I can't murder you, Becque," I said.

"You *have*," he replied. "Can't you complete your job? . . . No. . . . The Bold-and-Beautiful de Beaujolais couldn't do that—he could only gloat upon his handiwork and spin out the last hours of the man he had killed. . . . You and your Arab-debauching women from the stews of Paris. . . ." And he spat.

"One of those women worked over you like a nurse or a mother, Becque," I said. "She lavished her tiny store of cognac, eau-de-Cologne, antiseptics and surgery stuff on you——"

"As I said," he interrupted, "to keep me alive and gloat. . . ."

Silence fell in that hot, dimly-lighted tent, and I sat and watched this Becque.

After a while he spoke again.

"De Beaujolais," he said, "I make a last appeal as a soldier to a soldier. . . . Don't keep me alive, in agony, for days—knowing that I shall be a mortifying mass of gangrene and corruption before I die. . . . Knowing that nothing can save me. . . . I appeal to you, to you on whose head my blood is, to spare me *that*. . . . Put your pistol near me—and let Becque die as he has lived, with a weapon in his hand. . . ."

I thought rapidly.

". . . Come, come, de Beaujolais, it is not *much* to ask, surely. It leaves your lily-white hands clean and saves your conscience the reproach that you let me suffer tortures that the Arabs themselves would spare me. . . ."

I came to a decision.

"De Beaujolais—if I have the ghost of a chance of life, refuse my request. . . . If I have no chance, and you *know* I have none—as surely as you know the sun will rise—then, if you are a man, a human creature with a spark of humane feeling in you—put your pistol by my hand. . . . You can turn your back if you are squeamish. . . . Do it, de Beaujolais, and I will die forgiving you and repenting my sins. . . ."

His voice broke, and I swallowed a lump in my throat as I rose and went to where my revolver hung to the tent-pole. My sword had passed below his lungs and had penetrated the liver and stomach and probably the spinal cord. He would never leave that bed, nothing upon earth could save him, and his long lingering death would be a ghastly thing. . . . It *was* the one thing I could do for him. . . .

I put the pistol beside his right hand.

"Good-bye, Becque," I said. "In the name of France and Mary Vanbrugh I forgive the evil you tried to do to them both. . . . Personally I feel no hate whatsoever. . . . Good-bye, brave man—good-bye, old chap. . . ." And I touched his hand and turned my back.

The bullet cut my ear.

I sprang round and knocked the pistol from Becque's hand. "You treacherous *devil*!" I cried.

"You poor gullible *fool*!" he answered, with the wry smile that showed the gleaming fang.

The sentry raised the door flap and looked in, and Mary Vanbrugh rushed from the *anderun* half of the tent, as I picked up my revolver.

"*Oh! What is it?*" she asked breathlessly.

"An accident," replied Becque. "One of the most deplorable that ever happened. . . I shall regret it all my life. . . ." And he laughed.

There was no denying the gameness and stout heart of this dear Becque.

"More Duty, I thought, perhaps, Major de Beaujolais," observed the girl.

"It was. As I conceived it, Miss Vanbrugh," I replied.

After looking at Becque's bandages and giving him a sip of hot *soupe*, made with our compressed meat-tablets and a little cognac, she returned to the *anderun*, bidding me drink the *soupe*, for Becque could do little more than taste it.

"You win again, you dog!" said Becque, as soon as we were alone. "What a fool I was to aim at your head— with a shaking hand! . . . But I did so want to see those poor brains you are so proud of. . . . *Now*, will you kill me?"

"No," I answered.

"*I know you won't!*" he replied. "You haven't the guts. . . . *And I know I shall recover.* . . . Why, you fool, I breathe almost without pain. . . . My lungs are absolutely sound. . . . You only gave me a flesh wound and I heal splendidly. Always have done. . . ."

The poor wretch evidently did not know that the bandages hid as surely mortal a wound as ever man received. His talk of fatal injuries and certain death, which he had supposed to be a ruse that would gull and fool me, was but the simple truth.

"I'll be on my feet in a week, you witless ape," he continued, "and I'll get you yet! . . . Believe me, Beautiful de Beaujolais, I won't miss you next time I shoot. . . . But I hope it won't come to that. . . . I want to see you die quite otherwise—and then I'll deal with your Arab-debauching harlots. . . . But I'll get you somehow! I'll *get you*, my Beau Sabreur! . . ."

He raised himself on one elbow, pointed a shaking hand at my face, spat, and fell back dead. . . .

CHAPTER XVI

FOR MY LADY

"The wordly hopes men set their hearts upon,
　　Turn ashes—or they prosper;
Anon, like snow upon the desert's dusty face,
　　Lighting a little hour or two—are gone. . . ."

BECQUE'S body having been borne away at dawn for burial, I soon began to wonder if the events of the previous day and night had really occurred, or whether they were the nightmare imaginings of a delirious fever-victim.

My wounds were real enough, however, and though slight, were painful in the extreme, throbbing almost unbearably and making movement a torture.

I would not have been without them though for three times that day Mary Vanbrugh dressed them, and if I scarcely heard her voice, I felt the blessed touch of her fingers

But she attended me as impersonally and coldly as a queen washing the feet of beggars, or as a certain type of army-surgeon doctoring a sick negro soldier.

As she left the tent on the last of her almost silent visits, she paused at the door-curtain and turned to me.

"What exactly *was* that shot in the night, Major de Beaujolais?" she asked.

"It was Becque shooting at me," I replied. "You did not suppose that it was me shooting at Becque, did you, Miss Vanbrugh?"

"I really did not know, Major de Beaujolais," answered the girl. "I should not be so foolish as to set *any* limit to what you might do in the name of *Duty*! . . . Nothing *whatever* would surprise me in that direction, now, I think. . . ."

"A man's duty *is* his duty," I replied.

"Oh, quite," she answered. "I would not have you deviate a hair's breadth from your splendid path. . . . But since the day you informed me that you would have left me to the mercies of the Touareg—had there been but one camel—I have been thinking . . . a good deal. . . .

Yes, '*A man's duty is his duty*,' and—if I might venture to speak so presumptuously—a woman's duty is *her* duty, too. . . ."

"Surely" I agreed.

"And so I find it *my* duty to hinder you no further, and to remain in the Oasis with these fine Arabs—*under the protection of the Emir el Hamel el Kebir.* . . ."

"*What!*" I shouted, startled out of my habitual calm and courtesy. "You find it your '*duty*' to do *what?*"

I felt actually faint—and began to tremble with horror, fear, and a deadly sickness of soul.

"I think you heard what I said," the girl replied coldly, "and I think you know that I always mean what I say, and say what I mean. . . . Oh, believe me, Major de Beaujolais—I have some notions of my own on *duty*—and it is no part of mine to hinder yours. . . ."

I drank some water, and my trembling hand spilt more than my dry throat swallowed.

"So I shall remain here," she went on, "and I think too that I prefer the standards and ideals of this Emir. . . . Somehow I do not think that *anything* would have induced *him* to leave a woman to certain death or worse. . . . Not even a *treaty*!" and the bitter scorn of her accents, as she said that word, was terrible.

Her voice seared and scorched me. . . . I tried to speak and could not.

"Nor do I feel that I shall incur any greater danger here than I should in setting off into the desert again with a gentleman of your pronounced views on the subject of the relative importance of a woman and a piece of paper. . . . Nor shall my maid go with you. . . . I prefer to trust her, as well as myself, to these people of a less-developed singleness of purpose . . . and I *like* this Emir—enormously."

I found my voice. . . . Clumsily, owing to my wounds, I knelt before her. . . .

"Miss Vanbrugh . . . *Mary* . . ." I cried. "This is inhuman cruelty. . . . This is *madness!* . . . Think! . . . A girl like yourself—a lovely fascinating woman—*here* . . . *alone*. . . . You must be insane. . . . Think. . . . A *hareem*—these Arabs. . . . I would sooner shoot you here and now. . . . This is sheer incredible *madness*. . . ."

"Yes—like yourself, Major de Beaujolais," she replied, drawing back from me. "*I* am now 'mad' on the subject of *Duty*. . . . It has become an obsession with *me* too—(an example of the influence of one's companions upon one's character!)—and I find it my duty to leave you entirely free to give the whole of your mind to more important matters—to leave you entirely free to depart alone as soon as your business is completed—for I will be no further hindrance to you. . . . Good-bye, and—as I do not think I shall see you again—many thanks for bringing me here in safety, and for setting me so high a standard and so glorious an example. . . ."

I do not know what I replied—nor what I did. I was *all* French in that moment, and gave full rein to my terrible emotion.

But I know that Mary Vanbrugh left the tent with the cold words:

"Duty, Major de Beaujolais—before *everything*! We will both do our Duty. . . . I shall tell the Emir el Hamel el Kebir that I intend to remain here indefinitely, under his protection, and that I hope he will give you your precious treaty, and send you off at once. . . . My conscience—awakened by you—will approve my doing what *I* now see to be *my* duty. . . . Good-bye, Major de Beaujolais. . . ."

I sat for hours with my pistol in my hand, and I think I may now claim to know what suffering *is*. . . . Never since that hour have I had a word of blame for the poor soul who blows his brains out. . . .

§ 2

I saw no one else that day, but during the night I was awakened from a fitful and nightmare-ridden doze by the Hadji Abdul Salam.

One more he rehearsed his proposals and warnings, modified now by the elimination of Becque.

ONE: Would I, by his help, escape alone, immediately, and return with a strong French force and make him France's faithful (well-paid) vassal Emir Regent of the Great Confederation? Or

160

Two: Would I promise him a great bag of gold and my help in his obtaining the Regency of the Confederation, if he procured the death of the Emir at the hands of Suleiman the Strong, and solemnly swore to poison the said Suleiman at as early a date thereafter as convenient? (He could not poison the Emir, for that distrustful man took all precautions against such accidents.)

He fully warned me that by rejecting both his proposals I should most certainly come to a painful and untimely end, and my two women become *hareem* slaves. He was in a position to state with certainty and truth that the Emir had decided to kill me and the Arab-Egyptian, keep the money, camels, weapons and other effects of both of us, and then accept the earlier offer of the Great Sheikh el Senussi and make an offensive and defensive alliance with him.

I heard him out, on the chance that I might glean something new.

When he had finished and I had replied with some terseness, I pointed to the doorway and remarked:

"And now, Holy One, depart in peace, before I commit an impiety. In other words—get out, you villainous, filthy, treacherous dog, before I shoot you. . . ."

The Hadji went, and as he crept from my tent, he ran into the arms of the Sheikh el Habibka el Wazir—and I saw him no more in this life, and do not expect to see him in the next.

I heard that he fell ill and died shortly after. People are apt to do so if they obstruct the ways of desert Emirs.

I lay awake till dawn, probably the most anxious, distracted, troubled man in Africa. . . .

Mary Vanbrugh. . . . France. . . . My Service. . . . My uncle. . . . My Duty. . . . An outraged, unforgivably insulted despot, a fierce, untrammelled tyrant whose "honour" was his life—and in whose hands lay the fate of the two women for whose safety I was responsible.

§ 3

Things came to a head the next night.

The Emir el Hamel el Kebir and the Sheikh el Habibka el

Wazir entered my tent, and, as though nothing had happened to disturb the friendliest relationship, were cordially pleasant.

Much too friendly methought, and, knowing Arabs as I do, I could not suppress the feeling that their visit boded me no good. I grew certain of it—and I was right.

After formal courtesies and the refusal of such hospitalities as I could offer, the Emir said:

"Your Excellency has the successful accomplishment of this mission much at heart?"

"It would be a fine thing for your people and pleasing to mine," I replied. "Yes, I have it much at heart."

"Your Excellency has the welfare and happiness of the Sitt Miriyam much at heart?" went on the sonorous voice.

Was there a mocking note in it?

"So much so that I value it more than the Treaty," I replied.

"And the other night Your Excellency called me *dog* and *swine*, and *filthy black devil*, I think," was the Emir's next utterance.

"Yes," he went on, as I was silent. "Yes. And Your Excellency has these matters much at heart. He admires this fair woman greatly. Perhaps he loves her? *Possibly he would even die for her? . . .*"

The Vizier watched the Emir, stroked his beard, and smiled.

"Your Excellency would achieve a great deed for France? . . . But perhaps he loves France not so much that he would die for her? Perhaps this woman is as his Faith, since he is an Infidel? . . . Yes, perchance she *is* his Faith? . . ."

The two men now stared at me with enigmatic eyes, cruel, hard and unfathomable, the unreadable alien eyes of the Oriental. . . .

There was a brief silence, a contest of wills, a dramatic struggle of personalities.

"*Are you prepared to die for your Faith?*" asked the Emir—and I started as though stung. Where had I heard those words before? Who had said them?

I had. I had used those identical words to Becque himself at St. Denis, years ago. . . . Well, perhaps I could make a better showing than Becque had then done—as much better as my cause was nobler.

"I *am*," I replied in the words of the dead man.

"*You shall*," said the Emir, as I had said to Becque—and I swear that as he said it, the Vizier's face fell, and he smote his thigh in anger. . . . Was he my friend?

"Listen," said the Emir. "These two women shall go free, in honour and safety, on the day after Death has wiped out the insults you have put upon me. After those words '*dog*', '*son of a dog*', '*swine*', '*black-faced devil*', I think that we may not both live. . . . Nor would I slay with mine own hand the man who comes in peace and eats my salt. . . . Speak *Roumi*. . . ."

"What proof and assurance have I that you would keep your word, Emir?" I asked.

"None whatever—save that I have given it," was the reply. "It is known to all men who know me, that I have never broken faith; never failed in promise or in threat. . . . *If you die by your own hand tonight, your white women are as free as air.* I, the Emir el Hamel el Kebir, swear upon the Holy Q'ran and by the Beard of the Prophet and the Sacred Names of God that I will deliver the two Sitts, in perfect safety, wheresoever they would be."

"And if I decline your kind sugestion that I should commit suicide?" I sneered in my fear, misery and rage.

"Then you can slink away in safety; the signed Treaty goes with you; the Sitt Miriyam enters the *hareem* of the Sheikh el Habibka el Wazir; and the Sitt Moadi enters mine. . . ."

"You Son of Satan! You devilish dog——" I began.

"*Choose*—do not chatter," said the Emir.

Now my revolver was in its holster and my sword leant against the tent-pole. . . .

Let me think. . . . Kind God, let me think. . . . If I could shoot both these dogs and the sentry who would rush in—could I get the girls out of their beds and on to camels and away—I, single-handed, against the bodyguard of Soudanese, whose lines were not a hundred yards away, and against the whole mob that would come running? Such things were done in the kind of books that Maudie read, no doubt.

'No. I was utterly and hopelessly in the power of these men. And what of the Treaty, if it *were* possible for us to escape?

"Since you give your word that the Treaty shall be signed and loyally kept, or, on the other hand, that the two Sitts shall be escorted to safety—why not do these wise and noble actions without sullying them with murder?" I asked.

"Do you not punish those who mortally insult *you*?" asked the Emir.

"I fight them," I replied, and my heart gave a little bound of hope as an idea occurred to me. "I fight them —I do not murder them. Fight me tomorrow, Emir— and if I die, let the Sitts go, taking the Treaty with them."

"And if *I* die?" asked the Emir.

"It will be the Hand of Allah," I replied. "It will be a sign that you have done wrong. The Vizier must have orders to see that we all go in safety, bearing the Treaty with us.'

The Emir smiled and shook his head.

"A *brave* man would fight me with the condition that the Sitts go in any case and take the Treaty with them —and that I go if I win," said I.

"I do not fight those who come to me in peace and receive my hospitality," answered the Emir with his mocking smile.

He was but playing with me, as the cat plays with the mouse it is about to kill.

"No? You only murder them?" I asked.

"Never," replied the Emir. "But I cannot prevent their taking their own lives if they are bent upon it. . . . If you die tonight, the Sitts leave here tomorrow. You *know* I speak the truth. . . ."

I did. I rose, and my head went slowly and reluctantly to my holster. Life was very sweet—with Mary so near and dear.

I grasped the butt of the weapon—and almost drew and fired it, with one motion, into the smiling face of the Emir. But that could lead to nothing but the worst. There was no shadow of possibility of any appeal to force doing anything but harm.

I drew my revolver, and the hands of the two Arabs moved beneath their robes.

"Your pistol is unloaded," said the Sheikh, "but ours are not."

I opened the breech of the weapon, and saw that the cartridges had been extracted. . . .

"Get on with the murder, noble Emir—true pattern of chivalry and model of hospitality," I said, and added: "But remember, if evil befalls the Sitts, never again shall you fall asleep without my cold hand clutching you by the throat—you disgrace to the name of man, Mussulman and Arab. . . . You defiler of the Koran and enemy of God."

"If you mean that you wish to die that the Sitts may go free, and my honour may be cleansed of insult . . ." replied the Emir, and he softly clapped his hands, as the Vizier angrily growled an oath in his beard. . . . *Was* he my friend . . .?

The slave who was the Emir's constant attendant and whom he called El R'Orab the Crow, stooped into the tent.

"Bring the cur and some water," said the Emir.

El R'Orab the Crow left the tent and soon returned, leading a pariah-dog on a string, and carrying an earthenware bowl of water.

Producing a phial from beneath his sash, the Vizier poured what looked like milk into the bowl. The slave set it before the dog, and retired from the tent. Evidently the matter had been arranged beforehand. . . .

As such dogs invariably do, this one gulped the water greedily.

The imperturbable Arabs, chin on hand, watched.

Scarcely had the dog swallowed the last of the water, when it sneezed, gave a kind of choking howl, staggered, and fell.

In less than a minute it was dead. I admit that it seemed to die fairly painlessly.

I rose again, quickly produced the Treaty from the back of my map-case, and got sealing-wax and matches from my bag. . . .

"*Sign the Treaty,*" I said, "*and let me go. . . .*"

.   .   .   .   .

The Emir, smiling scornfully, signed with my fountain-pen, and sealed with a great old ring that bore cabalistic designs and ancient Arabic lettering.

The Vizier, grinning cheerfully, witnessed the signature —both making a jumbled mass of Arabic scratchings which were their "marks" rather than legible signatures. . . . I could understand the Emir's contempt, but not the obvious joy of the Vizier.

Again the Emir clapped his hands. R'Orab the Crow entered, and the dog and the bowl were removed.

"Bring us tea," said the Emir; and, returning, the slave brought four steaming cups of mint tea, inevitable accompaniment of any "ceremony".

Into one the Emir poured the remainder of the contents of the phial and passed it to me.

"We would have drunk together," he said, "you drinking that cup—and we would have wished prosperity and happiness to the Sitts. '*May each marry the man she loves,*' we would have said, and you would have died like a brave man. . . . Now cast the poison on the ground, O Seller of Women, and take this other cup. Drink tea with us—to the prosperity of our alliance with France instead."

And beneath the smiling eyes of the Emir and the fierce stare of the Vizier, I said in Arabic: "*The Treaty is signed and witnessed, Emir!*" and in my own mother-tongue I cried: "*Happiness to my Lady, and success to my Country,*" and, rising to my feet, I drank off the poisoned cup—clutched at my throat—tried to speak and choked . . . remembered Suleiman the Strong and tried to tell the Emir of his presence and his threat . . . choked . . . choked . . . saw the tent, the lamp, the men, whirl round me and dissolve—and knew I was falling, falling—falling through interstellar space into Eternity—and, as I did so, was aware that the two Arabs sprang to their feet. . . . Blind, and dying, I heard a woman scream. . . . I . . .

NOTE

THUS abruptly ends the autobiography of Major Henri de Beaujolais —which he began long after leaving the Great Oasis and the society of the Emir el Hamel el Kebir and his Wazir (or Vizier).

The abrupt ending of his literary labours, at the point of so dramatic a crisis in his affairs, was not due to his skill as a cunning writer, so much as to the skill of a Riffian tribesman as a cunning sniper.

Major de Beaujolais, being guilty of the rashness of writing in a tent, by the light of a lamp, paid the penalty, and the said tribesman's bullet found its billet in his wrist-watch and arm, distributing the works of the former throughout the latter, and rendering him incapable of wielding either pen or sword for a considerable period. . . .

It happens, however, that the compiler of this book is in a position to augment the memoirs of his friend, whom he has called Henri de Beaujolais, and to shed some light upon the puzzling situation. Paradoxically, the light came from dark places—the hearts and mouths of two Bad Men. Their wicked lips completed the story, and it is hereinafter set forth.

.   .   .   .   .

The narrative which follows opens at a date a few years previous to the visit of Major de Beaujolais to the Great Oasis.

PART TWO

Success

THE MAKING OF A MONARCH

Out of the Mouths of
TWO BAD MEN

" Love rules the camp, the court, the grove,
And men below, and saints above,
For Love is Heaven, and Heaven is Love."

CHAPTER I

LOST

GOLDEN sand and copper sky; copper sky and golden sand; and nothing else. Nothing to relieve the aching human eye, in all that dreadful boundless waste of blistering earth and burning heaven.

To the bright tireless eye of the vulture, an infinite speck hung motionless in the empyreal heights of cosmic space, was something else—the swaying, tottering, reeling figure of a man.

The vulture watched and waited, knowing, either from marvellous instinct or from more marvellous mental process, that he would not have long to wait. As the man fell, the predatory bird, with motionless wing, slid down the sky in graceful circling swoop, and again hung motionless, a little nearer to his quarry.

As the man rose, tottered on, staggered and again fell, the vulture repeated its manœuvre, and again hung motionless, nearer to its prey. . . .

Would the still figure move again? Was it yet too feeble to resist the onslaught of the fierce beak that should tear the eyeballs from the living head?

The vulture dropped a few thousand feet lower. . . .

§ 2

With a groan, the recumbent man drew up his knees, turned on his side, planted his hands on the hot sand, and, after kneeling prone for a minute, struggled once more to his feet, and bravely strove to climb the long billow of soft loose sand that lay before him.

Beneath the hood of his dirty white *kayfiyeh* head-dress, bound round with *agal* ropes of camel-hair, his dark face was that of a dead man—the eyes glazed, the protruding tongue black, the cracked skin tight across the jutting bones. Through the rags of his filthy *jellabia*, his arms and shoulders showed lean and black; his bare legs were those of a skeleton. . . . An Arab scarecrow, a *khaiyul*, endowed with a spark of life.

At the top of the ridge the man swayed, put his hand above his eyes, and peered out into the dancing heat-haze ahead.

Burning sand and burning sky. . . . Not even a mirage to give a faint hope that it might not be what it was—a last added torture.

He sank to the ground. . . .

An hour later the vulture did the same, and settled himself, with huddled head and drooping wings, to continue his patient watch with unwinking eye.

Anon he strutted towards the body, with clumsy gait, and foolishly jerking head, his cruel hooked beak open in anticipation.

§ 3

"Allah! What is that . . .? Look, brothers, something white on yonder sand-hill—and a vulture. . . ."

The speaker reined-in his camel and pointed, his long-sighted gaze fixed on the far-distant spot where he had seen something that to European eyes would have been invisible.

Lowering his outstretched hand, he unslung his rifle as the other Touareg came to a halt around him.

"A trap perchance," growled another of the Wolves of the Desert, from behind the heavy blue veil that hid all but his eyes. He was a huge man, more negroid of countenance than the rest.

"Go, thou, and spring it then," said the leader; and the score or so of raiders sat motionless on their camels while the black-faced man rode off.

Cautiously scanning the terrain from the top of each sand-hill, he circled round the motionless bundle of rags, as the vulture flapped heavily away to alight at a safe and convenient distance.

After a long and searching stare around him, the rider approached the body, his ready rifle in both hands. He brought the camel to its knees.

As he dismounted, the rest of the band rode towards the spot. By the time they reached it, the scout had turned the man upon his back and discovered that he was unarmed, unprovided, foodless, waterless, and utterly valueless. There was not so much as a rag of clothing that was worth the trouble of removing.

"A miserable *miskeen* indeed," said the scout to the leader of the band, as he rode up. "Not a *mitkal* on the dog's carcas. Not even an empty purse. . . ."

"Curse the son of Satan!" replied the leader, and spat.

"There may be something on his camel, if we follow his tracks back to where he left its carcas," observed a lean and hawk-faced rogue, who was trying to force his beautiful white *mehara* to tread upon the body.

"Yea, a sack of pearls, thou fool," agreed the leader, and added: "Come on. Shall we waste the day chattering around this carrion?"

As the band rode off, he of the negroid countenance jumped on to his kneeling beast, and as it lurched to its feet, he emitted a joyous whoop, and either in light-hearted playfulness, or as a mark of his disgust at the poverty of so poor a thing, he discharged his rifle at the body.

The body jerked and quivered, and, as the robber rode off, it writhed over on to its face, to the annoyance of the observant vulture.

Not a man of this band of mysterious blue-veiled robbers, the terrible "Forgotten of God", looked round; and all rode on as heartlessly indifferent to the dreadful fate of this fellow desert-dweller, as if it might not well be their own upon the morrow's morrow.

Life is very cheap in the desert.

CHAPTER II

EL HAMEL

TOWARDS evening of the same day, a desert caravan of semi-nomad Arabs—"peaceful" herdsmen, armed to the teeth, and desiring to fight no foe of greater strength than themselves, followed in the track of the Touareg raiders.

At their head rode their aged Sheikh, a venerable white-bearded gentleman, with the noble face of a Biblical patriarch, and much of the philosophy, standards, ideals and habits of such—a modern Abraham, Isaac, or Jacob.

Beside him rode an Esau, a hairy man, a mighty hunter before the Lord. In his dark face was nothing noble, save in so far as a look of forceful and ruthless determination makes for nobility of countenance.

"Yea—of a surety are we safest in the very tracks of these sons of Shaitan, these Forgotten of Allah—may they burn in Gehennum," said the Sheikh to his companions, and, turning on his camel, he looked back at the long and straggling column whereon the bobbing rolling *bassourabs* showed that prized and honoured women rode hidden from the eyes of men.

"Thou art right, Wise One," replied the burly younger man. "No bullet enters the hole made by another bullet, and no knife nor spear strikes a bleeding wound. No other raiding-party will follow this one, nor will these Enemies of God turn about in their own tracks."

And it came to pass that as the sun began to set, and the old Sheikh prepared to halt the caravan for the evening *asha* prayer—when all would dismount, and, kneeling in long lines behind their leader, would follow him in devout supplication to Allah, their heads bowed to the sand in the direction of Mecca—the eyes of his companion, called Suleiman the Strong, fell upon the bundle of rags on the distant sand-hill.

"By the Beard of the Prophet," he exclaimed, pointing. "A man! And he may not be dead, or that vulture would be at work."

"If it is one of the Forgotten of God he will soon be dead," said the aged Sheikh, laying his hand upon the silver hilt of the curved dagger that was stuck through the front of the broad girdle bound about the long white *jellabia* beneath his *burnous*.

"Not too soon, let us hope, my father," growled Suleiman.

"He may live long enough to suffer something of what my brother suffered at Touareg hands, before his brave soul went to the bosom of the Prophet. . . . May dogs defile the graves of their grandfathers. . . ."

The two rode to the spot where the man lay, followed by several of the caravan guards, fighting-men armed with flintlock guns, rifles, or long lances, and straight heavy swords.

"He is no Touareg, but a victim of the Touareg," said Suleiman, slipping down from his camel without stopping to make it kneel. "See, they have shot him, and he with scarcely any blood to flow. . . ."

"He may not be dead even yet," he added, after placing his ear to the man's heart and holding the bright blade of his sword to the latter's nostrils. "He is only shot through the shoulder. . . . Shall I cut his throat?"

"No. Give him water," replied the Sheikh, and crying, "*Adar-ya-yan! Adar-ya-yan!*" to his camel, brought it to its knees. "He who is merciful to the poor and needy is acceptable to Allah."

"Go, one of you, for Hadji Abdul Salam," he added, turning to the impassive fighting-men, who looked on with calm indifference, viewing this evidence of desert tragedy, this agony and death of a fellow-man, with as much interest as they would the fall of a sparrow to the ground.

Is not "Here is a stranger—let us cut his throat" the expression of a sound, safe and profitable principle?

Taking his goatskin water-bottle from where it hung at the high peak of his saddle, the Sheikh untied the neck of it, and dropped a little of the desert's most priceless and precious treasure upon the black lips and tongue.

A fellow-feeling makes us wondrous kind, and the fact that this derelict was a Touareg victim gave him a claim that he would otherwise not have had, and brought him kindnesses he might not have received. Skeletons and

175

dried corpses of men are, in the desert, too common a sight to warrant a second glance; wounded men are a burden; and dying men will soon be dead.

Hadji Abdul Salam, a fat and (for an Arab) jolly rogue, rode up from beside the camel that bore his two wives in a gaily striped *bassourab* (or balloon-like tent), and, putting on an air of wisdom, examined the body. He had a great reputation in the Tribe, by reason of having cured the Sheikh of a mortal sickness by the right use of a hair of the Prophet's beard, a cup of water, in which was soaked a paper bearing a very special extract from the Q'ran, and the application of a very hot iron to the old gentleman's stomach. He also had a most valuable prescription for ophthalmia—muttering another Q'ranic extract seven times, and spitting in the patient's eyes seven times after each mutter.

This learned physician pronounced life extinct.

"Starved to death," he said. "Then died of thirst. Whereafter he received a wound which killed him."

This bulletin satisfied all present, save, apparently, the corpse, whose eyelids fluttered as the blackened tongue moved feebly in a kind of lip-licking motion.

"But I have brought him back to life, as you see," the good doctor promptly added, and his great reputation was enhanced.

§ 2

And alive, just alive, the foundling proved to be.

Curiously, and inconsequently enough, and yet again naturally enough, the old Sheikh set great store by the recovery of the man whom he had saved.

Had he not thus thwarted the Touareg, undone what they had done, plucked a brand from their burning, and was not this human salvage his, and a record and proof of his virtue? The Sheikh had reached an age at which proofs of virtue may soon be wanted in the sight of Allah.

He had the sick and wounded man rolled up in *feloudji* tent-coverings, splintered with tent-poles, and slung at the side of a good *djemel* baggage-camel.

"See that the dog dies, you," whispered Suleiman the

Strong to the camel-man in charge of the *djemel*, as the caravan moved on again after the evening prayer had been said. "If he be alive at the next halt, squeeze his throat a little. On thy head be it."

Why add a burden and a useless mouth to a caravan crossing a waterless desert?

A little later the Sheikh sent for this camel-man.

"See that this stranger lives," said he. "The succour of the afflicted is pleasing to Allah the Compassionate, the All-Merciful. On thy head be it."

Abdullah, the camel-man, felt that there was altogether too much on his head; but the old Sheikh was still the Sheikh, and he had better "hear his words" and put prudence before pleasure. Abdullah was a good killer, and, like the rest of us, enjoyed doing that which he could do well.

At the next halt, the foundling was still alive, and was distinctly seen to swallow the water that was poured into his mouth.

Suleiman the Strong looked at Abdullah el Jemmal, the camel-man, and, with a decidedly unpleasant smile, touched the hilt of his knife. The old Sheikh praised Abdullah, and said it was well. Of this, Abdullah felt doubtful.

After some hours spent lying flat and still upon the ground, the Unknown was certainly better. He drank camel-milk and opened his eyes.

Doctor Abdul Salam also had time to give proper care and attention to the man's wound.

He wrote a really potent quotation from the Q'ran upon a piece of paper, and fixed it, with blood and saliva, just where it would do most good—over the entry-hole of the bullet.

As the bullet had passed right through the man's shoulder, the good doctor confessed that he was really only wasting time in probing for it with a pair of pliers generally used for gun repairs—though this was, in a manner of speaking, really a kind of gun-repair, as it were.

Doctor Abdul Salam explained further to the old Sheikh as they fingered the rather large exit-hole, that he would leave it open for a few days—in order that anything in the nature of a devil might escape without let or hindrance —and that then he would close it nicely with some clay, should they be fortunate enough to find any at the next oasis.

This, he explained, would effectually prevent the entrance of anything in the nature of a devil, and so the man really ought to be all right. And, in any case, whatever Allah willed was obviously the will of Allah. Quite so. *Inshallah.*

The doctor thought the Sheikh was getting a bit senile, to pursue a whim to this extreme—but if the Sheikh wished to oblige Allah, the doctor wished to oblige the Sheikh.

After another long rest at the next halt, the Unknown was again better—if his wound was worse. He drank *halib* and water greedily, and looked about him. But if he could use his eyes, he could not use his tongue, or else did not understand what was said to him.

After each halt he grew a little stronger, and by the time the tribe reached an oasis, he could totter about on his feet, and wash his wound for himself.

The good *hakim*, Hadji Abdul Salam, however, washed his hands—of the patient. He would take no further responsibility for the fool, since he thought he knew more about the treatment of gun-shot wounds than the doctor did; and either could not, or would not, swallow the doctor's words—written on wads of paper—precious *hejabs*, warranted to exorcise all devils of sickness and destruction.

Hearing the physician complain, Suleiman the Strong bade him waste neither words nor skill, for as soon as the Sheikh tired of his fancy, he himself intended to cure the Unknown of all troubles, with complete finality. He had a feeling against him, inexplicable but powerful.

And daily the Unknown grew in strength, and by the time the caravan reached its destination, some weeks later, the *qsar* of the Tribe, he could ride a camel, and could almost fend for himself.

But his wound grew worse, and for months he seemed like to die, for he could not get at the hole in his back, whereas the flies could.

The Tribe called him "El Gherib", the Poor Stranger, and "El Hamel", the Foundling, the Lost One, and waited for the old Sheikh to tire of him.

But as the months went by, the old Sheikh's fancy seemed to turn to infatuation, and, far from tiring of the man and ceasing to interest himself in his existence, he cherished and cared for him. When, eventually, he recovered, the Sheikh raised him to prominence and importance.

El Hamel was he whom the Sheikh delighted to honour, and Suleiman the Strong sharpened his knife and bided his time—for the Sheikh was getting old, and his sole surviving son was but a boy.

When the Sheikh was gathered to his fathers, the stranger would die, for Suleiman would be Regent of the Tribe.

Undeniably, however, El Hamel was a remarkable person. In the first place, he was afflicted of Allah and quite dumb; in the second place, he was unbelievably skilful with a rifle and with the throwing-knife; in the third place, he was incredibly strong; in the fourth, he was a most notable horseman and horse-master, even among Arab horsemen; in the fifth, he was indubitably a far better doctor than the *hakim* himself; and lastly, and most remarkable of all, he was a magician—and a magician of power.

This wonderful great gift had come to light in this wise. The Sheikh had lost his *djedouel*, his famous amulet, a silver box wherein reposed a Hair of the Beard of the Prophet, bought in Mecca for an enormous sum; as well as an extremely holy and potent *hejab* or charm—a knuckle-bone of one of the holiest *marabouts* who had ever adorned this terrestrial sphere.

Surely no one could have sunk so low as to have stolen so holy a thing from the Sheikh's own person, and so he must have lost it. Gone it was, anyhow, and great was the commotion throughout the big *dour* (encampment), and great the rewards offered for its recovery. . . .

On the seventh evening from the day of the loss, El Hamel, that sad and silent man, sat, as usual, before the little, low black tent that was his, and looked remote and wise. Cross-legged, on his small striped carpet, silent and inscrutable, he made a goatskin thong for his sandal, and, anon, regarded Infinity and the doings of his fellow- men.

A goat-herd slave-boy sat and watched him, one, Moussa el R'Orab, Moussa the Crow.

Anon the old Sheikh, terribly upset by his loss, and still more upset by the evil augury of such a loss, strolled past the seated man who salaamed with deep respect.

The Sheikh paused, turned, seated himself beside his protégé, and settled down for a good *faddhl*, the meandering idle gossip so dear to his old heart—as to that of most Arabs. And a gossip with this fine-looking dignified man was particularly agreeable, as the poor fellow's infirmity prevented his taking an active part in it, and rendered him an accomplished listener.

The Sheikh talked on—about his loss; Suleiman the Strong strolled up, accompanied by his good friend, Hadji Abdul Salam, and from time to time various other prominent citizens of this tent-city joined the growing circle of listeners and respectful talkers.

It was the first time since the Sheikh's loss that the evening *faddhl* had taken place outside the tent of El Hamel, a thing that occurred fairly frequently. . . .

The talk dragged on interminably, and the great full moon rose and illuminated the oasis, and the groves of date palms, the hundreds of low black goatskin and felt camel-hair tents of various sizes, the flocks and herds of goats and camels, the gossiping groups, the women at the cooking-fires, the water-drawers at the *shaduf*, and wide ring of watchful sentries.

Suddenly the dumb man raised both of his clenched fists above his head, pointed to the moon, again to where the sun had set, and then threw his open hands dramatically towards the sky in an attitude of beseeching prayer.

Soon a mass of snow-white foam issued from his dumb lips and flecked his black beard, and his eyes rolled back until only the whites showed.

He looked terrible, and the Hadji Abdul Salam prepared to become professional. The grave Arabs stared in awed wonder at this manifestation of the work of *djinns*, spirits, or devils, and a deep silence fell.

The man seemed to recover, put his hand behind him

into his tent, brought out a vessel of water, and drank.

He then stared with starting eyeballs at the ground before his feet. All eyes followed his gaze.... Nothing... nothing but flat trodden sand, no scorpion, snake, nor hornéd toad was there.

The dumb man made passes with his hands above the spot at which he stared. He poured water on the ground, as though pouring libations to the memory of departed friends.

More passes, more pouring forth of water, more impassioned gesticulations towards the unanswering sky—and then—did their eyes deceive them? Or even as the man sat, with eyes and hands strained beseechingly aloft, did a gleam of silver show through the sand, and *did the lost box of the Sheikh rise up through the earth at their very feet,* before their very eyes, as they stared and stared incredulous?

It did.

The large audience sat for seconds as though turned to stone, and then a shudder ran through it, a gasping sigh escaped it, and, as the old Sheikh's quivering hand tentatively went out towards this magic thing, a great cry went up, so that men came running.

§ 4

The Sheikh summoned up his undoubted courage and seized the box firmly, fondled it, opened it, restored it to its place in his bosom—and then turned and embraced the dumb man as warmly and fervently as he had ever embraced his favourite wife.

"Let him be addressed as *Sidi,* and let him be known as '*the Magician*' henceforth," he said. "*The Dumb Magician —the Gift of Allah,*" and again embracing the Magician, he arose, cast a leathern bag of money into the man's lap, heavy Turkish *medjidies*—and retired to pray apart.

Tongues were loosened.

"No—there was no humbug about it. It was no conjuror's trick."

"His hands were above his head, and his eyes fixed on the sky when it happened."

"No, he had not flung the box there, nor had it been

flung from the dark tent by an accomplice. It had suddenly appeared from below the sand and had quietly and steadily risen up to the surface and lain there, while all men watched."

"No, he had not buried it and then shoved it up with his toe. His feet had never been off the carpet on which he sat, and he had never once touched the sand from beneath which the box had risen. . . ."

It was a plain sheer miracle, worked in brilliant moonlight before the eyes of all! . . .

The dumb man sat silent and still, with abstracted gaze, while the rest broke into chattering, gesticulating knots of bewildered men, arguing and shouting in wild excitement.

He then prostrated himself in prayer, upon the site of the miracle, his head upon the ground, and thus the awed crowd left him.

§ 5

"Yea, brother," agreed Hadji Abdul Salam, as he and Suleiman the Strong, followed at a respectful distance by one, Moussa el R'Orab, Moussa the Crow, goat-herd and admiring slave of El Hamel, walked away in the direction of the tent of the former.

"It is, as thou sayest, time that he died."

"I will let that accursed dog Abdullah el Jemmal, the camel-driver, know that unless this dumb devil and father of devils dies before the next moon, it will be the last moon that Abdullah sees," growled Suleiman, grinding his teeth. Not for nothing was he known as El Ma'ian—he who has the Evil Eye.

"He has marvellous powers, and the strength of ten," observed the *hakim*. "But there are draughts which are more powerful than he. . . . A little something of which I know, in his *cous-cous* or curds . . ."

"The cunning dog has a portion of all his cooked food eaten by Moussa, the goat-boy, long before he tastes it," was the moody reply. "The hungry Moussa eats right willingly, knowing that none try to poison him who hath a food-taster. . . . No, it is a task for Abdullah. . . . A stab in the dark. . . ."

"And what would the Sheikh do?" smiled the good *hakim*.

"Impale Abdullah, living, on a stake, after hearing my evidence," replied Suleiman; "and thus shall we be rid of two nuisances at one blow. . . ."

The two gentlemen discussed the matter further, sitting at the door of Abdul Salam's tent, and—while Moussa the Crow, enthusiastic spy of El Hamel's, lay behind the tent and listened, feigning sleep—Suleiman sounded his host as to his willingness to consider a scheme, whereby their food should disagree with both the Sheikh and the Dumb Magician simultaneously, on the occasion of the next invitation to eat, extended by the Sheikh to his now glorified protégé. There would be no previous "tasting" then.

But Suleiman the Strong quickly saw that he was going too fast, and that he was proposing to Abdul Salam a risky thing, the doing of a dangerous deed for which the *hakim* saw no present reason, and in which he saw no personal profit either. And as he distrusted the Hadji as much as the Hadji distrusted him, Suleiman affected to be jesting, and turned the conversation to the miracle, to which he alluded as a rascally trick.

But it appeared that neither he nor the worthy doctor could offer the slightest suggestion as to how the "trick" was done, nor propound the vaguest outline of a theory in elucidation of the mystery.

Nor could any man of the few scoffers who were among the intimates, toadies, and followers of Suleiman the Strong; and the remainder of the tribe believed in the Dumb Magician to a man.

Nevertheless, there are those who, having beheld a similar miracle in other parts of the world, say that the miracle-worker excavates a hole at the required spot and then fills it with some material that expands rapidly and quickly when made wet—some such substance, for example, as *bhoosa*, yeast, sawdust, grain, or bran.

They aver that the miracle-monger presses the substance tightly together between four stones, covers it with a layer of sand, places the object (which is to spring miraculously out of the earth) upon the pressed expansive material, and lightly covers all with dust, earth and sand. The hour strikes, and soon after the material is wetted—up comes the hidden object.

It is said that Mother Earth has been safely delivered of many brazen gods in this wise, to the credit and enrichment of their even more brazen priests.

But those who talk thus of expansive "material" are obviously materialists, and certainly not of those to whom miracles appeal. . . .

That night Moussa el R'Orab had something to tell El Hamel, the latter smiling gently as the boy spoke and gesticulated.

§6

As the infatuation of the old Sheikh waxed, so did the jealousy and wrath of El Ma'ian, known as Suleiman the Strong; and it grew apparent to all men that the same *qsar* could not much longer contain both him and El Hamel, the Foundling, the Dumb Magician, the Given of Allah.

Even to the Sheikh it grew clear that one of them must go; so truculent, surly, outrageous, did Suleiman increasingly become; and the old man's heart was heavy within him, for he loved his strong, wise Foundling, this big man of dignity and strength and magic power, whom he himself had found and saved; and he feared the forceful and influential Suleiman.

But one of them must go, or there would be quarrels and strife, parties and factions in that united tribe. . . .

It was Suleiman the Strong who went. . . .

And he nearly went by *sirath*, the bridge that spans Hell. . . .

One evening, the sullen brooding temper that seemed to smoulder behind his cruel eyes, blazed up, and he was as one possessed by *djinns*.

The old Sheikh was standing by the lance (which, planted before his tent, bore his *bairaq* or flag and ensign of rule) talking to El Hamel and others of his favourites.

To him came Suleiman, a *mish'ab* camel-stick in his hand, and a black sullen scowl on his face. He was followed by fat and smiling Hadji Abdul Salam, Abdullah el Jemmal, and certain others.

Thrusting into the circle of gravely conversing elders, Suleiman confronted the Sheikh and poured forth a torrent of indignant and minatory words, pointing as he did so at the impassive, silent El Hamel—his outstretched shaking hand almost touching the latter's face.

The Sheikh rebuked him sharply, and raised his hand to point. "*Emishi!*" he snapped. "Go—thou growling dog—or by the Beard of the Prophet . . ."

And then the impossible happened. For, even as the venerable Sheikh uttered the word "Beard", the jealousy-maddened Suleiman seized the long grey beard of the Sheikh in his left hand, shook him to and fro, and raised aloft his right hand, clutching the *mish'ab*, as though about to strike!

But it was Sidi el Hamel who struck.

With incredible swiftness and terrible force, he smote the impious madman with his clenched fist, and men gasped in wonder as Suleiman the Strong reeled staggering back, and fell, apparently dead.

"Bind him," stammered the Sheikh, almost speechless with rage at the unbelievable, unforgivable insult. "I will have him impaled, dead or alive . . ." and the old man trembled with wrath and indignation.

Sidi el Hamel ventured to intervene. Touching his breast and forehead, he salaamed to the Sheikh, joined his hands in entreaty and then, stooping, seized Suleiman by the arm, and partly dragging, partly carrying him, bore him to where the women crowded round the *jalib* draw-well, and the *darraja* roller creaked and groaned above the *'idda* superstructure, as a harnessed camel hauled upon the well-rope.

At the foot of a kind of palisade of split palm-trunks that banked up the earth around the stone-built mouth of the well, he flung the man down, and made signs to those who had brought camel-ropes wherewith to bind him, that they should secure him to the wooden wall.

Tearing off Suleiman's *burnous*, El Hamel raised him to his feet, and held him upright while his outspread arms were lashed to the tops of two posts, and his feet secured to a stump by a stout cord that passed round it and them. . . .

What was the Magician about to do? Would he leave the sacrilegious villain, the almost parricidal criminal to die of starvation and thirst, or was he going to shoot the dog? Men crowded round, with growls of indignant wrath, and the women fled to the tents of their lords.

El Hamel dashed water, from a dug-out trough, in the face of Suleiman, and waited. In a few minutes he recovered his senses, opened his eyes, and stared about him. The Magician stepped back several yards and motioned the onlookers to stand aside. He drew his knife.

Ah! He was going to give an exhibition of knife-throwing, to plant the dagger in the black heart of the dog who had most foully insulted and outraged his Chief and Master, Allah's representative to the Tribe, the Prophet's Vicar upon earth, the Giver of Salt. It was well.

The Sheikh approached and stood beside El Hamel. That great man removed his *burnous*, balanced the dagger upon his hand, and with a swift movement—threw.

The silence was broken by the sound of a swift intaking of breath as the knife stuck and quivered, not in the broad breast of Suleiman the Strong, but in the wood beside his right ear.

El Hamel had missed for once! No matter—the more torture for the foul Suleiman.

With a merry laugh, Hadji Abdul Salam tendered his own knife that El Hamel might throw again.

"This one balances well, Sidi," said he.

El Hamel took the knife, balanced it upon the palm of his great hand, and, with a lightning swoop of his huge arm—threw.

The knife quivered—in wood; beside the left ear of Suleiman the Strong.

Again there was the sound of swift intaking of breath, and the good *hakim* giggled like a girl.

"Try again, my son, and may Allah guide thine arm," said the Sheikh, and placed his great silver-hilted dagger in the hand of El Hamel.

"Make an end, thou squinting, cross-eyed dumb dog," cried Suleiman the Strong, and stared hardily at his slayer, though his face had taken on a sickly greenish hue.

Once again the Magician poised the knife and his great powerful body and—threw.

With a thud the heavy knife stuck in the post above Suleiman's head, and all but touched it. The three knives seemed to hold and frame his face in glistening metal.

And then it dawned upon the watchers that El Hamel was *not* missing his mark, and all men marvelled.

Suleiman the Strong stood like a statue.

Abdullah el Jemmal respectfully tendered a long lean blade. A moment later it stood out from beside the shoulder of Suleiman, its point buried in wood, its blade an inch from his flesh. . . .

Another stuck exactly opposite that. . . . A dozen knives were offered to the thrower, and in as many minutes stood in pairs on either side of the motionless man.

Suddenly he cried, "Enough! Make an end, in the Name of Allah the Merciful, the Compassionate," and, as the thrower raised another knife, he collapsed and hung forward, fainting, in his bonds.

But El Hamel had heard from Moussa the Crow of plotted poisonings and the encompassing of the death of the kindly Sheikh by the vilest treachery and ingratitude.

Striding to the man, he again dashed water in his face, and soon Suleiman the Strong was strong once more, and held himself erect.

"Make an end, Sidi," he said. "In the Name of the Prophet make an end."

"*As thou wouldest have made an end,*" screamed Moussa el R'Orab, pointing—and Hadji Abdul Salam eyed the boy sharply.

El Hamel pulled out the Sheikh's knife from where it stuck above Suleiman's head, and Suleiman closed his eyes and awaited the cutting of his throat.

El Hamel took the knife to where the old Sheikh stood, and returned it to him, touching his forehead and breast as he did so.

He then made the sign of a man putting a rifle to his shoulder to fire it, and pointed to his tent, and Moussa the Crow sped thither and brought him the fine Italian magazine-rifle that the Sheikh had bestowed upon his favourite.

Men smiled and nodded. So this was how Suleiman the Strong was to die!

Throwing the rifle to his shoulder, El Hamel pointed it at the face of Suleiman the Strong.

"Look upon thy death, thou dog," cried the Sheikh, and Suleiman opened his eyes.

"*Now* make an end, Sidi," he begged, "in the Sacred Names of God," and El Hamel fired rapidly five times.

Suleiman the Strong sank to the ground—untouched—the cords that fastened his wrist severed against the posts, and hanging idly.

El Hamel pointed out into the desert.

"Yea, go, thou dog," cried the old Sheikh. "Thou bitter tentless dog, go forth and scavenge. With nothing that is thine, begone within the hour. . . ." And El Hamel nodded in approval, drew his hand across his throat significantly, and pointed again.

The feet of Suleiman the Strong were untied, and with blows and curses he was driven to his tents.

When he departed, well within the allotted hour, he was followed by a flight of stones, some of the best-aimed of which came from the hand of the good physician, Abdul Salam. . . .

But Hadji Abdul Salam thereafter fancied that El Hamel eyed him unduly, and perhaps more critically, than a *moub'abbir*, a pious and learned man, should be eyed by a desert Foundling. . . .

And so the fame and honour of Sidi el Hamel, the Magician, the Given of Allah, grew apace, and his standing and importance in the tribe waxed with them.

More and more the Sheikh depended upon him, and more and more the Sidi strove for the common weal.

He trained riflemen until a few were almost as skilful as himself, many were as good as Marbruk ben Hassan, the Lame, hitherto undisputed best shot of the Tribe, and all (who possessed rifles) were far above the desert average.

Dumb though he was, he also taught them, patiently and slowly, how to attack unscathed, instead of charging wildly into a hail of bullets.

After getting squads of fighting-men to lie in line, flat upon the ground, he would make a few wriggle forward, while the rest aimed their rifles at the imaginary foe; and these halt and aim their rifles while yet others wriggled forward; and so on.

He taught the enthusiastic and devoted fighting-men

the arts of volley-firing and fire-control. He made a whistle of wood, like a short *quaita*, and gave signals with it, standing afar off.

He taught selected leaders an elementary drill by signals, and these taught their followers. He showed the horsemen and camel-men many things that they did not know, such as the treatment of ailments, and he scowled angrily and dangerously upon any whom he found saddling a galled beast and neglecting back-sores.

Hadji Abdul Salam, who knew nothing more than the administering of *zarnikh*, an acid concoction, to sick camels, and the muttering of charms over sick horses, looked on with merry laughing face and unsmiling eyes. El Hamel also cultivated the Sheikh's Soudanese soldier-slaves, between whom and the Bedouin fighting-men there is always jealousy, and made a small camel-corps of them a nucleus of the *élite*.

He also made smiling overtures to an aged wonder called "Yakoub-who-goes-without-water" and his family. He and his three ancient brothers were famous for their gift of living, when others died, if lost in the waterless desert, or on finding the waterhole dried up, at the end of a long and terrible journey.

An ordinary man will make a *girba* of water last five or six days in winter and three in summer, but Yakub and his brothers would double the time—and, as a camel can only carry four *girbas*, this is a valuable gift. . . .

Later El Hamel made these men into a wonderful Desert Intelligence Department, and, as poor old worthless beggars, they hung about oases, *dousars*, *qsars* and desert camps, learning much and bringing invaluable inform-ation. . . .

§ 7

And when the day dawned, of which the old Sheikh feared he would not see the night, he gathered his *ekhwan* and elders and chief men of the Tribe about his couch, and bade them regard the Sidi el Hamel as Regent of the tribe during the many remaining years of the childhood and youth of his son, and commanded that his *aba* should

189

descend upon the shoulders of the Sidi during the boy's minority.

Upon the Sidi's hand he placed his ring, graven with the sacred seal, in token of his power, and lifting up his voice he blessed him in the Name of Allah and of Mahomet his Prophet, ending with the words, "*Rahmat ullahi Allahim*—"the peace of God be upon him."

And the first "Amen" was that of Hadji Abdul Salam.

A little later, the old man was gathered to his fathers, and was buried with great honour and much mourning in the *kouba* by the little mosque, which stood near the oasis and *qsar*, the headquarters and depot of this semi-nomadic tribe.

Shortly afterwards came the great fast of Ramzan, and at the end of that weary month, and on the occasion of the great feast that marked its termination, the Sidi (accepted by all men as Sheikh Regent) worked a new and wondrous miracle.

He worked it upon himself. For, as all stood awaiting the appearance of the new moon of the next month, he strode forth before them, and with upraised arms stretched out his hands towards the horizon.

He then turned towards the watching, waiting assembly and pointed to his mouth. What was about to happen? All stared and wondered in silence.

The moon rose and in that instant the miracle was worked. The dumb Sheikh, Sidi el Hamel, the Magician, opened his mouth, and in deep sonorous voice intoned the *shehada*.

Across the vast silence of the desert and the awe-stricken throng, rolled the solemn words, "*As hadu illa Illaha ill Allah wa as hadu inna Mahommed an rasul Allah*," and, as he turned in the direction of the *kubla* at Mecca and recited the *fatha*, the opening *sura* of the Q'ran, the people fell upon their faces.

The Dumb had spoken.

Thereafter the Sheikh, Sidi el Hamel, spoke seldom and briefly. He uttered only short orders, curt replies, concise comments. It almost seemed as though speech hurt him, and that his long silence—perhaps the silence of a lifetime—caused his Arabic to be halting, like the speech of a man who has sojourned in foreign parts for many years, speaking not the language of his people once in all that time.

But now that the miracle had come to pass and he could speak, his rule and influence became yet more powerful; and more easily he trained his fighting-men; rebuked and punished evil-doers; gave orders and instruction in agricultural industry, animal management, tribal policies, and pursued his strange fads of health-preservation, sanitation, care of domestic beasts, and justice to all prisoners and captives, mercy to slaves, women, and other animals.

Nor would he ever act as *Imam* and lead the prayers, leaving that pious duty to Hadji Abdul Salam, who on such occasions contrived to look as holy as Sidi Mohammed ben Ali, the Reformer of Islam, in spite of his round, fat, laughing face, sleepy narrow eyes and loose lips—for was he not a *hadji*, a man who had made the *hadj*, the journey to Mecca, the House of Allah?

Was he not a *zawia*-trained *khouan*, a holy man indeed? Who could doubt it, that heard his sonorous call to prayer, "*Haya alla Salat! Haya alla falah!*"—and his leading of the *fedjr*, *dhuhr*, *asr*, *mogreb* and *asha* prayers at morning, midday, afternoon, sunset and night?

Who so fanatical a good Moslem as he, and so fierce against the *Ahl Kitab*—the People of the Book (Jews and Christians) and all other unmentionable *kafirs*.

So good Hadji Abdul Salam, the *hakim*, was the chief *imam*, and, making himself the Sheikh's shadow and echo, aspired to be the Sheikh's *Wakil* and *Wazir*.

§ 8

It was not very long before the value of the Sheikh el Hamel's innovations was proven. One of his wonderful old desert-men, Yakoub-who-can-live-without-water, arrived one night on foot, his camel lying dead a day's journey to the north-west, with news of the great Touareg band that made this the southernmost point of its annual journey in search of plunder.

If unresisted by the Tribe it would rest and feast fatly at the expense of its unhappy hosts, set them to pack camel-fodder, have the date-harvest loaded on to the *hamla* baggage-camels of the Tribe, make a selection of children, young men, and maidens, and depart with such of the camels, horses, asses, goats, rugs, clothing, and money as could not be previously removed or hidden.

Slaughter there might or might not be—probably not very much, and that only in a quite playful spirit. . . .

Wholesale flight was out of the question. What tribe burdened with women and children, tents, property, goats, asses, and slow *hamla* camels, can flee before an unencumbered *harka* of fierce hawk-like robbers, mounted on swift *mehari* that travel like the wind?

The forgotten of God, the Blue-Veiled Silent Ones, would leave all their previously gathered booty at a depot, guarded by their precious and faithful black slaves (whom they breed on slave-farms, like cattle); and their lightning raid upon the fleeing tribe would be like that of eagles upon chickens. Moreover the extra trouble given to these Lords of the Desert would not be easily atoned. . . .

The *ekhwan* gathered at the tent of the Sheikh el Hamel, and each spoke his mind in turn, the oldest first.

Some were for following ancient custom and leaving the *douar* to unhindered plundering by the Touareg. The sooner they got what they wanted, the sooner they would be gone. The less they were thwarted, the less bloodthirsty would they be. The very pick of the youths, girls, and children might be sent off into the desert, with the very best of the camels, horses, asses and goats—but not too many must go, lest the Touareg wax suspicious and torture the elders until someone break down and confess. . . .

Some were for drawing up as imposing an array of armed camel-men, horsemen and infantry as was possible, and letting them hover near, in full view of the Touareg, in the hope that, as sometimes happened, the robbers would decide not to over-provoke so dangerous a force, but to rob reasonably and justly, leaving the victims a fair residue of their property, the bare means of subsistence, and many of their young relatives.

One or two, including Marbruk ben Hassan the Lame, showing that the Sheikh el Hamel's lessons in Minor

Tactics of War had borne fruit, actually wanted to put up a genuine fight—receive the visitors with volleys of rifle-fire, and if they did not succeed in driving them off, see the thing through and die in defence of tent and child.

"And what of tent and child when you are dead?" inquired the Sheikh el Hamel.

Marbruk ben Hassan the Lame shrugged his enormous shoulders.

"What of them in any case, Sidi?" he asked. "Shall our eyes behold their defilement or, closed in brave death, see nothing of their shame and misery?"

"What says the good Hadji Abdul Salam, the Learned and Holy One?" asked the Sheikh.

The Learned and Holy One thought it would be a sound move for all the wealthy and important men of the Tribe —themselves there present, in fact—to clear out for a space, with all that was theirs. After a sojourn in the desert, away to the south-east, they could return, console the survivors, and help to clear up the mess. . . .

It seemed sound sense to several aged patriarchs, who had seen too much of the Touareg and his ways to have any desire to see more.

"They cut off the hands of my little son and the feet of my favourite wife," wailed one white-bearded ancient. "Had I fled instead of fighting, they would have been alive now. . . ."

"Yea, Father," murmured Marbruk ben Hassan, "and the little son would have been a grandfather and the fair woman a toothless hag. . . . We die but once. . . ."

And all having spoken and given the counsel that their experience, their courage, their hope and their caution prompted, the Sheikh el Hamel lifted up his voice and gave decision.

"We will not flee," he said. "We will not send the best of what is ours out into the desert. We will not leave the Tribe and go afar off with what is ours. We will not make a show of strength and watch the enemy while he robs us. We will not defend the oasis. . . ."

All stared in silence upon this enigmatical strong man, the Sheikh Regent of the Tribe, the Sheikh Magician.

"We will go and find our enemy," he concluded, "and fall upon him and destroy him utterly."

And in the silence that followed, Marbruk ben Hassan fired his rifle into the air.

"*Wallahi!*" he cried. "Our Sheikh is a *man*, by Allah!"

"We will leave not one of them alive to return and tell the tale," said the Sheikh again.

"*Inshallah*," murmured the *ekhwan* doubtfully, and the Sheikh strode away, calling for the chosen leaders of the fighting-men and the aged scout Yakoub, who should be their guide.

To these he made a brief speech in short curt sentences, and illustrated his meaning by the ancient method of the writing-on-the-sand. Around a stone which represented the Touareg camp he drew a circle with his knife and then a smaller circle within it, and then another. And to each leader-of-a-score he spoke in turn, each hearing his words, smiling, and replying,

"*Hamdulillah!* It shall be so. *Inshallah!*"

An hour later these men, each followed by a score of men for whom he also had drawn a writing-on-the-sand, assembled at the north-west corner of the oasis and, led by the Sheikh el Hamel and the ancient guide, rode forth in orderly array by the light of the moon.

CHAPTER III

EL HABIBKA

ONCE again was it proven that attack is the best defence and that an invaluable principle of strategy is expressed in the apophthegm, "Put yourself in your enemy's place, and think as he would think."

The Sheikh Magician was well aware that the Touareg attacks at dawn, and therefore expects to be attacked at dawn.

For this reason he attacked at evening, when cooking-fires were alight, food being prepared, "tents" being made with camel-rug and sage-bush, camels being fed and watered at the *ghadir*, and all men busy.

Well aware, moreover, that the correct and orthodox attack is a wild rush and a hack-and-stab *mêlée*, wherein mounted men expect to ride down and overcome dismounted men, unprepared and at a disadvantage, he made a most incorrect and unorthodox attack, wherein a complete circle of hidden riflemen opened fire and shot down an enemy who rushed about in great excitement and in full view, as he prepared to receive the said wild rush of mounted men—that never came.

Instead of this, an ever-closing circle of accurate rifle-fire ringed them about, and offered no concentrated body of foemen upon which they might charge.

Always many were firing while some were crawling nearer.

Always many were crawling nearer while yet more were firing.

And from every point of the compass came the thudding bullets and the stealthily approaching men.

At which point of this unbroken circle should they rush? Where was the great ring thickest—or thinnest . . .? Nowhere.

From time to time a Targui brave, with a shout of "*Follow me! Ul-Ul-Ul-Allah Akbar!*" would dash forward at the head of a few swordsmen, towards some part of the ring of fire, only to fall with his followers ere steel could be blooded.

And, from point to point of the attack, rushed the Sheikh Magician, and wherever he paused and emptied the magazine of his rifle, men fell fast. He seemed to be everywhere at once, and to see everything at a glance. He both fought and led.

He alone kept to his feet, and scarcely a man of his well-trained force raised more than his head from the ground, even when wriggling forward a few yards that he might fire again from behind bush or stone yet nearer to the foe—silhouetted against his camp-fires or striving to capture and mount his beast.

Thus no attacker shot his brother on the opposite side of the circle, and no attacker suffered from the ill-aimed fire of the Touareg who endeavoured to imitate the tactics of their assailants.

When, here and there, an excited follower of the Sheikh

Magician, spurred by his presence to a desire to distinguish himself, would kneel up to rise beside his leader—he found himself flung back to earth and to remembrance of the fact that his sole business was to creep and shoot, to creep ever nearer and to shoot ever straighter, until disciplined co-operative tactics defeated unco-ordinated effort, and the well-used rifle asserted its superiority over the sword, the spear and the casual gun.

And so the net drew tighter, the end came in sight, and the cool brain of the Sheikh Magician triumphed over the hot courage and tradition-bolstered invincibility of the terrible Touareg.

Not till the battle was fairly won and the victory inevitable, did human nature triumph over discipline, and his followers, with a wild yell, rise as one man and rush upon the doomed remnant of their foe.

And not till this moment did they sustain a casualty. . . .

§ 2

As the moon looked down upon the scene of the battle, and beheld the Sheikh's followers, drunk with joy, intoxicated with the heady fumes of Victory, feasting and rejoicing about the camp-fires that had been lighted by their dead or captured foes, it saw a sight more horrible than that presented by the corpse of any man slain in the fight, more horrible than that of all the corpses piled together, and they were many.

A man had been tortured. His torturers must have been at their foul and ghastly work, even as the first shot was fired by the encircling foe, for he was still incredibly alive, although he had no face and was otherwise mutilated beyond belief or description.

With his own rifle the Sheikh Magician put an end to this defiled creature's sufferings, and then turned to where the shouts of some of his followers indicated that another victim of the bestial savagery of the Touareg had been found.

This man, trussed like a fowl, had evidently been awaiting his turn. He was untouched by knife, but almost dead from starvation, thirst and cruel treatment.

Him, the Sheikh Magician made his own special care.

Perhaps he thought of the time when he himself had been saved from death at the eleventh hour, and would mete out to this apparently dying man the measure that had then been his.

With his own hand he poured water from his own *zemzimayah* upon the face and mouth of the Touareg's prisoner, cut the cords that bound him, and chafed his limbs. As he did so, his face was suffused with a fine glow of humane and tender sympathy, adorned with a look of brotherly love, and animated with a new and generous fire.

Raising the body into a sitting posture, he put his arms about it, and embraced it—a Biblical picture of an Eastern father holding the body of his dead son.

Beneath the mask of Arab dignity and gravity, a repressed soul shone forth and sought brief expression in a moment of wild emotionalism.

The moon has seen the fierce tigress paw her helpless cub, the savage lion lick its wounded mate, the terrible and appalling gorilla weep above its slaughtered brother, and it beheld this fierce and blood-stained avenger sit among the dead and croon nurse-like above this inanimate salvage of the slaughter he had made.

Encamped near the scene of his victory—the bodies of his foes given to the vulture and the jackal, the wounds of his followers tended by his own hand—the Sheikh set himself to win back to life the man whom he had saved from the knife of the torturer.

Scores and scores slain, dozens yet dying, and this one to be nursed back to life even as he himself had been; this one to be dragged back from the portals of the House of the Dead, to be snatched from the jaws of Death.

As he himself had done, the almost-dead man made brave struggle for life, and, one day, opened his eyes in staring wonder upon his saviour.

The Sheikh laid his finger on the bloodless lips, sent all men away, and remained long alone with his piece of human salvage from the ocean of the desert, and its storm of war. . . .

They named him *El Nazil*, the Newcomer, and later *El Habibka*, the friend, as he became the chosen Friend of the Sheikh.

And in honour of his incredible victory over the dread Touareg, they gave the Sheikh el Hamel the name of *El Kebir*—the Lion.

And even as the old Sheikh had delighted to honour his foundling, El Hamel, the Gift of Allah, so did the Sheikh Magician delight to honour him whom he had thus saved and brought back to life.

When he and his fighting-men returned to the oasis-encampment, to be welcomed by the heart-stirring "*Ulla-la-een! Ulla-la-een!*"—the wild shrill trilling of the women, who screamed aloud as they rattled forefingers up and down against the teeth of their opened mouths—he sat the man upon his right hand, decked him in clean robes of respect, and with his own hand fed him, from time to time, with tit-bits from his own savoury stew of goat.

The tribe saw that their great Sheikh, the Great Magician, the Gift of Allah—yea, the Beloved of Allah the Merciful, the Compassionate—delighted to honour the Unknown, even as he himself had been honoured when unknown; and the tribe realized that a great bond of sympathy existed between the Sheikh and the Tentless One, in that the latter was dumb, even as the Sheikh himself had been!

Perhaps the Sheikh Magician would cure him of his affliction, as he had miraculously cured himself . . .?

And gradually it was borne in upon all men that the second Unknown had much else in common with their Great Sheikh, for he too was a very remarkable magician, a marvellous shot, a mighty horseman and horse-master, a great physician, and a man of curious and wondrous skill with his hands.

Like the Great Sheikh himself, the man knew that special form of *rabah* in which the empty hand is clenched, the thumb upon the first and second closed fingers, and a blow is delivered by shooting forward the hand in a straight line from the shoulder.

This was a very fine and terrible form of *rabah*; for a man may thus be smitten senseless, and apparently dead, by an unarmed smiter; or in a few minutes be beaten into a blood-stained feeble wreck, with closed eyes, scattered teeth, and horrid cuts and bruises.

Perhaps the Great Sheikh and this Foundling came of the same tribe—some distant southern tribe of great skill in war, great magic, great strength, and great wisdom?

§ 3

Public attention was first drawn to the remarkable powers of the Foundling, the Tentless One, by his calmly and quietly producing cartridges from the ears of Marbruk ben Hassan the Lame.

Marbruk was one of the best shots in the tribe—nearly as good as the Great Sheikh himself—for he had wonderful eyesight, and great strong hands, arms and shoulders.

Perhaps his terrible lameness led him to practise more than most men with the rifle, the one weapon he could use, since he could only hobble about like a half-crushed spider.

One day, as the Sheikh and certain elders and leaders of the fighting-men sat and *faddhled* before the Sheikh's tent, this Marbruk sidled up, patted his loved rifle, showed an empty pouch, and sighed that he had no ammunition.

Promptly the Sheikh's favourite, the Foundling, rose, and, thrusting forth his hand from beneath his *burnous*, produced a cartridge from Marbruk's ear!

Men stared open-mouthed.

He produced another; and then one from the other ear! Men gasped. Marbruk ben Hassan turned almost pale.

The Unknown took two more from beneath the camel-hair ropes that bound Marbruk's *haik*. Marbruk sat down and perspired, and an awed whisper of *Magic! Magic!* rose from the gaping onlookers.

The Foundling concluded this astounding performance by extending an empty hand and a bare arm—and extracting a cartridge from the circumambient air!

He then resumed his seat beside the unperturbed Sheikh, who smiled tolerantly as upon the creditable effort of a promising beginner in the science and art of the Magician.

§ 4

For long, El Habibka remained dumb, and when various of the *ekhwan* asked the Sheikh Magician if he would not cure him of his dumbness, the Sheikh replied that such was his hope and his intention.

He explained further that El Habibka was of his own Tribe, from the south; a tribe of men mighty in magic and in fighting, in knowledge and in wisdom,—but much afflicted by the Djinns of the Desert, jealous of the gifts so richly bestowed by Allah, the commonest of all their afflictions being this almost incurable dumbness which came upon them permanently when sick almost unto death.

However the Sheikh had little doubt that he would be able to work a cure in time.

When this was effected it would be found that El Habibka's speech would be halting and strange, even as his own had been since his recovery and return from the very Gates of the House of Death.

He assured the *ekhwan* and the leaders-of-twenty, when *faddhling* with them, that El Habibka would prove a very tower of strength to the Tribe, wondrous wise in Council, a lion in battle, the equivalent of ten wise elders and a hundred warriors.

He also delighted in making El Habibka display his astounding powers with the rifle, with the little-gun, with the knife, and with a long thin cord at the end of which was a slip-knot and loop; his superlative skill on the back of the wildest stallion; his wonderful adroitness and strength at *rabah*; and, above all, his magic.

And indeed the magic of El Habibka swiftly reduced the open-mouthed, staring onlookers to awed wonder, leaving them speechless, save for murmurs of "*Allahu Akbar!*" and "*Bismillah!*"

The things he could do were unbelievable until actually seen. Nor was he any less a physician than the Sheikh Magician himself, for his first great cure, known to all men, was followed by many.

This first instance was the saving of none other than the daughter of the late Sheikh, the Sitt Leila Nakhla, the "Beautiful Young Palm Tree", herself. She had been suddenly possessed of a devil which had entered her head, causing terrible pain and making the head feel as though it would swell to bursting.

To avert this catastrophe, she had bound a stout copper wire so tightly around her head that it was buried in the flesh. But this gave no relief. The Sitt Leila Nakhla had then sent a message, praying that the Sheikh Magician would come and exercise his wondrous art upon her, or she would die.

If she did not die she would kill herself, for the pain was unbearable and she had no sleep.

The old woman who brought the message prostrated herself at the feet of the Sheikh el Hamel el Kebir—as he sat on his carpet before his tent and talked to the dumb El Habibka in a low voice—and implored him to cure the Sitt, her mistress.

And the Sheikh had bidden El Habibka exercise his magic. Nothing loth, that doctor of medicine and science had followed old Bint Fatma to the tent of the Sitt Leila Nakhla, where she lay dressed and adorned in her best, on dyed rugs of camel-hair and soft cushions, awaiting the coming of the Sheikh el Hamel el Kebir.

Seizing her hot hands, El Habibka had stared long into her affrighted eyes.

He had then uttered strange sounds, as the dumb sometimes do; and, with quick passes and snatches, had removed from the girl's very brain—by way of her ears, nostril, mouth and eyes respectively, a rusty buckle, a pebble, a large splinter of wood, and, what was probably the worst offender, a big and lusty beetle, kicking and buzzing like the Devil, whose emissary it doubtless was.

The horror-stricken girl shrieked and almost fainted away.

El Habibka then removed the tightly twisted wire, as no longer necessary, and, presumably to ensure that the breath of life should remain in her, placed his lips firmly upon the girl's, moved them with a slight sound, and then retired swiftly from the tent. . . .

The Sitt Leila Nakhla never had another headache from that hour, and the reputation of El Habibka grew daily.

Men wondered that the Sheikh el Hamel el Kebir was not jealous, and that he did not slit the throat of one who bade fair to eclipse him as a healer.

Yet far otherwise was it, for the Sheikh moved not without El Habibka, and kept him ever at his side when, after prayers, he sat and *faddhled* before his tent at the hour of sunset, peace and food.

Few sang the praises of El Habibka louder than the

pious Hadji Abdul Salam, and none of those who wondered at this fact knew of the Hadji's long and quiet talks with one Abdullah el Jemmal, the camel-man, and the really tempting suggestions that the Hadji made for the poor camel-man's enrichment.

§ 5

The hope and expectation of the Sheikh el Hamel el Kebir that his protégé, El Habibka, would be restored to completest health and fullest enjoyment of all his faculties, was fulfilled—with a strange dramatic suddenness—for Allah suddenly gave him the gift of speech that he might save the life of his preserver!

It happened thus.

One evening, the Sheikh el Hamel el Kebir, El Habibka, the Hadji Abdul Salam, old Dawed Fetata, Marbruk ben Hassan and others of the *ekhwan* and chief leaders of the fighting-men had strolled beneath the palms of the oasis, after the *mogh'reb* prayer by the little white mosque.

Casting their eyes over the irrigation-plots, green with their crops of onions, radishes, bisset, pumpkins, and barley; over the rows and piles of sand-bricks drying in the sun; over the groups of women at the well, in their long indigo-blue, scarlet or orange *tobhs*; over the jostling, noisy, dust-raising flocks of goats at the water-runnels and troughs, the chieftains strode *faddhling*.

Anon darkness fell, the group dissolved (savoury smells of cooking being the solvent), and the Sheikh el Hamel el Kebir returned to his tent, passing as he did so, one before which the Sitt Leila Nakhla sat, with her young brother and two black slave-girls—that she might see and smile as usual at the Sheikh, when he went by.

The boy sprang up and ran to El Hamel, reaching up to play with his big silver-hilted dagger in its curly-ended silver sheath; and, with her soul in her eyes, the Sitt smiled upon the great and splendid man as he knelt and embraced the boy, the future Sheikh, of whom he was fond and proud as a father.

From the door of his tent El Habibka watched the scene, an enigmatic smile playing beneath his beard, and softening his hard eyes as he studied the lovely Leila.

Suddenly he shouted three words in a strange tongue and snatched at the belt of his *gandoura*, as an almost naked man bounded from the black shadow of the palms, straight at the back of the kneeling Sheikh—a long knife gleaming in his right hand.

At the sound of El Habibka's cry—the words of which he evidently understood—the Sheikh swung round, keeping his body between the assailant and the child, but not rising to his feet.

The girl sprang forward like a tigress; up flashed the keen knife of the assassin, and the Sheikh's great fist shot out and smote him terribly, below the breast-bone. As he staggered back, El Habibka's pistol banged twice, and only then the Sheikh rose to his feet.

But El Habibka had spoken, a dozen people had heard, and the Sheikh had understood.

For the moment, this portent was forgotten, as the overwrought girl threw herself upon the Sheikh's breast and entwined her arms about his neck, the boy clung to him in alarm, and men rushed up to seize the murderer.

Gently pushing the girl and child from him, the Sheikh shouted that the assassin was not to be further injured, just as El Habibka seized the wrist of Hadji Abdul Salam, even as the point of that pious man's knife was entering the murderer's neck at the very spot for the neat severing of the jugular vein.

It was surprising with what force the Hadji struggled to execute justice, and with what a remarkable twist El Habibka caused him to drop his knife and yelp with pain.

It was almost as though the Hadji did not want the man to be taken alive.

It was soon seen that El Habibka's two shots had crippled and not killed; and that when the captive had recovered from the Sheikh's terrible blow, he would be able to give an account of himself. Or rather would be in a condition to respond to treatment designed and applied with a view to persuading him to do so.

And when water had been thrown over the man, and, tied to a palm-tree behind the Sheikh's tent, he had been left in the excellent care of El R'Orab the Crow—men's minds were free to turn to the more wonderful, if less exciting, event of the evening—the fact that El Habibka the Silent, the Dumb, the Afflicted of Allah, had been the object of the Mercy of Allah, and had been given speech that he might save his master.

None slept that night, and great was the *faddhling* round every fire—especially when the news spread that the assassin had at length yielded to treatment and confessed that he had been sent on his errand of death by the great Emir, Mohammed Bishari bin Mustapha Korayim abd Rabu, at the instance and plotting of one, Suleiman the Strong, now his *Wazir*, *Wakil*, and Commander-in-Chief combined.

Curiously enough, the Sheikh el Hamel el Kebir did not torture the assassin—either for the purpose of extracting information from him or in punishment for his murderous attempt.

The sight of certain magics, worked before his astonished eyes by the Sheikh and by El Habibka, appeared to convince him that confession would be good for his soul, even more than the contemplation of preparations for his painful and protracted physical dissolution.

And his story was interesting, particularly those chapters of it that bore upon the professed intention of the Emir Mohammed Bishari bin Mustapha Korayim abd Rabu to assemble his army and make Suleiman the Strong the tributary Sheikh of the Tribe from which he had been cast forth, and to add the Tribe to the small confederation of tribes which the Emir ruled. . . .

As he began to gain strength and hope of life, the hireling murderer grew more communicative, and under the influence of magnanimous kindness, brain-shaking exhibitions of magic, and the ever-present fear of ghastly torture, became as ardently and earnestly the willing tool of the Sheikh Magician, as he had been of Suleiman the Strong, and the Emir to whom Suleiman had escaped.

Many and long were the councils held by the Sheikh, El Habibka, wise old Dawed Fetata, Marbruk ben Hassan, and the elect of the *ekhwan* and fighting-men; and after a decision had been reached, a great *mejliss* was held, a great public meeting, which was harangued in turn by the wise men and the fighting-men of the Inner Council, while the Sheikh gravely nodded approval of the eloquence of each.

At the end of the meeting, the hitherto dumb El Habibka arose, and in a voice creaking and rusty from disuse, and with words halting, and sometimes almost incomprehensible, cried aloud,

"*Hamdulillah! Hamdulillah! Ana mabsut! Ana mabsut!*" and, having recited the *fatha* with wide-stretched arms, he fell upon his face before the Sheikh, his body quivering with sobs, or the wild hysterical laughter of a joy too great to bear. . . .

And the decision of the council approved by the *mejliss* was that at the coming season of sowing, when all the tribes scatter far and wide for the planting of barley for the next year's food-crop, the Tribe should migrate and travel steadily north-west towards that wonderful land where there was known to be a hundred square miles of palm trees and of all green things, a land flowing with milk and honey, Allah's own Paradise on earth. . . .

It had always been towards the north-west that the Sheikh had looked, and of the north-west that he had talked, night after night, to the *faddhling* circle and to the eagerly listening El Habibka.

Meanwhile, Yakoub-who-can-go-without-water, and his shrivelled colleagues disappeared, and none of them was seen for many days. By the time the first of them returned, much of the organizing work preparatory to the migration had been completed, and the Tribe was almost ready for another of its many moves.

This exodus, however, was to differ from former ones, in that the Tribe was going to move as an army that is accompanied by a big baggage-and-sutler train, instead of a straggling mob of men, women and children, and their flocks and herds.

Four drilled and disciplined Camel Corps, proceeding as an advance-guard, two flank-guards and a powerful rear-guard, were to form the sides of a mighty oblong; and inside this oblong the Tribe and its animals would march, each family being responsible for its own beasts and commissariat. . . .

Great was the sound of the querns throughout the *qsar* as the women of every tent laboured in pairs at the grinding of barley-meal for the filling of the sacks for the journey; and high rose the prices of pitch and *zeit* oil, as leaky *girbas* were made water-tight.

Day-long and night-long was the making and sewing of *khoorgs* for loads of dates and of camel-fodder, since the Tribe would "live on the country" where it could, and be self-supporting where it must, and every fighting-man's date-fed trotting-camel eats a sack of dates a day.

It was a hard and busy time, but a spirit of cheerfulness prevailed, for change is the salt of life, and great was the trust reposed by the Tribe in their wonderful Sheikh, so full of ideas, of organizing power, and of energy; and in his trusted lieutenant El Habibka, now Commander-in-Chief of the fighting-men.

It was felt that the Sheikh Regent would safely and surely lead the Tribe to the conquest or occupation of the Great Oasis, and that he who had defeated a great Touareg *harka*, would defeat anybody who opposed their passage. . . .

CHAPTER IV

THE CONFEDERATION

A few miles from the Pass of Bab-el-Haggar, Yoluba, the black Wadai slave and fighting-man, nearly seven feet high, and famed for long sight among desert men famous for their long sight, sat sideways on his camel that he might watch the horizon to which all other backs were turned.

He was alone, far in the rear of the rearguard, behind which rode the Sheikh el Hamel el Kebir.

From time to time, Yoluba of the Strong Eyes would halt and turn his camel about, the while he stared with unwavering gaze along the broad track made by the migrating Tribe. . . . Suddenly he whirled about, waved his long *mish'ab* stick towards his camel's head, and sent it along at its top pace, until he drew alongside the Sheikh.

"One comes," he said gutturally, from deep down in his thick throat. "A small man on a big camel. In great haste. It will be Yakoub-who-goes-without-water."

At an order from the Sheikh, the rear-guard halted, turned about and deployed. Camels were *barraked* in line, and behind each knelt a man, his loaded rifle levelled. . . . A piece of drill introduced by the Sheikh, and much enjoyed when once grasped, by his fighting-men. . . .

Yakoub it proved to be, and with a tale of weight to tell.

"Well done, thou good and faithful servant," quoth the Sheikh, on hearing it. "Ten silver *medjidies* and the best camel thou canst pick, if all go well. . . . And so the great Emir will do even as I did unto the Touaregs, and attack at the hour of camp-making, will he?"

"Ya, Sidi! But we will ring the camp about with rifles and await him, *Inshallah!*" grinned Yakoub.

"We will do better than that, Father Yakoub," replied the Sheikh, and sent three of his specially mounted messengers to El Habibka commanding the advance-guard, and to Marbruk ben Hassan and to Yussuf Latif Fetata, commanding the flank-guards, respectively.

The orders were simple. The vast caravan was to push on at its best pace through the deep dunes and vile loose sand that was the only way—churned to fine dust by fifty centuries of caravan-traffic in a rainless land—through the pass between the Bab-el-Haggar rocks, a few miles of precipitous out-crop over which camels could not go.

At the far side of the pass, the advance-guard and flank-guards were to halt and await the coming of the rear-guard, while the caravan pushed on.

§ 2

A few hours before sunset, the Pass of Bab-el-Haggar was silent and apparently deserted, but a quarter of a mile to the north-west of it the camels of an obviously well-drilled Camel Corps were *barraked* in orderly lines, in charge of camel-guards and sentries. On the distant horizon, a mighty cloud of dust indicated the passing of a vast concourse of men and beasts. . . .

An hour before sunset, a typical Arab *harka* swept like a torrent into the wide pass; hundreds and hundreds of well-armed fighting-men on magnificent buff, grey, and white camels.

At their head rode a splendid group, one of whom bore a

green silk flag on which was a crescent and the device of the Lord of Many Tents, the Emir Mohammed Bishari bin Mustapha Korayim abd Rabu, spiritual and temporal head of a small, but growing, confederation of Bedouin tribes.

The pace of the beautiful camels of the Emir and his Sheikhs dropped from a swift mile-eating trot to a slow walk, as they reached the area of flour-like yielding dust-dunes into which even the broad feet of camels sank deeply. The setting sun shone blood-red upon rich silken *caftan*, gay *kafiyeh* bound about with golden *agals*, flowing *burnous* and coloured camel-rugs with dangling tassels. . . .

After their leaders, ploughed the mass of fighting-men, brave as the lions of the desert and as undisciplined as the apes of the rocks.

"The curse of Allah on this corner of Hell! It will upset my plan," growled the Emir, an impatient man, as his camel dragged one foot painfully after another through the bottomless dust.

"There is no need for haste, Lord," replied Suleiman the Strong, who rode beside him. "*Inshallah*, our ways will humbly resemble those of Allah Himself this day, for is it not written, '*Allah fleeth with wings of lead but striketh with hands of iron*'?"

"This cursed pass will spoil my plans, I say," growled the Emir again.

It did.

A curious long whistling sound was heard, like a sustained note on a *quatia*, the Arab flute, and, as all eyes were raised to the rocks that bounded and formed the defile, a sudden crash of musketry followed, and the pass became a shambles.

Many flogged their camels as though that would give them wings or firm ground on which to tread. Many wheeled about, to escape by the way they had come, making confusion worse confounded.

Many attempted to *barrak* their camels and fire from behind them at the well-concealed enemy, only to find that their unprotected backs were turned to another foe.

"*Kismet*," groaned the Emir, putting his hand to his bleeding chest. "*El Mektub, Mektub . . .*" and fell from his camel.

The man to whom he spoke, this Suleiman the Strong, brought his camel to its knees and then lay flat, close beside it, feigning death.

Wild, almost unaimed, discharging of rifles by fully exposed men, replied but for a brief space to steady, careful short-range shooting by men lying, with resting rifles, behind rocks.

The inevitable end came quickly, and the Sheikh el Hamel el Kebir was prompt to save life.

To the surprise of the vanquished, not a throat was cut; and to each wounded man the same help was given that would have been rendered by his son.

But the defeat was utter, bitter and irretrievable, for not a rifle, a round of ammunition nor a camel remained to the leaderless army of the confederation of tribes, lately strong and arrogant in the mighty hand of the Emir Mohammed Bishari bin Mustapha.

Well acquainted with the truth of *væ victis*, it did not take the Sheikhs of the prisoners long to accept the small change of plan whereby the confederated tribes became attached to the Tribe, instead of the decimated Tribe being attached to the confederated tribes.

Nor did they see any loss in exchanging the leadership and rule of the Emir Mohammed Bishari bin Mustapha Korayim abd Rabu for that of the Emir el Hamel el Kebir who had conquered him in war; who had behaved with the noblest magnanimity to the vanquished, in the very finest Arab tradition, now more often honoured in the breach than in the observance; and who was undoubtedly a great and remarkable man, who might be relied upon to lead the confederation from strength to strength, until it could dwell in unmolested safety, making sure to each his own, that he might reap where he had sown. . . .

So the tribal Sheikhs gave hostages of their sons and daughters and of their flocks and herds and treasure; and the Sheikh el Hamel el Kebir became the Emir el Hamel el Kebir, the Victorious and Blessed of Allah the Merciful, the Compassionate.

His days now being filled with labours of military and civil organization, the new Emir appointed El Habibka to be Sheikh Regent of the Tribe, and brought joy upon the *ekhwan* and fighting-men by promising that he would himself dwell with the Tribe, and none other.

At a great *diffa* given in the new Emir's honour by aged

Dawad Fetata, the Sitt Leila Nakhla delighted to honour him by waiting on him herself.

The Emir was conscious of the honour, but not of the fact that the girl pressed to her own lips and breast, the bowl from which he drank, and let none but herself touch it in future. . . .

Other nomadic and semi-nomadic tribes, some in wisdom and some in fear lest they be eaten up, sent envoys to the Emir, proposing that they should join his confederation and enjoy his countenance and protection, in return for tribute and the services of fighting-men.

These he visited, accompanied by his famous Camel Corps of men who drilled and manœuvred like the *Franzawi* and other *Roumi* soldiers, and who were reported to be invincible.

And slowly the great and growing confederation moved north-westward to the fabled Great Oasis of a Hundred Square Miles of Palm Trees and green grass, where the Emir el Hamel el Kebir talked of a permanent *douar*, that the Tribe might occupy the land and possess it, waxing mighty, self-supporting agriculturists and herdsmen, strong and safe, as being the centre and focus of a powerful tribal alliance.

He even talked of the building of a walled city with a protected caravan-market, a great *sūq* that should become famous beneath his shadow, and attract caravans from the north laden with sugar, tea, cotton stuffs, soap, needles, scent and sandal; from the south with ivory and feathers and Soudanese "orphans"; from the east with coffee from Arabia; and from the west with the products of Nigeria, Lake Tchad and Timbuctu. . . . A walled city with schools, mosques, *zaouias*, *serais*, *hammams*, *madressahs*, and cool houses with beautiful gardens. . . . And the *ekhwan* stroked their beards and smiled at the Emir's pleasing fantasies. . . .

Inshallah . . .!

And, as unto him that hath shall be given, more and more power was given to the Emir el Hamel el Kebir, as more and more Sheikhs sought his protection and countenance; and his Confederation waxed like Jonah's gourd, until its fame spread abroad in all the land, north, south, east, and west.

In the north and west it attracted the attention of certain deeply-interested Great Ones. . . .

The first intimation that Fame had come to the Emir took the shape of an overture from the great Lord of the Senussi, who sent one of his most important Sheikhs, escorted by an imposing retinue bearing gifts and greetings and proposals for an offensive and defensive alliance, and the exchange of hostages for its better observance.

In full *mejliss* assembled, the Emir listened to the words of the Senussi emissary, and made suitable replies.

After some weeks of intermittent conversations, much *faddhling*, feasting and ceremonial drinking of mint tea, the ambassadorial caravan departed, taking with it a deep impression of the strength of the Confederation, the wisdom, and greatness of the Emir, gifts for the Lord of the Senussi and little else. . . .

"The Emir would deeply consider of the matter, confer with his tribal Sheikhs, and send his messengers, anon, to Holy Kufra with his reply. . . ."

CHAPTER V

A VOICE FROM THE PAST

IT was the prudent custom of the Emir el Hamel el Kebir and his Vizier, the Sheikh el Habibka, to sit apart from all men, that they might converse of high matters of state in the completest privacy.

This they did upon a rug-strewn carpet, above which a roof-canopy of felt was supported by four poles. At the corners of an imaginary square, four Soudanese sentries, a hundred yards each from the other and from their Lords watched that no man approached without invitation. . . .

To them, seated thus one evening, there came the Emir's faithful body-servant, R'Orab the Crow, escorting the aged but tough and enduring chief of the scouts who formed the Intelligence Department of the Emir.

The two men prostrated themselves, salaaming reverently. "Speak," said the Emir.

"Lord Shereef, thy servant, Yakoub-who-goes-without-water, hath news for thine ear," announced El R'Orab.

"Speak," said the Emir to the ancient.

"Lord Kalipha, a small caravan comes. Its leaders are strange men. One is an Egyptian or an Arab from Egypt. He is of the great Al Azhar *Zaouvia* of Cairo. The other speaks and dresses as the Bedouin, but his ways are strange. . . . The two speak together in a foreign tongue. They seized me and made me their guide"—the old man grinned toothlessly—"and I slept against the wall of their tent for warmth and shelter from the wind—but their talk was in a strange tongue. They have much money and their servants are faithful. Their hired camel-men could not tell me much. They were engaged at Siwah and have come by way of Holy Kufra. They think it possible that the chief leader is a *Roumi*, but he carries papers that great Sheikhs, Emirs, Kaliphas, Shereefs and Rulers kiss and place against their foreheads and their hearts. . . . It is said that much honour was shown them at Siwa and also at Holy Kufra by the Lord of the Senussi. . . . I left them at the last water-hole, escaping by night upon my fast camel. . . ."

Three days later two heavily-bearded strangers sat and talked long and eloquently with the Emir el Hamel el Kebir and his Vizier.

Most of the talking was done by a curious hybrid product of modern civilization who had been a student of the great Al Azhar University at Cairo, and of the Paris *Sorbonne* as well. He had been an employee of the *Bureau Arabe* and had sojourned in Algiers. He had resigned his post and visited Constantinople, departing thence for Baghdad. The wanderlust or some other lust had then taken him to Europe once more.

All that he said was confirmed in terse speech by his master, a man whom the Emir and his Vizier studied more carefully than they did the voluble cosmopolitan Arab-Egyptian.

And what he said was of deep interest—a thrilling and intriguing story. . . .

He told these simple desert chieftains of a Great *Roumi* Kings of Kings, one clad in shining armour, who had long since been moved by Allah, in a dream, to see the error of his ways and to embrace the True Faith. . . . So great was he that the very Father of the Faithful himself had called him Brother and had invited him to Stamboul that he might embrace him. . . . So great was he that, once upon a time, the very walls of the Holy City of Jerusalem were thrown down that he might enter, when he went there on pilgrimage, using no common gate trodden by the feet of common men.

The simple devout chieftains, much impressed, were too deeply enthralled to talk—until the Emir, stroking his beard, sought enlightenment as to what all this had to do with him.

He received it.

Stirred by the knowledge that there is no God but God and that Mahomet is his Prophet, and shocked by the sight of Islam groaning in bondage—yea, beneath the heel of the *Franzawi Roumi* here in Africa, this mighty King of Kings was about to urge his Brother, the Father of the Faithful, in Stamboul, to preach a *jehad*, a Holy War, for the overthrow of all oppressors of Islam throughout the world—and especially in Morocco, Algiers, Tunisia and the countries adjacent. . . .

And to all great Chieftains, Emirs, Sheikhs, Kaliphas, Shereefs, Rulers, and leaders of Tribal Confederations, he was sending word to be prepared for the Great Day of Islam, the Day of the creation of the Pan-Islamic State in Africa, and the utter overthrow and extermination of the *Roumi*. . . . Already the greatest Islamic power in Africa, the Senussi, were pledged to obey orders from Stamboul, and it was hoped and believed that the Emir el Hamel el Kebir would attack the French when the Senussi attacked the English in Egypt. . . . Meanwhile—gifts, arms, money, promises . . .

This first audience being concluded, and orders having been given for the pitching of a camp for the strangers' caravan, the Emir el Hamel el Kebir and the Sheikh el Habibka el Wazir stared long and thoughtfully into each other's faces.

"D'you place him, Bud?" asked the Emir.

"Search me, Hank Sheikh," replied the Vizier, "but I cert'nly seen him before. . . . He's got me guessin' and he's got me rattled. . . . There's a catch in it somewhere. . . . I'm real uneasy. . . ."

The Emir smiled; a slow and thoughtful smile indeed.

"He's going to be a whole heap uneasier than you are, Buddy boy. . . . Remember a sure-enough real thug, way back at Tokotu when we was in the Legion? . . . Came to us at Douargala with a draft from the Saida depot. The boys allowed it was him, and him alone, started that big Saida mutiny, though it was never brought home to him. . . . Same game at Tokotu. . . . Always had plenty of money and spent it on gettin' popular. . . . Reg'lar professional mutineer and trouble-brewer . . . a spellbinder—and a real brave man. . . . Get him?"

"Nope."

"He had been in the French Cavalry, he said, and got jailed for mutinying there too, and later, he joined the Legion to carry on the good work. . . . He was on that march with us from Tokotu to Zinderneuf—the place those two bright boys burnt out and killed old Lejaune—and Old Man Bojolly shot this guy with his empty revolver, and then put him under arrest—for refusing to obey orders. . . . He tried to work up a mutiny again that time, and he very nearly . . ."

"*Rastignac!*" cried the Vizier, and smote his thigh. "*Rastignac the Mutineer!* Good for you, Hank Sheikh. . . . That's the guy! I knew I knowed him, the moment I set eyes on him. . . . Had too many drinks out of the old crook not to know him. . . . Used to wear a pointed beard and big moustache waxed up like you would stick corks on the ends for safety."

"You said it, Bud. It's Old Man Rastignac. And what in hell is the stiff doing in *this* outfit, I want to know. Last we saw of him, he was for General Court Martial and the Penal Battalion."

"Doin'? Earnin' some dirty money again, I s'pose. From the same purse too, I guess. . . . What'll we do with him, Hank?"

"Teach him poker, Son, and get all he's got. . . . Think he reckernized us any?"

214

"Not on your life. I watched him mighty careful. We was clean shaven, those days, and he wore a hairy face. . . . That's why we seemed to know him and he didn't know us. . . . *You* look more like an ole goat in a bush than a soldier, behind that flowin' door-mat of whiskers. . . . '*Hank!*' Huh! Sure—*a Hank of Hair*. . . . Gee!"

"And you, Buddy Bashaw, you look just e*gg*sactly like a monkey in a haystack. . . . You ain't a little Man with a beard on him, Son—you're a Beard with a little man in it. . . ."

The two simple desert chieftains eyed each other critically, their strong faces impassive, sardonic, hard; their eyes enigmatic, inscrutable, faintly humorous perhaps. . . .

Sending for one Yussuf Latif Fetata, grandson of the High Sheikh, Sidi Dawed Fetata, the Emir bade him bivouac a company of the Camel Corps beside the camp of the strangers, for their honour and protection, and to protect them so effactually that not a man of the caravan left their camp by day or by night. Their camels were to be "minded" for them in the *fondouk*, their rifles were to be taken from them to be cleaned and also "minded"; and daily they were to receive ample rations and water—for that day alone. (No man could leave the Great Oasis without swift camels and a good supply of food and water.)

"On my head and my life be it, Sidi," salaamed young Latif Fetata, and departed to see that the honoured guests were also honoured (and strictly guarded) prisoners. . . .

But though they could not leave their spacious and comfortable camp, others could enter it—others, that is to say, who had authorized business there—and no one dreamed of hindering that influential and pious priest, Hadji Abdul Salam, chief *imam*, and spiritual head of his Tribe, from paying a ceremonial visit of honour to the Emir's honoured guest.

He paid many visits, in fact, which were not ceremonial and in the course of which this prophet, who was not without honour in his own country, showed that honour might not be without profit also. . . .

When a certain soldier, one Gharibeel Zarrug, a young man who feared and reverenced the Hadji, and whom the tongue of malice declared to be the Hadji's son, was on sentry over the tents of the leaders of the expedition, the pious Hadji visited them by night, and much curious and interesting conversation ensued.

After one such heart-to-heart talk, and the departure of Hadji Abdul Salam, the Egyptian-Arab, who affected patent-leather dancing pumps, silk socks, scent, hair-pomade and other European vices—and who yearned exceedingly for a high stiff collar, frock-coat, *tarbush* and the pavements of Paris—observed to his colleague and employer:

"Might do worse. . . . He'd be ours, body and soul, both for the money and because we should know too much . . . If he killed this Emir and his jackal, or had them killed, he would be the power behind the throne—until he was the throne itself. . . ."

"Yes. . . . Might do much worse," agreed the other man. "He would be Regent for this boy that the Emir is nursing—until the time came for the boy to die. . . . I don't like this Emir. . . . He say too little and stares too much. . . . He's a strong ruler, and no tool for anybody. . . . And it's a *tool* we want here. . . ."

"No. I don't like him either," agreed the other, "and he doesn't like us or our proposals, I fancy. I have an idea that the French were here before us. Do you think we are in any danger?"

"*Great* danger, I should say," rejoined the leader, and smiled mockingly at his companion, whose invaluable gifts he knew to be rather those of the fox than of the lion.

"Then we must get down to real business with the Hadji, the next time he comes," was the reply of the Egyptian-Arab. "We shall have deserved well of our masters if we do nothing more here than remove the Emir, a potential enemy of great importance. . . ."

"We shall do more than that," prophesied the other.

CHAPTER VI

MORE VOICES FROM THE PAST

In pride, peace, prosperity and patience sat the Emir el Hamel el Kebir upon the rugs and cushions of the carpet of his pavilion, a few days later, splendidly arrayed, exhaling dignity, benevolence, and lordship.

Beside him sat his almost equally resplendent Vizier, known to all men as the Sheikh el Habibka el Wazir.

Between their bearded lips were the mouth-pieces of their long-stemmed *narghilehs*, from which they inhaled deep draughts of soothing smoke.

A man came running, halted, and prostrated himself.

"Speak, O El R'Orab the Crow," murmured the Emir.

"Lord," said the man, "the leader Marbruk ben Hassan has returned, with none missing. He brings three prisoners, two of them women. The man prisoner says he comes to the Emir with messages from the Rulers of his Tribe."

"Go to the Hadji Abdul Salam and say that the Emir bids him receive these people and offer them hospitality for three days in the Guest-tents. '*Are not we all the guests of Allah?*' saith The Book. . . . When they are rested and refreshed, let him bring the man before me. . . . I have spoken."

The Emir and the Vizier sat in silence, their eyes resting on the pleasant view before them, a scene beautified by feathery palms, green grass and running water, on which rested the benediction of the setting sun. . . .

Anon men approached, in the midst of whom walked a French officer in full uniform.

The Vizier's elbow pressed that of the Emir.

"Sunday pants of Holy Moses!" murmured the Vizier. "*It's Old Man Bojolly . . .!* Run us down at last!"

"Game's up, Bud," murmured the Emir. "This is where we get what's comin' to us. . . ."

And with severe dignity, and calm faces of perhaps more than Oriental inscrutability, they received the officer, in open *mejliss* or durbar.

After the return of the French officer to the Guest-tent, the Emir and the Vizier sat cross-legged upon their cushions, and gazed each upon the face of the other.

"Well, Hank Sheikh, and what do you know about *that*?" asked the Vizier of his Lord.

"Our name's mud," replied the Emir. "Our monicker's up. . . . Old Man Boje and his '*great and peaceful message!*' Be more great than peaceful when his troop arrive. . . ."

"They say they always get you, in the end," reflected the Vizier. "I wonder what force he's brought and where he's left it?"

"That's what's puzzlin' me, Bud. I allow no desert-column, nor camel-corpse, nor squadron of Spahis, nor company of the Legion, could have got within three days of here without us knowing it."

"Sure thing, Son Hank—if a gang of Touareg Bohunks couldn't, French troops couldn't. . . . I s'pose it *is* us he's after?"

"Who else . . .? It cert'nly isn't this Rastignac guy. . . . Anyhow, we'll play Sheikhs till Hell pops, and 'see him and raise him' every time, Bud."

"You've said it, Hank. We got better poker-faces than Old Man Bojolly, I allow. . . . But what'll we do if he gets up in *mejliss* and says:

"'*I rise to remark I've come to fetch you two hoboes outa this for deserters from the Foreign Legion on reconnaissance duty in the face o' the enemy an' the Lord ha' mercy on your sinful souls amen, and you better come quiet or I'll stretch you and call up my Desert Column,*' eh, Hank Sheikh?"

"Bluff him out and say he's got a touch o' the sun and oughter turn teetotal. . . . If we can't talk anything but Arabic we *can't* be deserters from the Foreign Legion. . . ."

"Or else tie him up in a neat parcel an' run him into Egypt," he continued. "That's British Territory. . . . Sit on the walls o' Jerusalem an' sing *Yankee Doodle* to him. . . . Jerusalem *is* in the Land of Egypt, ain't it, Bud?"

"Yep. . . . House of Bondage and Children of Israel, an' all that. . . . But we needn't vamoose any. We can turn the Injuns loose on him, if he starts handing out the rough stuff and is all for marchin' us to the calaboose in Zaguig or somewhere. . . . Or let his old friend Rastignac get him. . . ."

"*Can* it, Buddy Bashaw. Cut it out. We don't turn Injuns on to a lone white man, Son. . . . No, and we don't set 'em up against Christian machine-guns nor civilized artillery either. . . . Not after they elected us to Congress like this, and made me President and all. . . . Put their last dollar on us for Clean Politics and the People's Party, Monroe Doctrine and No Foreign Entanglements. . . . No, I guess we gotta hit the high places again, and hike. But shan't I laugh some *if he gets Rastignac too*!"

"Gee! Ain't it the hard and frost-bitten pertater, Hank Sheikh—after we been livin' so respectable? Like a Hard-Shell Baptist Minister in a hard-boiled shirt. . . ."

"It surely would jar you, Buddy. . . . We had our ups and downs, Son, and now we're booked for a down."

"Some tracking Old Man Bojolly's done! He's a cute cuss and the fierce go-getter. . . . He's got a nerve too, to ride straight in here like a Texas Ranger into a Mex village—an' I hand it to him, an' no ill-will. . . . But I'd certainly like to go and paste him one. . . . And me just thinking of marrying and settling down and all. . . ."

"'Nother thing gets me guessing, Bud. . . . What's he brought the two girls here for? They ain't labelled *A Present from Biskra* . . . *For a Bad Sheikh* . . . are they?"

"No. He's French, Hank. Shocking morals they've got—but I don't see that it's any affair of ours if Bojolly travels comfortable. . . . But if he does gather us in for the Oran General Court-Martial an' we're sentenced to death, I shall get my own back, sure."

"As how?"

"When he's finished his evidence, I shall say, quiet like, but with all the nacheral dignity and weight of Truth, '*Oh, you Rambunctious Ole Goat,*' I shall say—an' leave it at that. . . ."

"Well—look at here, Son. . . . He hasn't showed his hand yet. We've staked him to a hashparty to-night, an' told him to bring the girls. We'll play light till Marbruk ben Hassan comes in—I whispered to Marbruk to scout clever and find out if there was an escort hiding anywhere

—and we know for sure whether there's French troops around. And until there is—what we say *goes*. . . . Gee! Ain't it some world we live in? Major Bojolly and Rastignac the Mutineer, both leavin' visitin'-cards on *us*. It's our At Home day, Son Bud. . . ."

"We'll be wishin' it was our Go Home day, before long, Hank Sheikh," replied the Vizier. "Anyhow, we'll see that Boje and Rastignac don't meet yet awhile."

§ 3

That evening, after the feast and the departure of their guests, the Emir and the Vizier observed a long silence, each apparently respecting the feelings of the other. At length the Vizier groaned.

"Can you beat it, Son?" quoth he. "Do I sleep? Do I dream and is Visions about? . . . Bite me in the stomach if I'm wrong, Hank Sheikh—but I believe I've been talking to an honest-to-God, genuine, sure-enough American girl, and held her hand in mine. . . ."

"I'm dazed and weak, Bud," murmured the Emir, "but I testify you certainly held her hand in yours. I thought it *was* yours. . . ."

"*It's goin' to be*," pronounced the Vizier, with a fervour of resolution. "It's goin' to be!" he repeated. "Say, Son Hank—don't go and fall in love with that li'll Peach, or I shall hand in my checks and wilt to the bone-orchard. . . . *I'm in love*, Hank Sheikh, for the first time in my life! . . ."

The Emir emitted a rumble of sarcastic laughter.

"Huh! And yesterday you were going to marry four Arab Janes and settle down respectable!"

"That ain't *Love*; you old fool! Not by a jugful. . . . That's matterimony and respectability, instead of living like a sky-larking lone wolf. . . . Say, Hank, old Son, you *ain't* goin' to fall in love with that li'll lovely Peach yourself?"

"No, Bud, I am not. . . . But I'll rise to remark that Old Man Bojolly *is*. . . . Yep, sur thing! He's fallen for that little looker, all-right."

The Vizier closed a useful-looking fist and shook it above his head.

"*What!*" he ejaculated in a whispering shout. "He'd come here to arrest us an' get us shot—*and* he'd steal our girls from under our very noses too! . . . He would? . . . I allow that's torn it! . . . Old Man Bojolly better git up an' git. . . . Let's ride him outa town and tell him to go while the goin's good! . . . B'Gees! *I'll* paste him one to-morrow. . . . Sheikh Hank, Son—I'm goin' to propose to that sweet and lovely American girl, and lay my heart and life and fortune at her feet. . . . She wouldn't look at that damn' Wop then, sure*ly*?"

"He ain't a Wop. And you ain't got a fortune," replied the Emir patiently.

"Well, he's French, an' that's the same as a Wop or worse. . . . And I allow I'll dern soon rustle a fortune if she'll have me."

"*That's* the spirit, Son! Good luck to you, Buddy-boy —and I'll back you up. You court her gentle and lovin' an' respectful an' I'll give you a character. . . . Time you had one too. . . . But we sure got to tell her all about ourselves, Bud. . . . All the truth about us, so there's no deception like. . . ."

"Sure thing, Hank Sheikh, I wouldn't deceive her—not for anything."

"No, Son. . . . I'll mention about those four Arab Janes—just to show you got the serious marryin' mind, and prob'ly been collectin' the sticks o' furniture for the Home. . . ."

"Cut out the funny-stuff, Hank Sheikh. . . . It's fierce, ain't it? I got to talk this Arabic gargle while Ole Boje gets away with it in English—and French—and American too! How I'm goin' to lay my feelin's before her in Arabic? She won't reckernize 'em fer the respeckful love-stuff. . . . Hell!"

"You got away with it in Agades, Son. . . . You remember that black Jane. . . . You was *dumb* then, too. . . ."

"*Can* it, I tell you, Hank, or you'll get my goat. . . . This is different. . . . This is a girl that's Real Folks. . . . You don't know what love is, you ugly low-life old moron. . . . The laughter of fools is as the cackling of prawns in a pot. . . . You never bin in love, I tell you!"

"Me? Love? No. Sure. . . . What you know about Miss Maudie Atkinson, Bud?"

"Some looker—if Miss Mary Vanbrugh wasn't there. . . .
An' not bad fer British. . . . Yep, I'd surely have fallen
for her, if the American girl hadn't been there. . . ."

"You certainly would, Bud. . . . Thou Fragrance of
the Pit!"

"Say—I got an idea, Buddy," continued the Emir.
"S'pose we could tell Miss Vanbrugh all about us, and
say we trust her not to tell Ole Boje until he springs it on
us himself? . . . I got a hunch he *ain't* after us, and don't
reckernize us either. . . .

"If I'm wrong, he's got the best bluff and the best poker-
face on any man I met yet—an' we're innercent children
beside him. . . . Him an' his *great and peaceful message!* . . .
We'll wait until Marbruk comes back, an' then we'll
force Boje to a show-down. . . . *I* don't believe the old fox
is on to *us* at all. . . ."

"Then what is he here for, Son?" asked the Vizier.

"You got me guessing, pard," was the reply, and the
Emir drained a glass of lemon-water without enthusiasm.

Silence fell. The Emir and the Vizier sank deep into
thought. From time to time the solemn face of each was
lighted by a reminiscent smile.

"Say, Hank—didn't she just jolly us! I nearly bust
with laffin' when she sang that *Bul-bul Emir* stuff. Gee!
Isn't she a sweet Peach! . . . *Allah Akbar*—she's a *houri*! . . ."

"Sure—and that li'll British girl. . . . '*Oh, Sir, ain't
the big one a lovely man!*' . . . That's *me*, Buddy Bashaw—
and don't you forget it. *I* got that bokay! It gave me the
fantods that I couldn't back-chat with her. . . ."

"*Lovely man!* . . . Sufferin' Moses!" groaned the
Vizier. "You ever see a g'rilla, Hank?"

"And I'll tell you something else, Bud," observed the
Emir. "I got a hunch that Miss Mary Vanbrugh isn't
such a fool as you look. . . . What about if she was joshing
us *double*? . . ."

"Eh?"

"Women are funny things, Bud. They see further
through a brick wall than you can spit. . . . They got a
sort of second sight and sixth sense, worth all your clever-
ness, Son. It's what they call . . ."

"Instink?" suggested the Vizier.

"Yup, an' something else. . . . Institootion? . . . No.

Intooition. That's it. An' I got a hunch Miss Vanbrugh was clean through us—and out the other side!"

"*Gee!* . . . Think she's put Bojolly wise—if he wasn't already?"

"No. . . . No—I think not. . . . I allow she'd watch and wait. . . . If we weren't planning any harm to Boje, she'd plan no harm to us. . . . But I may be wrong. I usually am. . . ."

"Sure, Son," agreed the Vizier.

"I got to get Miss Vanbrugh alone tomorrow . . ." mused the Emir. . . .

"Me too. *Some,*" murmured the Vizier.

Two minds with but a single thought.

§ 4

The next morning the Emir, in the presence of the Vizier, granted an interview to his latest visitor.

Thereafter the two rulers sat in council.

"I said it, Son! *I said it!* He don't know us from Adam," said the Emir, as the French officer returned to his tent.

"Nor hardly from Eve, in these damn' petticoats," agreed the Vizier. "You *said* it, Professor—and I hand it to you, Son. . . . Sunday pants of Holy Moses, *he ain't after us at all! Inshallah!*"

"No, Judge, he ain't," replied the Emir. "We thought he had come gunning for us with half the French army—and he's come to bring us a million francs. . . . Can you beat it, Colonel?"

"How much *is* that, Sheriff?"

"Two hundred thousand bucks, Senator. . . . *Some* jack!"

"*Hamdulillah!* What'll we do with it, President?"

"Earn it, Governor. And do good with it."

"Good to *us,* too, Judge?"

"You said it, Colonel! We'll have our rake-off. The labourer is worthy of his wad. . . . Says those very words in the Bible. . . ."

"Sure thing, Pastor. *Allahu Akbar!* . . . Yea, verily the face of Allah the Merciful, the Compassionate, is turned unto these, his servants; and Muhammed, his Prophet, hath spoke up for us like a li'll man. Small prophets and quick returns maketh the heart glad."

"Glad goes, Son," agreed the Emir, and the two sat sunk in deep thought.

"We'll go riding this evening," said the Emir at length. "You can ride with Miss Vanbrugh, and I'll take Miss Atkinson. . . . But let me have a turn with Miss Vanbrugh too—on the way back, say—and if she starts joshing, I'll own up and confess—if it's plain she's called our bluff. . . . An American girl won't queer the pitch for two poor American men in a tight place and pulling off a big deal, 'specially if they own up and put it to her honest. . . ."

"What about the li'll Britisher?" asked the Vizier.

"By the Beard of the Prophet she's all-wool-an'-a-yard-wide. *She* wouldn't butt in an' spoil things. 'Specially when Miss Vanbrugh had a talk with her. . . . Then I can say my spiel to *her* in good old U.S.A. language—bye'n' bye. . . ."

"Yep—an' by the Beard of the Prophet *and* the Whiskers of Moses I can talk some good he-talk to Miss Mary," agreed the Vizier.

"Sure—but we gotta go careful, Bud. . . . We don't wanta get lead instead of gold out of Ole Man Bojolly. . . And b'lieve me, Son, it's Miss Vanbrugh for his—if she'll fall for him. . . ."

"I'll cut his throat first," growled the Vizier.

"Cut nothing, Son," replied the Emir. "You're alway falling in and out of love. . . . We aren't goin' to lose two hundred thousand bucks and the chance of settin these Injuns up for life, just because you haven't got self control of your passions. . . . Old Man Boje has come here in his innocence, wanting to give us a fortune—and we aren't going to hinder him any. . . . If Miss Vanbrugh'll have you, Bud, I'll be the happiest Sheikh of the Sahara—and I'll do all I know to bring it off. And i she won't have you, Son, you gotta take your gruel (*and* your sack of gold dust!), an' that's all there is to it. . . Get me, Steve?"

"I get you, Father. . . . But by the Ninety and Nine Names of Allah, I'll sure plaster Old Boje till . . ."

"Cut it *out*, I say, you thug. . . . If she's in love with

Bojolly we gotta remember that all the rest of the Universe don't matter a hill of beans to *her*—and the kinder we treat *him*, the fairer she treats *us*. . . . So go in and win if you can—and keep a poker-face if you can't. . . ."

"Huh! *You* aren't in love, you perishin' politician!"

"Nope? Well then p'raps I'll have the clearer head to steer us past the doors of the Oran Gaol and through those of the Bank of France, oh, Sheikh el Habibka. . . . Thou love-sick lallapaloozer."

§5

"And you really are perfectly certain that you can bluff it through to the end, and that Major de Beaujolais won't place you?" said Miss Mary Vanbrugh, as she and the Emir el Kebir rode side by side in the desert.

"Certain sure," replied the Emir. "We've been bluffing Arabs with our lives depending on it, and got away with it. . . . It'll take more than a Frenchman to . . ."

"He's one of the cleverest men that ever lived," interrupted the girl.

"Sure thing," agreed the Emir. "But he isn't an Arab. Why should he suspect anything wrong when he sees the Bedouin taking us as Bedouin? It wouldn't enter his head. It isn't as though he was looking for European or American crooks, or ever dreamt there was any about. I may tell you there's another Frenchman here too, who has lived in the same barrack-room with us! *He* hasn't an idea we're not Arabs!"

"How you did it, I don't know."

"Easy enough. Buddy and I were wandering in the Sahara for years—with a couple of bright boys, and with our eyes and ears open. We stayed dumb but we learnt a lot.

"Then I got lost, and this Tribe picked me up—with one foot in Heaven and the other twitching feeble but full of hope. . . . I stayed dumb until I surely knew Arabic better than American. . . . Got it from a three-year-old kid mostly. As he learnt to talk so did I. . . . Then I did a miracle on myself and came undumb. Even then I never said a sentence nor a word that I hadn't heard and learnt by heart. It was easy as fallin' off a log.

"The poor Injuns thought I was from a strange tribe, if they thought anything at all, when my pronunciation was funny, or I hadn't got quite the right religious dope. But I wasn't far out anyway, for I'd been studying that like Hell—for years."

"Your life must have hung by a thread at times."

"Well, it never hung by a palm-fibre rope, Miss Mary Vanbrugh, which is what it deserved," and the Emir smiled.

"And does still," replied the girl. "And where did you pick your friend up?"

"What, Buddy? Why, he and I have been friends since I was a road-kid. We've been soldiers, sailors, hoboes, cowboys, hoss-wranglers, miners, lumber-jacks, Wild West Showmen, conjurors, Foreign Legendaries and Sheikhs. . . . When I got lost in the desert, he got away to safety—and what you think he did? Rustled some camels and a nigger, and *come back to look for me*, right where he'd nearly died himself. . . . And when I got sort of top-sergeant there, I uster send scouts all round that same country to see if they could get news of another poor Bedouin picked up there like I was. . . .

"I never did—but I got news of a gang of Touareg who'd come up that way. . . . They'd got him—and I got them, good and plenty and just in time."

"What sort of a man is he? He has certainly got good taste, for he gives me the eye of warm approval. . . . Virtuous?"

"No. He isn't what I'd call that. I allow he's broken all the Commandments and looks to to do it again. . . . No, he hasn't got any virtues that I know of, 'cept courage, and loyalty, and gratitude, and reliability. . . .

"There isn't much to Buddy beyond that he's braver than any lion—for a lion hasn't got imagination—and that he never did a mean thing in his life nor went back on his word or his pal. No. He's only got a fine head and a great heart, and doesn't know the meaning of the words fear, despair, failure, selfishness, nor any kind of meanness. . . . Just an 'ornery cuss'. . . ."

"You want me to like him, I see . . ." smiled the girl, "so you damn him with faint praise. He sounds very like a man to me."

"No, I'm praising him with faint damns like 'ornery

226

cuss'. . . . You see, I'm one myself, and so Bud and me suits. . . . As to your liking him—you couldn't help that—but it would be a dark day for me if you married him an' took-him-home-to-Mother. . . ."

"Don't worry, Mr. Emir! . . . What would happen if you two fell in love with the same girl?" asked Mary Vanbrugh.

"Poor girl would be left a widow like, before she was married. I wouldn't butt in on Bud and Bud wouldn't butt in on me. . . ."

"And how long do you plan to stay in on this Sheikh game?"

"Till the li'll kid's ready to come into the business and sit on his father's stool. I promised his old Dad I'd see the boy through teething and high-school. . . . There's one or two sharks want his job."

"And will your friend stay here with you?"

"Sure. . . . Unless you take him away, Miss Mary Vanbrugh."

"Keep a stout and hopeful heart, Mr. Emir."

"Or unless Major D. Bojol*lay* takes us both away in the middle of a camel-corps of *goums* and things. . . ."

"Why should he want to do that?" asked the girl.

"He wouldn't *want* to, but it would be his painful 'Duty'—when it came out that we were swindlers and Americans, a big man and a little man, the same being wanted for departing from the Legion. . . . They'd prove it on us too, as soon as they got our whiskers off. So if you get mad with us any time, and tell him—it's us for big trouble. . . ."

"It's the very last thing in the world I'd tell him—if you were my worst enemies. . . . I'd give *anything in the world* for him to bring off this Treaty successfully. . . .

"If you only knew what it *means* to him . . . ! He has spent his life—and as hard a life as yours has been—in fitting himself for just such a stroke as this. It's not for himself either—it's for France. . . . He thinks of *nothing* but France—and Duty. . . .

"It's his one longing, to feel that he has *done* something for France, and that his labour hasn't been wasted. . . . His uncle is Commander-in-Chief and Governor-General and he's almost God to Major de Beaujolais. I think he'd value a pat on the back from the old man more than the Grand Cross of the Legion of Honour. . . ."

"How did you come to know the Major?" asked the girl suddenly.

"He was mule-walloping with a detachment of the Foreign Legion."

"And you actually served under him?"

"We did."

"How jolly—as they say in England."

"Yup. *Beau*-jolais—as they say in France."

"I wonder he doesn't recognize you."

"Well—we were clean-shaven in those days. A door-mat of whiskers and a *kafiyeh* make a lot of difference. . . . He might, yet—but people generally only see what they're looking for. . . ."

"It must be splendid to serve under him," said the girl.

"We hid our joy," replied the Emir. "We even tore ourselves away. . . ."

"And of course you'll make this Treaty?"

"Sure. Why not? Provided there's no 'peaceful penetration' nor the Blessings of Civilization, I'll make it. . . . France protects us, and we keep this end o' the Sahara quiet and healthy. We get a rake-off from France, an' we wax rich and prosperous because the caravan-roads and trade-routes'll be kept open and peaceful. . . ."

"You mean you and your friend will get rich?" asked Miss Vanbrugh.

"I surely hope we make our modest pile. . . . We aren't in the Sheikh business solely for our health. But what I meant was that these Injuns should prosper and get a bit in the bank. I'd like to hand over the whole outfit as a going concern when the young Sheikh's old enough. . . . And I'd like to be one of the few white men who have left the native better than he found him. It's a plumb silly idea of mine. . . ."

"You want to 'make two blades of grass grow where one grew before'?"

"Well—not so much grass, as *loobiyeh*. It's better grazing."

They approached the outlying palms of their corner of the Oasis.

"It's a bargain, then, Mr. Parlour-Sheikh," said the girl. "You'll do your utmost to keep Major de Beaujolais thinking you two are real Arabs, and you'll make the Treaty with him and see that it is kept—and I'll do my best for you. . . ."

"Sure. I'd sooner face a sack of gold twenty-franc pieces than a firing squad, any day, Miss Mary Vanbrugh. There's everything to gain for everybody on the one hand, and everything to lose for everybody on the other. . . ."

"There certainly is, including your beloved Arabs, remember . . . I shall be just a tiny bit anxious until we're away again, but oh, I do enjoy seeing you two solemn boys playing Sheikhs!"

"*Bismillah arahman arahmin. En nahs teyibin hena*," boomed the Emir el Hamel el Kebir, as they neared the tents.

"Why certainly," replied Miss Vanbrugh. "You've said it, Mr. Emir—whatever it is. . . ."

§6

At eventide, the Sheikh el Habibka el Wazir was dining with his lord, the Emir el Hamel el Kebir, as usual.

In sonorous Arabic these grave men discussed matters of importance to the *haute politique* of the Tribal Confederacy—until the servants had removed the tray of bowls, and brought the earthen cups of black coffee and the long *narghilehs*.

As soon as they were alone, they ceased to express their thoughts in the ancient tongue of the followers of the Prophet.

The Emir, smiling broadly, nodded his head.

"I was right, Son," he said. "Soon as we were alone, I turned a hose of Arabic on to Miss Mary Vanbrugh—best Arabic I ever shot; real Hot Dog. . . . What did she reply? Tell me that, O Father of Lies and Son of a Gun. . . . '*Cut it out, Bo*,' says she. '*Talk your mother-tongue and let's get next. What's the game with Major de Beaujolais?*' or words to that effect. And I fell for it, Son. I could not look that young woman in the face and get away with it. . . ."

"You talked *American* to her?" interrupted the Vizier.

"I'm telling you, Bud. . . . She had me back-chatting like two old Irish women—almost before I knew it. . . ."

"Jiminy!" breathed the Sheikh. "The li'll devil!"

"Why?" inquired the Emir.

"Because she wouldn't talk a word of American when *I* rode alone with her! She only knew French! . . . Gee! She surely did get my goat! When I tried a bit of broken English on her, as a sort of thin end of the wedge to letting her know we also were hundred-per-cent Anglo-Saxon Americans from God's own Country, she says:

"'*Commong-vous porty-vous*' an' '*Doo-de-la-day.* . . .' I mostly forgot my French since I left the Legion, but I twigged she was pulling my leg. . . . I said:

"'*You spik Engleesh.* . . . *Las' night you spik 'im,*' an' she replies, '*Nong Mossoo. Vous étiez ivre.*' (That means *drunk!*) '*Vous parlez Arabique,*' and every time I tried to say something kind and loving in English, she says, '*Parly Arabique Mossoo le Sheikh. Je ne comprong pas Anglais.* . . .' An' she don't know a word of Arabic, I swear."

"How d'you know she don't?"

"Well—she'd have fell off her hoss if she had understood what I said. . . . And there was me tryin' to talk plain American, and her axin' me in French to talk Arabic. . . . An' I didn't get any forrader. . . ."

"Gee! Can you beat it?" smiled the Emir. "Well, Buddy, my experience was more joyful than yours. Yea, verily, O Rose of Delight and Charmer of Many . . . Thou Son of None—and Father of Hundreds."

"Did you make love to her, Hank Sheikh . . . Thou Son of Hundreds—and Father of None?" asked the Vizier threateningly.

"Search me, Son! I hadn't the time nor the temptation. We talked good, sound, solid business, in good, sound, plain American. And let me put you wise, Son, and you quit dreaming love-stuff, and listen. . . .

"I've told Miss Mary Vanbrugh that we're two genuine low-brow American stiffs, honest-to-God four-flushers and fakers. . . . She says she could see that for herself. . . ."

"You speak for *yourself*, Hank Sheikh," interrupted the Vizier.

"I did, Son . . . Miss Mary spoke for *you*," replied the Emir.

The Vizier looked elated.

"She says, '*Where did you pick up that li'll ornery dead beat that side-kicks with you, Mr. Emir? Did the cat bring it in, or did the wind blow it along, or was it left on the beach by the tide? . . .'* or words to that effect, like."

The Vizier's face fell.

"Then *I* spoke for you, Son. I said, '*The pore guy ain't sich a God-awful hoodlum as he looks*, Miss Mary,' I said, and she replies kindly—'*No, Mr. Emir, I'm sure he couldn't be!*' and then I spoke up for you hearty, Bud, and I said there isn't your equal in Africa. . . ."

The Vizier beamed.

". . . to cut the throat of a goat, skin it and gut it, while another man'd be sharpening his knife. . . . But you interrupted me and I'm wandering around trifles. . . . Well . . . I had to admit that we're Americans, Boy, and wanted by the police . . . wanted badly—for doing a glide outa the Foreign Legion. . . . And I owned up that Old Man Bojolly had got me scared stiff, and that you and I allowed that we'd either got to find Boje a lone desert grave, or get up and hike once more—or else give in and go quietly. . . .

"Then Mary . . ."

"Who you calling 'Mary' so familiar, Hank Sheikh?" asked the Vizier, scowling indignantly.

"Then Miss Vanbrugh put her cards on the table too. A clean show-down, Son. . . . Boje *ain't* deserter-huntin'. He's got something better to do! . . . And he hasn't a notion about Rastignac. . . . That bunk he pulled on us about '*bearing a great and peaceful message*,' wasn't bunk at all! What he said to us in the Great and Solemn interview was *the Goods*. . . .

"We must have had uneasy consciences, Son. . . . He surely thinks he's on a Mission for his Fatherland. He ain't told Miss Vanbrugh too much about it—he being a diplomatist and all, but she knows that much for sure . . . And what do you know about *this*, Son? He's a Big Noise in their Secret Service—not just a Major in the Mule-Wallopers. . . ."

"By the Beard of the Prophet and the Name of Allah *I'll* wallop him," growled the Vizier.

"Well, as I was going to say when you injected that vulgar remark, Miss Vanbrugh and I have done a deal. She won't tell Bojolly that we're genu*ine* swindlers and

231

deserters from the Legion, provided we treat ole Boje kind and loving, and fall in with all his schemes. . . ."

"We'll fall in with those two hundred thousand dollars without a kick or a moan," observed the Vizier, "and I rise to remark that Viziers are Treasurers in this undeveloped rural State. . . ."

"So we're on velvet again, Bud. . . . All Old Man Bojolly wants to do, is to press the dough on us. All we gotta do is sign this Treaty not to let the Senussi in on the ground floor, and to have no truck with low foreigners. That means all people that on earth do dwell who aren't French. . . . Shall we boot Rastignac out an' tell him to go while the going's good—or keep him around and make a bit on the side? . . . But it's old Boje's Treaty we'll sign!"

"You can't sign '*Hank*' in Arabic, Father, can you?" inquired the Vizier.

"I certainly can, and you can sign '*Bud*' too. You only do a lot of pot-hooks upside down, with their tails turning to the left, and then scribble on it. . . .

"And mind, you gotta do it from right to left, too. I saw that boose-hoisting old rum-bound, Abdul Salam, doing it. . . . No Arabs can't get their signatures forged, because they never do 'em twice alike, and nobody can read 'em—least of all those who wrote 'em. . . . 'Sides, I've got the ole Sheikh's family ring . . ." and he indicated a great ancient seal ring that he wore on a slightly withered finger, of which the top joint was missing, the only finger that it would fit.

"Well, as I was trying to say, Buddy Bashaw, Miss Mary is as set on Bojolly getting away with it as we are. . . ."

"Why? What's the graft?" inquired the Vizier.

"Well—as I figger it—he's the golden-haired, blue-eyed boy. Saved her life in Zaguig. Shot up some stiffs who were handing out the rough stuff. Then brought her safe out of Zaguig—where her own brother must have got *his* by now, she says. Whole garrison shot up, and him with 'em. . . ."

"Old Man Boje must have been mighty set on paying a call here if he lit out from Zaguig while they were fighting. . . ."

"Sure thing, Son—you spoke the truth for once. . . . Mary—I mean Miss Vanbrugh—says it's *the* Big Thing of his Life, and if he pulls it off he's a made man. . . . He wouldn't stop in Zaguig for anything—though his comrades and his life-long pard and chum were in the soup. . . ."

"Then we raise our price, Hank Sheikh! What's a measly million francs if it's as important as all that . . .? Let's keep him guessing, and get some more in the jackpot. . . . Tell him we got other offers too. . . ."

"Well—Son of Temptation and Father of Joyful Ideas —we won't hurry any. I certainly like having the girls around—I could have wept bitter salt tears of joy all down my whiskers when those two girls stepped into our li'll home. . . ."

"Me too, Hank! I went all wambly in my innards and got a lump in my throat. . . . I nearly hugged 'em to my bosom. . . . I may yet. . . ."

"Not both, Son," remonstrated the Emir. "In the Name of the Prophet let the Reins of Moderation restrain the Stallion of Frowardness. Yup!"

"Only in the way of showing respect, I meant. I ain't a Mormon, am I? If Miss Mary'll marry me . . ."

"Well—don't go indulging your mind too much, Bud. It'll only make it worse for you later. . . . The way Miss Mary talked—I reckon she's a spinster for life or Mrs. Boje for ditto—if he has the sense to ax her. . . . She wouldn't do us any *harm*—not till Hell pops—but it's Old Man Bojolly's good *she's* thinking of. . . ."

The Vizier rose to his feet and strode up and down the tent like a caged lion.

"Look at here, Hank Sheikh," he said at last. "Can't we fix it for Mister Blasted Bojolly to take his punk Treaty and *go*—leaving the girls behind?"

The Emir pondered the suggestion.

"We could put it to him, Son," he said at length, "but I don't think you get old Boje right. . . . I could live the rest of my young life without Boje, I allow—but I believe he's a blowed-in-the-glass White Man, if he is a Wop or a Dago or a Frenchman. . . . We haven't had a sporting bet for some time, Bud—I'll lay you seven to three in *medjidies* that Boje won't stand for it. . . . He isn't going to leave two white girls in the wigwams of a camp of Injuns, while he gets away with the goods. . . . Nope . . . I'll make it ten to one on Boje and . . ."

"Done! *Shake!*" snapped the Vizier, extending his hand, and the two "shook". "I should certainly enjoy marrying his girl on his million francs. . . . Teach him not to come here frightening people . . . *and*—don't forget— *he left Dufour and Achmet and the others to die while he made his getaway!* . . ."

"But we won't hurry things, Hank," he added. "Let Boje get a bit anxious first. We'll coop him up some—an' pull the fierce and treacherous Sheikh stuff on him. We might pretend we was double-crossing him with the Rastignac outfit."

"You can have it your own way and run it how you like, Son," agreed the Emir, "but I promised Miss Vanbrugh we'd not hurt a hair of his lovely hide, bless him. . . ."

"He's a brave man, and he's straight. But I say he'd leave the girls in the lurch to get that Treaty," said the Vizier.

A silence fell.

The Vizier, his head on his hand-clasped knees, made the cooing sounds that showed his friend he was indeed again in love.

"Hank Sheikh, old Hoss," he said anon, "she is the plumb loveliest girl from Egypt to 'Frisco an' from Hell to breakfast. . . . *Yes,* Sir!"

"Mary or Maudie?" murmured the Emir, from the depths of his own long thoughts. . . .

L'HOMME PROPOSE

ONCE again the Emir el Hamel el Kebir and his guest Miss Mary Vanbrugh, rode alone.

". . . And why do you consult *me*, Mr. Emir?" said the girl. "Unlike yourself, I'm no matchmaker."

"If you're alluding to poor Buddy, I only spoke up for him because you were breaking his heart, Miss Mary Vanbrugh. . . .

234

"And why I wanted to consult you about Miss Maudie Atkinson is because she's your hired help, and I don't want to take her away from you while you're in the Desert —if you can't blow your own nose. . . .

"Also you're a woman—and you'd know better than a rough and common man like me, how a girl'd feel, and if it's a fair proposition. . . .

"Also you're clever, and can see if it's likely to pan out well for a girl like Maudie—who's been uster living in gay and populous cities. . . .

"Also if you think you could persuade Major D. Bojol*lay* that it is all right to leave her behind with us low In-juns. . . . In fact what do you think about it? . . ."

"Well, I think that Love is the *only thing that matters*," replied the girl, flushing warmly. "I think that Love is Heaven and Heaven is Love.

"No, I'm *certain* it is. . . . And if Maudie really loved you and you really loved Maudie, I'd say, 'Go to it, and God bless you, for you couldn't do a wiser thing! . . .'"

"It's Maudie I'm thinking about, more," said the Emir.

"So'm I. . . . And I believe she'd be as happy as the day is long, for she's the most romantic soul that ever lived —and one of the staunchest. . . .

"I know you'd be kind and good to her, and I know you'd have a splendid wife. . . . She's real pure gold all through. . . . And she'd worship the ground you trod on, for she's madly in love with Love. . . ." The girl gazed wistfully at the horizon. . . .

"But remember," she continued, "she's very simple, and she's no 'Janey that's Brainy'. She won't brighten your wigwam with high-brow thoughts and bee-you-ti-ful aspirations to make you lead a higher and better life of culture and uplift."

"Sure—God bless her," agreed the Emir.

"And how long did you plan to deceive her and play this Sheikh-game with *her*?" asked the girl.

"Just up to the day when she realizes that she's fair fed full with Arabs and Desert Sheikhs, and begins to wish I was an ornery White Man. . . . As soon as I see it in her eyes that she misses the shops an' movies an' street-cars an' candy an' the-pianner-an'-canary-home-sweet-home stuff, she becomes Mrs. Hank of the U.S.A. . . ."

"That's sense. She'll want another woman to talk frocks and scandal with, some day, however much she might love you. . . ."

"Sure. But me being willing to pull stakes and light out as soon as she gets real weary of the Injun life—d'you think it's fair to her if I? . . . "

"Yes. If she loves you. . . . She's seen how you live; and it's been the one great yearn of her young life to behold the Desert Sheikh Sheikhing in the Desert. . . . Shall I say anything to her? . . ."

"Not on your life, Miss Mary Vanbrugh! I'm going to do the things as I believe she dreams it. . . .

"All women are cave-women at heart, and would like to be swept off their feet once in their lives. . . . It's when they've got to wash the cave-man's shirt and pants, an' he will leave his nasty stinking tobacco-pipe on the cave drawing-room plush table-cloth; and bawls her out when he can't find his slippers, that cave-life wears thin. . . . Yep, they do cert'nly like to be swept off their feet and swept right away by a Strong Silent He-Cave-Man, once in their lives. . . ."

Miss Mary Vanbrugh sighed.

"Well, I hope you'll both be very happy—and if Maudie can stand desert life, you *will* be—for you're made for each other."

"And what about Major D. Bojol*lay*?"

"What do you mean?"

"Will he agree to leave her behind?"

"Yes—if I can persuade him that she'll be happy here. . . . To these European aristocrats she's just a 'servant and her tastes unaccountable. . . . Besides, if Maudie *won't* go back, he can't take her by force. . . ."

"Would he leave her if he thought she'd get a bad time? . . . *Would he leave the pair of you—in return for my signing the Treaty*, say?"

"I don't think you quite understand a gentleman—if you talk like that," answered the girl.

"No. Sure. I haven't had much truck with gentlemen, Miss Mary Vanbrugh. Only low common men like me and Buddy. . . . Sure. . . . 'Sides—to tell you the truth *I was thinking of Dufour and the others that he left to die*, for the sake of his Treaty . . .! I knew old Dufour. He was a man. He was Sergeant-Major with Major D. Bojol*lay* when he was mule-walloping at Tokotu. . . . I knew Achmet too. . . . He was a real fine he-man and *some* scrapper. . . ."

"Yes, yes," broke in the girl, "but it was *duty*. Duty is his God. . . ."

"Sure. It's what I'm saying, Isn't this Treaty *still* his Duty? It'll be real interestin'. . . . All a matter of what's your own private *Bo Ideal* as they call it. . . . 'Sides, Major D. Bojol*lay's* French, and as you said, he'd give his soul to get that Treaty for his beloved France. . . ."

"His *soul*, perhaps—not his honour," was the proud reply, but the Emir, closely watching, had seen her wince.

"I always mistrusted people that go about with a wad of 'honour' bulgin' outa their breast-pockets. . . . I've found . . ."

But Miss Mary Vanbrugh spurred her horse forward and the Emir's further words of wisdom were lost.

§ 2

Miss Maudie Atkinson, bred and born in Cockaigne and the sound of Bow Bells, stood at eventide on a sandhill of the Oasis and gazed yearningly towards the setting sun.

She was a happy, happy girl, but the cup of her happiness was not full. She had, she felt, been, in a manner of speaking, captured by Sheikhs, but not by a Sheikh.

True, the great and beautiful man, the *lovely* man, in whose presence she had thrice feasted, had looked upon her with the eye that is glad—and Miss Atkinson, as an extremely attractive girl who had grown up in London, was experienced in the Glad Eye. . . .

She had had it, she was prepared to swear, from the Great Sheikh, and, moreover, he had held, and squeezed and stroked her hand. . . .

But, as one who knew joyous days on the Mondays that are holy, Bank Holy Days, at Easter, at Whitsun, and eke in August, Miss Atkinson knew a sense of something lacking.

Young pages and footmen of on-coming disposition had to be slapped and told to Give over, to Stop it, to Come off it, Not to be so Fast, and had to be asked What they thought they were Doing—pulling people about until their back hair came down and all. . . .

But there seemed to be no hope that the Great Sheikh was going to earn a slap and an admonition to Stop it. . . .

Not his to chase, with flying feet, a shrieking damsel who fled across the daisy-pied sward to a quiet spot. Not his to hug, wrestle, and mildly punch, a coy nymph, who scolded laughingly.

Not his to behave thus, nor issue invitation to the quiet walk that leads to "walking-out".

No; a calm and dignified man, alas, but oh, so big and beautiful, and so authentic. . . . And his eyes fair burnt into you. . . . Just as the lady had written in the book, the lovely Book of Sheikhs. . . .

Maudie dreamed. . . . And remembered passages from the Book. . . .

"*With a thunderous rush of heavy hoofs, the Desert Sheikh was upon her, and ere she could so much as scream, she found herself swung like a feather to his saddle-bow and whirled afar across the desert. . . . On, on, into the setting sun—while his hot lips found hers and drank deep of her beauty the while they burnt her very flesh like fire. . . .*"

Ah-h-h-h-h. That was the stuff. . . .

And even as the Cupid's bow of Maudie's mouth trembled with the words, there *was* a thunderous rush of heavy hoofs, two huge and powerful hands took her beneath the arms, and she was mightily hauled from the ground and dumped heavily on to a hard saddle—("*Oo*-er!")—and whirled afar across the Desert—on, on, into the setting sun. . . .

Maudie all but swooned. Half fainting with joy, and with the hope fulfilled that maketh the heart too full for speech, she summoned the strength to raise her arms and her eyes.

The latter gazed straight into those of the Great Sheikh Himself, and the former settled firmly about his neck.

His lips found her in deed and very truth, and with a shuddering sigh of the deepest content and the highest gratitude for the fruition of a life's ambition, Maudie gave the Great Sheikh Himself the First Kiss of Love—a long, long clinging kiss—and was grateful to God for His wondrous goodness.

When Maudie came to earth again, wondering to find

the earth still there and Maudie still in the strong arms of this Wonder of the World, she wiped her eyes (and nose) with the sleeve of her *barracan*, sniffed, and gave a little sob.

The Emir reined in his horse, dismounted, and lifted her to the ground. Her knees betrayed her, and she sat down with some suddeness, on the soft warm sand.

The Emir seated himself beside her and took her hand.

"Li'll girl," he said, "will you marry me?" and Maudie cast herself wildly upon his broad bosom.

"Oh, *Sheikh, darling!*" she said, and again flung her arms about his neck.

"We'll get married by the mullah-bird here," said the Emir later. "Then bye'n-bye we'll hike to where there's a Christian marriage-dope man, an' get married some more. Have *another* wedding, Maudie!"

Maudie snuggled.

"And have *another* honeymoon, darling," she whispered.

They kissed until they could kiss no longer. . . .

Anon she dragged herself from him and stared wide-eyed.

"Why—you spoke *English!*" she stammered in amaze. . . .

"Sure. I learnt it since you came—so's to talk to you, Maudie." said the Emir modestly, and again gathered the girl in a huge embrace.

"But mind you, Maudie," he said impressively, when they rose to go, "that Major de Bojolly mustn't know I've learnt English or else he'd want to talk English all the time —and get me muddled in business perhaps, while I'm a beginner—or p'raps he'd think I wasn't a Sheikh at all!"

"Oh, him!" murmured Maudie languidly. "He's only a Frenchie. . . ."

§ 3

In the *hareem* portion of the chief Guest-tent were four women, two white and two black.

The black women were slaves, brought as "orphans" from Lake Tchad by a Senussi caravan, and sold to the old Sheikh twenty years before.

The bad old days of the fire-and-slaughter Arab slave-raider are gone for ever, but there is still some slave-dealing carried on—chiefly in children.

These are sold by their parents, or adoptive parents in the case of genuine orphans, to caravan-leaders, who sell them again at a profit in the distant oases, where negroes, other than slaves, are not.

The shocked European Authority confiscates the entire caravan if a slave is found with it—but the caravan does not seek the spots honoured by Authority.

And if Authority goes out of its way and seeks the caravan, it finds none but happy adopted children, staring big-eyed from the backs of camels, or toddling along beside kindly men, or seated patting scarcely "fair" round bellies, beside the cooking-pot.

The unshocked Arab Authority buys the healthy little animal, and treats it well, because it is valuable property; and, when it grows up, puts it in regiment or *hareem* according to its sex—where it may rise to high rank and power as a military commander, or to the position of Sheikh's favourite, and mother of future Sheikhs.

Slave-raiding is the foulest and vilest pursuit ever engaged in by man, but a great deal of misunderstanding exists about slavery as an Arab institution. . . .

And certainly the two black slave-women, who squatted in the *hareem* side of the guest-tent, were happy enough, as they produced beautiful Arab stuffs and clothing, *henna* for the nails and hands, *hadida* for the hair, *djeldjala* "golden drops", *khalouk* rouge, *koh'eul* for the eyes, and other matters of feminine interest, from the big *bahut* trunk they had carried over from the tents of Sidi Dawad Fetata.

The four women chattered; the chirping sounds of a Senegalese dialect mingled with the Cockney accent of London and the refined tones of a Boston high-school and college; and though in language they were divided, in interest they were one, as the slave girls showed the uses of the stuffs, clothing, unguents, paints and powders that they had brought. . . .

Anon came the aged Sidi Dawed Fetata, smiling sweetly, and saying that his long white beard was a perfect chaperon and his age-dimmed eyes were blinded by the beauty of the Sitts.

"*Salamoune aleikoume Esseleme, Sitt Roumya,*" he said. "*Marhaba, marhaba,*" and proceeded to hope that life might be as sweet as *Mekhtoume*, the Wine of Paradise;

as beautiful as *jahwiyan* daisies in the desert; as satisfying as the dates of Nabt al Saif; and as long and flowing as the Tail of the Horse of the Prophet. . . .

"The old dear is making a beautiful speech, Maudie, if we could only understand a word of it," said Mary Vanbrugh, and smiled graciously upon the visitor, who promptly produced gifts—a silver *khams* Hand-of-Fatma charm, and silver *maroued* box to hold *koh'eul* for Mary; with a *sokhab* tiara of small coins and a *feisha* charm (to keep a husband's affections) for Maudie.

The old gentleman then announced a *diffa*, clapped his hands, and the slave girls brought in a huge *sahfa* dish, on which was an appalling heterogeny of bowls and platters, of *berkouks*, pellets of sweetened rice; cous-cous; *cherchem* beans; *leban* curds; *burghal* mince-meat and porridge; *asida* dough and onions; *fatta* carrots and eggs; strange sweetmeats, fruits, and drinks.

"As good a death as any, Grandpa," replied Miss Vanbrugh, to the old Sidi's "*Bilhana!* With Joy! *Bilshifa!* With health!" and they fell to. . . .

"Coming round, Maudie?" asked Miss Vanbrugh later, when they were alone, comatose, replete, bursting with food.

"I'm *getting* round, Miss," replied Maudie.

"We shall be as round as one of those lovely fat Arab babies dressed in a string of beads, if we go on like this, Miss," she added. "I shall fair lose my figger."

"We'll offer a reward for it, Maudie . . . *Lost—a lovely figure. . . . Anyone returning the same to Miss Maudie Atkinson at No. 1, High Street, Emir's Camp, Great Oasis . . .*"

"Oh, *Miss*," murmured Maudie, "may I tell you something? I'm not going to be Miss Atkinson much longer."

"You've told me already, Maudie."

"Oh, *no*, Miss!"

"But you have! You've been mad, Maudie, ever since it happened. Perfectly insane—going about like a dying duck in a thunderstorm; trying to do my hair with a toothbrush; trying to manicure my nails with sandpaper. You don't know who you are nor where you are; nor whether you're on your head or your heels. . . . Now tell me all about it. . . ."

Maudie told. . . .

. . . . .

"If you see Major de Beaujolais, to speak to, don't tell him that some of the Arab Sheikhs know English, Maudie," said Miss Vanbrugh, when Maudie's rapture-recital was finished.

"*No*, Miss," replied Maudie. "The Great Sheikh told me not to. He said the Major might take advantage of his innocence and make him talk English when he was bargaining—and do him down. . . . It would be a shame to impose on him, wouldn't it, Miss?"

"I don't think the Major will impose on the Emir, Maudie," said Miss Vanbrugh, a little coldly perhaps. "Anyhow—say nothing about it."

"I'd sooner rather *die*, first, Miss," asseverated Maudie warmly.

"Well—if you do let it slip—you'll die *after*," observed Miss Vanbrugh, "for I'll certainly kill you, Maudie."

§ 4

During the days that followed, the Emir noticed a change in the temper of his trusty Vizier.

Perhaps no one else would have seen it, but to the Emir, who loved his friend with a love passing the love of women, including Maudie, it was clear that the Vizier was really suffering and unhappy.

Never, nowadays, in the privacy of the open desert, did he sing,

> "*O ki yi yip; O ki yi yi,*
> *O ki yi yip; and ki yi yi,*
> *Get along you stinkin' camels, don't you cry,*
> *We'll all be in Wyoming in the sweet bye-an'-bye,*"

or any other amended version of any of the eighty verses of "The Old Chisholm Trail". Nor did he utter vain longings for his old mouth-organ. . . .

His hard grey eyes, that saw so much and told so little, enigmatic, ironic, unreadable, humorous, were humorous no longer. . . .

The Emir was troubled, torn between two emotions, and quite unreasonably ashamed. . . .

The object of his thoughts rode past on a lathered horse, staring grimly before him, looking neither unto the right hand nor unto the left. . . . He looked dangerous.

"Oh! Sidi Wazir!" called the Emir. "Come and *faddhl*," and El R'Orab the Crow ran and took the Vizier's horse and led it away to its stable of plaited palm leaves in in the *fondouk* horse-lines. . . .

"Good job this is a Dry State, Hank Sheikh," growled the Vizier, seating himself beside the Emir, "or I should cert'nly lap the *laghbi* this night. . . . *Hamdulillah!* I'd sure be off the gosh-dinged water-wagon, *some*!"

"What's the trouble, Son?" asked the Emir, although he knew too well.

"Trouble is, I'm going to bust that Sheikh-wrangler, Bojolly. . . . *Rahmat Allah!* Treaty or no Treaty. . . . And tell him some talk in the only sensible language there is. . . ."

"What's he done now, Son?" inquired the Emir.

"Put me in Dutch with Miss Vanbrugh. . . . The Infiddle Dorg. . . ."

"I allow he'd play a square game, Bud."

"I mean it was through him I spoke rude to a lady an' showed myself the low-life ornery bindle-stiff I am."

"You was never rude to any lady, Bud."

"Yes, I was, Hank Sheikh. I axed her if she was engaged to be married to a scent-smellin', nose-wipin', high-falutin dude French officer. . . ."

"What you do that for, Son?"

"She turned down my respeckful proposal of matteri-mony."

"And then you fired up about Bojolly?"

"Sure."

"And what did Miss Vanbrugh say when you did that? She talked American at you all right this time, then?"

"Yep. You bet. When I began to call Bojolly down . . ."

"What did she say when you asked if she was fixed up with the Mayor?"

"She says, '*It's a beautiful sunset tonight, Mr. Man,*' an' she thought she was ridin' with a decent an' courteous American, and that Major D. Bojo*llay* was the finest and noblest and bravest man she'd ever met, an' thank you, she'd prefer to ride back to the Oasis alone. . . ."

"What you do then, Son?"

"I says, 'I thought *you* was American, Miss Vanbrugh,' an' then I over-rode my hoss like the mean coyote I am."

243

"So you're sore and ashamed, Son. You hurt a hoss an' a woman, the two best things there are. . . ."

"I'm tellin' you. . . . And I'm goin' to eat sand . . . and I'm goin' to bust that Sheikh-wrangler, Bojolly. . . ."

"As how?"

"He can shout his own fancy—knives, guns . . . rifles if he likes, P'raps he'd prefer to use that sword he's brought all this way to impress us and the girls. . . . I'll back my Arab sword against it, if he likes."

"What d'*you* like, Son?"

"Knives. I ain't had a knife-fight since when. And it's a satisfying way of expressin' your feelings to a man you don't much like. . . ."

"And Miss Vanbrugh, Son? Miss Vanbrugh, who you love so much, and who thinks Major D. Bojo*lay* the finest an' noblest an' bravest man she ever saw . . .? Didn't I *tell* you, right back at the very first . . .? Didn't I say to you, '*Don't you go kidding yourself, you Bud—for she's going to be a spinster or Mrs. Boje*'?"

The Vizier scowled glumly.

"Now I'll tell you something for your good, Buddy Bashaw. . . . You aren't in love with *any*body. . . . You're just plumb jealous of a better man than yourself, because he's got away with it. . . . Who was first in the field? . . . You talk about busting Boje! And why for? Because you can't get his girl away from him! . . . *Gee!*"

"Spill some more, you oozin' molasses-bar'l," growled the Vizier.

"Certainly. . . . If you haven't got the innercence o' the dove nor the wisdom of the serpent, you *can* have the sense of a louse. . . . Ole Man Bojo*lay* brought Miss Vanbrugh here, and he's goin' to take her away again. . . . You made your firm offer of marriage and it was declined with thanks. . . . Now behave your silly self . . . and be ashamed of you."

"Sure. But look at here, Hank Sheikh. I'm *plumb jealous of a better man than me*, am I? Well—no objection to makin' *certain* who's the better man, is there?"

"Yep. You aren't goin' to fight Major D. Bojo*lay*, so don't think it. I dunno what's bitin' *you*, Buddy Bashaw. . . . *Wallahi!*"

"Why not fight him?"

"Because he's our guest. . . . Because he's going to give us a wad of jack. . . . Because we don't want any French army here looking for him. Because Miss Vanbrugh thinks he's the noblest, bravest, and . . ."

"Gee! I got a think come!" interrupted the Vizier. . . . "We'll sure try the brave man out. . . . We'll see if he *is* worthy o' Miss Vanbugh—which nobody is."

"'Cept Buddy Bashaw the Wild and Woolly Wazir," murmured the Emir.

The Vizier pursued his great idea.

"You say he's the Almighty Goods, an' *you* seem to want him to marry Miss Mary—well, *we'll try him out. Inshallah!*"

"Now look at here, Son," interrupted the Emir again. "Get this straight. . . . See that hand o' mine, Boy?"

"*Some! Allahbyjiminy!* I could see it seven mile away, without a telescope neither—an' then mistake it for a leg o' mutton. . . ."

"See that hand o' mine, Bud," repeated the Emir solemnly. "God's my witness, I'd cut it off, if that'd make you an' Miss Mary happy for life. I cert'nly would. . . . But I got sense, tho' I ain't a clever li'll man like you—an' I say no girl ever did a plumb sillier thing than marry a man she didn't love. . . . Nor any man ever did such a *damn*, silly thing as wanta marry a gal that didn' love him. . . . I'd sooner see Mary marry you and live on goat's flesh and barley-bread in a tent, than marry the Major and live in High Sassiety, provided she loved you. . . . But she don't. And won't. . . ."

"Very well, Pastor, an' that's *that*. . . . Now then! We're goin' to find out how much this French parlour-snake and lounge-lizard *does* love Miss Vanbrugh. . . . First of all I'm goin' to take ten *medjidies* off'n you, an' if I don't, then you're goin' to take a hundred off *me*."

"How's that, Son?"

"You forgot that li'll bet we made? We're goin' to knock him up in the dead o' night an' offer him the Treaty, signed, sealed and witnessed—*provided* he saddles up an' lights out tomorrow *without* the girls. . . ."

"Which he cert'nly won't."

". . . An' if you're right you get your ten. *And* soon after that, we'll give him a *real* test. . . . Now I'd lay down my life for Miss Vanbrugh, or any other nice girl . . ."

"Sure thing, Son. *Any* girl."

". . . and if Boje *really* loves Miss Vanbrugh, let him lay down his'n. . . . We'll give him the opportunity. . . . He oughta be proud of the chance to do it! . . . He won't though, you betcha, and I put a hundred to one on it."

"*Done*. Shake. Put it there, Son," and the two erring men shook hands.

"It's robbing you, Son—and I didn't oughta do it," pondered the Emir thereafter, "but you gotta live and learn."

"You live till tonight and you'll learn you've lost ten bucks, Hank Sheikh," was the cold reply.

"I'll live, Son, if Rastignac don't get me," answered the Emir. "He'd poison our coffee when we visited him, or shoot us unarmed as soon as look at us, if he thought he could get away with it—and nominate his own Emir here. . . . How *I* didn't shoot *him* when he started in about murderin' Boje and doin' worse for his two female spies, I do *not* know."

"Me, neither," agreed the Vizier. "I promise myself a quiet heart-to-heart wrangle with Rastignac when the time comes. . . . Reckon we should be layin' up trouble for the tribes if Rastignac was never seen again?"

"Sooner or later. . . . It's bound to come though, when we hitch up with the French, as we must. . . . The foul filthy coyote—I'd like to hang him on a tree."

"I allow he's got the face of a shark and the heart of a shark," observed the Vizier.

"No, no! That's an exaggeration, Son," reproved the Emir. "There never wasn't any shark with a face as much like a shark's as Rastignac's is. Nor any shark with a heart as much like a shark's neither. . . . Still, he's a brave man—and he shall die a man's death if we don't let him go."

"Right, Hank Sheikh," agreed the Vizier. "Let me fight him. . . . *Knives!*"

"We'll see how things pan out with Boje before we settle Rastignac's hash," replied the Emir. "I should smile to stick 'em in a ring, with any weapons they liked, and say, 'Now fight it out for yourselves'—*after* tellin' Boje what Rastignac offered us big money to do to him *and the girls*. . . ."

"*Rastignac!*" growled the Vizier, and spat in a vulgar and coarse manner.

"You low common man," observed his lord. "You don't seem to improve in your ways although you live with *me*."

"*No*," replied the Vizier significantly.

CHAPTER VIII

LA FEMME DISPOSE

YOLUBA, the seven-foot Soudanese slave, on sentry-go outside the Guest-tent, heard the murmur of voices rising and falling within.

That did not interest him in the least.

Nothing interested him greatly, save to get the maximum of food, love, fighting and sleep. And the approbation of his Lord the Sidi el Hamel el Kebir, Commander of the Faithful and Shadow of Heaven.

To do this, orders must be obeyed promptly and exactly.

Present orders were to prevent the *Franzawi* Sidi from leaving the Guest-tent—firmly but respectfully to tell him he must stay within, because the sun (or moon) was very hot without.

Suddenly the voices ceased and then the *Franzawi's* rose to an angry and abusive shout! Should he rush in?

No—for the Emir and the Vizier were coming out.

"I hand it to you, Hank Sheikh," admitted the Vizier, as the two entered the pavilion of the Emir. "Boje cert'nly spoke up like a man. . . . He's made good *so far*."

"You can hand me ten chips too, Son," observed the Emir. "And if you go on with it, you'll hand me a hundred. I'll let you back out if you wanta quit. . . . In fact I'd like you to. I hate playing a low-down trick on a brave man. . . ."

"Cut out the sob-stuff, Hank Sheikh," was the prompt

reply. "If he's the blue-eyed hero, let him live up to it—or *die* up to it. He won't know it's a trick either, the way I figger it. 'Sides, you're so all-fired anxious about Miss Vanbrugh—let's see if he's solid, before you give him your blessin' and a weddin'-present."

"What's the frame-up, Son?" asked the Emir.

"Why—we're goin' to be the fierce and changeable, treacherous Sheikhs on him for a bit, and get him buffaloed. Then we'll pay another midnight call on him, an' tell him he's sure hurt our tenderest feelin's—callin' us dorgs an' pigs an' such. . . . Got to be wiped out in blood. . . . But we don't want to wipe a guest ourselves—so if he likes to do it himself, we'll let the girls go free and uninjured immediately."

"And if he won't?"

"Then we say, 'Very well, Mr. Roumi. Then the gals come into our *hareems*, the Treaty gets signed, an' you can get to Hell outa this with it. . . .'"

"And if he says, '*How can I trust you to do me a square deal when I'm dead?*'"

"Then we say, '*You* GOTTA *trust us. No option. But when we noble savages give our word on the Q'ran—it goes.*'"

"And how do we work it . . .? Tell R'Orab to pull the cartridges outa his gun beforehand, and then let him shoot himself with an empty gun. . . . When it clicks, our stony bosoms relent and we embrace him in tears. . . . That it?" asked the Emir.

"Nope. Too easy a death. Nothing in shootin' yourself. 'Sides, he might *find* his gun had been emptied, an' double-cross us. Shoot himself with the empty gun, grinnin' up his sleeve meantime."

"What then?"

"Nasty sticky death. Poison."

"He might drink it, feeling sure it was a bluff and grinning to himself while hopin' for the best."

"He's goin' to *know* it's poison. Good forty-mile, mule-slayin', weed-killer. . . . What we took off old Abdul Salam. . . . He's going to see it kill a dorg."

"Well, it'll kill *him* then, won't it?"

"Nope. The poison'll be in the poor dorg's drinkin'-water *already*. Then I'll pour half a gill of *pure milk* into it, an' the li'll dorg drinks an' hands in his checks *pronto*. . . .

Then I give the rest o' the milk to Boje in his cawfee. . . .
Then it's up to him. . . . *If* he drinks, you get a hundred
bucks, an' Boje gets Miss Vanbrugh. . . ."

"An' if he don't?"

"We'll ride him outa town an' tell Miss Vanbrugh that
the li'll hero—what was goin' to live for her—didn' see
his way to *die* for her."

"*You* can tell her, Bud. . . . I'll be somewhere else at
the moment. . . ."

"Well—we ain't goin' to put him in in any danger, nor
do a thing *to* him, are we?"

"Not a thing. . . . And you're going to a girl to bear
the glad news that her hero's slunk off and left her because
his hide was in danger and to get his Treaty signed. Shake,
Son, I admire a brave man."

"But it'll be *true*, won't it?" expostulated the Vizier.

"Yes, Son—and that's what she'll never forgive you,"
replied the Emir.

"But it won't be," he added. "Boje'll lap that fake
poison of yours like you'd drink whisky. . . . And he'll
come outa this job better'n we shall. . . . I don't like it,
Son. Sure thing, I don't—but it'll come back on your
own silly head. . . . Mary'll love the Major all the more,
and our name'll be Stinkin' Mud. . . . The Major'll love
Mary all the more, because he tried to die for her. . . ."

"Die nothing!" jeered the Vizier. "He's only a furriner
an' a scent-smellin' ornament. . . . Drinkin' poison at
three o'clock in the morning's a tougher proposition
than shootin' off guns in a scrap. . . . 'Sides—s'pose he did
play the li'll hero an' drink the fatal draught to save his
loved one's life—he won't tell her about it afterwards, will
he? 'Specially when he finds it was all a fake?"

"No. He won't say anything, Son. But *I* shall. If
Boje swills dorg-slaying poison on an empty stomach in
the nasty small hours o' the morning, he's goin' to get the
credit for it—an' I'll see he does. . . ."

"Well—he won't, Hank Sheikh, so don't spend those
hundred bucks before you collect. . . . Well, I'm goin'
to hit it for the downy. . . ."

The Emir sat stroking his beard reflectively, and murmured, "*Wallahi!* Verily '*he worketh well who worketh
with Allah*,' saith The Book. . . . Bust me if *I* know—

Anyway, it'd settle that li'll girl's doubts once for all—an' poor Ole Man Dufour's ghost won't worry her. . . . If I guess her right, she hates one little corner of Boje and worships the rest of him with all her soul. . . . It's an awful low-down trick in a way—but it'll settle things once for all for Miss Mary Vanbrugh. . . . If Boje is a dyed-in-the-wool and blowed-in-the-glass bachelor, with his work as his wife and his job as his mistress, she better know it—the sooner the quicker. . . . It is a low-down game, Bud—awful mean and ornery—but those Secret Service guys cert'nly spend their lives in bluffing and playing tricks. . . . It's their job. . . . And they ought to take it in good part if they're bluffed themselves. . . . *Bluff!* Gee! What a bluff to pull on the bluff-merchant. Well, let it rip. . . ."

"Sure thing," replied the departing Vizier. "G'night, pard. *Emshi besselema.*"

§ 2

As the Emir and his Vizier rode back from visiting the camp of the emissary of the Sultan of Stamboul and his great Brother; and from watching the drill of the camel-corps recruits; inspecting the *fondouk* and lines; and generally doing the things that most Oriental Rulers leave to others to leave undone, the Emir asked his Vizier if he had slept well, and if he had risen in a better frame of mind.

"I'm goin' to try Bojolly out, I tell you," replied the Vizier.

"And you got it clear that whether he stands or falls, it won't do you any good with Miss Vanbrugh?"

"Yup. I done with women. My heart's broke—but I shall get over it. I don't ask any girl twice. She refused me flat. Quite nice but quite certain. *And,* when I called Bojolly down—quite nasty an' still more certain. . . . No, Hank, my heart's broke, but I'm facin' up to life like a man. . . ."

"Sure thing, Bud. . . . Now drop this foolishness about the Major. It won't do any good. . . ."

"Do some good if it saves Miss Vanbrugh from a fortune-huntin' French furriner, won't it? American girls should marry American men. . . ."

"And American men should marry American girls, I s'pose?" observed the Emir.

"You said it, Son. . . . Say—ain't that li'll Maudie-girl some peach? . . ."

"She surely is. . . . Pity your heart's broke, Bud. Still—American men gotta marry American girls, anyway."

"Well—Anglo-Saxon men oughta marry Anglo-Saxon girls, I mean. *Course* they ought. . . . No frills an' doo-dahs about Maudie, if she *is* British. . . . Make a fine plain wife fer a plain man. . . ."

"You cert'nly *are* a plain man, Bud," admitted the Emir reluctantly.

"Maudie may be engaged already," he added.

"She don't wear any ring. . . . I looked to see . . ." replied the Vizier.

"Well—I *have* known engaged girls not wear a ring, Son," admitted the Emir.

"Then they was engaged to mean skunks," decided the Vizier, and burst into song.

His broken heart evidently *was* mending, and cool dawn in the desert is a very stimulating, lovely hour.

The Emir smiled tolerantly as he listened to one more variation of "The Old Chisholm Trail". All was well with Buddy when Buddy sang. . . .

"Wish I got my ole mouth-organ," observed the Vizier.

"Your mouth is an organ in itself, Son," replied the Emir, as the Vizier again lifted up his voice and informed the wide Sahara that,

> *"Ole Hank Sheikh was a fine ole Boss,*
> *Rode off with a gal on a fat-backed hoss,*
> *Ole Hank Sheikh was fond of his liquor,*
> *Allus had a bottle in the pocket of his slicker."*

"How you know I rode off with a girl on a fat-backed hoss, Son?" asked the Emir, as the Vizier paused for breath.

"I didn't," admitted the Vizier. . . . "Did you? Sorta thing you *would* do. . . . Many a true word spoken in jest. . . ."

"Sure, Son. And many a true jest spoken in words," agreed the Emir.

They rode on.

"Sing some more, Son," requested the Emir. "Thy voice delights me, O Father of a Thousand Nightingales. It's good training for these high-strung Arab hosses. . . . Make the animals calm in a mere battle. . . ."

And the Vizier continued the Saga, in the vein of the history-recording troubadours of old:

> *"Foot in the stirrup and hand on the horn,*
> *Worst old Sheikh that ever was born.*
> *Foot in the stirrup, then his seat to the sky,*
> *Worst old Sheikh that ever rode by."*

§ 3

Beside a little irrigation-runlet Miss Maudie Atkinson sat—and waited, her mental attitude somewhat that with which she had been familiar all her life at the hour of one on the Sabbath Day, "*For what we are about to receive. . . .*"

Emerging from the Guest-tent, at what, after much peeping, she considered to be propitious moment, she had strolled past the tents of her *fiancé* (her *fiancé!*), the Great Sheikh, and walked slowly towards a strategic spot.

Here she threw off her *barracan* and stood revealed, Maudie Atkinson, in a nice cotton frock, white stockings and white shoes. Much more attractive to Arab eyes, she was sure, than shapeless swaddlings of a lot of blooming night-dresses and baggy trousers.

Silly clo'es for a girl with a figger. . . .

Would he come?

Sure to, if he wasn't too busy, or hadn't got to take Miss Mary for a ride. . . . When would that nice Major come up to the scratch, and take what was waiting for him . . .? Oh, what happy, lucky girls she and Miss Mary were! . . .

Would he come?

A shadow moved beside her and she turned.

Golly! It was the little one. Didn't he look a nib in those gay robes!

"Good evening, sir," said Maudie.

"'Evening, Miss," replied the Vizier. "Shall we go for a li'll stroll under the trees?"

"*I* don't mind if we do, sir," said Maudie, rising promptly. (*Sheikhs!*)

"I been admiring you ever since you come, Miss," observed the Vizier as they strolled off.

"No! Straight? Have you *reely?*" ejaculated Maudie.

"Sure. All the time," replied her companion with conviction. "In fact, I follered you tonight to say so— an' to ask you if you thought you an' me might hitch up an' be pards. . . ."

"*I* don't mind, sir," said Maudie. "Fancy *you* speaking English, too. . . ."

"Yes, Miss. . . . Er—yes. You see, I sent for a hand-book as soon as I saw you that night."

"No! Not *reely?*"

"Sure! Fact! Would I tell you a *lie?* But you must never let Major Bojolly know."

"Oh no, sir. Miss Vanbrugh said she'd kill me if I did. . . . As if I *would!* Besides, I never see him now. Why are you keeping him a prisoner?"

"Oh, we're just making sure he doesn't run off an' take you two ladies away from us. . . ."

"He don't take *me!* *I'll* watch it," asserted Miss Maud Atkinson.

"My heart would cert'nly break if he did. . . . Miss Maudie, will you marry me?"

"Oh, *sir!* If you'd only spoke sooner!" Maudie looked down and blushed.

"I'm engaged to the other Sheikh. . . . We're going to be married twice and have two honeymoons. . . . It's reely very kind of you, sir, but things being as they are, I . . ."

Maudie looked up. But the Sheikh had gone. . . .

A few minutes later he thrust his head into the sleeping-tent of the Emir, where that gentleman, dressing for dinner, was washing his feet.

With a horrible scowl and a display of gleaming teeth, the Vizier gazed upon his Lord.

"O you Ram*bunc*tious Ole Goat," he hissed, and withdrew his Gorgon head from the aperture.

§ 4

But, being a man of noble forbearance and generosity, this was the only allusion made by the Vizier to the human frailties of his Lord.

The soul of determination, and slow to accept defeat, he remarked during the course of the evening *faddhl*:

"Say, Hank—how you like to be a *real* brother-in-law to a Sheikh?"

"Fine, Bud. . . . You got a sister for me to marry?"

"No, Son. And if I had I'd be pertickler who she married to. . . . No, I meant a real Sheikh, and I was referring to me bein' his brother-in-law."

"You got me buffaloed, Pard. Spell it."

"S'pose I was to marry Miss Leila Nakhla, then? I'd be brother-in-law to the young Sheikh, wouldn't I?"

"Yup. And own brother to a damn' fool."

"Jealous of me again, Hank Sheikh?"

"You got marryin' on the brain, or where your brain oughter be, Buddy Bashaw. . . . You had a rise in salary—or feelin' the spring?"

"It's partly your bad example, an' partly seein' these lovely white girls, Hank. . . . I'm all of a doodah. I wanta marry an' I wanta go Home. . . . I sets on end by the hour and sings "The Old Chisholm Trail . . ." and then I keeps on sayin' '*Idaho, Montana, Utah, Oregon, Nevada, Colorado, Kansas, Oklahoma, Texas, California*'—till you'd think I was going potty. . . ."

"No, I'd never think you was *going* potty, Son," observed the Emir, regarding the face of his Vizier benignly.

"How long you had this consumin' passion for Leila?" he asked.

"I got up with it this very morning, Hank Sheikh. I s'pose it *is* your bad example? . . . *I* dunno. . . . I think I'll go an' have a talk with ole Daddy Pertater and see what he knows about me an' Leila gettin' engaged. . . . As you made him guardian, I s'pose he gets the rake-off?"

"Sure, Son. . . . I allow I'd better go down the bazaar and buy the weddin' present. Have a toast-rack or fish-knives, Brigham-Young-and-Bring 'em-Often?"

"Gee, Hank! If your brains was a furnace there wouldn't be enough fire to scorch your hat. . . . I'm goin' to call on Daddy Pertater right now. . . ."

But when, after speaking with old Sidi Dawad Fetata of all other subjects on the earth, in the heavens above, and in the waters under the earth, the Vizier inquired—with meaning—as to the health and happiness of the Sitt Leila Nakhla, he learned a strange thing.

"My heart is sore for her, Sidi," announced the old man. "She is possessed of *djinns*. . . . She cannot sleep. . . . Every night she rises from her cushions and goes forth to walk beneath the stars. Old Bint Fatma follows her, and she says the girl talks with spirits and *afrits*. . . . Always, too, she stands near the tent of the Emir and calls the protection of the Prophet and the blessings of Allah upon him. . . . No, she sleeps not, and neither does she eat. . . ."

"Marriage worketh wonders with women," suggested the Vizier.

"Ya, Sidi," agreed the old man. "But the poor Leila's pale bridegroom will be Death. . . . She will not live to marry my grandson—and he will pine for her and die also. . . . I am an old man, Sidi, but the grave will close upon her and upon him, while I yet cumber the earth. . . ."

"And what do you know about *that* for a merry old crape-hanger, my son?" the Vizier asked himself as he strolled to his tent.

§ 5

Hadji Abdul Salam, doctor and saint, entertained visitors the evening.

"Often they sleep in the big pavilion where they have sat and *faddhled* till nearly dawn," he said to the more important of his two guests. "More often they sleep each in his own tent. . . . There is usually a Soudanese sentry on the beat between the Guest-tent and those of the Emir and the Vizier."

"We can wait till your man is on duty," said Suleiman the Strong, called El Ma'ian, "or if it be a Soudanese, we can kill him."

"There might be a noise, and if you are caught—I do not think you will leave his presence alive, a second time. . . . He knows it was you who sent the Emir Mahommed Bishari bin Mustapha abd Rabu's assassin, too. . . ."

"There will be no noise," said Suleiman the Strong, grimly.

"Nor must either the Emir or the Vizier make a sound

255

in dying," warned the good Hadji. "They are lions possessed by devils, and each would spring to the help of the other. . . ."

"Yea. See to it, thou Abdullah el Jemmal, that thy man dies swiftly and in silence," growled Suleiman.

"Right through the heart, Sidi—or across the throat a slash that all but takes the head off," smiled Abdullah, "according to how he lies in sleep."

"Bungle not—or the Hadji here will put a curse upon thee that shall cause the flesh to rot from thy bones."

"Oh, *yes*!" chirped the doctor. "Surely! . . . Be not taken alive in thy bungling, sweet Abdullah. A quick death will be a lovely thing in comparison with what I will arrange for thee, shouldst thou spoil our plans."

"And if I do my part well, I have *medjidies*, camels, women, tents—to my heart's desire, and be made a man of consequence in the Tribe?" said Abdullah the camel-man.

"Yea! Verily! After the dawn that sees the death of the Emir and the Vizier, thou wilt never work again, Abdullah—never sweat, nor hunger, nor thirst again, good Abdullah."

"Dost thou swear it, Sidi Hadji—on the Q'ran?" asked the camel-driver.

"I swear on the Q'ran, and on my head and my life and by the Beard of the Prophet and the Sacred Names of Allah that thou shalt never hunger nor thirst again, Abdullah, after thou hast slain the Vizier."

"Yes," added Suleiman the Strong, with a sinisterly humorous glance into the merry face of the Hadji, "I myself will see to it that thou shalt *never hunger nor thirst again*, gentle Abdullah," and he displayed gleaming teeth in a smile that quite won the camel-man's heart.

How delightful to bask in the smiles of the future rulers of the Tribe, and to know that one was shortly to become a Person of Quality and a Man of Consequence! . . .

"And now—return to this tent no more," said the Hadji in speeding his parting guests, "for it is dangerous to do so.

"At times they visit me—though not often at night—and I have a fancy that the accursed El R'Orab the Crow spies upon me, and also the aged Yakoub. . . . Let them beware—and watch their food, I say. . . .

"Go in peace and with the blessing of Allah, and remain hidden with the caravan-men in the *fondouk* of the lower *sūq*. . . . Gharibeel Zarruk will bring thee word. . . . *Emshi besselema*. . . ."

CHAPTER IX

AUTOCRATS AT THE BREAKFAST-TABLE

"Well, son Bud, what you know about *that* for a fight?" asked the Emir of his Vizier as they broke fast after the duel between the French officer and the *agent provocateur* from the East. "What price Boje at the killing game?"

"I allow it was the best sword-fight I ever seen," replied the Vizier. "I never denied that Rastignac nor Boje was real *men*. . . ."

"And I'll tell the world that if Boje gets Miss Mary, she gets a husband to be proud of," interrupted the Emir.

"Yep—as a he-man that can hold up his end of a dog-fight, all right, Hank. But I tell you a woman wants a man that's something more than a bad man to fight. . . . S'pose he loves fightin' better than he loves her—what then, Hank Sheikh? And s'pose his real views of women is that they're just a dead-weight on the sword-arm or gun-hand, and a dead-weight on your hoss's back?"

The Vizier paused and pondered mournfully.

"Don't stop, Son," requested the Emir. "You remind me of Abraham Lincoln. It's almost po'try too. . . . I can lend you a bit. . . . Hark:

> '*White hands cling where your wool is thickest :*
> *He rideth the fastest who rideth the quickest.* . . .'"

"Where you get that from, Hank Sheikh?" asked the Vizier suspiciously. "'Tain't *Q'ran*, is it? Sounds more like Shakespeare to me."

"No, Son, you're wrong for once. Bret Harte or Chaucer. . . . I had to say it at school. There's a lot more:

> *'Fallin' down to Gehennum or off ef a throne,*
> *He falleth the hardest who falleth alone.'"*

"Well! I allow he *would*," commented the Vizier. "Because if he weren't alone and fell on the other guy, he'd fall softer. . . ." he added.

"You're right, Bud, as usual," admitted the Emir. "My mistake. I oughta said:

> *'Climbin' down to Gehennum or up on a throne*
> *He goes by himself who goeth alone!'*

"Yes—that's the poem—and, as I said, it's by Josh Billings or a Wop named Dante. . . . I forget. . . . They *did* tell me at school, when I had to learn it. . . ."

"Don't believe there's any such pome, nor that you ever was at school, Hank Sheikh. Put your tail down! And let a yell for some more of this porridge-hash. . . . Yes—I allow Boje is a good boy—he's straight; there ain't a yeller streak in him; he's got sand; and it's pretty to watch him fight. . . . But that don't make him the man for Miss Mary Vanbrugh."

"What *would*, Bud?" asked the Emir.

"Lovin' her more than anything and everything else in the world. . . . Bein' ready to lay down his life for her. . . ."

"He'd do that, Son."

"*That's* nothing! . . . Bein' ready, I was going to say, when you butted in, to give up his army prospects an' his chances, an' his promotion—*you* know—what they call his career and his—future and all. . . . *To let everything go for the woman he loves—even his country.* . . ."

"Say some more, Walt Whitman," the Emir stimulated his flagging friend. "I'll lend you a bit for that too. Listen to this:

> 'He made a solitude and called it Peace,
> (Largely because there weren't no P'lice)
> The world forgetting, by the world forgot
> He took her to that lovely spot.
> Saying I have now but you, my dove, and that's what the papers call.
> *The World well lost for Love.*'

258

"That's Byron, Son. But you shouldn't read him till you're older."

The Vizier stared long and critically at his lord.

"What's biting you now, you old fool?" he asked.

"Miss Mary Vanbrugh," replied the Emir. "Ever since she came here I sit and think of all the things I learnt at school—and how I uster talk pretty an' learn lessons . . . and recite po'try . . and play the pianner. . . ."

"And I s'pose you wore a plug hat and a Prince Albert and a tuxedo and lavender pants and white kid gloves and pink silk socks on your pasterns in those days? Here —get a lump o' this tough goat and chew hard instead o' talking, Hank," advised the Vizier. "You got a touch of the sun or else swallered a date-stone and it's displaced your brain. Chew hard an' listen to me and improve your mind. . . . What I say is, that Boje's got to do something more than killing Rastignac to prove he's the right husband for a way-up American girl—and I don't agree to it until he shows *and* proves that she's the Number One Proposition of all his life, and nothing else isn't worth thirty cents in the same continent. . . . Get me? . . . And the quicker the sooner, for he's the wounded hero and she's nursing of him—and women always falls in love with what they nurse. . . . Amateur-like, I mean. . . . It isn't the same with professional nurses o' course. . . ."

"Right again, Son. I was in a Infirmary once and at Death's Door, and if that old nurse had started lovin' me, I'd certainly have crep' through that Door to escape. . . ."

The Emir was apparently in sardonic mood and of flippant humour that morning—not an infrequent symptom, in his case, of a troubled and anxious soul.

His friend was well aware of this peculiarity, and classed it, in his puzzled mind, with other of Hank's idiosyncrasies —such as his way of being dumbly taciturn for days, and then having a mordantly loquacious hour; or his habit of occasionally speaking like an Eastern dude instead of talking properly like a genuine rough-neck hobo and a he-man. However, whatever Hank chose to say or to do was right in the sight of the man whose narrow, deep stream of affection flowed undeviatingly and eternally towards him, his hero, friend and ideal. . . .

"Well—we better try Boje out as soon as possible or

sooner," continued the Vizier. "He only got a bit chipped in the fierce shemozzle this mornin', and he'll be able to sit up and do business tomorrow. . . . Reckon Rastignac will pull round?"

"No. Rastignac has got his, this time, and a damned good job too, the swine! . . . He's for the land where the tombstone bloometh beneath the weeping willow tree, and the wild whang-doodle mourneth for its mate," opined the Emir.

"Well—we and the world can spare him, though I rise to remark he died like he lived, makin' trouble, and seekin' sorrow with a high and joyful heart," and the Vizier turned down an empty cup—of clay—and poured a libation of coffee-dregs. "What'll we do with that mouth-flappin', jabbering, shave-tail breed he brought with him, if Rastignac goeth to organize mutinies against the Devil?" he asked.

"Send him back with the soft answer that turneth away wrath—and a soft and empty money-belt," replied the Emir.

"You allow Boje's proposition is the best?" inquired the Vizier.

"Sure thing, Son. It is. Yea, verily. And I got a special reason for lending ear unto the words of Boje too. We'll go in solid with him."

"You're right, Hank Sheikh. We don't wanta hitch up with a gang of niggers, Turks, Touareg, Senussi and anti-white-man trash. . . . We ain't French and we ain't got no great cause to love 'em either—but we got our feelings as White Men. . . . Yep—and we got some sacks that'd just take a million francs too. . . . And if ever we got caught out by the Legion hogs, and it was a firing party at dawn for ours, the French Big Noise would say, 'Forget it—they're good useful boys, and we want 'em whole and hearty in the Great Oasis.' Wouldn't they?"

"You said it all, Son," agreed the Emir, and clapped his hands, that *narghilehs* might be brought by the slave waiting at a respectful distance.

§ 2

"Who *was* this poor creature whom Major de Beaujolais found it expedient to kill?" asked Mary Vanbrugh during the evening ride with the Emir el Hamel el Kibir. "He was a Frenchman too, so why was he treated as an enemy?"

"He wasn't treated as an enemy by *us*, though he soon would have been," replied the Emir. "We received him politely and we listened to all he had to say. . . . Listened too long for our comfort. . . ."

"And it was interesting?" asked the girl.

"Some of it certainly was," replied the Emir. "He got to know that there was a French officer here, openly wearing his uniform, and accompanied by two white women. . . . He told us exactly what I ought to do with the three of them, and offered me quite a lot of money to do it."

"What was it?" asked the girl.

"I won't put it in plain words," was the reply. "But you just think of the plumb horriblest thing that could happen to you, and then you double it—and you'll hardly be at the beginning of it, Miss Mary Vanbrugh."

"Oh!" said the girl. . . . "And was that why Major de Beaujolais fought him?"

"Partly, I guess—along with other reasons. It certainly didn't help the man's chances any, that the Major knew what was proposed for *you*. . . ."

"How did he get to know?" asked the girl.

"That's what I've got to find out," was the reply, "if I have to pretend he won't get his Treaty unless he tells me. . . . He'd do *anything* to get that safely signed, sealed and delivered."

"Not *anything*," said the girl, staring ahead unseeingly.

"Well—*that* we may discover, perhaps, all in good time," was the doubting reply. . . . "Life is very dear—and a life's ambition is sometimes even dearer. . . ."

The Emir was speaking English, with the words, accent, and intonation of a person of culture and refinement; and his companion eyed him thoughtfully, her face wistful and sad.

CHAPTER X

THE SITT LEILA NAKHLA, SULEIMAN THE STRONG, AND CERTAIN OTHERS

At dead of night, the Sheikh el Habibka el Wazir awoke with the feeling that there was something wrong. For as long as he could remember, this invaluable gift had been his, perhaps because, for as long as he could remember, he had lived, off and on, in danger, and under such conditions that light sleeping and quick waking had been essential to continued existence.

Also the fact that, in the month before his birth, his mother had slept alone in a log cabin, with a gun leaning against her bed, and an ear subconsciously attuned to the sound of the approach of stealthy terrors—Indians, wolves, mountain "lions", Bad Men, and, worst of all bad men, her husband—may have had something to do with his possession of this animal instinct or sixth sense.

Someone had passed the tent with stealthy steps. . . . The sentry had done that a hundred times, but this was different.

The Vizier passed straight from deep dreams to the door of his tent, his "gun" at the level of the stomach of anyone who might be seeking sorrow.

"*Min da?*" he growled, as he peered out.

Nobody. . . . He crept towards the Emir's pavilion. . . . Nothing. . . . Yes—a shadow beside the Guest-tent sentry, a young recruit, one Gharibeel Zarrug.

There should be no shadow on a moonless night. . . .

The shadow stooped and went into the tent by the entrance to the men's part of it.

Had it been the other entrance, the Vizier would have fired; for persons wearing black clothing, for the sake of invisibility, do not enter *anderuns* at midnight for any good purpose.

The Vizier circled the Guest-tent in the darker darkness of the palm-clumps, approached, and lay down behind it. Ah! . . . The good and pious Hadji Abdul Salam! . . . *What* was that? . . . *Murder*, eh? . . . The lowdown, treacherous swine! . . .

And Suleiman the Strong was back again, was he? . . .
And who might *he* be? . . . Good old Boje! . . . Spoken
like a man. . . . Wouldn't leave the girls, wouldn't he?
He would—to save his life, and get the Treaty, though. . . .
Wouldn't stand for assassination of the Emir nor the
Wazir, eh? . . . Yep. Boje was certainly a White Man! . . .

The Vizier crept round to the front of the tent and the
knees of Gharibeel Zarrug smote together, as a figure rose
beside him, and the voice of the Sheikh el Habibka el
Wazir gave him sarcastic greeting. . . .

A few minutes later, the Vizier also gave the Hadji
Abdul Salam sarcastic greeting, and said he would see him
safely home to his tent: he would take no refusal of the
offer of his company, in fact. . . .

§ 2

As the Emir el Kebir emerged from his pavilion before
dawn the next morning, and strode to where El R'Orab
the Crow led his master's great stallion up and down, he
was joined by the Vizier.

When the two were clear of the headquarter tents of the
"capital" of the Oasis, the Vizier told the Emir of the
events of the night.

"The worst of these holy *marabouts* and *hadjis* and
imams and things is that they *stay* holy in the sight of these
ignorant hick Injuns, no matter what they do; and you
can't get away from it," observed the Emir. "There'd
be a riot and a rebellion if I took good old Abdul and
hanged him on a tree. . . . I'd be real sorry to do it, too. . . .
I like the cute old cuss . . . always merry an' bright."

"He's gettin' a whole heap too bright, Hank," opined
the Vizier. "But as you say—there's no lynchin' Holy
Sin-Busters in this State. . . . They can cut their mothers'
throats or even steal hosses, and they're still Holy Men an'
acceptable in the sight of Allah. . . ."

"We better have a talk with old Dawad Fetata," said
the Emir. "He knows the etiquette of handling Holy
Joes when they get too rorty. . . . *Bismillah!* We mustn't
make any false moves on the religion dope, Son. . . . There'd
be an 'Ell-of-an-Allahbaloo. . . ."

"Sure," agreed the Vizier. "But Old Daddy Pertater won't stand for havin' Abdul plottin' the death of the Emir. . . . He'll know how to hand it to him. . . . We'll have li'll *mejliss*, with Abdul absent, by request. . . . What are we going to do about this Suleiman guy that's got it in for you? Who *is* he?"

"Don't you remember the gink I told you about—that left our outfit before you came—and joined the Emir Mohammed Bishari bin Mustapha Korayim, that we shot up—at Bab-el-Haggar? *He* was this Suleiman the Strong, and he sent that thug to get me—the one you shot. . . . Let him come when he feels like it. I allow he'll get his, good an' plenty, this time," replied the Emir.

"Why not get a posse an' have a man-hunt?" suggested the Vizier. "Man-hunts is good sport, and prowlin' thugs lookin' for your liver with a long knife is bad sport. . . . Catch him alive, and skin him at poker, Son."

"I allow it was all lies of Abdul's," replied the Emir. . . . "Suleiman's dead long ago, an' if he was alive he wouldn't come snoopin' round here. . . . He's on'y too willin' to keep away—with both feet. . . . Forget it. . . . What you do with poor old Abdul?"

"Frightened him white. . . . *'Lhamdoulah!* . . . I certainly did put the fear of God in Abdul. . . . Did a magic on him. . . . *Pro*duced things from him that he hadn't got. . . . Told him to watch his eyes and teeth as they'd soon fall outa him; watch his arms an' legs as they'd soon wither; watch his food becos it'd soon turn to sand in him; watch his secret *laghbi* becos it'd boil in his belly; watch his women becos each one had a dancin' partner—secret, like his fermented palm-juice—an' watch all through the night becos Death an' the Devil was coming for him. . . . He's *watchin'* all right! . . . He surely is a sick man this mornin'. . . . I reckon he'll die. . . ."

"Poor old Abdul—I must go and hold his hand and cheer him up some," said the Emir. "Promise him a real rousin' funeral and start buildin' him a nice tomb. . . . Place of pilgrimage for thousands. . . ."

"Say, Son," he added, "I'm glad the Major played a clean game. I told you he was a hundred per cent white."

"He was straight enough," admitted the Vizier. "But I don't like him any. . . . Too all-fired pompshus. . . .

Thinks he could play his Ace on the Last Trump. . . . Too golly-a-mighty own-the-earth. . . . Thinks he's God's Own Bandmaster, Lord Luvvus, Count Again, an' the Baron Fig-tree. . . . And he's one o' the hard-faced an' soft-handed sort—that women fall for. . . ."

"You're hard-faced, hard-handed, hard-hearted, an' hard-headed, Son Bud. . . . Yep. . . . Head solid bone. . . ."

"We'll settle his hash one night, Hank Sheikh," replied the Vizier, ignoring his Lord's rudeness. "Then we'll *see. . . . Abka ala Kheir.*"

§ 3

They saw.

Never had the Emir and his Vizier cowered and fled before armed men as they cowered and fled from the wrath of the angry woman who burst into their presence, that night, at the loud choking cry of the man whom they had foully murdered.

She was a raging Death-angel, her tongue a flaming sword.

"My God—*you killed him*! . . . You murdered him! . . . Poisoned him like a sewer-rat. . . . What the Hell *happened*, you ham-handed buffalo?" panted the Emir as the two fled from the Guest-tent and went to earth in the pavilion of the latter chieftain. . . .

"Search me!" replied the Vizier, obviously badly shaken.

The Emir seized his friend's arm and glared into his face.

"You didn't double-cross me and *poison* that fine man a-purpose? . . . Not *poison* him? You wouldn't be such a damned yellow dog?" he asked sternly.

"Don't be a fool," replied the Vizier. "I gave him camel's milk. Part of what we had at supper. . . . *He's* double-crossed *us*. . . . Yelped so as Miss Vanbrugh sh'd hear him, an' then threw a fake fit. . . ."

"Don't be a mean hound. . . . He saw that dog die— an' drank what he thought killed the dog. . . . *And* he choked like the dog did, and then collapsed—he went white an' cold an' limp. . . . He's *dead*, I tell you. . . . *God! How'll I face Mary?* . . . Bud—if I thought you . . ."

"You make me tired, Hank. If he's dead—the milk killed him. 'Nuff to kill anybody too. . . . I near died myself, first time I drunk milk! . . . Hank, Son, you hurt my feelin's. . . . You seen me kill a few men. . . . Ever know me *poison* 'em behind their backs? . . . You gotta beastial mind, Hank Sheikh. . . ."

They sat silent for a moment.

"Say, Hank," said the Vizier suddenly. "Think she'd turn crool an' tell Bojolly on his death-bed that we're a pair of four-flushers? . . . Or tell him tomorrow if he lives?"

"No, Son, she'd die sooner. She allows the Major would blow his brains out, in rage an' disgust an' fear o' ridicule, if it came out that the Mahdee whom he'd circumvented with his superior Secret Service Diplomacy had circumvented *him*, the Pride o' the whole French Intelligence Bureau, an' signed a treaty for a million jimmy-o'-goblins. . . . Folks saying he didn't know a Mahdee from an American high-jacker! Gee! . . ."

The Emir rose.

"I'm going back," he said. "If he's dead that girl will go mad. . . . She ain't screamin' any. . . . She's got a gun too. . . . Hope she shoots me first. . . . I take the blame, Boy—for allowin' such monkeying. . . . I hadn't oughter stood for it. . . . Shake, Son—you didn't mean any harm. . . ."

"I sure didn't, Hank pard. . . . I only meant it for her good. . . . No I didn't! May I burn in Hell for a liar! I *was* jealous of a better man. He *is* a better man. . . . *Was* I mean. . . ."

"I'll put my gun in his dead hand and shoot myself. . . . That oughta satisfy him," he added, as the Emir crept out of the tent. . . .

§ 4

The Emir returned beaming.

"*They're cuddling!*" he cried. "*Cuddling*—fit to bust! . . . I didn't mean to intrude, and they didn't see me. . . *He was kissin' her face flat.* . . . You cert'nly brought it off,

266

Buddy Bashaw . . . and serve you damned well right! . . . They got *you* to thank. . . . Boje oughta ask you to be Best Man, B'Jimminy Gees! . . . Allahluyer!. . . "

"But what *happened*, if he didn't throw that fit on purpose?" asked the bewildered Vizier.

"Why—I'll tell you, Son. He was so blamed sure that he *was* drinking poison that *he felt all the effects of it.* He felt just like he saw that dog feel. . . . I knew an Injun once, an Arapaho or a Shoshone, I think he was, back on the Wind River Reservation at Fort Washakie—no, it wasn't you goat—it was in the Canyon, and the man was a Navajo breed—and the boys played a trick on him one dark night —stuck a fork in his heel and yelled '*Rattler*'—an' he up an' died o' snake-bite, *pronto*."

"*Can* it!" said the Vizier. "Cut out the funny-stuff."

"Fact, Son! . . . Yep—like old Doc' Winter, back in Colorado in the old days. He sent out two letters, when he couldn't go himself—one tellin' a sick man he'd better make his will, and the other telling a Dude from the East he was healthier than a mule. . . . Put 'em in the wrong en*vell*ups! . . . The Dude made his will and died, and the sick man got up and ate a steak. . . . Never felt another pang or sorrow!. . ."

"Sure," agreed the Vizier. "Same sorta thing happened in Idaho. . . . Only it was a young bride was sick, and a lone ol' bachelor cattle-rustler that *thought* he was. . . . Same mistake like yours, Hank. . . ."

"What happened?" inquired the Emir.

"Old bachelor had the babby o' course," was the reply. "Only case on record I believe. . . ."

"Probably," agreed the Emir. . . . "And that's what happened to the Major."

"What! Had a? . . . " began the Vizier.

"No," interrupted the Emir. "You got a *very* coarse mind, Bud. . . . He thought the milk was poison, and he thought it so hard that for a while it *was* poison, and it acted according!. . ."

"It's a fierce world, Hank. . . . Let's pound our ears, right here. It'll be daylight in an hour. . . . God help us in the mawnin', when Miss Vanbrugh gets us! . . . I'm glad you're the Emir and not me, Hank Sheikh. . . ."

The troubled statesmen slept.

267

Meanwhile, two men of simple passions and simple methods of expressing them, prepared for strenuous action.

Wearing the minimum of clothing and the maximum of razor-edged knife, Suleiman the Strong and Abdullah el Jemmal crept from darkness to darkness until they could see the pavilion of the Emir, wherein burned a single candle in the wind-proof *shamadan* holder, that hung from a tent-pole.

Not far from the big tent, a sentry, one Gharibeel Zarrug, leaned heavily upon his rifle, his crossed arms upon its muzzle and his head upon his arms. . . .

Rightly considering that the place of the strategist is a place of safety where he may strategize in peace, Suleiman the Strong bade Abdullah the Camel-man reconnoitre the tent and report.

Like a dark snake in the darkness, Abdullah crept to a blacker spot beside the Guest-tent, whence he could see a portion of the interior of the lighted pavilion.

No one moved therein, and, after a period of patient observation, he crawled, writhed and wriggled until he reached the aperture where a hanging curtain of heavy felt did not quite close the entrance to the tent.

Perfect stillness reigned within, and a silence broken only by the sound of breathing.

How many breathed?

It was unfortunate, but intentional on the part of the occupants, that the light hung just where anyone entering would see nothing but the light—the back of the tent being in darkness, and the front well-lit.

Abdullah accepted the situation and moved slowly, silently, almost imperceptibly, across the lighted carpet. Once the light was behind him, he saw that the Emir el Kebir and the Wazir el Habibka lay on their rugs, sleeping the deep sleep of the innocent and just; the Vizier the nearer to him.

What about two quick stabs?

No. These were not ordinary mortals. The Vizier would, perhaps, make some sound as he died, and the

Emir's great arm would shoot out and seize the slayer. . . .
Abdullah had seen both these men in swift action. . . .

No, he must stick to the programme and obey the orders
of his leader, to the letter.

He writhed backward as silently as he had come, and
wriggled crawling from the tent. . . .

"He did that very neat and slick," observed the Emir
as Abdullah departed.

"Not bad," agreed the Vizier. "He's a bit slow
though . . . You ain't too near the side o' the tent, Hank,
are you?"

"Plenty o' room, Son; but he won't bother to come
under while he can come through the front door. . . . See
his silly face?"

"Nope. I allow it's that Suleiman guy what the Hadji
was talkin' to Boje about."

"Guess again, Son. . . . Suleiman the Strong's a real
big stiff. Twice the size o' that galoot," and the Emir
yawned hugely.

"What you reckon he's gone for, Hank?"

"Why, his bag o' tools or his plumber's-mate, I s'pose."

"Wish he'd hurry up then, I'm real sleepy. . . . S'pose
we'd better hang Mister Gharibeel Zarrug bright an' early
tomorrow."

"We'll hand him over to Marbruk ben Hassan and the
body-guard. They can use him for a li'll court-martial
mejliss. Keep 'em happy all day."

"Pore Mister Gharibeel will be Mister Skinned-ell, time
they done with him. They'll treat him rough."

"Learn him not to double-cross—but it's poor old
Hadji Abdul Salam that oughta hang."

"Sure, Son. He's a bad ole possum. . . . G'night, boy."

"They are both there, Sidi," whispered Abdullah the
Camel-man to Suleiman the Strong. "Sleeping on their
rugs like drunken *kif*-smokers, but the Emir lies beyond
the Vizier and cannot be reached. El Habibka must die
first. . . ." And he proceeded to explain exactly the position of affairs and of the victims.

"Now listen—and live," growled Suleiman, when all was
clear. "Go you back into that tent and crouch where
you can strike home—when the moment comes."

"When will that be?" asked Abdullah, whose knife was brighter and keener than his brain.

"*Listen*, you dog," was the reply. "Crouch ready to strike El Habibka at the moment I strike El Hamel. Watch the tent-wall beyond him. I shall enter there. . . . And our knives will fall at the same moment. . . . As your knife goes through El Habibka's heart, clap your left hand upon his mouth. . . . They must die together and die silently. . . . Then we flee back to the *fondouk*—and tomorrow I will appear to my friends and proclaim myself Sheikh Regent of the Tribe. . . ."

"And I shall be a camel-man no more," said Abdullah.

"No—you will not be a camel-man after tomorrow," agreed Suleiman, and carefully repeated his instructions.

"Now," he concluded. "Dawn's left hand will be in the sky in half an hour. . . . Remember what will happen if you bungle. . . ."

Kneeling beside the sleeping Vizier, Abdullah el Jemmal poised his long lean knife above his head, and stared hard at the tent wall beyond the recumbent form of the Emir. . . .

In his sleep, the Emir rolled his heavy head round and lay snoring, his face towards the very spot at which Abdullah stared.

A bright blade silently penetrated the wall of the tent. Slowly it travelled downward and the head of Suleiman the Strong was thrust through the aperture, as the knife completed the long cut and reached the ground.

Gently Suleiman edged his body forward until his arms and shoulders had followed his head. As he raised himself on his elbows, Abdullah lifted his knife a little higher, drew a deep breath, and, ere it was completed, the silence was horribly rent by the dreadful piercing scream of a woman in mortal anguish. . . . A rifle banged. . . .

Abdullah, unnerved, struck with all his strength, and his wrist came with a sharp smack into the hand of the waiting Vizier, whose other hand seized the throat of Abdullah with a grip of steel.

Suleiman, with oaths and struggles, backed from the tent, and the Emir, bounding across the struggling bodies of the Vizier and Abdullah, rushed from the tent, with a low exhortation of, "Attaboy, Bud! Bust him up," and dashed round the tent—in time to see Suleiman the Strong drive his knife into the breast of a woman (who grappled with him fiercely), just as El R'Orab sprang upon the slayer from behind.

Another woman stood and shrieked insanely, sentries came running, and the French officer burst from his tent, sword in hand. . . .

The murderer was secured after a terrific struggle and bound with camel-cords.

As soon as the Emir had shaken the shrieking woman into coherence, it was learnt that it had become the custom of the Sitt Leila, who slept badly, to rise and walk in the hour before dawn—"when she had the world to herself," as the old woman pathetically sobbed, "and unseen could pass the tent of the Emir and pray for blessings on his sleeping head. . . ."

On this occasion, as they went by the road that ran behind the Emir's pavilion, they had seen a man lying prone, with his head beneath the tent-wall and inside the tent.

Realizing that this could mean but one thing, the girl had uttered a terrible scream and thrown herself upon the man. . . . She had seized his foot and held on, with the strength and courage of love.

The man, moaned the old Bint Fatma, had kicked and struggled, knocking the girl down, had wriggled out backwards, risen, and turned to flee, as the girl again sprang at him and clung like Death. . . .

As gently as any mother nursing her sick child, the big Emir held the dying girl to his breast, her arms about his neck, her eyes turned to his as turn those of a devoted spaniel to its master—and if ever a woman died happily, it was the little Arab girl. . . .

Yussuff Latif Fetata arrived, at the double, with the guard, and, even in such a moment, the man who had made them what they were, noted with approval that it was a disciplined guard under an officer, and not a mob of Soudanese following an excited Arab. . . .

"Keep that man here and hurt not a hair of his head," ordered the Emir, "I return," and he strode away, with the dead girl in his arms, to the tents of Dawad Fetata.

. . . . .

As he came back, the Vizier emerged from the pavilion.

"Sorry, Son," he whispered, "I croaked him. . . ."

"Good," growled the Emir. "You'll see me croak the other . . ." and it was plain to the Vizier that his friend was in that terrible cold rage when he was truly dangerous.

He himself had enjoyed that for which he had recently expressed a wish—an intimate and heart-to-heart discussion in a righteous cause and with a worthy foe.

Abdullah had really put up quite a good show, the Vizier considered, and it had taken several minutes and several good twists and turns and useful tricks, before he had had his visitor where he wanted him—clasped immovably to his bosom with his hawser-like right arm, while his equally powerful left forced the assassin's knife-hand back and over—until the hand was far behind the sharply crooked elbow, in a position that Nature had never intended it to occupy. . . .

Abdullah had screamed like a wounded horse as the arm and joint snapped, the knife fell from his hand, and the Vizier seized his neck in a double grip. . . . Minutes had passed.

"That'll learn you, Mr. Thug," the Vizier had grunted, and released the murderer's throat.

But alas, it was the final lesson of his unlearning misspent life.

"Let the guard charge magazines and form single rank," said the Emir to Yussuf Latif Fetata—who, beyond a greenish pallor of countenance, showed nothing of what he felt. None would have supposed that this stoic had just beheld, borne in the arms of another man, the dripping corpse of the girl for whom his soul and body hungered. "If the prisoner tries to escape, give him fifty yards and a volley. . . ."

The Emir then bade El R'Orab and the sentries who had seized Suleiman the Strong to unbind him and to chafe his limbs.

"Do you thirst, dog?" he asked.

"For your blood, swine," was the answer.

The Emir made no reply, but waited a while, that the prisoner's strength and the daylight might increase.

"Give him his knife," he said anon, and gripped his own.